The Trouble
with Fairies

Books by Liz Roadifer

Peace & Prosperity series

The Trouble With Fairies

The Trouble With Pirates

The Oracle Suspense series

This Time Justice

Ambushed

Wind Riders of R.A.H.M. (YA series)

Morning Star

The **Trouble with Fairies**

Liz Roadifer

Liz Roadifer Books

Published by Liz Roadifer Books
P.O. Box 22
Pine Bluffs, WY 82082-0022

LizRoadiferBooks.com

Cover art by Duvall Design
Edited by Sharon Mignerey

ISBN-10: 1-942335-05-9
ISBN-13: 978-1-942335-05-4

To the members of CAWG, the Cheyenne Area Writing Group, past and present, for your critiques, comments, support, and laughter. This book was made possible because of your talents and friendships. Thank you.

Chapter 1

With a heavy heart, Harradorn Lawson brushed his hand over the bronze memorial plaque just delivered to his office. Slowly he traced the names of Kelly Bjork and her husband Ragnar. Like death, the engraved letters were cold to the touch. His shaking fingers refused to go near the name of their newborn babe Harradorn Bjork. His namesake. His godson.

Barely a month had passed and still his grief was raw.

Solemnly, he placed a hand on the plaque. "I swear, no one in Peace & Prosperity will ever come to harm again, not if I can help it. Not while I'm mayor." He paused, then corrected himself. "At least mayor of the Peace side of town."

As if to seal the vow, a sudden flash of day-glo red lightning coated the plaque in a bright, bloody hue. Startled, Harradorn glanced out the windows. The Montana evening sky was gentling to a soft denim blue. Not a cloud in sight.

Damn magic.

Grabbing his leather jacket, he raced to the entrance of the Mayor's Hall and Residence. His twelve-foot tall assistant, Agamemnon, lumbered out of an office. The huge hazel eye in the middle of his forehead widened in shock when another bolt, stronger than the first, shook the building.

"Is Zach leaving?" Harradorn asked, aware that when the town's wizard went traveling, he took along his tower.

Zach's magical motorhome needed power. A lot of power. But whether the storms were conjured to supply that power or were the result of the build-up of the magical charge, Zach refused to say. Since he'd matured into a full-fledged wizard, Harradorn's childhood friend had become vague and secretive. And a prick.

The Cyclops stepped outside the two massively tall entry doors and scanned the sky in all directions. "There's no gathering storm," Agamemnon said.

Harradorn joined him. They looked to the west, to the half of town called Prosperity where Zach's tower normally parked. Above the buildings, they could see the upper floors of the black tower. Parallel to it loomed a huge vertical cloud, maroon in color, with two wispy strands like horns on top.

"Look!" Agamemnon pointed to the cloud. "An electrical charge is crossing between the horns. It's—"

Red lightning flashed towards Zach's tower. Before it hit, a white bolt shot out from the black tower and intercepted it like a Patriot missile.

"The wizard must be testing his defense systems," Agamemnon said.

Harradorn frowned as the deflected red bolt shot toward Peace, crackling when it zoomed overhead, shaking the ground with its intensity. In the park across the street, children shrieked and ran for home. Tourists strolling on the grass stopped and stared at the wizard's tower.

Another red thunderbolt zipped toward Zach's tower and another white bolt deflected it, this time hurling the garish red lightning up into the sky where it disappeared from view.

Harradorn ground his teeth. It wasn't like Zach to be this careless. "Get our wizard on the phone," he told his assistant. "Tell him to stop his experiment. He's scaring the children."

And me.

* * *

In the upstairs bathroom of her New Jersey home, Joy Flint had just squeezed the last of the hair dye on her head, her grungy dyeing t-shirt already spotted with reckless drips, when she heard a moaning squeak from the inside door to the garage. At this time of night, the rusty hinge would have normally signaled her sister was home from the night class she taught at the local community college.

But Merry was four thousand miles away in Italy exploring caves for *National Geographic!* Only yesterday Joy had taken her to the airport.

She swallowed hard and shifted to the open door leading into the hallway. Hair dye bled down her forehead. She nervously wiped it away with gloved fingers and listened.

The moaning squeak from the door to the garage had not repeated itself, which meant whoever had entered the house was still inside.

Mike. It HAD to be Mike. Their brother had keys to the house. That was it.

But he always used the front door. And he never entered without knocking or ringing the bell first.

She stripped off the dyeing gloves, tossed them in the sink, then pulled out the phone from her jeans. She thought about the house behind her that had been burglarized two weeks ago… and the flyer from the local Neighborhood Watch warning a sex offender had moved in down the block… and the horror movie on TV last night where a woman home alone had been sliced, diced, and made into a soup of her own blood.

Her stomach clenched, remembering the eyeballs floating in the bloody soup.

In the corn syrup and red dye soup, she reminded herself. *Get a grip, girl. There's a perfectly logical explanation for what you heard.*

But she refused to go downstairs and find out. Call it intuition, cowardice, too many horror movies, or the warning shudder that shook her from head to toe. She wasn't going to join the ranks of silly victims who should have known better.

Instead, she peeked into the hall, thumb hovering over the speed dial for 911, and strained to hear a footfall, a sneeze, an evil laugh, anything that would indicate someone was in the house.

The furnace thrummed keeping the house warm while down the street a distant siren heralded a fire truck leaving the station. Thunder drifted in and a branch grazed the roof above her. The wind had picked up. The storm forecast for tomorrow had decided to come tonight, the weatherman wrong again, which meant everything was as it should be. No crazed killer was stalking her. Just exhaustion playing with her imagination.

Sighing in relief, she repocketed the phone and stepped into the hall. She probably hadn't latched the door completely when she got home from work. The change in air pressure from the approaching storm must have shifted the door open enough to—

Shredder, her silver-gray cat, charged up the stairs. Joy jumped back as he streaked down the hall and into the bedroom, claws scrabbling at the hardwood floor under the bed as he frantically sought to hide.

Her heart slammed against her chest. *Ohmigod! Someone is in the house! Someone Shredder doesn't know, doesn't like.* She tried to breathe. *Someone he's afraid of.*

She ducked into the bathroom and locked the door. With trembling fingers, she dug out the phone. The lock wouldn't keep out the intruder. More for privacy than protection, even a coin could open it. Who would think to put a dead bolt on a bathroom door?

Mike would. Ever since her brother moved out, he'd been warning Joy and her sister to make the house more secure, create a safe room, be armed, be prepared. To halt his torturous nagging, she and Merry had compromised. They took the self-defense classes he signed them up for, installed motion-sensor lights on both the front and back porches, and then added another set of locks on all the outside doors.

The place was a fortress. It should have been enough. She should be safe.

Lightning crackled. New Jersey's first storm of the spring had arrived. Thunder shook the house. Seconds later, she heard a crash from downstairs. She gasped. Hands clumsy with fear, she fumbled with the phone and dropped it. Lightning flashed again, so brilliant she could have sworn it was day-glo red.

It had to be an afterimage. Lightning wasn't red.

She scrambled for the phone. Her skin prickled, the hair on her arms rose, the air suddenly charged with the hot smell of electricity. She winced as crazy red lightning burst all around. Then the lights went out.

Had the intruder turned off her power? No. A quick glance outside revealed the surrounding blocks of suburbia were dark, yet in the distance tall buildings were lit. Lightning must have hit the local substation.

Darkness was good. It'd be harder for an intruder to see her, find her. With a shaking hand, she speed-dialed 911.

For once in her life, she wished she had a gun.

Mike had bought them guns. They promptly, stupidly, gave them back, opting for the more feminine line of defense—baseball bats. Merry kept hers in the car—college campuses were rape magnets. Joy's was downstairs where she'd used it to kill a nasty-looking spider on the ceiling. Dented the plaster but the spider was dead. She hugged herself and waited for the emergency dispatcher to answer her call. She'd killed the spider out of fear, but the fear she felt now was different. It soaked into her bones, chilled her from the inside out.

Most household items can be used as a weapon or deterrent, her self-defense instructor had repeatedly told the class. With the light from the phone she searched the bathroom. Shampoo bottles, hair dryer, curling iron, a stack of *Vanity Fair*. The only thing even close to a bat was the toilet plunger. Grabbing the plunger, she hefted it with one hand and frowned at how light it was.

On the fourth ring, a recording answered her call. Operators were busy. Please stay on the line. *Darn it!* With the partial power outage, the whole neighborhood must be calling for help. She'd never get through.

Thunder rumbled, rain pummeled the bathroom window, and in the middle of it all, a fierce knocking reverberated from downstairs.

Ohmigod! What the hell was that?

She gave up on the police and speed-dialed her brother. Mike lived only a few blocks away. He was Army Special Forces, trained to kill, to protect, to save.

Through the tiny speaker, she heard his phone ring.

Pick up, Mike! Pick up!

From downstairs came a loud thump, followed by a heated curse. She'd seen enough movies to know the only thing worse than a sex-crazed intruder was an *angry* sex-crazed intruder.

Toilet plunger in one hand, phone in the other, she frantically whispered, "Please, Mike! Pick up!"

*   *   *

While Agamemnon called the wizard, Harradorn studied the dangerous vertical cloud. Bolt after bolt of red lightning was deflected this way and that. Most had gone skyward, disappearing into the upper atmosphere, and a few continued to do so. Tourists hurried to the hotels and bed and breakfasts circling the park, where they would presumably hide out until the magic tapered off.

The evening Tie-Dye Tai Chi group he had been participating with before the memorial plaque arrived, decided to give up trying to reduce stress and restore peace, and beat a hasty retreat to their homes. Phones rang inside the Hall. He listened to his staff calm the callers, and nodded in approval. He ran a tight ship. It was heartening to know all the training had paid off.

An errant bolt crossed the sky, just missing the Hall. He flinched in spite of himself and put on his jacket. He shot a scathing glance toward the vertical maroon cloud and wondered how his younger brother Rick was handling things on his side of town. They were the youngest mayors in the town's history, and a reckless streak ran through his brother's veins. Knowing Rick, he was probably taking bets on where the next bolt would hit. The maxim on the Prosperity side of town was "Anything to make money," while in Peace the citizens treasured restful beauty at a fair price.

And yet, in spite of Rick's roguish way of governing, partying, and gambling, he always managed to keep Prosperity prosperous. It was the damnedest thing.

While I sweat fourteen-hour days keeping Peace shipshape.

His phone alerted him to an incoming call. Sound calm, he reminded himself. There's nothing to worry about. Everything's taken care of. He shook his head cynically. Even the weather. All part of the job.

With a smile he hoped would translate into his voice, he said, "Hello, this is—"

"Mike!" a woman's frantic whisper erupted from the phone. "It's Joy! Help me! There's someone in the house!"

Without warning, a frisson of heat flashed through his body. Every muscle quivered, eager to take action. The curse—damn magic—always took hold when any woman's cry for help reached his ears, and it wouldn't let go until he resolved the problem.

He clenched his teeth. *Best get this over with.*

Harradorn gripped the phone and peered at the caller ID. Joy Flint. Not a familiar name—he knew everyone in town. Must be a tourist. Then he noticed the number and his mouth opened in shock. It wasn't a local call.

He said, "You have—"

"To call the police," Joy Flint said, speaking fast, clearly overwrought and interrupting his attempt to tell her she had the wrong number. "I've already tried. I can't get through. The cell towers are maxed out with the power outage. Please, Mike, hurry. Wait! I heard—"

The call was cut off.

Harradorn stared at the phone. With the mystical security measures enveloping his town, he shouldn't have been able to receive an outside call. Those same security measures should prevent him from phoning her back, yet, on the off chance the strange fluke would continue, he tried her number and wasn't surprised when the call didn't go through.

Dammit! A woman thousands of miles away thought someone named Mike was coming to her rescue. But Mike wasn't, and he had no way of letting Joy Flint know she was on her own and should keep calling the police, find a place to hide. Try to escape.

He ran to his assistant's office. "Agamemnon, we have a problem."

"I know." From behind his giant desk, Agamemnon set down the huge phone proportioned to his size. "That was your brother. There's a wizard duel in progress. The rogue FearfulFran is in town. That's her cloud-encased tower next to Zach's. She's attacking him with lightning, trying to break through his defenses. Our wizard has his hands full until she leaves."

A wizard duel.

He'd been a child the last time one occurred. Portions of the town had suffered serious damage, along with four deaths and many injured. Zach's dad had been mortally wounded, but in the waning moments of his life, he'd prevailed against the usurper. Afterwards, Zach's aunt took over safeguarding the town until her nephew came of age. Unfortunately, fate had other things in store for Harradorn's childhood friend, and Zach was forced to mature a lot quicker than expected.

"Have Rick keep us apprised of the duel. We have another problem." Harradorn handed over his phone. "This woman's in trouble, maybe only minutes before she's harmed."

"I'll send for the sheriff."

He shook his head. "Look at the area code."

Agamemnon squinted at the small phone in his massive hand. "This is impossible."

"Agreed. We'll figure it out later. Right now Joy Flint thinks I'm coming to save her."

Agamemnon stared at him in alarm. "The curse?"

"Already taken hold. I have to save her whether I want to or not." Or the curse would slowly burn him alive from the steadily increasing adrenaline.

"The wizard cannot transport you until he defeats FearfulFran."

"Which leaves only one other person who might be able to help."

Agamemnon rolled his enormous hazel eye. "Sirena."

"Can't be helped," Harradorn said. "In the meantime, make sure all the lightning rods are deployed. Have the sheriff and his deputies help. And make sure Rick does the same in Prosperity."

He turned to leave but stopped when Agamemnon said in a tight voice, "The town council will soon be aware of your absence. Lance Warbird, in particular, will take note."

Like he didn't have enough on his plate to worry about. "This should take only a few minutes. With any luck, I'll be back before I'm missed."

"*Luck*." Agamemnon wrinkled his massive brow. "There's an old Greek proverb: When God throws, the dice are loaded."

"Maybe for once Odin's on my side." He headed for the front doors and yelled over his shoulder, "Call Sirena! Have her ready by the time I get there!"

"She'll make you pay!" Agamemnon shouted after him.

Don't I know it.

He sped through the park, gathering curious glances— Harradorn Lawson never ran anywhere. Always calm, in control. Or at least gave the appearance of being so. He was priding himself on getting to the far side of the park without any delays when a small orange fairy flew in front of him. He dodged around her and continued onto Pleasant Street.

The pesky fairy quickly caught up and flew backwards at eye level. "What's up, Mayor Harradorn?"

"No time to talk, Felicity. I have an emergency. Make an appointment with Agamemnon and I'll get back to you."

He careened around the corner onto Smiling Way and ducked under a low tree branch. He couldn't help but chuckle as Felicity barreled into a cluster of new spring leaves. He thought he'd lost her until she reappeared in front of his face.

Her diaphanous yellow-orange wings flapped madly, trying to keep up with him. With an impatient gesture, she straightened the tiny diadem of woven copper threads decorated with a chip of Montana blue sapphire, which had slipped in her unruly orange hair, and asked, "Another damsel in distress?"

Harradorn grimaced. Everyone in town knew about the curse.

"Fourth one this month," she pointed out. "Maybe my team and I could help."

He almost laughed. Fairies and help. Now there's an oxymoron. "She's very far away. Out of your reach." *And mine.*

"Going to see Sirena?"

"You got it. See you later."

Behind him, Felicity's tiny voice squeaked in warning. "She'll make you pay."

Hopefully the price won't be too high.

On that troubling thought, he entered Mistress Sirena's Shop of Quiet Contentment. A merry chime announced his presence. Water softly babbled from several stone fountains situated on either side of the door, and the faint scents of frankincense and myrrh drifted in the air. Sirena had designed the sound of water and the scents to ease the cares of all who entered, usually with enough success that her customers left with filled shopping bags.

It never worked on him.

He scanned the shop. "Sirena! Did Agamemnon call?"

Sirena's melodious voice floated from the backroom. "In here. I'm just about ready."

He swiftly bypassed the displays of exotic statuary, scented candles, and bottled aphrodisiacs and stepped behind the counter to where a lace curtain acted as a soft door to the backroom. Moving the curtain aside, he found his sister Sirena at a work table.

Ringlets of honey-brown hair fell to her shoulders, interwoven with thin gold and purple ribbons. The neckline of her dark purple velvet dress plunged down to her waist, teasing customers to look but not touch. Frosted purple eye shadow, purple blush along the high cheek bones, and purple lips accented her smooth caramel complexion.

Her multi-ringed fingers added two vials of foul-smelling oil to the mixture, followed by a pinch of blackness. Though only twenty-five years of age, a few years younger than himself, she was already advanced in the art of alchemy.

Sirena looked up when he entered; her dazzling smile of welcome balanced the worry in her eyes. She tsked. "Dear, dear Harry. What are you thinking—dashing off to save a stranger. And in the outside world no less?"

"Can't be helped. The curse has already taken hold. If I don't go—"

"You'll die." Her forehead scrunched in misery. "A misplaced call in a storm of magic—Fate has dealt you a bad hand." She shook her head. The ringlets and ribbons in her hair shook as well, punctuating her disapproval. "One of these days, you won't be able to solve someone's problem."

"Don't worry. I'll find a way to lift the curse before then. Even so, I couldn't live with myself if I didn't try to help this woman."

"Aye, you're a good person, Harradorn Lawson. It's why you were elected mayor of Peace and not Prosperity. You're the glue that holds this community together. Now pick a color that will trigger your return."

"Purple." Around Sirena, it was always the first color that came to mind.

"How sweet." She grinned, obviously taking it as a compliment. With her long gold-painted nails, she added a generous pinch of purple to the concoction. "You're not going like that, are you?" She eyed the tie-dyed tai chi clothes under his jacket.

"No time to change. Outsiders who see me will think I'm

nothing more than a geek." Harradorn approached the floor-length black mirror in the rear of the room. He'd used the ominous device twice before, once as a boy to visit his mother when she was critically ill, and once when his brother was lost at sea.

He stood before the mirror, hands fisted, ready for action. Ready to save Joy Flint from her intruder. "Let's do it."

"Not so fast. We haven't agreed upon my price."

He stared at her in disbelief. "This is an emergency."

"And the perfect time to set the price."

He clenched his teeth. Sirena could be as stubborn as a cat. Ordering her around would only make her balk, and he didn't think Joy Flint had time for that. "Very well. What's your currency and price: yen, euros, doubloons, or dollars?"

Sirena wriggled her nose in distaste. "No money," she said. Then she raised her chin and said, "I want to be able to live in my home again. The Lawson Manor."

"There's a reason you were kicked out," he replied evenly.

"And now I have a reason to be let back in, *brother*."

He scrutinized her face. Sirena's purple lips smiled with a mischievous tilt, but her eyes were sad and desperate. After all these years, she still hurt, still yearned to be let back in the family's good graces.

"I can't make that decision," he told her. "As the family's main residence, I'd have to get everyone to agree. Rick alone might take days to convince, if ever, and the rest are spread around the world."

Her smile drooped into a bitter frown, and he saw her hope for restitution wither along with any desire to speed him on his way. "I can't meet your price," he said, "but I can offer an alternative. You can live in the Mayor's Residence."

Her face brightened.

"For a month." Though it probably would seem more like a year.

Sirena shook her head. "Not good enough. Make it for as long as *you* live there or I throw the potion away." And to prove her intent, she started toward the sink.

"Wait!"

She turned to him.

By Thor's thunder. Her demand was extravagant, ridiculous, and completely unacceptable. "I agree. Now let's do it."

All smiles, Sirena joined him at the tall black mirror, her voice once again soft and melodious. "One more thing," she said. "You don't want *outsiders* seeing that, do you?"

He followed her gaze to the gold medallion with a large blue sapphire in the middle of it, which hung on his chest. His symbol of office, Mayor of Peace.

"I can hold it until you get back," she purred, and extended a hand to take it.

"Thanks, but I've got it covered." He hid the medallion inside his shirt.

With a pout, she withdrew her empty hand. "Don't you trust me?"

No.

"Since receiving this, I've never taken it off. Now send me on my way before it's too late."

"Very well. What's the address?"

"I don't know. I only have the phone number."

"You don't make things easy, do you?"

He shrugged. "I'm a Lawson."

"As am I, though everyone tends to forget." She dipped her finger into the mixture and wrote the number he gave on top of the mirror, then dabbed a small amount on the back of his hand where it tingled and vanished into his skin. Using a feather caster, she sprinkled the mirror with the potion, mumbling mystical words under her breath.

Harradorn watched, gut churning with expectation, ready to pass through the mirror the moment the spell took effect.

There.

As Sirena continued to sprinkle the mirror, their reflections disappeared. The droplets no longer fell on the surface but through it. The passage was open. Without a second thought, he leapt into the mirror and entered the Stygian Gap.

Chapter 2

In the somber gloom of the bathroom, Joy's phone sizzled, spitting static and giving every indication it was in the throes of a horrible death. Afraid of being tasered by her own phone, she dropped it to the floor where it sputtered into silence. A warning flashed on its display: the battery was low.

Joy groaned. It couldn't be. She'd just recharged it.

That wasn't the worst, for when she picked it up and hit redial to find out how soon Mike would come to her rescue, she noticed the number displayed wasn't her brother's. Wasn't even close. Not even the right area code!

Her phone dimmed. What little life remained in the battery was almost gone, perhaps seconds left. She texted one word to Mike—HELP—then pushed SEND. At the same time, her phone died, plunging the room into total darkness.

Did it get sent? She couldn't be sure. Even if it did, there was no way of knowing how soon Mike would see it, how far away he was, or how long it would take to get here.

There was no getting around it. Cowering like a rabbit in the bathroom wasn't something a Flint did, no matter how scared she was.

Lightning brightened the room for a teasing moment, followed by a rumble of thunder that shook the rafters. At least the lightning was back to being white. Before her courage shriveled completely, she boldly stepped into the bleak hallway, toilet plunger in hand, determined to confront the intruder. Or at least sneak out the front door.

For a brief second she thought about taking Shredder with her, then decided the cat was safer under the bed. She considered joining him. But the killer in that horror movie had found his last entree under a bed. The way her luck was going, the intruder probably had watched the same show. Might as well stick a sign on top of the covers that said: *Here she is.*

Joy started toward the stairs, toilet plunger raised threateningly, nerves quivering, forcing herself to move through sheer stubbornness. The power outage had given her one advantage. Even in the dark, she knew her way around. Her intruder didn't. Holding her breath, she crept down the steps and prayed the next flash of lightning wouldn't show the intruder coming up when she was going down.

Everything was going as planned until she stepped on what had to be the loudest, most arthritic, creaky step in the entire house. She cringed in terror.

Please, please, please, don't let him have heard it!

From the darkness below, a beam of light speared her face.

She froze, her mind a blank. All her self-defense techniques vanished.

Her brother's angry voice growled, "What the hell are you doing?"

"Mike?" she cried out. "Is that you?" Dizzy with relief, she covered her pounding heart with one hand. Of course! That explained Shredder's actions. Her cat hated Mike. Whenever he visited, Shredder disappeared.

"You're lucky it *is* me," Mike said. "What the hell are you doing, not locking the door to the garage? How many times do I have to tell you to keep every door in the house locked?"

"I figured the garage-door opener should be good enough to keep anyone out."

"You figured wrong. Jeez Louise, Joy. You know how easy it is to bypass the code?" Mike trained the flashlight down her arm to the plunger. "And what were you planning on doing with that? Make an intruder fall on the floor laughing while you escape?"

Not amused, and feeling stupid for mistaking her own brother for a burglar, she changed the subject. "Is that how you got in? Through the garage?"

"Yeah. It was starting to rain. I pounded on the front door. When you didn't answer, I checked the garage on the off-chance you didn't lock up. Which you didn't." Grumbling, he headed toward the kitchen, flashlight leading the way.

She followed. "You know you scared me half to death. Still, I'm glad you got my message. Thanks for coming."

"What message?" Mike grabbed a towel near the sink and ran it through his rain-soaked hair.

"I texted you for help."

"What are you talking about?" He tossed her the towel and pointed to her forehead where hair color had trickled down. While she cleaned her face, grateful not to be using permanent dye, he said, "I decided to get a second piece of that chocolate cake you made for dinner tonight." He pointed to her cheek where she'd missed a spot. "Walked over but forgot my keys." He pulled out his phone and checked. "No messages."

"Believe me, I called. Actually, I called the wrong number, then texted you."

"If you say so." In the rear of the kitchen, he retrieved a dust pan and broom from a nearby closet and began sweeping up dried flower petals along with pieces of a small glass bowl in which she had kept the potpourri.

She stared at the mess. "What happened?"

"Dunno. Probably your cat. Gets into everything. Worst pound cat I've ever seen."

Joy trained the flashlight on the entry table where the bowl used to be and saw her handbag on its side, the contents scattered about. "With the lights out, maybe you accidentally broke it when you came in."

"Uh-uh. I grabbed a flashlight from the garage. Saw the shards on the floor before I walked in."

She tried replaying the sequence of events. Everything had happened so fast. "I could swear Shredder was already upstairs when I heard it break."

"Fear has a way of playing tricks on the mind." Mike emptied the pieces in the trash. "Damn cat probably knocked the bowl over trying to get something to eat."

She held up a pack of mint gum to the flashlight. It was still intact, with no discernible bites or claw marks. She shrugged and placed the gum back in her handbag along with her wallet, coupons, hand sanitizer, and Wonder Woman key chain. Maybe Mike was right. Shredder had dug through her bag to get to the gum, only to be scared off by his sudden intrusion. Poor Shredder. The cat was a rascal and a troublemaker and got into everything, but he was her cat and she loved him.

She secured the bag in a closet. "If you're going to scare my cat every time you come over, maybe I should change the combination on the garage door so you can't get in."

"As if that would help. Knowing you, you'll give the new code to half the neighborhood. How many have it now?"

"Only Mom and Dad, Merry's friend Gina, Mrs. O'Keefe across the street," who was in her nineties but could still whack an intruder with a shovel, which she did last month when New Jersey PSE&G forgot to warn her they were sending someone over to change a connection in her basement. "And Jeff, of course." Her next-door neighbor and fellow teacher. Each also had copies of her house key and she theirs in case everyone got Alzheimer's at the same time and locked themselves out.

Mike continued to grouch while getting out the cake. He'd always objected to her inordinate trust in the neighbors. Chances were her brother had done background checks on all of them before he moved out.

He poured himself a hefty serving of milk, then used the still very warm water in the hot-water dispenser to make Joy's nightly cup of herbal tea. She smiled in appreciation. For all his gruffness, when it came to family her brother was a real sweetheart.

While he sliced the cake, Joy lit three cookie-dough scented candles and arranged them on the table. She shut off the flashlight to save on the batteries—no telling how long the power would be out. She sat down. Her brother got out another fork and handed it to her.

"Thanks." She speared a forkful of cake loaded with gooey frosting and ate it, licking her lips, savoring the rich taste of chocolate. "Did you see that strange red lightning earlier?"

"Yeah, I did."

"You think it has to do with global warming?"

"Dunno. Saw purple lightning over Denver a few years ago. Just a few bolts."

"Really? Anywhere else?"

"One other place, but I'm not at liberty to say where."

Undoubtedly, another of his super-secret deployments. She sipped her raspberry tea, its warmth sliding through her.

He raised a candle to her face and surveyed her slimy, foul-smelling hair. "Bad day?"

"Bad week."

"It's only Monday."

"Don't remind me." She checked her watch. Five minutes until she rinsed out the dye.

"What color is it going to be this time?"

"Persian Plum."

"Looks more like Frightful Purple." He eyed the dark tint to her hair with a critical frown. "Hoping to scare your students into doing their work?"

"If only."

"Changing your looks every time you're bored is only a temporary solution."

"Bored? Are you crazy? If anything, I'm stressed out." She

19

paused and listened. "Did you hear something?"

"No, and don't change the subject. You can handle stress." He pointed the fork at her. "The problem is you're bored with normal students and normal classroom problems. The two years you spent with VISTA ruined you. You're not an ordinary teacher. You're a Flint. We love challenges."

She rubbed her fingers on the table, disturbed her brother might be right. But he couldn't be. Though she had loved helping poverty-stricken students at risk, she had also come back from Appalachia sick and exhausted, in need of rest and normalcy. She liked living here safe and secure with her sister in their hometown. "Next year will be better."

"That's what you said last year, and it hasn't. Face it, sis. When the bad gets worse, it's time to change territory."

"Is that what you do when things get worse? Cut and run?"

Mike grabbed the knife to slice more cake, bristling with indignation. He hated that phrase, which was why she had used it. "That's a whole 'nother thing," he said, his voice rising.

"Is it?" She stood up. This was an old bone of contention between them, and way past due for her to win. "Every time you come home half-starved, beat-up, injured," she glanced at the wound still healing on his cheek, "Mom, Dad, Merry, Gramps—all of us—keep praying it'll be the last time. But you always go back. Always answer the call."

He pointed the knife up at her. "That's my job."

She grabbed the plunger and shook it at him." And mine is teaching, even normal students, no matter how bad the class is, so back off."

* * *

Without warning, the Stygian Gap spat out Harradorn like a troublesome clump of snot. The vertigo passed quickly while his eyes adjusted to the dim light. The power outage Joy Flint had mentioned was still in effect, for he found himself in the rear of a kitchen lit solely by candles. A woman stood with her back to him, shaking a stick—was that a toilet plunger?— at a sinister-looking man sitting at a kitchen table with a knife pointed at her.

Thank Odin, he'd arrived in time.

He seized the plunger and pushed aside the woman. "Stand back, Joy Flint. I'll handle him." He risked a sideways glance at the woman, expecting a smile of welcome, a sigh of gratitude, a typical damsel in distress. Instead, she grabbed the plunger from him and jabbed the stick end into his stomach.

"Oof!" He doubled over in pain and disbelief. She hooked the stick behind one of his knees and pulled. With a loud thud, he fell on his back. The next thing he knew, she was standing over him, the rubber end of the plunger placed directly on his privates, threatening his ability to procreate, with the added promise he'd be singing soprano if he moved.

Joy Flint peered down at him. In the shadows of candlelight, she resembled Medusa, with dark shaggy strands of wet hair framing her face.

"Who the hell are you?" she demanded to know. "And what are you doing in my house?"

Gut bruised and hurting, he stammered, "I came to rescue you. From him!" he added in alarm. The knife-wielding intruder approached. Lightning flashed, momentarily brightening everything in the room. Harradorn recognized murderous intent when he saw it. "Watch out!" he warned Joy.

Lightning flashed again. Something must have caught her eye, for she abruptly glanced to the side, an odd expression on her face. Her eyes darted up and down, as if following a dust mote in the air. "What the...?" The room swiftly dimmed to candlelight. Joy glanced at the man with the knife and said, "Did you see that?"

Harradorn moved fast. Always one for recognizing an opportunity and taking advantage of it, he rolled away from the menacing plunger, spun, and leapt to his feet. He snatched the toilet plunger away from Joy and pointed it at the intruder.

The man with the knife shone a monster of a flashlight in his face, blinding him.

Something wasn't right. Raising a hand to shield his eyes, he was surprised to see Joy Flint standing calmly next to the intruder. The woman he had come to rescue looked puzzled, not scared. Whereas the man next to her, well, he'd seen bears in the Enchanted Forest who looked friendlier.

He redirected his gaze at the woman and spoke fast. "On the phone, you said somebody was in your house. You thought I was someone named Mike. We got cut off before I could tell you that you had the wrong number. Since I couldn't call you back, I used my caller ID to track you down. I'm here to rescue you."

"Rescue me?" Her mocking smile asked how he would have managed that when she had so easily set him flat on his back. But then she must have reconsidered his explanation, for her face scrunched up into a doubtful frown and her eyes lowered in regret. With an embarrassed smile, she placed a hand on the intruder's arm and nudged the megawatt beam away from his face.

Beauty and the Beast, that's how he perceived Joy and the hefty man who sported a fresh scar on his cheek. He checked her hands. No glint of a wedding band on her finger. What little he could see of her in the blaze of light revealed a pleasing face, though her shaggy black hair needed work. It had an odd tint to it. Then again, her figure in jeans and snug t-shirt was eye-catching. The lady had great curves.

The man beside her grunted. Every word came out rock hard. "I want your name, address, social security number, and a complete explanation of how you got in here."

Harradorn aimed the toilet plunger at his face. "Would you like a driver's license and birth certificate to go with that?"

The man snarled.

Okay, so the guy didn't have a sense of humor.

The man stepped ominously closer. Harradorn backed off, not so much from the man but the wicked glint of his knife.

Joy rushed forward. "That's enough, you two. Everybody take a breath and calm down. Let's start with introductions. Everyone seems to know who I am." She turned to Harradorn. "The man next to me, who's about to skewer your intestines if you don't start taking him seriously, is my brother Mike, the person I was trying to call."

Harradorn nodded stiffly in greeting, but Mike refused to lower the knife. Harradorn kept the plunger raised. "What about the intruder?"

"It was Mike. A comedy of errors combined with the storm knocking out the power."

When the magic curse heard Joy wasn't in danger, it released Harradorn from its grip. Cool relief washed through him. His heart calmed; his breathing eased.

"We still don't know who you are," Mike said. "How'd you get in here?"

Like I'm really going to tell you. "How did *you* get in here?"

Joy rolled her eyes, then poked her brother in the arm. "Did you lock the garage door after you came in?"

Mike winced. He lowered the knife. "I didn't think there was any need, not with me in the house."

"And you yelled at me for being careless?" She gestured toward Harradorn. "So now we've got this guy in the house."

Harradorn found it increasingly difficult to take her bravado seriously, what with the way she planted her hands on the enticing curve of her hips. It was all he could do not to smile in appreciation. But he tore his gaze away when she added, "You have exactly one minute to answer my brother's questions or I'm calling the police."

He lowered the plunger. "My name's Harradorn Lawson. I'm from a small town out west. Somehow I got your call for help and since I was in the neighborhood—" *actually, the curse wouldn't let me ignore you,* "I decided to see if I could help. Since you seem to have everything under control, I need to be on my way." *Back to a real emergency. The wizard duel.*

He started for the living room, to the front door. He'd step outside into the cover of darkness so these outsiders wouldn't see how he traveled.

"Wait!" Joy hurried after him. "What about—"

"Yeah, not so fast," Mike said. Brandishing the knife, he stepped in Harradorn's path. "I want to see some ID first."

"What are you, a cop?" Harradorn asked.

"Guys. Guys." Joy stepped between them and held up her hands "Let's not be hasty." She turned to Harradorn. "I make a mean triple chocolate fudge cake. How about a slice? It's the least I can do to thank you for coming to my rescue."

Truth be told, he'd like to spend a few more minutes with Joy, alone, and take advantage of the candlelight to flirt among the shadows and discover if she was as interesting as she seemed to be. Plus he loved chocolate cake. But if meddling Warbird found out he'd taken an unauthorized jaunt through the skelter mirror, he'd tell the rest of the council and there'd be Hel to pay. He had enough problems without adding to them.

He edged toward the front door, determined to resist her tempting offer. But luck, or fate, interceded.

The lights came back on and Harradorn noticed three things right away.

First, Mike Flint was a lot bigger and meaner looking with the lights on than off.

Second, Joy Flint had the warmest, brightest, loveliest smile he'd ever seen. If someone could package her smile, there'd be instant world peace.

Third, the color of Joy's hair. It wasn't black like he'd originally thought. It was dark purple. Purple dye dripped down her face and onto her ratty t-shirt. He was so startled by her ridiculous appearance, he laughed and blurted out, "You're purple!"

A familiar tingling sensation rippled across his skin. Black sparkles burst all around him. In the next instant he was in the Stygian Gap, traveling back to the skelter mirror in Sirena's store, cursing himself all the way for inadvertently speaking the color that would trigger his return. And he still had the toilet plunger in his hand.

Dammit.

* * *

Joy gawked, dumbfounded.

Harradorn Lawson had vanished into thin air!

Actually, he'd disappeared in a mist of black sparkles, after which the sparkles disappeared, too. "What the hell?" she said, and turned to see her brother's reaction, wondering if he was as bewildered as she was. To her surprise, Mike was on the phone.

"Who are you calling?"

"My section head. I want a team brought in to do a sweep, see if there's any hallucinogenic gases, EMFs, or soundwaves in here."

While he keyed in a flurry of numbers, a movement across the room caught her eye. Something orange was hovering behind her African violets, the same thing she had seen fly away from Harradorn while he was fending off her brother. She thought she'd imagined it, an optical illusion brought about by the sudden flash of lightning. But then she'd caught sight of it again when Mike and Harradorn were verbally testing each other's testosterone levels.

It was definitely alive, shifting back and forth behind the plant. A large moth or butterfly, or a small bird. Poor thing was probably scared. And it had a right to be. Joy didn't know exactly what super secret group in the military Mike was assigned to. From the way he refused to talk about it, she always figured only someone with the President's security clearance knew what he did. If Mike was any indication of what his co-workers were like, a die-hard, no-nonsense group would soon be invading her home, and she was sure they wouldn't think twice about cutting open the orange bird or insect to see if it contained clues to Harradorn's mysterious disappearance.

Aghast at the possible vivisection, she placed an anxious hand on her brother's arm. "You really think that's such a good idea?"

"Seeing someone do a David Copperfield in the middle of your living room isn't normal. I need to know what just happened."

"Of course you do. But what if it was menacing sound waves or psychotropic gas? Would that mean we're infected? Our brains scrambled? What if the cause has dissipated, or is undetectable? Wouldn't you be classified not-fit-for-duty until they figured out what happened to us?"

Her brother frowned. Not being able to do his job, whatever it was, was comparable to being classified a ninety-pound wimp with a pocket protector.

"Maybe someone slipped some silly weed into the cake batter," she said.

Mike stared at her in horror. "You didn't?"

"Of course not. What I'm saying is we should look at other causes before my house is torn apart by the Men In Black." She held her breath while Mike thought it over. He ended the call but kept his phone out.

"Joy, I have my blood and urine tested on a regular basis. Please tell me you didn't put anything illegal in the cake."

"Dark chocolate may be so addictively yummy that it's sinful, but it's not illegal. I swear, my cake is made up of one hundred percent pure decadent wholesomeness."

Mike studied her face for a long second, searching for any hint she was fudging the truth. Out of the corner of her eye, Joy saw the orange thing move.

Don't look at it. Don't look. Keep your eyes on Mike. Smile.

She smiled sweetly. Mike shook his head. He dropped a brotherly kiss on her cheek then went to the spot where Harradorn had disappeared. Crouching down, he rubbed the carpet, looking for anything besides cat hair, and sniffed his fingers. "Smells like church. Incense maybe."

He stood and looked around. Joy edged closer to the African violets, blocking her brother's view of the orange thing hiding behind them.

Mike put his phone away. "I'm figuring this Harradorn, if that's his real name, is some kind of magician. Used diversionary chaff to divert our attention while he slipped away."

Magician? That might explain the small orange thing he'd left behind. Probably one of those trained birds hidden in clothes, part of a magic trick.

"He might still be in the house. Stay here while I do a sweep. And lock that door to the garage."

While her brother left to reconnoiter her home, she dutifully locked the door, and then went back to the living room to look for the bird. She doubted Harradorn was still in the house. After the way she and her brother had treated him, she couldn't blame him for making a fast exit. Too bad. The quick glimpse she got of him after the lights came on, before he did his vanishing act, had her heart beating in approval. Late twenties, early thirties, lean but not skinny lean, hair the color of dark honey, with a twinkle in his feral gray eyes when he'd confronted her brother, and a wolfish grin to match.

Harradorn was remarkably striking. She was inclined to think the feeling was mutual, for she'd noticed the way his gaze had traveled up and down the length of her body, twice. A double once-over could only be interpreted as interest bordering on attraction.

She glanced at her reflection in a nearby mirror, and groaned. Not only was her hair icky purple, but rivulets of dye had streaked her face and neck and seeped into her old dyeing shirt. No wonder Harradorn had laughed. Talk about bad first impressions.

By the time Mike finished his search of the house, she was in the kitchen, toweling her hair after rinsing out the dye. "I didn't find him," he said.

"Duh. He came to rescue me and we both treated him like a felon. You really think he'd stick around?"

"We only have his word as to why he was here." Mike opened the door to the garage and looked around. "Hold on." Moments later, he returned, frowning. "Did you leave the window open in the garage?"

"I might have. It's been getting warmer and I wanted to air things out."

"Well, the screen is torn. Could have been the wind. Or this Harradorn taking advantage of your motion-sensor lights being off during the blackout."

"A magician-thief? Hard to believe with the way he looked. He was quite handsome, like a sexy elf from one of the Tolkien movies, only taller, more muscular—and a tad geeky. Who wears a tie-dyed tai chi outfit?"

Mike shook his head. "No one looks that good naturally."

"When was the last time you took a peek in a mirror?" she asked and gave him an affectionate hug. "Come on, let's go finish that cake."

"What about pretty boy? What if he comes back when I'm not around?"

"I've got a baseball bat, cake knife, and a scary-looking plunger, and I know how to use all three." She laughed, trying to ease her brother's worry. "Plus, thanks to the self-defense classes you had me take, I can handle myself really well, like I did tonight."

"That's not what I meant." He lifted her chin, forcing her to meet his somber gaze. "It's not how a man looks on the outside that counts. I've met so-called saints whose souls are black as hell. Besides, he took your plunger."

She scanned the living room in surprise. If Harradorn was so anxious to slip away unnoticed, why would he take her plunger?

"It's the only thing he touched," Mike said with a scowl. "The only object that might have his fingerprints on it. It'll make it harder for me to track him down and find him, but I will. You can bet on it."

She looked up at her brother and didn't like what she saw. This was the consummate warrior who did his job until it was finished or he was dead. "Why are you so sure Harradorn isn't who he said he is?"

He placed his hands on her shoulders, the same gesture she used when giving a student unexpected bad news. He said, "It's still raining outside."

She searched his face, not getting his point.

"If this Harradorn didn't enter the house until after you called, why wasn't he wet?"

Chapter 3

In the central park of Peace, dew on the grass glistened like fallen tears in the light of Harradorn's lantern. It seemed a sacrilege to walk upon it. But he had work to do, an old friend to say good-bye to. While away in his meaningless attempt to save Joy Flint, the Valkyrie Oak, the oldest living tree in town, had been hit by a stray bolt during the wizard duel. All night he had stood vigil. The pungent scent of scorched wood still haunted the park.

Dawn turned the sky from indigo to dismal grey, and a mournful song filled the air. Elves were coming across the bridge from his brother's side of town. People filled the park, holding lamps and candles, lending light to the somber task ahead. At the elves' request, there were no flashlights; lightning had dealt the mortal blow and its kindred, electricity, was not welcome.

Sprites and fairies had already stripped away the lush green finery, making the mighty oak seem naked and violated. The elves set their ladders on the trunk, and an unspeakable sadness filled his heart. The Valkyrie Oak had embodied strength and stability to the town. Now it was dead. The rune diviners would say it was an omen of things to come.

Harradorn surveyed the hotels lining the park. When word had gotten out that a wizard duel was in progress, most of the tourists had packed up and portaled away. Tourism was the lifeblood of the town's economy. The wizard duel would cause a recession, but he'd worry about that later.

High among the branches, fairies held aloft globes of captured moonbeams as the elves began their sorrowful task. With a loving touch and sharp blades, they took down the tree, branch by branch, limb by limb.

While the elves worked, tiny glowing tree sprites chittered and cried inconsolably. On the ground, Harradorn ministered to the crowd, including a respectable showing from his brother's side of town. He passed out handkerchiefs, answered children's questions, and placed a comforting hand on many shoulders. By the time the sun rose above the surrounding mountains, the ancient tree had been taken down except for the enormous stump, which would be dug out in the weeks ahead.

The lightning-split trunk had been cleaved in half and was fitted onto two massive slings of rope and salvaged branches. Now came the hard part. Letting go. He looked around for his brother. As co-mayor, Rick should be helping. Strange he wasn't here.

With sorrow in his heart, Harradorn addressed the crowd. "It's time to say good-bye to our dear old friend. Let us take comfort in knowing not a splinter nor leaf nor drip of sap of the Valkyrie Oak will be overlooked or wasted. The leaves will line the nests of sprites and fairies, the twigs will be given to the squirrels and birds.

"In the weeks to come, the elves and woodcrafters of our town will transform our beloved tree into walking sticks, flutes, furniture, chimes, bowls, and jewelry so everyone can honor its memory by keeping some part of the Valkyrie Oak in our lives and in our homes."

The elves wept freely, so did the sprites and fairies. Women and children dabbed their tears, and moisture glistened the eyes of more than a few men.

Harradorn forced a smile he didn't feel and said, "Come forward and touch the Valkyrie Oak one last time and thank it for sharing its life with us." Rick had sent the best singing group from a casino on his side of town. Accompanied by musicians playing lurs and lyres, the Nordic singers intoned an intensely sorrowful death chant that lamented the passing of the sacred oak.

Harradorn went first and laid his hands on one of the halves of the trunk. With an aching heart, he bowed his head and said good-bye. Others came forward to say good-bye until everyone in the park had touched the tree. When done, the elves hefted the halves and began a funeral procession back to their home in Prosperity. They were accompanied by a drum beating slowly, the heart beat of the town mourning the loss of one of its oldest members. Through the streets of Peace, all followed as far as the bridge where the river bisected the town—the east side Peace, the west Prosperity. Those from Prosperity continued across. For those of Peace, families returned to their homes while others opted for reminiscing about the Oak at the local bars and coffee houses.

Harradorn followed the procession across the bridge. He would stay with the Oak until the elves reached their homes.

When he had returned through the skelter mirror, the sky above his town had raged with bolts of lightning. Thanks to the lightning rods, the strikes had been minimal. He supposed he should be grateful the Valkyrie Oak was the only casualty.

He looked to the northwest. The two towers stood eerily quiet; FearfulFran must be planning her next attack. The duel would continue until she or Zach conceded or surrendered. It all depended on what had caused the duel in the first place. But no one would know that until it was over and the victor announced.

Suddenly, the funeral march came to a halt. On the far side of the bridge, he saw Rick talking with the leaders of the procession. Like many who resided in the Prosperity side of town, his younger brother took pride in his ancestry, which included wearing what outsiders would probably call a more modern version of their Viking forbears—a pirate costume: black pants, boots, white blowsy shirt with a red sash around the waist, and a matching red scarf tied over his hair, along with gold hoop earrings. On his chest hung his symbol of office, Mayor of Prosperity, a gold medallion with a large flame-red ruby embedded in its center.

Rick began wearing the clothes in high school along with some of his friends. Now Harradorn couldn't remember him wearing anything else.

While Rick talked, the elves looked at each other in alarm. Those hauling the trunks repositioned their load and took off running, not through the center of Prosperity to their homes, but south along the river. Elves are inherently strong and deft. Even so, Harradorn was amazed at how quickly they disappeared from sight while hauling two massive loads. He'd never known elves to do anything in a hurry, certainly not a funeral procession.

What in Thor's hammer was going on?

Rick met him halfway across the bridge. "The duel has resumed." With an urgent frown, Rick gestured for the two of them to return to Peace.

Harradorn glanced back at the towers, then up at the sky. "At least they're not using lightning."

"Don't count your blessings," Rick said. They strode to the Mayor's Hall. "Remember the magical treat Zach gives out during the Founders Day Festival?"

"You mean Blithe-Mist-on-a-stick?" It was a sticky yellow droplet on the end of a toothpick. Touch it to one's skin, or anyone's skin, and the recipient had the giggles for at least a minute.

"The same. Now picture it oozing out of Zach's tower in the form of a mist, climbing over everything it comes in contact with, including FearfulFran's smoggy tower."

Aghast at the implication, he stared at his brother. "No!"

"Aye. Only the residue seems more oily than sticky. I've spent the last few hours having a wall built around the towers to hold it in, but there's so much of it, we couldn't keep up. At twelve feet, the Mist has already gone up and over and will soon spread throughout Prosperity. Then it'll cross the river into Peace." Rick glanced worriedly at him. "Except for the Hall, none of the buildings on your side of town are as tall as those in mine."

Harradorn ignored the criticism of his zoning restrictions. He had his security measures and Rick had his. "Where did the elves go?"

"They thought it best to circle south to get to the trees before it reaches their homes. They should be fine if they stay up high and inside. On the straightaway the Blithe Mist is only at eight feet. I've got the sheriff and my assistants alerting everyone to stay on the upper floors of their homes and businesses. Within a quarter hour, the Mayoral Palace will be completely surrounded. Until then, I've opened up the Palace to all ground dwellers and anyone who needs a higher place to stay."

"Even trolls?" Harradorn asked, suspicious of his brother's surprising generosity.

"Aye. But they have to pay a damage deposit up front. Even so, I have my assistants moving all the breakables up to the attic."

Harradorn got out his phone.

"I called Agamemnon," Rick said. "He'll place someone by the bridge to sound the signal horn when the Mist starts to cross over from Prosperity."

He nodded in gratitude. Already he could see some of his assistants running door to door to alert everyone in Peace about what was going on. Hardware stores were putting up signs advertising duct tape and plastic sheeting. Likewise, shop owners who sold soaps and cleansers were advertising their wares, anticipating the need to clean the oily residue once the Mist dispersed.

"Lemonade from lemons," Rick said. People were leaving cafés and restaurants laden with takeout boxes. "On my side, the bars and casinos are going to make a killing. Happy patrons are an easy mark. I've been invited to two poker games to celebrate the occasion. Should be interesting to see how much of a poker face one can have when everyone has the giggles."

"How can you possibly win?"

"I'll figure it out. I always do. With all the tourists popping out, I had to do something to help the economy." Rick stopped short and sucked in his breath. They had entered the central park to cut across to the Mayor's Hall & Residence. The sight of the huge stump where the stately Valkyrie Oak had once stood took even Harradorn's breath away.

Rick's voice cracked. "I can't believe it's gone."

"Watching the elves take it down was hard," Harradorn said. "So many memories went with it. My first kiss was under that tree."

"Mine, too."

"I remember the day you broke an arm falling out of it." Rick flexed the selfsame arm and Harradorn added, "You always pretended you were climbing the mast of some ship."

"Aye." After a long moment of silence, Rick turned away. With a heavy stride, they headed to the Mayor's Hall. "Won't be the same without it."

"I have the fairies searching among their stores for Valkyrie acorns, and the tree sprites are talking with the squirrels. With luck and the elves' help, we'll soon have one of its descendants taking its place. The circle of life."

"And all that crap." Rick glanced at Harradorn. "You're such an optimist."

"Someone in the family has to be." He clapped his brother on the back and together they climbed the stairs. They entered the Mayor's Hall and found Agamemnon putting duct tape around the windows.

The Cyclops greeted them. "Mayor Rick. Mayor Harradorn."

Harradorn handed the lantern to an assistant. "Need any help?"

"Robert Burns always warned the best-laid plans of mice and men often go awry. But for now, all have been alerted. Everything is almost covered or taped. The last will be the plastic sheeting over the front doors."

"What about those in need of shelter?"

"Chairs, cots, and refreshments have been set up in the upstairs ballroom. Last count, we have forty-three guests."

"Good work." Harradorn smiled, pleased by the efficiency of

his staff. The last mayor had left him a bickering, back-stabbing group of political appointees as apathetic as they were self-serving. He'd downsized to get rid of those too stubborn to change, brought in Agamemnon, and rebuilt the spirit and goals of the staff until they learned how to work as one.

"Your family…" he started to say, remembering Agamemnon and his kin might seem to live in a two-story house, but actually it was only one level because of their inordinate stature.

"They're here and safe," Agamemnon replied. "Thank you for asking."

"Good. If there's anything I can do, let me know. Oh, almost forgot—when you have time, get us a satellite phone."

The Cyclops raised his single massive brow. Contact with the outside world was permitted only with prior approval. "Is the council aware?"

He gave Agamemnon a knowing look. "Not yet. Have your son create a program to bounce the signal off multiple satellites so it can't be easily traced back to us."

"He'll enjoy that."

"I thought so." The Cyclops' son, though all of nine years, was the town's tech whiz. A true genius, it was a shame his skills would be wasted here. But the outside world would never allow a Cyclops to have the normal life Peace & Prosperity could provide.

In the mayor's office, Rick flopped into a leather chair and Harradorn sat on the edge of his desk. He picked up a fishing lure from the desk and absently turned it over in his hand.

Rick noticed the toilet plunger on a nearby table and jerked his thumb toward it. "Having problems with the plumbing?"

"A memento from my last trip to the outside." He told Rick about the curse taking hold and his disastrous attempt to rescue Joy Flint from her intruder. By the end of the tale, Rick was laughing so hard he fell out of his chair.

Harradorn tried not to smile. On the retelling, it did sound comical. He grabbed the plunger and twirled it like a baton. "Don't laugh. This is the closest thing to sex I've had in a long time."

"Really?" Rick climbed back in the chair and hooked a leg over one arm. "How long has it been? Weeks? Months?" With each increment, his eyes continued to widen in disbelief. "A year? Two?"

"Ever since I became mayor."

Rick shook his head in disapproval. "Since the day we were elected, the lasses have been hanging onto me like barnacles on a ship. If not for Cynthia scaring them away this past year, they'd still be shanghaiing me to their beds." Rick chuckled, no doubt amused by the pleasurable possibilities, which made Harradorn suspect having a possessive lover like Cynthia was wearing thin.

Rick's brow lowered and he studied Harradorn in concern. "You're not having trouble with the plumbing, are you?"

"Hardly. Problem is the women on my side of town aren't into one-night stands. They want something more permanent and the title that goes along with being married to the mayor. I'd give anything for a casual date or two."

"Like with the fair owner of said plunger?" Rick's mouth curled into a devilish slant. "Is that why you ordered a satellite phone? To keep the plumbing shipshape with a little phone sex?"

Harradorn smiled to himself. In the few minutes he'd spent in Joy's presence, he'd decided she was resourceful and feisty, feminine yet tough. A wild and dangerous combination that was sexually appealing. But the last thing he needed was an outsider in his bed, no matter how good the sex might be.

"It'll never happen." He shrugged out of his jacket and tossed it onto a nearby chair. "She's from the outside world, a potential security hazard." Rick arched a brow, a clear signal he wasn't buying the excuse. "Besides, except for a great looking figure and a wonderful smile, her straggly purple hair was more disturbing than exciting."

"A great figure and smile are more than sufficient. The last time we went to Mardi Gras, the lass I saw you with had outrageous violet hair, but it didn't stop you from adding to your collection of beads."

"That's before we became mayors." Harradorn dismissed his brother's mocking smile with a wave of his hand. "Forget it. I'll never see her again. The satellite phone is insurance. If I ever get another call from the outside, I can straighten out the problem from here."

"So you say." Rick pulled out the jeweled dagger he kept in his sash and began trimming his nails. "Tell you what. When Zach kicks FearfulFran out of town, I'll throw a bash at my place and invite a few wenches who'll have you raising your anchor in no time."

The offer was tempting. Rick had great taste in women, and it'd been far too long since he'd been able to relax and be himself, whoever that was. The Harradorn Lawson who had fun at the drop of a hat was now buried beneath the ever thickening layers of Peace's mayoralty.

"This Joy and her brother," Rick said. "They saw you disappear right in front of them. Think they'll cause trouble?"

"Maybe an outlandish article in the supermarket tabloids. As soon as the next UFO is sighted, it'll be old news."

The signal horn sounded. The Blithe Mist had crossed the river.

"Here it comes." Harradorn got up to look out the windows towards the west. Within minutes, Mist oozed around a corner into view. The yellow cloud was four feet high, but its oily tendrils rose several feet higher, snaking up the sides of buildings, searching for any hole or crack that would allow it entry. He couldn't believe Zach would endanger the town with such magic. And yet Rick said it was Zach's tower creating the Mist.

A giggling pink fairy smacked into the window directly in front of him. Harradorn drew back, startled. She fell to the grass, laughing, yet her small eyes stared up at him, pleading for help. It was all that was need to activate the curse. His blood heated, muscles fired, ready to take action.

He gestured for her to stay put. "Don't fly!" he shouted

through the window. The fairy giggled in response. The Mist approached. Soon she'd be drowning in it, forced to laugh without stopping. "Rick, get my jacket and the plunger."

Quickly, he removed the duct tape and opened the window. Rick handed him the jacket. He knotted the end of one sleeve and, using it like a mitten, grabbed the plunger and leaned down to the giggling fairy. "Grab on. I'll pull you up."

By now the Mist had reached the fairy, producing bouts of laughter that made it impossible for her to hold onto the plunger.

Yellow tendrils of Mist snaked up the stick toward Harradorn. "Climb into the suction bulb. Hurry!"

Tittering, she retracted her wings and crawled inside. He drew the plunger in and Rick shut the window. Immediately, the curse withdrew from Harradorn. Coolness washed over him.

Oily Mist dotted the fairy. As long as it remained, she'd be forced to laugh. Rick took off his red head scarf and gently enveloped the fairy inside it. Careful of her wings, he eased the fairy inside a drinking glass, then poured a carafe of water over her, rinsing off as much of the Mist as he could. Harradorn stepped out into the hall and yelled for Agamemnon. The Cyclops soon came stomping into the office with a box of cleansing wipes.

Giggling, the fairy climbed out of the glass and began cleaning herself with one of the wipes. The Blithe Mist magic in her system would continue to make her laugh until it wore off.

"Where's Felicity?" Harradorn asked. He recognized this particular fairy, Sessi, a member of her team. Given the situation, he was surprised they weren't staying together.

Sessi laughed. "I don't know. No one's seen her since yesterday."

"Where's the rest of the team?"

"Oh, this way and that." The fairy giggled, hands pointing in all directions. "Most are high up in the trees, but I saw a cookie on the ground outside of Mordred's Bakery and thought I could get to it before the Mist did." She giggled. "Guess I was wrong."

"Well, you're safe now. Agamemnon will take you upstairs where we've set up a shelter. You'll find cookies and fruit juice there."

Sessi laughed and danced into the Cyclops' waiting palm. Agamemnon's massive hand closed enough to keep her from falling out. "I'll take good care of her," he told Harradorn, and left with the giggling fairy.

"This is getting dangerous," Harradorn told Rick, who was using wipes to clean the oily Mist from the plunger. "There's no telling how many others are out there unable to get indoors."

"Aye, but I don't see what anyone can do." Rick set the plunger down and started cleaning Harradorn's jacket. "Ahoy. Something fell out of the pocket." He picked up a small, copper object from the floor. "Felicity's diadem. What's it doing in your jacket?"

Harradorn stared at it in shock. Sessi said no one had seen Felicity since yesterday. "By Odin, she must have hitched a ride with me to the outside." His stomach tightened in dread. "If someone sees her, captures her, makes her talk—"

"We'll have outsiders searching for us like crazy. It'll be Shangri La all over again." Rick clicked his tongue. "Wait till your town council finds out about this. Warbird will string you up on the yardarm like a scurvy dog."

"You mean start a petition to have me removed from office. Hmph. He's already tried three times and failed."

"I hate town councils. Puffed up peacocks trying to tell you how to do your job. You should have dissolved yours like I did mine."

"I don't work that way."

A woman's voice asked, "Why's everyone so sad?" Sirena swept into the office in a swirl of purple skirts, purple shirt, and a gold shawl. She casually walked around like she owned the place, one finger trolling along the desk, checking for dust.

Rick scowled. "What the Hel is she doing here?" He stared at his brother. "Well?"

"I, uh, left something out of my story. In payment for using the skelter mirror, I'm allowing Sirena to stay here for a while."

"Live here?" Rick snarled. "For how long?"

"As long as Harry is here, I'm here," Sirena said in a haughty voice. But then she crossed her arms and said to Harradorn, "Of course, I didn't expect a storage room in the basement."

"Serves you right for taking advantage of him." Rick pulled Harradorn to the side and said, "Are you daft? Since when did this place become a hotel?"

"Hey!" Sirena said, sounding insulted. "I'm family. Family has a right to visit."

Rick ignored her. "Give her an inch and she'll take a mile. Always has and always will. No good will come of this."

"It was a fair deal," Sirena whined.

"I think not." He handed Harradorn the plunger. "All you got was this." Rick headed for the door. "Take my advice and get rid of her."

"If he does," Sirena said, "he'll lose his only chance of getting rid of the Blithe Mist." She crossed to the windows and gestured outside. "Look. It's expanding in the morning heat. Rising. Soon it will be up to the second floor. If it keeps rising, it'll seep down through the chimneys and vents. No one will be able to escape it." With a grin, she turned to her brothers. "You need my help to stop it."

Rick sneered. "Only a wizard can stop a Blithe Mist."

She planted her hands on her hips."So can I."

Rick laughed in derision. "You're an alchemist, and a poor one at that. You have no magical powers."

"I can," she insisted. She focused on Harradorn. "Let me try. You have nothing to lose and so much to gain."

Rick eyed her with well-earned suspicion. "And what will you ask in payment?"

"I want a suite on the same floor where Harry lives."

Harradorn frowned. Rick was right, Sirena always got the better of the deal. "Laughing might be good for a change. Therapeutic." But then he looked at the small copper diadem in his hand. With Zach in the midst of the duel, their sister was the only person in town who could send him back to rescue Felicity from the outside world. And the sooner the better. With each passing moment, the chance of the fairy being caught increased.

Rick studied Harradorn. He scowled in disgust, "I can't believe you're actually considering it. I'm outta here." He headed down the hall.

Harradorn followed, trailed by Sirena. "You can't go out there," he told Rick while his brother removed the tape along one edge of the plastic sheeting which covered the doors. "The entire area is filled with Mist."

Rick glanced over at Sirena. "I'd rather endure Mist than her. Besides, I have a poker game to go to." He gave Harradorn one last measured look. "One of these days you're going to learn staying on an even keel isn't all it's cracked up to be."

Rick slid between the sheeting, then re-taped it shut. With a devil-may-care grin, he opened one door, threw his arms wide, and yelled, "Embrace chaos!" The Mist flowed over him. Within seconds of closing the door, Harradorn heard him laughing.

With his brother lost to the Blithe Mist, there was nothing left to do but hold fast to his decision. If Sirena could remove the Mist so they could get to the mirror in her shop, he'd hear her out. "What did you have in mind?"

Her eyes sparkled with more than gold eye shadow. "Do you agree to my terms?"

The deal was going to bite him in the ass, but he didn't think he had much of a choice. "Agreed. Now, what do you need to pull this off?"

"Nothing. It's already done." She glanced at her watch. "I put everything up on the roof with a ten minute fuse. In fifteen more seconds, the Mist will be gone."

"What? Wait a minute! What chemicals are you using? Don't

you remember what happened the last time you did a roof experiment?"

"Don't worry. That was years ago. Since then I've learned a lot about mixing herbs and chemicals."

Harradorn heard a huge "Whoosh" from the top of the building. He raced to the nearest window and looked out. Above the yellow Mist, a bright fuchsia-colored cloud was swiftly descending upon the town. The two began to intermix. A thunderous roar erupted.

The last thing Harradorn heard was Sirena say, "Oops."

Chapter 4

Four hundred years ago, New Jersey gave birth to the first brewery in America, a tiny yet important historical fact because tonight Joy needed a beer. There was still one left from the six-pack her brother had brought over. She dragged herself in from the garage; she could already taste the hops.

At school, two boys in her class had decided to see how many times they could jab each other with pins before one of them said "Ow!" Five, according to the red marks on their skin. The mutual assault had probably taken all of ten seconds. But the disruption to the class, the time it took to summon the assistant principal, take the boys to the school nurse, then return to class, calm everyone down, and try to teach for the rest of the day as if nothing had happened took hours. The interrupted lessons for two subjects would have to be squeezed into the next few days so her class wouldn't fall behind the other fifth-grade classes.

Then there was the pile of paperwork documenting what had happened, why it had happened, and how she would make sure it wouldn't happen again. Of course, the boys were given out-of-school suspension for three days, which meant they'd be three days behind the rest of the class when they returned. Getting them caught up while continuing with the class's regular lessons would take a minor miracle.

If only she could clone herself.

She didn't even want to think about the censuring stare the assistant principal directed at her Persian Plum hair, insinuating the color instigated her students' misbehavior. Why couldn't the boys have tested each other's macho by playing violent video games like everyone else?

Though exhausted, she had dreaded coming home. Last night, she'd stayed up past midnight searching for the thing her mysterious would-be rescuer had left behind. Whatever it was, by now her cat must have eaten it.

She entered the kitchen, expecting to see a pile of orange feathers, and gasped. Cabinets and drawers were ajar, boxes of food tossed about, their contents scattered over the counters and floor. Likewise, the refrigerator was open, containers overturned, milk, syrup, dressings, ketchup, mustard dripping from the shelves; lettuce and tomatoes gouged as if mice had nibbled on them.

She whimpered. Her lovely bottle of lite beer lay broken on the floor. Nothing had escaped the attack except for a snack-sized box of orange juice. The carton was still upright with a straw in it. Huh?

Her cat couldn't have done this. Well, at least not all of it. There was a reason why they'd named him Shredder. But he certainly wasn't capable of opening the fridge. On that troubling thought, she got out her phone to call the police... and found herself face to face with a tiny orange woman hovering near the tip of her nose, her gossamer wings flapping madly. The slender body was as tall as Joy's finger and clad in a scanty, translucent tangerine dress.

Startled, Joy stumbled back and fell into a heap of sugar, tuna, beer, and corn flakes.

There was an orange Tinker Bell in her home!

The buxom beauty flew down to her. "This place is so boring. Did you hear what I said? Borrrrring!"

Joy gaped in disbelief. "You're a... a... fairy!"

The tiny woman planted tiny orange hands on her tiny orange hips. "Name's Felicity Morningstar, and don't you dare call me *it*, Hey You, or Pea-brain. Got that?"

"I'm hallucinating." Joy squeezed her eyes shut. "All those chemicals from the purple dye must have seeped into my brain.

Fairies aren't real."

A tiny fist clunked her on the head. Joy reopened her eyes.

"Don't be so dense. I am, they are, so get over it." Felicity hovered at eye level. This close, her wings created a slight breeze. "I thought the outside world would be fun. Exciting. Full of treasure and exotic food. The only thing worth eating around here is orange juice and honey. Then there's that rude cat."

"Shredder?" Joy scrambled to her feet.

"A little fur-removal showed him who's boss. Scaredy-cat is cowering under your bed." Felicity patted a tiny pouch on her belt. "The team's going to love using his fur for pillows. I might snatch some more before going home."

"Don't you dare!" She noticed water running in the sink. Not even wanting to think how huge next month's utility bill was going to be, she turned it off and raced upstairs. Poor Shredder was squeezed into a corner under the bed, back arched, fur raised, hissing in warning and fear while the belligerent orange fairy fluttered next to where Joy knelt.

"Na na na-na na! Who's afraid of the big fat cat? Not me!" Crowing in derision, the fairy cartwheeled in the air.

Joy narrowed her gaze. As a teacher, she knew what to do with a bully. Removing her skirt and top, which stank of tuna and beer, she slipped into a pair of jeans and t-shirt, then entered the bathroom. The bored fairy followed. Immediately, Joy dashed out and closed the door.

"Hey!" Felicity yelled. "I'm still in here!"

"And you're going to stay in there until you start behaving."

"You can't do this to me! I'm Felicity Morningstar! Leader of the best search and gossip team in all of P—er, in the whole world."

"Well, you're in my world now. And you're not getting out until you say you're sorry for what you did to my kitchen and my cat."

Joy heard the fairy blow out an exaggerated breath. "You're no fun."

"Thank you. Neither are you."

"Come on. Let me out. I can do tricks that will make you laugh."

Joy noticed the doorknob slowly start to turn. She grabbed it and held on tight.

Felicity banged the doorknob with her tiny fists. "Let me out!"

From inside the bathroom, she heard a plastic water cup bounce on the floor and shampoo bottles bang in the tub. The door of the medicine cabinet was repeatedly slammed; items fell out and clattered in the sink. The toilet was repeatedly flushed.

It seemed fairies had temper tantrums just like children.

The doorbell rang.

Joy raised her eyes to heaven. *Why me?*

"Stay put," she ordered the fairy. "And keep quiet."

She ran down the stairs. *Please, don't let it be Mike.* One look at the fairy and he'd come up with a hundred ways to make her into a strategic weapon. If the Men In Black didn't dissect her first.

She gazed through the peep hole and breathed a sigh of relief. It was Jeff, fellow fifth grade teacher, next-door neighbor, and all-around sweet guy. Over the years she'd formed a cozy friendship with him and his family, borrowing the occasional sugar, flour, coffee, and frozen pizza from his wife while Patsy Demarco reciprocated by asking her to babysit. Their two young kids were great, as kids went. They'd taught her a lot about video games. Because of them, she could hold her own against spell-casting, time-traveling, blood-sucking, Roman gladiators who were genetically enhanced with alien DNA.

She opened the door partway and smiled. "Hi. What's up?"

"May I come in?" Jeff asked. "It's about school."

She hesitated, worried he might discover the fairy. Yet his frown and the fact it was about work balanced her apprehension, and she let him in.

"What is *that?*" Jeff asked. His eyes almost popped out of his head just like the time-traveling, blood-sucking Roman gladiators genetically enhanced with alien DNA whenever she blasted them with her turbo-charged Phase Stunner Mark IV.

Oh, no! The fairy! He's seen Felicity!

He rushed to the kitchen and surveyed the disaster. "What happened here?"

"Oh, uh, ever since the storm last night, Shredder's been upset. When I came home, I found this." All true, yet not all the truth. Which meant she hadn't just lied to a good friend. Hopefully she could keep it that way.

"I'll help you clean up." Jeff began picking up boxes of cereal and pasta.

"Thanks, but I'll take care of this later." Joy took the boxes from him and put them on the counter. "Believe me, after the day I had, cleaning this up will probably be good therapy." Actually, all she wanted to do was soak in a hot bubble bath, sipping a beer and making believe she didn't have a fairy hiding out in her bathroom. Instead, she asked, "What did you want to talk about?"

"I heard what happened today. I wanted to let you know I had three boys do the same in my class last week."

"You did? I didn't hear anything about it."

Jeff shrugged. "Why call in the principals and the school psychologist over a little macho rivalry? After all, boys will be boys. I simply scared them half to death about infections from unsterilized pins and they promised not to do it again. And, because I used discretion, there's no follow-up paperwork, no gossip in the teachers' lounge, and no note put into my file that questions my classroom management skills."

"You think they put something in my personnel file about today's incident?"

"You might want to look. I know the law says you can remove whatever you want from your file, but believe me, these administrators keep a private file on all of us that we never see."

She chewed on her lip, aghast one small incident by two mischievous boys might ruin her career. "But we're supposed to report all incidences of violence or abuse, even those by mutual consent."

"Yeah, big stuff like hitting, kicking, groping, but not this petty stuff." He placed a comforting hand on her shoulder. "I know you thought you did the right thing, but if you're into teaching for the long haul, you have to learn not to sweat the small stuff." He gently squeezed her shoulder then removed his hand. "I better go. With both kids home with the flu, Patsy's worn out. I offered to cook tonight."

"That's sweet of you." She saw him to the door. "Thanks for coming over."

"What are friends for?" Jeff stopped in the doorway. "One more thing. Forgive me for what I'm about to say, but your hair."

"What about it?"

"You've been changing it this school year: platinum blonde, red, tri-tone, frosted. I've enjoyed the surprise of seeing what color it's going to be. But the purple…"

He paused, and she remembered the critical looks from the principals today.

"Don't take me wrong, I love the purple. Makes you look exotic, mysterious, kind of sexy. But are you sure that's the impression you want to give your fifth graders?"

"No," she grudgingly replied. "The class is reading a Harry Potter book and I thought it would fit in. You know: supernatural, out of the ordinary, teacher of magic."

"In that case, leave it alone. But maybe add some moon-and-stars jewelry to delineate it for your students. And the administrators."

She forced a smile. "Thanks for the advice."

After he left, and she leaned against the closed door, thinking. Was Jeff right? Had she overreacted? Nowadays boys weren't allowed to be rough and tumble like in the past. But jabbing each other with pins seemed more than just boys being boys.

A slight breeze stroked her face. Draft from Felicity's wings.

"I thought I told you to stay put."

"He's a peeper," the fairy said.

"Who is?"

"The man who was here, the one with the puppy-dog eyes and wire-thin lips. He's a peeper. Saw him take a quick peek through your living room window after he left."

"I don't believe it," Joy said. "He wouldn't."

Felicity raised and lowered a tiny shoulder. "Then someone who looks like Wire Lips."

Joy crossed to the window. If Felicity had been hiding from view, she probably hadn't gotten a good look at whoever had been peeping. Joy pulled back the curtain and looked out. A young teen walked by bouncing a basketball, a man carried a bag of groceries, and an elderly woman wheeled her oxygen cart. A few unfamiliar cars were parked on the street, one with the motor running with someone in it. A police car drove by, another car, a van, and a truck.

She ran her hands up and down her arms, feeling uneasy, watched.

The Neighborhood Watch flyer on the nearby table caught her eye and she examined the photo of the sex offender who had moved in down the street. The man looked nothing like Jeff. He had a rounder face, bent nose, and vacant, droopy eyes. Since receiving the flyer, she'd been trying to make light of the monster's presence. Truthfully, she'd been shaken to the core. And with good reason. Her college roommate had been assaulted. Date rape, but rape all same. The memory of her friend's painful recovery was a constant reminder that a woman has to be on guard more often than a man.

Felicity zoomed in front of her. "Let's do something fun."

Joy eyed the fairy, and was suddenly grateful for her company. "Yes, let's do something." She went up to the bathroom. Felicity followed. Like before, Joy dashed out and shut her inside.

"Hey!"

"You still owe me an apology."

A long silence followed. Then Felicity cooed, "If you let me out, I'll tell you all about Harradorn."

"So, I was right. He did bring you here."

"Sort of. I hitched a ride."

"From where?" If it was close enough, she could return Felicity and see Harradorn again. He really was easy on the eye, and she hadn't had a good date in a long time, assuming no wedding ring on his finger meant he was available.

"I can't tell you where I'm from," Felicity said. "It's a secret."

Hmm. Maybe Harradorn was a cryptozoologist, one of those scientists who searches for mythological creatures. She'd look him up later on the Internet. "I'm surprised he hasn't realized you're missing," she said. "Does he have a lot of fairies? Is that why he doesn't know you're gone?"

"Harumph! Harradorn doesn't *have* fairies. We're not property. And we're not pets like your stupid, lazy cat. We have the same rights like everyone else. Now let me out. Please."

Please. Finally, a half-hearted request instead of an order. It was a start, but still not good enough. "Are you sorry?"

"Yessss!" Felicity replied in exasperation.

"For what?"

"For everything. Anything. I'm sorry! Now will you let me out?"

"I guess fairies have never been taught how to apologize correctly. You need to say you're sorry and then say what you specifically did wrong."

"You're kidding?"

"Those are the rules. Even my 5th grade students know that."

A bout of swearing was followed by lot of grumbling, then a long silence. And then, "I'm sorry for making a mess of your kitchen and scaring your cat. How's that?"

"What about the bathroom?"

"Oh. I'm sorry I trashed your bathroom. Now can I come out?"

"You did a very good job of apologizing, but there's one more thing. You have to make amends."

"Is that like work?"

"It means you have to undo what you did. In this case, clean up the mess you made."

"That *is* work. Will I get paid?"

Joy rolled her eyes. Having Felicity Morningstar in her home might be more of a problem than a novelty. Maybe she should rent *Peter Pan* or a Tinker Bell movie for pointers.

"Let me ask you this," Joy said. "Who's going to pay for all the food you ruined?"

"Gotcha. You drive a hard bargain, Joy Flint. Tell you what, you're such a nice person, I'll clean up everything, free of charge."

I'm going to regret this. I know I will. But she opened the door anyway.

The fairy zoomed out and flew in circles around Joy's head. "I'm free! I'm free!"

"Wonderful. Now get to work. And leave my cat alone."

Felicity saluted her. "Yes, Ma'am." She flew downstairs.

Joy straightened the bathroom. Noise burst from the kitchen, more banging and breaking than what cleaning should sound like. Before going down, she stopped in her room to comfort her cat. Shredder was still under the bed. His hackles were no longer raised, but his eyes seemed to blame her for Felicity, and he hissed when Joy tried to pet him. "Sorry, Shredder. I had no idea what she was when I left this morning." Maybe Jeff had a birdcage she could borrow. One with a lock.

In the kitchen, Felicity was creating more of a mess than cleaning. To her credit, the fairy was trying. With her little hands, she could only pick up two corn flakes at a time. Working together, they soon got the place cleaned up.

Joy glanced out the window. The sun had already set. She was tired, hungry, and had papers to grade and lessons to prepare.

"I'm hungry," Felicity said while Joy put away the mop and pail.

"Any rose nectar around? Or juice?"

"Is that all you eat? Liquids?"

"Mostly, though we fairies have been known to indulge in a good cookie now and then."

"Well, I've got some lemonade concentrate." Joy rummaged in the freezer for the container and found a spinach lasagna to microwave for herself. "I have no idea where I can get rose nectar. How about I make us a batch of chocolate chip cookies instead?"

"Super. Could you make it with honey?"

"I don't think I have enough." Felicity had spilt most of it during her feeding frenzy.

Felicity landed on her shoulder. "Are you still upset over what Wire Lips said?"

"Not really." Though it bothered her Jeff had kept quiet about the misbehaving boys in his class. Not reporting the incident didn't seem right.

"Because you shouldn't. He doesn't know what he's talking about. I love your hair."

"You do?"

"Sure. It almost looks as good as mine."

Joy laughed. The fairy's hair was a riot of bright orange, with strands sticking out in all directions. What a pair they made.

Felicity grabbed some of Joy's Persian Plum hair and wrapped it around her hand. "It's so silky and thick. I could weave the strands into belts. We'd make a lot of money. Fairies love purple. So do—"

A cloud of black sparkles appeared all around them. Joy gasped. Exactly like when Harradorn disappeared.

The fairy tugged on Joy's hair and squeaked, "Uh-oh. We're going for a ride."

Chapter 5

Endless black engulfed Joy, so thick it was almost tangible. So she did what any sane person would do when mind-numbingly scared. She screamed.

Felicity yanked her hair. "Quit yelling. This is the fun part."

Fun? She'd been swallowed by a cloud of black sparkles in her own kitchen and was now… moving? No air pummeled her skin, yet her stomach did flip-flops as if she was traveling up and down and sideways, maybe even upside down once when her stomach switched places with her mouth. She couldn't see a thing, not even Felicity, who jerked her hair every time she whimpered in distress.

"Brace yourself," Felicity said.

"Why? What's going to—"

And then there was light. And a solid footing underneath.

Joy squinted while her eyes adjusted, and took in her surroundings. Worktables were the major decor, several laden with jars, mortars & pestles, and Bunsen burners. Herbs and flowers hung overhead, their sweet and sour scents intermixing. Someone's workshop, maybe a craft store, for there were decorated walking sticks and a partially painted statue of an apple tree with a snake slithering up its trunk. On one table, beads were sorted, some already strung into jewelry. Bookcases covered one wall, their shelves sagging under the weight of leather-bound tomes.

"Where are we?" she asked Felicity.

"Mistress Sirena's Shop of Quiet Contentment." The fairy took off from Joy's shoulder and buzzed the room. "I'm hungry. I bet

Sirena has rose nectar around here somewhere."

While Felicity made herself at home, Joy looked about. Behind her stood a tall black mirror. Its dark surface shimmered like water. Across the top, seemingly floating in midair, were a set of numbers written in purple. Her phone number!

Fascinated, she reached for the numbers to see if they had any substance to them. "Felicity, is this how we got here? Through this mirror? I can't see my reflection in it."

Felicity tackled her finger before it met the flickering surface. Frantically, the fairy flapped her wings and pulled Joy away. "Don't touch! You can't go through. Not until I have a chance to check in with my team."

Joy glanced back at the mirror. "Why is my phone number on it?"

"The mirror zeroes in on addresses. Harradorn only had your phone number, so he took a chance it might send him to your phone. Lucky for me, it worked."

"What if I have my phone with me while I'm here?"

Felicity looked startled. "Do you?"

"Why? What would happen?"

"I have no idea."

"But I can go back through to my home any time I want, right? Because I can't stay long. I have a lot of work to do, and I haven't missed a day all year." She was babbling. Joy sucked in her breath and tried to get control of the situation. Be logical. "It's some type of transportation device in the shape of a mirror. A transporter."

"Sort of." Felicity let go of her finger and flew toward a white lace curtain masking a doorway. "This way. I'll show you around. Bet you'd like to see Harradorn again. A good looking guy, our mayor."

"Harradorn is a mayor?" He seemed awfully young for such a weighty responsibility.

"Sure. Single, too. Supposed to be great in bed—the tales I could tell you. But it's been a while, or so I hear from all the women waiting for him to ask them out. A workaholic definitely in need of some fun. Come on."

Felicity zipped through the edge of the curtain. Joy followed, curious not only about the studly mayor, but also about what kind of town he was in charge of that was home to fairies. Must be pretty safe and secure if a transporter could be left unguarded in a curtained workroom.

The front of the shop was full of interesting new-age novelties: dribbling water fountains, gemstone jewelry, feel-good banners, dowsing rods, prisms and candles in all shapes, sizes, and colors. Shelves contained statuary of elves dancing and playing musical instruments, and also colorful fairies, one of which looked a lot like Felicity.

But it was the objects on a table that had Joy doing a double take. Scattered among green jade Chinese dragons and red jade dogs were several lifelike nudes in evocative poses. One couple in particular had her sighing with envy. No one had ever made love to her that way.

To her surprise, the image of Harradorn doing it—doing it with her—suddenly popped into her head. Her face flamed hot, aroused by the possibility of making erotic love with the dashing mayor. Why on earth was this shop called a place of quiet contentment?

Her nose twitched. Myrrh and frankincense. Church smells. The scents Mike had detected in the area Harradorn had disappeared. And her thoughts returned to the intriguing mayor. Her gaze slid back to the statue. Maybe she could buy it before she went home.

Felicity grabbed the front doorknob and struggled to turn it. "Give me a hand, will you?"

Joy obliged. "Where are we?" she asked. They stepped outside. In New Jersey, the sun had already set. Here it still shone, though long shadows indicated it was late in the day. Possibly two or three time zones away from where she lived, Mountain West or Pacific. Fierce mountains guarded the town to the east and northwest, snugging the place in what looked to be a cozy alpine valley.

Harradorn said he was from out west. Perhaps Colorado or Utah?

"This is my home." Felicity grinned proudly. "I'll show you where Mayor Harradorn lives, then I have to go find my team." She patted the pouch on her belt. "They're going to love this cat fur. Maybe I'll take you to see Maggie. She used to be an outsider like you. Runs a yarn store a few blocks from here, Stitchers Delight."

"You have people from the outside world living here?"

"Sure. We're not prejudiced. Well, not all of us. Robin who owns Feline Fashions, and Sharon, one of our teachers, all used to be outsiders."

"How did they get here? Through the mirror?"

"Love. They fell in love with someone from here. Once you marry, they can't keep you out. A stupid rule. Might as well say the truth: sex buys your way in."

Joy choked back a laugh, still getting used to the fairy's bluntness. "Sex and love are not always the same," she pointed out.

"You got that right. One costs more than the other."

Felicity zoomed down the street. Joy jogged after her. All the buildings were two stories tall and built with cream-colored stone or brick. Flower boxes decorated all the windows with brilliant spring colors of grape hyacinths, yellow daffodils, and red tulips. The tan cobblestone streets were narrow, but the beige sidewalks were broad, level, and devoid of cracks, giving the impression pedestrians ruled. Looking about, not a single vehicle could be seen on the litter-free streets.

The streets possessed cute names like Smiling Way and Pleasant Avenue. Windows were crystal clean, all the sidewalks tree-lined. With military precision, every tree conformed to the same height, about twelve feet. The entire place was almost storybook in its uniformity.

She gazed around in wonder. "Everything is the same."

"Not quite." Felicity stopped to hover. "Helga Holderson planted pink hyacinths in her window box. If she doesn't change them to purple by week's end, she'll have to pay for their replacement and spend some time in Dulgrun Prison."

"You go to prison if you have the wrong colored flowers?" And her students thought she was strict.

"In Peace, the law's the law. Which is why I spend most of my time in Prosperity."

Peace and Prosperity What strange names for towns.

Are you talking about twin cities?"

"Nah. One town. But I tell you, it's a lot more fun in Prosperity."

Joy frowned. Was Harradorn really such a hard-ass? Her first impression said he was playful, mischievous, daring, like the man in the statue she wanted to buy. Easy for her imagination to make him into the ideal date material. But ignorance is bliss. She might not even like him this time around. Yet she hoped otherwise.

Quaint stores and cafés filled the area. All empty, from what Joy could see. An eerie silence blanketed the town. "Where is everyone?"

Felicity shrugged. "The tourists must have left. It's not safe in town during a wizard duel."

Wizard duel?

Wizards!

"You have wizards here?" she asked. The ludicrous look that Felicity shot her said the answer was too obvious to bother with, so instead she asked, "Where do the tourists come from?"

"Other towns, but I think ours is the best."

Other towns with fairies and wizards? How did they keep them all a secret? Or were they the source of fairy tales?

Approaching a large park, an odd smell permeated the air, a peculiar mixture of cotton candy and burnt wood. From what Joy could see, the park seemed planned out like the rest of the town. Except for the trees. Unlike the shorter ones along the streets, these were permitted to grow over seventy-feet tall. The grassy expanse had several picnic tables in organized clusters. A white bandshell was positioned in one corner, clumps of trees in two others, and a huge stump in the fourth.

Felicity cried out, "The Valkyrie Oak! It's gone!" Tears sprang to her eyes. Overcome with grief, her orange wings barely fluttered. Joy swiftly reached out to catch her. Felicity collapsed into her palm, sobbing. "Our softest nest was in the Valkyrie. And our biggest stash. By the dryads of Eden, what's happened?" She raised her watery eyes to Joy, her face awash with tears. "I was gone less than a day. My team. My home. All gone." She covered her face with her hands and sobbed.

A faint chirp drew Joy's attention to a nearby tree where she spied a robin on an upper branch. The head was down, eyes closed, its beak tucked under a wing. "Felicity, look up there. It's a bird sleeping."

The fairy sniffed and wiped her eyes. "Birds don't sleep during the day."

"That one is."

Felicity flew up to the bird. "I know this one. It's Richurp. He and his mate are building a nest by the Mayor's Hall and Residence. Hey, Richurp, wake up." She clunked the bird on the head with one of her orange fists. "Do you hear me? WAKE UP!"

The bird chirped a high-pitched snore and kept sleeping.

Felicity flew down to Joy. "There's a small twig in his beak, as if he was taking it to his nest when he suddenly decided to take a nap. I don't get it. Hold on. I'll go scout."

Felicity soared into the huge trees of the park, then flew to the windows of several buildings before returning to Joy. "All the birds are asleep. I can't wake them. The hotels are empty, but in an apartment I saw the Anderssons sitting at their kitchen table, asleep. Has to be magic, a spell, it's the only explanation. Maybe something to do with the wizard duel. We need to find Mayor Harradorn. I bet he knows what's going on. This way."

Felicity sped toward a tall building at the far end of the park. Joy followed. Halfway there, something red caught her eye. She ran over and stared in surprise. On the ground lay a man dressed in a pirate costume with a large gold medallion on his chest.

A pirate?

His lips were parted, smiling, as if he had fallen asleep in the midst of laughing. She knelt down and tried to wake him. But his sleep was deep, his smile strangely enticing. She recalled Felicity's bizarre explanation that the sleep was induced by magic, some sort of spell. It reminded her of Sleeping Beauty and Snow White. A kiss woke them up. A kiss broke the spell.

A laugh tickled her throat. It was a ridiculous thought. Girlish. And yet, when she gazed down at the handsome pirate and his tempting lips, she decided what harm would it do to try out her theory. After all, who would know? Everyone was asleep.

She bent over the sleeping pirate. He chuckled lightly in his sleep, as if amused by what she was about to do yet welcomed it all the same. Her lips drew close, desirous to know what it would be like to kiss him.

"Hold," a booming male voice called out.

Startled, Joy drew back. A block away stood a lone figure cloaked in black robes, the hood drawn forward, hiding his face. One hand was raised, emphasizing his command that she not kiss the pirate. In his other he held a six-foot white walking stick with a black obsidian sphere nestled in its top.

Embarrassed to have been caught trying to kiss the sleeping pirate, she quickly stood.

He lowered his hand and started towards her. His stride was slow and steady, his footfalls silent like the town. If not for the steady click, click, click of his staff striking the cobblestones, she would have sworn he was floating. It reminded her of the opening lines of one of Emily Dickinson's poems. *Because I could not stop for Death— He kindly stopped for me—*

It suddenly occurred to her: the man approaching wasn't asleep. Probably the only one in the whole town who wasn't. That couldn't be good.

She turned her head in the direction of the tall building and yelled, "Felicity!"

The dark figure stopped on the other side of the pirate. From within the depths of the cowl she heard a chuckle, yet all she could see was a rosy tan chin with a cleft in it.

"You're not from around here, are you?" he said, a hint of amusement in his voice.

Attackers prey on the weak and the fearful, her self-defense instructor had constantly reminded the class. Always appear confident.

Crossing her arms, Joy widened her stance and raised her chin. "What gave me away?"

"Besides the *New Jersey is Hot For Lovers* t-shirt? The fact you called a fairy for help. Most here know better." He leaned forward as though trying to get a better look at her. "May I ask how you got here?"

"If I answer your questions, will you answer mine?"

"Since all we seem to be doing is asking, it seems prudent to agree. You first."

"I came through the transporter."

"Transporter?"

She smirked. "That's two questions."

"I'll keep track." He held up two long fingers, one with a fire opal ring. "I say again: transporter?"

"The black mirror in the back of Mistress Sirena's Shop."

The cloaked figure stiffened. His grip on the white staff hardened, and Joy noticed a coiled snake tattoo on the back of his hand. "Sirena," he groaned. "I should have known. Was she in her shop, asleep?"

Joy started to answer, but paused, eyeing him until he held up another finger to mark his third question. "I haven't seen anyone except you and him," she said, indicating the man on the ground between them.

"Then how did you come through the skelter glass?" he asked, and raised another finger.

"Felicity Morningstar knows what happened. I get the feeling she brought me here."

"She was with you in the outside world? How? And that's a single question," he stated, raising but one finger.

"I think she was left behind by Harradorn. Felicity says he's the mayor of this town."

"He is. As is his brother, Rick, who sleeps between us."

Joy gazed down at the sleeping pirate. "I thought he looked familiar. Huh, two mayors."

"Indeed. Now please explain as to why Harradorn was in the outside world."

Outside world? He sure had an odd way of speaking. She couldn't wait for him to start answering all her questions. She gave a brief rundown of the reason Harradorn showed up in her home and how he had disappeared in a cloud of black sparkles.

"Interesting. It would seem our mayor's good deed sparked the good deed needed to undo what has been done." He gazed around at the empty streets, and for the first time Joy noticed how heavily he leaned upon his white staff, as if it was the only thing holding him up.

The black embroidery in his thick robes moved. She stared, entranced, while the patterns changed. They shifted and swirled, drawing her in, snaring her in the ebb and flow of the threads, holding her in a mesmerizing whirlpool of ever-darkening shades spinning all around her. She lost control of who she was, where she was. If she was. All she had to do was let go, give in to the pull, and all her worries about her job, her dismal love life, would disappear. It'd be so easy. So restful. A dark peace beckoned, irresistible and waiting. She longed to accept what was being offered.

But then images of Mike and Merry appeared. And her parents. Her students. Her classroom. And, surprisingly, Harradorn.

She took a strengthening breath, grounding herself in the memories of all she loved, all that she cared about. She stared at the face in the shadow of the hood, and refused to look at the ever shifting patterns of his cloak. "You were saying something was interesting."

"Indeed," he said, and the embroidery of his cloak settled and calmed, and became mere decorative designs. "Before I say more, I believe you have some questions of your own to ask. But be swift. I don't have much time before the duel resumes."

The man had five fingers raised. Five questions out of the hundreds she wanted to ask.

"What duel?" she asked. Could this be the wizard duel Felicity had mentioned?

With his staff, he beckoned her to follow. She accompanied him to where a street ran east and west. He looked toward the west. So did she. In the distance, beyond the gentle sameness of all the two-story cream-colored buildings, was another town. Its buildings were a riot of different materials, different heights, colors, and shapes, some leaning in defiance of gravity. In their midst loomed a stark black tower. A maroon cloud seemed to be hugging its side.

"I am Zacharias Blackhawk. You may call me Zach. The tower is my home. And that ugly red monstrosity next to it is the home of FearfulFran. She's furious that I won't sell her one of my roses, so she's decided to take them by force. If she can," he added in a steely voice that promised sharp retribution to anyone who tried.

Joy shook her head, utterly confused. The guy lives in a tower. The woman he's dueling lives in another tower, though it looks more like a vertical cloud. And he's a horticulturist who doesn't like to sell his prized roses, at least not to this FearfulFran.

Okay, this wasn't Oz or Kansas, and she hadn't fallen down a rabbit hole.

"Let's try this again," she said. "Where am I?"

"I'm not at liberty to say." He started back toward the sleeping pirate. "Even I must obey some of the rules."

"Then you owe me a question. Do you know how I can return

home?"

"You already know the answer." They were back to standing on either side of Rick. "Think. What were Harradorn and Felicity talking about when the skelter glass was activated?"

She searched her memory. "My hair. Specifically, the color of my hair. Pur—"

Zach moved fast. In an instant he was at her side. A finger hovered near her lips. The closeness of his touch sizzled, but not with pain. "Don't say the color," he warned. "I believe it to be the trigger Harradorn must have agreed upon with Sirena that would return him here. Once said, it will send you home."

She looked up from the finger enticingly close to her mouth and peered into his cowl. But before she could get a good look at his face, he withdrew. Darn.

"So, because Felicity had a hold of my hair when she said the color, I was brought back with her?"

"So it would seem."

"Interesting."

"As I said."

"Why is everyone asleep?"

"When FearfulFran couldn't force me to sell her a rose, she decided to use coercion and attack my town. Her tower discharged a Fear Fog, which, when inhaled, would cause the townspeople to be afraid of everything: a speck of dust, their shadows, even their children. To counter it, I released an oily version of Blithe Mist, which makes people laugh. One cannot be afraid when laughter takes hold. I suspect someone tried to counter my spell with one of their own, not knowing about the underlying Fog. Did you notice anything when you arrived? Perhaps a peculiar scent?"

"Burnt wood."

"That would be from when lightning killed the Valkyrie Oak."

"And cotton candy."

"Ah." The shrouded head nodded. "Someone used Serious Smog to counter the laughing. Probably added an explosive sweetener to dampen the side effects. Mix fear, laughter, seriousness, and sweetness, and the results are?"

"Sleep?" It couldn't be that simple. Zach's patient silence indicated more.

Joy smiled and bowed her head to him, acknowledging the same technique she utilized in her classroom. The power of silence always spurred her students' minds into providing the solution to a problem. And, like in her classroom, the answer came suddenly.

"I get it. An overload of opposing emotions. Turns the brain fluffy, confused, spun about, like cotton candy. Shuts down the mind into a dream-filled sleep in order to deal with it."

The flash of white teeth within the hood indicated Zach was grinning. "Very intuitive. As is your solution."

"Really?" She glanced down at the pirate. "A kiss will wake everyone up?"

Zach nodded. He swept a hand over the obsidian sphere on his staff and stared at it. Then he looked at her. Then at Rick. A bottomless sigh followed. "It has begun. The beginning of my end. Who would have thought a purple-haired woman from New Jersey would signal it." He sighed heavily again, then gestured at Rick. "Think carefully how you will kiss him. He is not for you, though he thinks he is. The one for you is waiting, though he waits for no one."

"Do you always speak in riddles?" Joy asked. "And what's with the outfits? Was there a costume party going on when this duel started?" Zach tilted his cowled head as if puzzled, and she added, "Rick's dressed like a pirate and you look like someone out of a Harry Potter book."

He chuckled. "I assure you, our clothing is quite common here. But where you come from, purple hair is not, so don't be calling the kettle black. Now, be quick and wake Rick, for I am tired and need his help to return to my tower before FearfulFran realizes I'm not there."

Chapter 6

Joy knelt beside the sleeping pirate. His lips, the roguish smile, enticed her. But something told her to heed the wizard's warning and she only kissed Rick Lawson on the cheek.

His eyes slowly opened. Vivid Norse blues looked at her in a daze. She rose to her feet and stepped back. Rick sat up, stretching and yawning, taking stock of his surroundings. "Must have been some party. Long time since I fell asleep in the park." He scratched the growth of beard and noticed the black-robed figure first. "Hey, Zach. What's up? Is the duel over? I got a lot of money riding on you."

Zach shook his head. "It will soon begin anew. As such, I need your help to return to my tower, then wake everyone in Prosperity."

"Everyone? Must have been one Hel of a party. Can't remember a thing."

"I'll explain on the way. We must hurry."

Evidently, they were old friends or drinking buddies, for with one last yawn, Rick got to his feet and readily accepted the wizard's arm around his shoulders. Then he noticed Joy. His eyes gleamed with interest. "Ahoy there, beautiful. Who are you?"

"A friend of your brother's," Zach replied. "She will attend to everyone in Peace. We must go quickly before it is too late."

"If you insist," Rick said, though he sounded disappointed. Before leaving, he offered Joy a rascally smile and an appreciative wink, and for a second she regretted not kissing him on the lips.

The strange pair walked away, and she heard Rick ask, "So, how do I wake everyone up?" The answer produced a hearty laugh from Rick and he added, "Yo ho, this is going to be fun. But I'm only waking the pretty lasses. I'll leave the rest for Leif and Sanders to kiss, especially the dwarfs."

She stared after them in wonder. *Dwarfs?*

The two turned in the direction of Zach's tower and soon disappeared within the lengthening shadows. To the west, the sun brushed the mountains, reminding her of the time. Tons of school work waited for her, plus an angry, scared cat in need of adoration and food.

All right, then. Kiss and leave. What could be simpler?

The two wooden entry doors of the white marble building were enormously tall and wide. Both were carved in bas-relief. The one door slightly ajar pictured three Viking longships with a steady flow of passengers—humans, dwarfs, fairies—crossing a beach toward a vast forest and the mountains beyond. The scene was curiously inviting and she lightly fingered the dragon ships, the ocean waves, and the people leaving it all behind for a new life.

As for the other door... her fingers recoiled in horror. Its carvings depicted a guillotine with severed heads on the ground. People were fighting, dying, screaming in anguish. In the background, a multi-rayed sun rose over the mountains. Or was it a sunset? Most of the people who were looking at it appeared to be smiling and cheering, while others cringed, covered their heads, and fled.

The doors made her feel both welcomed and warned.

"I should have brought Mike with me."

Plastic sheeting covered the doorway. She slipped past it and entered a spacious entrance hall sumptuously decorated with exquisite paintings and sculptures Dubai would outbid the Louvre for. Right away, her attention was drawn to two people lying on the floor, a woman in purple and gold, and a man.

Harradorn.

Even in sleep, his face lacked the carefree image of his brother, Rick. His features were troubled, his brow knitted. Considering all he had to contend with, from the Fear Fog and the Blithe Mist invading his town to the failed attempt to alleviate them with the Serious Smog, it was a wonder he hadn't fallen asleep bellowing in frustration. She sat on the marble floor by his side, and her judgment softened. Last night, even with the wizard duel, he had used precious time to come to her rescue.

His face was boldly handsome, not pretty as her brother had said, with a strong chin and a faint scar along the left brow. A slight bump on his otherwise straight nose indicated it had been broken at one time, making him as normal as any man in New Jersey. Like Rick, he had a medallion on his chest, though this had a large blue sapphire in its center. Also like Rick, he had a slight shadow of a beard, making her wonder how long everyone here had been asleep.

She reached out to finger his hair but stopped at the last second, remembering Zach's intrusion when she had been about to kiss Rick. She glanced around. There was no movement, no sounds; everyone in Peace was still asleep.

Tentatively at first, she twiddled his short sandy hair, then ran her fingers through the strands, and was rewarded with a faint twitch of his lips. Her fingers combed his hair again, enjoying the soft feel of the strands, the varying hues of gold and buff, butterscotch and caramel. He smiled. She smiled back, pleased to have eased his worries. "Hello, Harradorn Lawson, Mayor of Peace, my would-be rescuer. I've come to return the favor."

She brushed his smiling lips with her own, and he breathed into her mouth, warm and welcoming, inviting her to linger. She obliged, sampling his lips, pressing a little more, playing with his mouth, enjoying the feel of him, the taste, the bold beat of his heart matching hers, and she savored their kiss.

Then he stirred and, not wishing to be caught taking advantage of his magical sleep, she pulled away. But his hand came up behind her head to hold her in place, to lengthen the kiss, and deepen it. His lips pleasured hers like waves on the shore, sweeping across her mouth, back and forth, taking and giving. Sharing. The ebb and flow of his mouth made her thirst for more, and when his tongue sought entry, she willingly gave way. The surging pressure of his lips begged her to stay, priming a fire deep in her heart. Reaching up, she chased her fingers through his hair, moaning in pleasure and drinking him in.

Harradorn dreamt he was lying on a couch at Rick's place, being kissed by one of the wenches his brother had invited to a party. If the rest of her body was skilled like her mouth, he never wanted the dream to end. Yet, in spite of his efforts to stay asleep, he could feel himself waking. The couch became hard and uncomfortable. It felt more like a floor. He shifted to get comfortable, and the wench's lips pulled away along with the dream.

Still half asleep, he stretched and smiled. "Rick, you sure can pick them."

A woman's voice chuckled. "Oh, he can, can he?"

His eyes shot open. He hadn't expected the woman in his dream to answer him.

Startled, he sat up and stared at the purple-haired woman sitting next to him. "You're Joy Flint!"

"You remembered." She laughed, clearly trying to make light of the situation, but it caught in her throat and her cheeks took on an interesting tinge of pink.

"What's happened? How did you get here?" He saw Sirena on the floor and rushed to check her vitals. Alive, yet definitely unconscious.

His assistant would know what was going on. "Agamemnon!" he yelled.

Silence answered his call. There were no stomping feet. No phones ringing. Out the Hall's opened front door, he could hear no children playing, no fairies gossiping. Nothing.

He glanced at Sirena, then leveled his gaze at Joy, the one

unknown factor. "What's wrong with her?" he demanded to know. "What did you do to her?"

"I didn't do anything. She's asleep. The whole town is asleep. Zach said it was the result of someone using Serious Smog."

"You've met Zach?!"

"Black robe. White staff. Talks funny. And what's with the hood? He never let me see his face."

"Our wizard is suffering from a curse."

"Of course he is." Her smile brimmed with disbelief. "What is it, a beauty-and-the-beast thing?"

"Quite the opposite, actually." He rubbed his face, bewildered. Why and how Joy had met Zach? And during a wizard duel, no less. "I need to know everything Zach told you."

Joy related the reason for the duel and Zach's explanation for why everyone had fallen asleep. Including how to wake them all up.

"Really? A kiss?" He lowered his brow. "Is that why you were kissing me?"

"No, I'm a nymphomaniac who goes around kissing men when they're asleep." Grumbling, she got to her feet and brushed off her jeans. "You're welcome, by the way. Now, if you don't mind, I've got papers to grade and lesson plans to write. Felicity!" she yelled.

"Felicity's here?"

The orange fairy came zooming down the stairs. She hovered in front of Joy. "Oh, Joy, it's terrible! Everyone's asleep! I keep trying to wake Sessi but all she does is snore. I don't know what to do."

Joy leaned forward. "Give her a kiss on the cheek."

"Really?"

Joy nodded. Without even acknowledging him, Felicity zoomed back up the stairs. Harradorn stared after her. Then he looked at Joy, worried. Fairies were opportunists, only helping people when they were paid. And paid a lot. Which meant this outsider was not innocent or selfless.

He left Sirena and stalked toward Joy.

Alarmed by the dangerous glint in his eyes and his cool,

determined stride, Joy searched for a way to divert his attention. She glanced at the woman asleep on the floor. "Aren't you going to wake her?"

"Later. I want to talk to you first."

Harradorn had been a lot more manageable when asleep. The man advancing toward her suddenly seemed quite sure of himself, and predatory. She took a step back. "What do you want to talk about?"

"You told Felicity she can wake anyone with a kiss on the cheek." He stopped in front of her, seductively close. "So why were you kissing me on the lips?"

Uh-oh. Busted.

Flushed with embarrassment, she looked everywhere but at him.

"Maybe you are a nymphomaniac." He fingered her purple hair. "Your hair seems to say as much. Wild. Unconventional. Erotic."

Erotic. She swallowed. "Maybe I like the color."

"Or maybe you really do like kissing men." With a wicked glint in his gray eyes, he focused on her mouth. "That was no chaste kiss you gave me."

"I—" Whatever excuse she was about to give was lost when his lips met hers.

Harradorn took her breath away in a penetrating, powerful kiss that had her melting. She swayed on her feet and leaned into him. Oh, yeah. This guy could kiss, hot, heady, full-bodied, burning through her like an unstoppable fire while his arms encircled her with a firm yet tender touch that made her tremble with desire.

She wanted him to take her, here, now, up against the wall, down on the floor—hell, even on the stairs. With this man, she was game for anything. It didn't make sense, it wasn't like her. Maybe it had something to do with the magic that had put his town to sleep. Some of it might still be lingering in the air or on his lips, making her common sense go fuzzy like cotton candy, her inhibitions sleep. His tongue stroked hers and blazed a lusty path around her mouth, and she had to face the fact this had nothing to do with magic or the weird town she was in and everything to do with the powerful maleness of the man holding her like he never wanted to let her go.

When the kiss ended, she opened her eyes. Harradorn looked as puzzled as she was by what had passed between them. "Why did you do that?" she asked.

"Seduction is a two-way street," he said, his voice low and sensual. "Remember that the next time you kiss someone without permission." He stroked her cheek with a finger, prolonging the intimacy produced by the kiss. "Now, how much did you pay Felicity to bring you here?"

"Nothing."

He lowered his hand and shifted away. The warmth between them cooled, so did his voice. "How much?"

"Look, I don't know how things are done here in Peace, but where I come from not everything or everyone has a price. And for your information, Zach gave me permission to kiss you—yes, on the lips—after I woke your brother up."

"My brother?"

"Good-looking guy in a pirate outfit named Rick. He was out by the park. The first person I kissed."

That seemed to surprise him even more. His posture shifted from demanding to guardedly curious. He cleared his throat and asked, "What did you think of him?"

"Rakishly handsome. Freewheeling. Probably got a lot of suspensions when he was in school. Definitely enjoys life a lot more than you do."

He raised one brow. "You could tell all that from a kiss?"

Was that jealousy she detected in his voice? "You'd be surprised."

Harradorn frowned, strangely annoyed, though why he couldn't say. Because Rick had tasted her lips first? He shoved his hands in his pockets. "And what could you tell from kissing me?"

"The first time or the second?"

He was about to ask if there was a difference when Felicity flew down the stairs with Sessi by her side.

"It worked! It worked!" Felicity circled Joy's head three times before pausing in front of him. "It worked, Mayor Harradorn! Just like Joy said. Isn't she wonderful? Teachers are so smart!"

He glanced around the fluttering fairy at Joy. So, Joy Flint was a teacher. Regardless, the woman was *too* smart. He'd never known an outsider to adapt to Peace & Prosperity so fast, especially an uninvited visitor who might blab about what she had seen. He had to make sure Joy would keep her mouth shut. If not, she'd have to stay. Forever, if need be.

But first things first. "Felicity, I have a job for you and your team. I want you to wake everyone in Peace." From what Joy had told him, Rick was already taking care of Prosperity.

Felicity saluted him. "Yes, sir, Mayor Harradorn. How much?"

"An ounce of rose nectar and a cup of geranium potpourri." To his annoyance, Felicity glanced at Joy as if seeking her approval, then looked back at him.

"Hm. That's a big job, Mayor. We'll have to enter every residence, squeeze through vents and locks and chimneys. It could take days. The sprites alone have a lot of hiding places. For such a huge task: three ounces of rose nectar and two cups of jasmine potpourri."

"That's outrageous." He crossed his arms in refusal. He'd have the sheriff and his deputies wake all the humans in Peace, then get the sprites from Prosperity to wake up all the sprites and fairies in Peace. Of course, sprites were even less reliable than fairies. Scatterbrained. Still, it would teach Felicity a lesson about greed.

He opened his mouth to tell Felicity the deal was off when Joy stepped forward.

"Sorry to interrupt your negotiations," Joy said, "but I really must be going." She looked at him. "I wouldn't say it was nice seeing you again, but it was interesting. So is your town." She turned and smiled at Felicity. "I really enjoyed meeting you. Maybe someday you can visit me again."

"No!" Felicity shrieked. "Don't go!" She fluttered to Joy's shoulder. "Not without me."

"Wait a minute," he said. "Neither of you are going anywhere."

"Why not?" Joy asked.

"Felicity has a job to do here. As for you, you know too much."

Joy slapped a hand over her heart. In a mocking voice that irked the Hel out of him, she said, "I promise not to tell anyone about Peace, fairies, or you."

"And I promise," Felicity said, putting a small hand on her heart in imitation of Joy, "my team will kiss everyone in Peace for the price of three ounces of rose nectar and two cups of jasmine potpourri. Got that, Sessi?"

The pink fairy bobbed her head in agreement.

He looked from Joy to Felicity and back again. "You don't have my permission to leave."

Joy laughed. "As if I need any man's permission to do anything."

With a smirk, he crossed his arms and inclined his head toward the woman on the floor. "But you do need her help to use the skelter mirror to return home. And she's still asleep."

Joy shook her head. "Men," she said to Felicity. "They think they know everything. Hold on tight, girlfriend. We're going for a ride."

Felicity grabbed a handful of Joy's purple hair. Both waved whimsically at him. Then Joy smiled that smile that had warmed his heart the first time he saw it, the one that made him feel good about the world and himself. She pursed her lips as if to kiss him and his heart sped in anticipation. Then she breathed, slow and sexy, "Purple."

Immediately Joy and Felicity were surrounded by black sparkles.

He couldn't believe it. This shouldn't be happening. "Wait!" he yelled. But they were already gone, the black sparkles fading. Not only had he let Felicity slip back into the outside world, now an outsider knew of the town's existence. A woman.

Dammit! He didn't know any woman who could keep a secret.

* * *

There's a lot to be said about traveling by magic, Joy thought while they sped through the dark void. No packing. No tickets. No money. And when you got mad at someone, you could leave without taking a single step. Trouble was, when you left that quickly it didn't give the other person time to apologize and say he was sorry for being such a jerk, then try to make up for it by giving you a kiss that could curl your toes and make you completely forget why you were angry with him in the first place.

When Joy appeared in her home, she decided magic wasn't as great as fairy tales made it out to be. The glum feeling of having left something unfinished shadowed her while she fixed a thimbleful of lemonade and a thin slice of canned peaches for Felicity, as requested. As for her cat, Shredder had taken out the stress of having a fairy in the house, and Joy's neglectful disappearance, by shredding her bedspread while she and Felicity were in Peace.

Joy held up her beautiful torn bedspread and sighed. Over the years Shredder had clawed a lot of things in the house, but this was the first time he'd taken out his frustration on her bed. He was back under it, still acting scared, still not wanting to be touched. She cooed and offered sincere apologies, telling Shredder how much she loved him, that she wasn't angry at him for what he had done, with the promise she wouldn't let Felicity yank out any more of his fur.

Shredder seemed unconvinced. Knowing only time would soothe his ego, she bagged the bedspread, then brought up his food and water bowls and set them close to where he cowered in fear. She commandeered a spare blanket to use as a temporary bedspread, then went downstairs and asked Felicity to stay out of her bedroom until Shredder got used to having her around. In case that took a while, Joy moved the cat's litter box into her bedroom.

With a yawn, Felicity wished Joy happy dreams and flew to the African violet in the living room where she retracted her orange wings and stretched out on the soft, living bed of leaves. With a flower as her pillow, she was soon asleep.

The house and its occupants taken care of, Joy fixed herself a large pot of coffee and dealt with the stack of papers needing to be graded before morning. With the assistant principal displeased with what had happened with her students, the last thing Joy needed was to show up unprepared. The hours passed into morning. Joy climbed the stairs, and Felicity hummed merrily in her sleep. From the look of things in the bedroom, Shredder had gotten something to eat and drink and used the litter box. Joy carried it into the bathroom and scooped it clean, then left it there for the night.

Lights out, she snuggled under the covers, allowing her thoughts to stray to Harradorn as they had all evening, lingering on his irresistible mouth.

He said her purple hair was erotic.

Erotic.

Softly, she rubbed a finger back and forth across her lips, longing for his touch, the heat of another kiss.

His own hair was the color of sand dunes along the Jersey shore. Thoughts of the beach led her to wonder how he'd look in a Speedo. Her mind pictured him lean and tight and oh so male. She groaned and turned over. Morning was a few short hours away and this wasn't helping her get to sleep.

Go to sleep.

Go to sleep.

Stop thinking about him and go to sleep.

But she couldn't. Her thoughts drifted back to him. Being mayor of a secret town with wizards, fairies, and a pirate for a brother must be unbelievably difficult. She couldn't fault him for taking his responsibilities to heart. Poor guy. It'd probably take the rest of the night to supervise the waking of everyone in Peace.

And then he'd use the skelter mirror to fetch Felicity home!

She sat up in bed. Well, she certainly wasn't going to allow that to happen. After all, this was America. Freedom was an inalienable right. Which meant she couldn't leave Felicity home alone for him to find.

The full implication hit her, and she moaned.

I have to take a fairy to work.

Chapter 7

Since the break of dawn, Harradorn had been sitting in the council chamber. He needed to do something physical. Lift weights. Swim laps. Run the perimeter of town, twice.

Instead, he sat in his chair while the meeting droned on and glanced at a report about two areas of Peace where tree heights weren't conforming. The ones in front of Sirena's shop were an inch taller than the surrounding trees, but those by Councilman Lance Warbird's home were at least two inches shorter. He made a note to have the gardeners prune the former and fertilize the latter, then put his pen down and tried to look interested.

Every Lawson for the past thousand years had served at least one term as mayor of either Peace or Prosperity, a longstanding obligation to maintain what their ancestors had created, even if it meant sitting through long, boring meetings.

Harradorn believed in community, in forming a consensus. Lance, a prominent restaurateur and hotelier, always opposed his ideas. Over the years, they had compromised, but today Lance wasn't budging.

Lance wanted revenge.

The fairies kissing everyone awake had discovered Lance in bed with two women, neither one his wife. The oddsmakers in Prosperity were having a field day. Harradorn himself had wagered that when Kathy Warbird came home, she would finally throw the bastard out and file for divorce. Most, though, expected her to be showing off a new collection of diamond and platinum jewelry, payment for tolerance of her husband's philandering ways. Time would tell.

For now, revenge simmered in Lance's clear red eyes. He was an albino with porcelain skin and bright white hair streaming down the back of his white silk clothes. In contrast, a long braid beginning at each temple, ran down onto his chest plaited with flame-red stones etched with runic symbols. The effect was striking, maybe appealing to the opposite sex. Knowing the man's morals, it always surprised Harradorn any woman would have anything to do with him. Including his wife, Kathy.

She could have picked me.

He frowned. Water under the bridge. He took a swig of citrus water, hoping to drown old dreams of what might have been, and discovered the tangy taste brought thoughts of two kisses with a zesty outsider named Joy Flint.

Unlike Kathy, Joy didn't seem the type to put up with anything. She certainly didn't like being ordered around. And he wondered if Joy liked being in control in bed.

Lance slapped his hand on the round table. "Things wouldn't have gone from bad to worse if Mayor Harradorn hadn't authorized Sirena to put the entire town to sleep."

"Actually," Harradorn calmly replied, not missing a beat, "Sirena was asked to get rid of the Blithe Mist, which she did."

"By putting everyone to sleep," Lance reiterated with a sneer. "And with grave consequences. Tipsy O'Neill was taking a bubble bath at the time. Healers are yet treating her skin. Only fortune prevented her from drowning. Legally, she could sue us."

"A miracle she could fit in a bathtub," the councilwoman next to Harradorn muttered.

Several heard the comment and chuckled. Tipsy O'Neill was notably rotund and proud of it. Gossipers claimed she might have a few errant troll genes in her DNA.

"It's unfortunate about Tipsy," Harradorn said, keeping a neutral tone. "However, the town was in a state of emergency. The

Blithe Mist was sweeping into Peace. We can't be sued for someone's foolishness.

"That's not to say I disagree with Lance," Harradorn added, seeking a way to keep emotions tempered. "Sirena was only contracted to take care of the Mist, unaware of the Fear Fog hidden within its midst."

"So you agree Sirena screwed up." Lance snickered. "She should be fined for her incompetence. Maybe a week in Dulgrun Prison. Or is the mayor trying to protect her because she's a Lawson?"

Harradorn's temper rose a notch, but he refused to be baited. "I admit Sirena made a mistake. But you also have to admit she saved both communities a ton of money."

"How so?" the councilwoman next to Harradorn asked.

"While we slept, Sirena's Serious Smog removed every trace of Mist." He looked at each councilmember in turn. "Do you realize how much time and effort it would have taken to clean the entire town of the droplets of oily Mist? Shops would still be closed, workers scrubbing and cleaning, children not allowed outdoors for fear of getting it on their skin from the grass and swings and trees."

He sat back in his chair. "I think she did the town a favor. In fact, I wouldn't be surprised if she asks for further compensation."

The council nodded in assent, but not Lance, who grumbled and said, "I'd say living here with you is more than payment enough. Perhaps too much."

"Family members staying in the Mayor's Residence is a long and honored tradition," he countered.

"Even for those baseborn?"

There was a sharp intake of breath from many in the room. In the stark silence that followed, Harradorn could hear his own heart hammering in fury. No one had ever dared mention Sirena's parentage, at least not in public. From the sympathetic frowns and downcast eyes of everyone around the table, even Lance had to realize he'd stepped over a line not tolerated by the town.

Harradorn glared at him, silently demanding an apology.

Lance shifted in his seat. "As you know, the ordeal of suffering through a wizard duel makes even the most patient person irritable and tactless. Like many of my fellow councilmembers, I've been dealing with a multitude of complaints. If I spoke out of turn, then I apologize."

Harradorn fumed. Lance had dissembled his words with *if* and *then*, not directly apologizing. Not apologizing at all. He was more of a bastard than Sirena.

Lance surveyed the room, looking for favorable reactions. When none were forthcoming, he was forced to add, "If I can make amends in any way, do not hesitate to ask."

He wanted to tell Lance this was one time he couldn't buy his way free of transgressions as he did with his wife. But such a response might cause divisions on the council, and right now Harradorn had everyone on his side, which probably pained Lance more than the apology.

"Sirena is the one you need to make amends to. Once that's done, we won't talk of this again."

Lance nodded and the tension in the room evaporated. Everyone gathered up their things, eager to call it a day, but all stopped when Lance said, "We have two more matters to discuss. The reprehensible situation of Felicity Morningstar being in the outside world, and the security breach in the person of Joy Flint." He fixed his eerie red gaze on Harradorn. "Perhaps you'd forgotten about them."

Truthfully, all Harradorn kept thinking about was Joy. Every five minutes, the image of her lying naked in his bed, her exotic purple hair splayed out on a white pillow while he made love to her, sprang into his mind. Sex with Joy would be a lot more satisfying than smashing in Lance's face. Take longer, too. If her kisses were any indication, he couldn't imagine making love to her for anything less than all night long.

He should have told the fairies to waken the councilmembers

last. Then he could have started the morning by visiting Joy before she went to work, maybe while she was still in bed, after which he could have brought Felicity home before being stuck in this meeting all day.

His thoughts were still on Joy and sex and purple hair when he was startled to hear Lance say, "I move we authorize Mayor Harradorn to return to the outside world and impel Joy Flint and Felicity Morningstar to return to Peace."

Harradorn sat up straight. *What's going on? What have they been talking about?*

Lance stared at him, clearly aware Harradorn hadn't been paying attention. "All in favor say aye."

"Aye," the tired majority said, everyone anxious to leave.

"Wait a minute," Harradorn said in astonishment. "There was no call for discussion."

"None was needed." Lance stood. "You have our mandate."

He stood as well. "What do you expect me to do, kidnap them?"

Everyone looked at Lance, deferring to him to deal with the mayor.

"Felicity was not given permission to go into the outside world," Lance said. "If need be, the law allows you to bring her back by force. With regard to Joy Flint, the town's well-being takes precedent over her rights. You're to apprehend her, Mayor Harradorn, and bring her here immediately or face reprimand."

Harradorn was stunned. He recovered quickly, ready to launch into a persuasive argument about acting with more circumspection by reminding them about Joy's dangerous brother and his Special Forces background, when Agamemnon appeared.

The Cyclops stood smiling in the doorway. "Good news, Mayor. Council. The wizard duel is over. Wizard Zach won. All are invited to Prosperity to witness the concession ceremony."

Cheers went up around the room. With laughter and smiles, everyone rushed out. But not Lance and Harradorn. Alone, they stared across the table at each other.

"I understand why you want Felicity back," Harradorn said. "But you and I both know no one in the outside world will believe anything Joy Flint might say about us."

"What if she took pictures of Peace while we were asleep?"

"She didn't have a camera with her."

"What about a phone? They have cameras."

He hadn't thought of that. But a sneaking, cheating husband like Lance would. "Photos can be deleted," he replied evenly. "So the question remains: Why do you want Joy Flint here? What are you really after, Warbird?"

"What I always want. Change. To turn this tired little community into a thriving enterprise that rivals Prosperity."

Harradorn shook his head. "Peace has always been a refuge from greed and magic."

"Then perhaps we'll also need to change the town's name." His red eyes dropped to the medallion hanging on Harradorn's chest and his mouth twisted into a sinister smile. "Unclench your fists, *mayor*. I'm not after your job. Just your attitude."

"Maybe it's time you moved to a community that better reflects your interests."

"We'll see who's forced to leave first." With a cold chuckle, the councilman left.

* * *

In Prosperity, a large crowd from both communities gathered around the two wizard towers, waiting for Zach and FearfulFran to appear. Harradorn stood next to Rick, who was drinking a large tankard of grog in celebration. Many of the scalawags and dwarfs from Prosperity were drinking, and would continue to do so far into the night. In Rick's side of town, any excuse to party.

Agamemnon leaned down to Harradorn and whispered, "St. Jerome said never look a gift horse in the mouth. But I'm of a mind to always keep the receipts."

"What did Agamemnon say?" Rick asked. He held out his tankard for a refill from a barmaid serving the crowd.

"He believes the sudden end to the wizard duel is too good to be true."

"Party pooper." Rick scowled and drank deeply.

Children ran by with balloons, pinwheels, and confetti to mark the happy occasion. From on high, fairies dropped colorful streamers and flower petals on the crowd while elves played flutes and danced. If not for the horrendous mandate to kidnap Joy, Harradorn would have been enjoying himself.

Along the fringe of the crowd, he noticed Sirena. Always when in public, she traveled alone, shunned by all the women and secretly assessed by all the men. Being seductive and beautiful was both a blessing and a curse. Sirena could have any man she wanted—and wanted none. What she desired was love and acceptance. Because of her heritage, the only thing men wanted from her was sex.

Sirena's mother was Darlia, daughter of a selkie and a sea nymph, who had magically raped Harradorn's father while the family vacationed in the Highlands of Scotland soon after Rick was born. Hybrids of humans and supernatural creatures were preternaturally stronger in magic than most purebloods, and males ran in the Lawson family. Darlia wanted a powerful son.

And she got him.

What she didn't want was her son's nonmagical twin sister, so on Sirena's seventh birthday—when any magic she might possess would finally manifest, and didn't—Sirena was dumped on Sven Lawson's doorstep like worthless trash.

Traumatized by her mother's abandonment, and faced with the lingering bitterness of her stepmother, Sirena tried to learn magic to prove herself useful to the Lawson household. But her abilities were no better than her cooking skills, and when she turned to alchemy to compensate, disaster took on a new definition. A conditioning shampoo she created made their youngest sister temporarily bald. An aftershave lotion grew so much hair on their father's face, he looked like a Sasquatch. Harradorn smiled. That one had been funny. Not to their father, of course. But he and Rick had laughed their heads off for days afterwards.

Her preteen attempt at making lavender-scented rain destroyed the roof of their home and produced the first threat from their father that she'd be kicked out if she didn't stop experimenting. Things calmed down until one Mother's Day. Knowing how much her stepmother loved cut flowers, Sirena concocted a bouquet that would last forever. But the flowers turned into man-eating plants and snacked on their housekeeper's fingers. It was almost the last straw.

Almost.

Fortunately for Sirena, elves are a forgiving and tolerant race, and after her final transgression they agreed to take her in for the remainder of her teen years.

A child chasing a balloon ran into Harradorn and jarred him back to the present. He steered his way through the merrymakers to Sirena's side. "What's that?" He nodded at an object cupped to her chest.

"A crystal ball!" Sirena lowered her fingers for him to see. "I just got it. For it to work, I need to carry it about my person for seven days so we bond, though I could swear there was an instant connection between us." She smiled down at the four-inch ball as if it were a kitten or a puppy.

"Just because Rick's girlfriend is into crystal balls doesn't mean Rick likes everyone who uses them."

A frown skirted Sirena's lips, but was quickly banished by a girlish grin. "Oh, I know that. I just thought it would be fun to have one. A new skill to add to my many talents."

And another persuasion in a long line of inducements to make Rick treat her like a sister. Harradorn pitied her and Rick, but there was nothing he could do to mend the rift between them. Thor knows, he had tried.

"You look tired," she said.

"I was up all night supervising the fairies while they woke everyone in Peace."

"And making sure they didn't help themselves to the sleepers' valuables?"

He matched her knowing smile. "That, too."

"There's something different about you," Sirena said, studying his face. "I've never known you to walk past the Svenson twins without a second look. Dehbie and Dehlila gave you their best slutty winks—in unison, no less—but you didn't notice."

He glanced back at the two young women. Both winked at him again, with Dehlila adding a slow enticing lick of her bottom lip. Strangely, the tempting stir he usually felt when they flaunted interest in him failed to appear

"And yet there's a look in your eyes," Sirena added. "A spark. Someone in the mind's eye. Someone who's not here but whom your memory keeps before you."

He glanced down at his feet, away from his sister's perceptive gaze. But it was already too late.

"Ha! That's it. Someone has caught your eye and won't let go. Who is she?"

"No one," he said, doing his best to sound bored.

"You may be able to fool yourself, dear brother, but not me. If only my ball was working already, I could see who she is."

He shuddered. The thought of her prying into his personal life with that damn crystal ball was a thousand times worse than having her live in the Hall with him. "I thought you needed a person's permission to do a reading on them? Isn't there a seer's code you have to abide by?"

Sirena stuck out her bottom lip in a rebellious pout. "That's what Cynthia said. Something about mixed messages and fuzzy images."

"And false readings?"

Her frown soured. "There are so many rules to follow. No advice is better than bad advice. No warnings about an impending death. No lottery numbers. Blah, blah, blah." She glowered at the crystal ball as if it were a naughty puppy, then relented and cuddled it again. "I heard what you did for me in front of the council, how you defended my use of Serious Smog. Rumor has it Lance has started another petition to remove you from office."

"He's failed three times to get rid of me."

"But the last by only five signatures." Her brow wrinkled in worry.

"He blamed me for the collapse of the sewer system." His voice turned rough. "And the Bjorks' deaths. People will believe anything, look for any scapegoat when things go wrong."

"Wizard's First Rule. Even so, it was risky taking my side before the council."

He shrugged. "You're family. I could do no less."

"You're so special, Harry. Always watching out for me. Not only the glue that holds the community together, but our family as well." With a heartfelt smile, she gave him a peck on the cheek. "I wish Rick was more like you."

He followed her wistful gaze to where their brother was toasting the town's good fortune with several of his mates. "Give him time. He'll come around."

"I hope so." She looked down at the crystal ball in her hands. "Sometimes I don't think he'll ever accept me, let alone love me. Not like you do."

Harradorn raised her chin to look at him. "Know this, my sister. Rick doesn't hate you. He hates what your mother did to our father. Having you around is a constant reminder that a lot of what happens to us seems beyond our control. And you know how much Rick likes to be in control, though he gives the illusion he's a scalawag without a care in the world."

"Still, I would do anything to have his approval. At the very least his respect." She pulled her purple shawl tighter around her shoulders. "Regarding the skelter mirror, per your request, I've examined my books, trying to figure out how Joy was able to use its magic to return home from the Hall."

"And?"

"My best guess is a form of residual magic, like passing on a cold. Felicity traveled with you to Joy's, so she was subject to the same return trigger as you were. Just like she hitched a ride with you, Joy hitched a ride with her, probably by Felicity holding onto her hair."

"So, because Felicity used *purple* to travel here, the residual magic of the spell allowed Joy to use the same trigger to take her home?"

Sirena nodded.

"So all I have to do is find a way to get Felicity to say it again and my hitchhiker will return. If she's touching or holding onto Joy, Joy will be brought here, too."

"Yes, but it's risky. Having two traveling back forth that way can drain the magic from the mirror like a battery. Used too often, they might be stuck in transit when the power gives out."

"How long is the magic good for?"

"No longer than three days. After that, traveling could be dangerous."

"So, tomorrow would be the last day they could safely use the mirror." He scratched his head, thinking. "Would using a fresh spell on me strengthen the magic?"

"Not likely. If anything, a new spell would reset the mirror and negate the previous magic. Why do you ask?"

"Because the council has mandated I fetch Felicity—and Joy—whether they want to return or not."

"Kidnapping isn't your style, brother."

"True. Rick would be better at it, but this is my problem, not his."

"When do you wish to leave?"

"After the concession ceremony."

"And the payment?"

"Consider it a favor. After all, I did defend you before the council, and you are living in the Mayor's Residence on the same floor as I am." Along with all her incense, potpourri, chimes, and water fountains. She must have moved half her store's inventory into the suite with her.

Sirena simpered. "Rumor has it Lance owes me restitution. For payment, I want a seat on the council."

He choked. "You can't be serious."

"With council approval, a mayor can appoint a representative-at-large. You've never done that, so the seat remains vacant. I want that seat."

"What on earth for?"

She glanced at Rick, who was leading another toast. "Respect." She turned to Harradorn. "Lance needs to make amends, so he won't oppose it. A council seat, that's what I want. Take it or leave it." And before Harradorn could convince her otherwise, she slid into the crowd and was gone from view.

Harradorn was in a foul mood when he rejoined Rick. He paid for a tankard of ale from a barmaid and emptied half the mug before coming up for air.

"Has everyone been wakened?" he asked Agamemnon. The Cyclops and his family sat on the grass nearby so they wouldn't block anyone's view.

"The fairies have taken care of the vast majority of Peace's inhabitants," Agamemnon said, "and have subcontracted out kissing the lower lifeforms to the sprites."

"Ditto on my side," Rick said, "except for the Sasquatch. Can't find a single person, fairy, or sprite to kiss even one of them. They're all still asleep."

"You're joking," Harradorn said.

Rick laughed. "Don't worry. I'm running a raffle. And it's free. First person to have their name drawn wins a hundred doubloons."

"That's extraordinarily generous of you."

"I thought so." Rick took a long pull on his grog. "However, the second name drawn has to kiss the least putrid Sasquatch we can find. Then the Sasquatch can kiss their own.''

"And how many have decided to risk joining this raffle?"

"Everyone in Prosperity." Rick grinned. "Including me."

A chorus of French horns announced the beginning of the concession ceremony. From Zach's tower, a spray of gold bubbles rained down. They burst open; tiny rainbows shot forth like gentle fireworks, showering everyone in a myriad of colors and floral scents.

Zach appeared on top of his tall tower, dressed in his ceremonial black and gold robes, head hooded like always. He waved to the crowd below. Everyone cheered, waved, or clapped in response. While they waited for his opponent to appear, Harradorn said, "FearfulFran must have underestimated Zach's abilities. Usually these duels go on for weeks."

"Aye. I've heard one town had a duel that lasted two months." Rick met his eye and must have realized his words echoed Agamemnon's earlier suggestion that it was too good to be true because he added, "Don't go courting trouble where there is none. Let's be grateful."

On top of the maroon cloud-enshrouded tower, a thin woman with straggly black hair appeared, garbed in black and wine-red robes that looked more ragged than ceremonial. In her hands was a gold chest, filled with whatever wizards consider valuable, the gift a concession for starting the duel and then losing it.

Wizard duels have one of three purposes: to test a wizard's abilities; to force one wizard to share new magic or hand over a magical item no one else has; or to claim territory—towns.

Being town wizard is one step removed from a seat on the wizards high council. Since there are more wizards in the world than magical towns in which they can openly exist, a duel is a gateway to respectability. If Zach had lost and if FearfulFran hadn't been after one of his rose bushes, she could have claimed his spot of official wizard of Peace & Prosperity and forced him to leave. From what he'd learned abroad, Zach was one of the most generous, peaceful wizards in the world. The town was fortunate to have him. Except for the damn roses he grew.

The gold chest rose from FearfulFran's outstretched arms and floated across to Zach. The crowd cheered. Zach stood his staff aside and reached up with both hands to accept the gift.

Then all Hel broke loose.

As Zach's fingers touched the chest, a wand appeared in each of FearfulFran's hands. She targeted them at Zach's tower. Cannon fire flashed from her tower to Zach's; a resounding boom shook the ground. Sparkling, magical cannon balls penetrated one of his floors, blowing out the stone walls.

The elves fled. Rock trolls hunkered down and formed into boulders; dwarfs hid behind them. Fairies and sprites sought cover in the surrounding trees. People ran, parents protectively covering their children from the shards of granite raining down.

Zach dropped the gold chest and grabbed his staff. But the damage had already been done. Debris fell. FearfulFran cackled in glee. She raised her wands and twirled them. Deafening peals of thunder filled the air. The maroon cloud, which encased her tower, twirled and rose above it. It swirled above what was now revealed to be a plain gray tower with cracks along its length. Then she and her tower disappeared, leaving behind the maroon cloud that spiraled malevolently overhead.

Fighting the gale that threatened to become a tornado, Zach struggled to stay on his feet. Harradorn feared he'd be blown off his tower. Through sheer effort, Zach managed to raise his staff toward the expanding whirlwind. His mouth opened, yelling, but whatever was said was lost among the thunderous sound like a freight train approaching. A pale blue beam shot from the crown of Zach's staff, aimed at the funnel. The blue mixed with the maroon of the vortex, swirling, changing it to purple. The color lightened, the violent wind eased, the cloud thinned and broke apart. Within seconds, the sky was clear and blue. On the black tower, Zach collapsed and disappeared from sight.

Harradorn moved to help, but Rick held him back. "No one can go in the wizard's tower until Zach opens the door, you know that. Until then, he's on his own." Rick gripped his arm for a long second, his face grim. "He'll be fine, Harry. You'll see."

Harradorn hoped his brother was right. He looked around. People were coming out of their hiding places. The rock trolls straightened and the dwarfs moved off. Fairies and sprites took to the air but stayed safely close to the trees. One elf reappeared. The rest would stay home and await news, unwilling to get involved, like always. After what had just happened, he couldn't blame them. Among wizards, such treachery after a concession was not unprecedented, but it was rare. When later found, the treacherous wizard was stripped of his powers and banished to the outside world forever.

FearfulFran had to be insane. Or desperate.

From on top his tower, Zach staggered to his feet and looked down. "No!" He had suddenly realized which floor of his tower had been attacked.

So had Harradorn. His stomach turned to stone. FearfulFran had destroyed the floor housing Zach's greenhouse. It seemed if she couldn't have one of Zach's roses, neither would he. Colorful petals filled the air. Soon the breeze would spread them over the entire town.

A white rose petal landed softly at his feet. Rick's boot crushed it into the ground.

"That's one less disaster in the making," Rick said.

Harradorn nodded in agreement. Amidst a flurry of red, yellow, orange, and pink petals falling like snow, he searched for the white ones. "Only a thousand more to go."

Chapter 8

Entry into a wizard's tower was rare. Those granted permission considered themselves lucky. Privileged.

Or in deep deep trouble.

On this occasion, Harradorn regarded it as an obligation born of friendship, though it felt more like torture.

On the fifth floor of the tower, all the windows lining the circular walls of Zach's greenhouse had been blown out. During the concession ceremony, the shields had been lowered to receive the gift. But now a slight ripple beyond the missing windows indicated the shields were up and running. From the outside, the black granite walls appeared windowless and solid, the illusion provided by the mystical privacy of the structure.

Harradorn stopped a few steps inside the door. Rick lingered behind, reluctant to venture further. The entire floor was one massive greenhouse. The air, usually moist and perfumed by hundreds of rose bushes, reeked of burnt vegetation. Shredded and scorched plants, pot shards, and soil littered the floor. In the midst of the destruction, the town's wizard stood hunched over, hands covering the face inside the hood, shoulders shaking while he sobbed uncontrollably.

Rick fidgeted, plainly uncomfortable. "They're just plants," he whispered to Harradorn. "Aren't they?"

"I always thought so. But now..." He shook his head. Zach had shown no inclination toward horticulture until he had been forced to accept the mantle of his father's tower. Now he seemed obsessed with it, particularly roses.

The bushes near them were still in their pots. All had been blown over, yet their distance from the blasts had saved them. Harradorn righted some and noticed every pot had a gold plaque on it, each engraved with a name. John Thrush. Philippe Menendez. Katarina Engstrom. Stefan Szbeczenski. Not fanciful flower names. More like names of people.

The roses in this area had flowers dull in color with veins of black running through them, petals shriveled, edges curled and blackened, many malformed, giving the impression they were infested or diseased. He set one pot upright; his nose wrinkled in distaste. The henna-red flowers had a brackish scent, like rotting seaweed and spoiled fish. Sap oozed from a harsh slash along the main stem. He peered closer, not sure if he was seeing correctly, then jerked back in abhorrence. Not plant sap. It was red. Blood red.

The plant was bleeding!

He shuddered. "We shouldn't stay long," he told Rick. "I don't think it's safe."

With Rick on his heels, he picked his way through the wreckage to where the wizard now crouched, fingers delicately touching the tattered remnants of a white rose bush. From inside the hood, murmurs of regret fell like teardrops. The snake tattoo on Zach's hand pulsed dark and fast. Not a good sign.

"They were mine," Zach said, his voice thick with emotion. "Trusted unto me. In my care. Some have been here since before my father. All relying on me, needing me. Their only hope." His head drooped. "I failed them."

Harradorn noticed all the rose petals in this area were white, so pure and bright it almost hurt to look at them.

With one hand, Zach swept up white petals from among the debris. "Would you like one? You might as well. Both of you, take one. Take two."

Harradorn took a step back, appalled, whereas Rick looked

down at the petals and licked his lips. "Don't even think about it," Harradorn warned him.

"Thinking and doing are miles apart," Rick answered.

"When tempted, they become two sides of the same coin." Afraid Rick might accept Zach's dangerous offer, he swatted the petals out of the wizard's hand. They tumbled to the floor.

Zach gasped. The embroidery on his robes turned from black to red to orange to yellow, the threads hot and bright. Zach rose, shaking in rage. "How dare you!" He pointed the finger wearing the fire opal at Harradorn. It glowed with power. "Do you know who I am?"

"Yes, I do." Harradorn fisted his hands, more to keep the wizard from seeing his hands quaking in fear than as a challenge. "You're Zacharias Morgan Blackhawk. The snot-nosed kid I beat the crap out of when he made out with my little sister. The mate I let copy my book report on *Ulysses* after I spent three months trying to understand it while you and Rick went fishing. The guy who took us to Mardi Gras and taught me how to make love to a woman's breasts. The one who risked his life to bring a healer from Macklin's Mark to save our mother's life."

Ignoring Rick's protest, he reached out and placed a hand on Zach's shoulder, knowing it was going to hurt like hell but believing it was the only way to penetrate the wizard's grief and raging anger, and reclaim his friend.

The threads burned into his palm, but he kept his hand determinedly on Zach's shoulder. "You're my friend. You're hurting. You've just had your tower and roses blasted by that bitch FearfulFran. She's blown wizard's petals all over our town—Odin only knows what they're being used for. The real question isn't *who* you are." He gave the shoulder a shake. "It's *what are you going to do about it?*"

A tense silence passed. The embroidery under Harradorn's hand burned into his skin. Rick stepped forward in alarm, but Harradorn flashed him a stern look not to interfere. He gritted his teeth and held on.

Zach grabbed his hand and thrust it away. Seething, his body shaking beneath the robes, he raised his arms to the ceiling and roared. Flames shot out from his fingertips. Harradorn and Rick ducked. The fire swept across the ceiling in billowing waves of yellow, orange, and red. Zach continued to roar until the fire from his fingers sputtered and gave out. The embroidery on his robes cooled to black. The tattoo on his hand stopped pulsing. He lowered his arms and turned to the brothers.

"Glad you got that out of your system," Rick said. They rose to their feet. "For a while there I thought you were going to invite the town to a barbeque."

Zach chuckled and shook his head. Then he turned his hooded face toward Harradorn. "That was stupid."

Though his seared hand throbbed in pain, he tried to sound indifferent. "It worked."

Zach grabbed his wrist. A wand appeared in Zach's other hand. He circled it over the wounds, chanting something under his breath. The pain eased, the skin formed patterned scars that soon thinned into silvery threads on his palm and fingers. Likely the scars would be permanent, but the redemption of his friend was more than worth it.

"The nerves will be sensitive for a few days, but they'll continue to heal." Zach inspected the hand to make sure he had taken care of all the damage. The wand disappeared. He looked at Harradorn and shook his head again. "Better if you had kneed me in the balls," he said, an unmistakable smile in his voice.

Harradorn grinned. "I'll keep that in mind for next time."

* * *

In Joy's fifth grade classroom, a student pointed at a solar system mobile hanging from the ceiling. "A fairy's sitting on Jupiter."

Joy winked at Felicity and said, "Good job, Jaden."

She'd told her students Felicity was a high tech gadget in the guise of a fairy, fragile and extremely expensive—irreplaceable, a new vocabulary word for them to work with—so no one was permitted to touch it or she would never bring it to class again. It was the end of the day and as a reward for the class's good behavior, she'd let Felicity play hide-and-seek with them.

"Okay, class, there's the bell. Leave by rows, starting at the windows. Remember, spelling test tomorrow." Of all the schemes she'd devised on how to bring a fairy to work, hiding her in plain sight had seemed the best tactic. And the simplest. When everyone was gone, Joy locked the door and pulled the shade. "That went better than I thought."

"Easy for you to say." Felicity flew down from Jupiter and made several circuits of the classroom. "I hate sitting still. I don't know how your students do it."

"Practice. Don't the students in Peace do the same?"

"Sure, but that doesn't mean they like it. It's why fairies only go to school for a few years. It's not in our nature to be still."

Felicity zoomed around. Joy took advantage of their privacy to search the Internet. She found several photos of fairies similar in appearance to Felicity, all slightly blurred, which wasn't surprising considering fairies only seemed to stop moving when asleep. Concerning Peace & Prosperity, she'd discovered several tall tales about the town. For centuries, Indians, trappers, hunters, and hikers in the Rockies had reported falling asleep after eating with the inhabitants, only to wake up hundreds of miles from where they had been.

One eyewitness insisted it was actually a UFO base.

A thousand years ago Vikings visited the New World and settled in Newfoundland, eventually returning home, yet according to the door in Peace, some of them remained and relocated farther inland—along with fairies and dwarfs!

Of course, the time it would take to cross-reference fairies and dwarfs with Norse history wouldn't be necessary if Felicity would tell her about the town's founders, but the ditzy fairy always turned stone-cold serious whenever Joy brought up the subject.

Further searches uncovered a journal from the Civil War with an entry regarding a feverish soldier ranting about a tree town full of pointy-eared people and tiny women with wings. Elves and fairies? The really interesting thing: the town was in the Blue Ridge Mountains.

"Felicity, is there a town like Peace & Prosperity in the Blue Ridge Mountains?"

The fairy dove in between the desks like a gymnast practicing an aerial routine. "You know I can't answer that."

"I'll take that for a yes. What about elves?"

Silence answered her question. Another yes.

There was a knock on her door. Jeff.

"Just a sec!" She gestured for Felicity to find a spot. With a frown, the fairy sat on Joy's desk in a lotus position, eyes closed so she wouldn't blink, the pose she'd used most of the day when not sleeping behind one of the plants in the room.

"Ready?" Joy whispered. Felicity nodded and Joy opened the door

Jeff walked in. "I heard about your new toy. Where is it?" She gestured to the desk. Jeff went over to get a closer look. "Wow. It's so lifelike. Pretty, too."

Men, Joy thought when she noticed him staring at Felicity's buxom breasts.

To her credit, Felicity didn't flinch when his fingers reached out to touch her. Joy snatched his hand away. "She's very fragile," Joy explained. "Please don't touch."

"No problem. Where'd you get it?"

"I found her at home. Mike's always been into unusual gizmos," she said, throwing bits of truth together so she wouldn't have to lie. "She probably got left behind. I decided to take your advice about making my hair color reflect mystery and magic. The fairy seemed perfect."

"Glad to be of help." Jeff glanced at the door and lowered his voice. "Just overheard the assistant principal talking about you to the principal. Thought you'd want to know what was said. That new Coffee & Buns is supposed to be good. How about we go there and talk?"

"Thanks, but Mike's invited me over for supper and I want to finish up here before I go."

"You sure? I could give you a few pointers, help you get on the assistant principal's good side. With contracts coming out and tenure only a few weeks away, you don't want to blow it."

No, she didn't. Getting tenure meant job stability for a teacher. Maybe it wouldn't hurt to take a few minutes to have coffee with him. But then she saw Felicity yawn and Joy's eyes widened in alarm. She shifted in front of the fairy to block his view.

"Maybe another time," Joy said, and quickly changed the subject. "By the way, how are your kids? I noticed they weren't in school again today."

"Still sick. You know the crud. It can last for days. Weeks."

"Well, then, you probably want to hurry home and help Patsy."

"I'm sure she has everything under control," he muttered. "She always does."

Uh, oh. Sounded like Jeff and Patsy had another fight. Normally she'd lend a sympathetic ear, but she could hear the fairy shifting impatiently behind her. She had to get rid of Jeff, fast. "Well, I better get my work done before I go." But she didn't move. Instead, she stayed between Jeff and Felicity, waiting for him to get the hint and leave. Unfortunately, it only seemed to make him suspicious.

He put a hand on her shoulder. "Are you all right? You look tense."

"I haven't been getting much sleep lately." *Because I have a real live fairy staying with me. And last night I visited a town where everyone was under a sleeping spell. And I met a handsome pirate and an honest to goodness wizard. Then there's Mayor Harradorn, whose kisses are pure electric and can jump-start my engine more than any man I've ever known.*

"Just need a night off." She faked a yawn.

He gave her an affectionate squeeze on the shoulder and said, "Get some rest."

After he left, Joy turned to Felicity. "Let's get out of here."

"No argument from me." Felicity flew to her shoulder. "Wire Lips likes touching you."

"You mean the hand on the shoulder? Jeff's always done that." She retrieved the hard-sided cylinder purse she'd punctured with air holes. "It's just a friendly gesture."

"If you say so." Felicity climbed into the purse.

Joy spied a stash of objects among the padding and removed four paperclips, a Croc ornament, a hair clip with blue rhinestones, several pennies, and a dime. "What did I tell you about taking things?"

"Fairies don't steal. We just keep whatever we find."

"I bet it was a fairy who came up with the saying: Finders keepers, losers weepers."

The fairy looked at her in surprise. "How did you know?"

"A wild guess." She was about to close the purse when she noticed Felicity fretting. Orange eyes peered up at her, and for the first time since they met, the fairy looked concerned.

"Maybe humans are different about friendly gestures," Felicity said, "but I've never known a stud to be satisfied with only being friends with a chick."

Stud. Chick. *Male and female?*

"In my experience, studs are only after two things. Sex. And more sex. Especially during mating season."

"Fairies have a mating season?"

"One month of wild, glorious, unbridled sex." Felicity fluttered her wings. "Just thinking about it makes me all hot and twittery. Beau Monde and Tom Scarlet are always after me."

"You have two partners? Husbands?"

"Three, actually. Aslo usually shows up last, but since he's the best, he can afford to take his time."

Joy gazed down at the fairy with new respect. Felicity had three studs that made love to her. Three! And she had... none.

She sighed miserably and wondered if wizard Zach could turn her into a fairy.

* * *

While Joy drove to her brother's, Felicity popped out of the purse and sat on the dashboard like an ornament. They continued their conversation about sex, male fairies, mating season, and the amazing detail that studs raised the children after they're weaned from their mothers.

No wonder Felicity seemed so carefree.

After several questions about parentage, she gave the fairy a brief lesson in biology, including a woman's egg being viable for twelve hours but the sperm good for up to five days.

Felicity's mouth dropped open. "You're kidding?!"

"I don't know anything about fairy physiology, but in humans, when the egg is ready to be fertilized, usually whoever's sperm is already inside her will be the father."

Felicity stared at her, aghast. "But that would mean Aslo is... is..."

"Not even out of the gate when your other two partners have satisfied their biological urges. Unless you can get Aslo to show up first, few of your progeny will be from him."

"That explains why none of my children are blue like Aslo." Felicity's wings drooped.

"Maybe fairies should stay in school longer, at least until they've taken biology."

"Maybe you should come to Peace and teach us."

"Thanks, but I have my hands full taking care of human children."

"At least in Peace you wouldn't have anyone following you around. Wire Lips is two cars back. Has been since we left the school."

Joy scanned her rearview mirrors while navigating traffic. Hmm.

That did look like Jeff's car, right behind the PSE&G truck. "He lives next to me," she told Felicity. "He's probably going home. Wait and see, we'll go past it on the way to Mike's and he'll pull in his driveway."

Minutes later, Joy followed a police car past her home. So did Jeff. "The supermarket is in this direction," she explained to the fairy, who kept looking at her with an I-told-you-so expression. "His kids are sick. Patsy probably asked him to pick up some things on the way home."

Two blocks later, she turned down the street to Mike's condo. So did the utility truck. Jeff's car continued without turning. "There." Joy glanced at the rearview mirror. "He's going to the store."

"Whatever." Felicity climbed into the purse.

She'd put the purse in her brother's spare bedroom so Felicity could stretch her wings, and sneak her some food later.

At the entry to the condos, she called Mike on the intercom. The door buzzed to indicate it was unlocked. She started to open it when Felicity pounded on the side of the purse.

"There he goes!" the fairy yelled.

"Shh." Joy raised the purse to her mouth and whispered, "Who are you talking about?"

"Wire Lips! I just saw him drive by. Go look before he gets away. Go! Go! Go!"

"All right already, I'm going." What looked like Jeff's car was moving slowly down the street. It turned in the direction of his home, yet she couldn't see the driver. Couldn't even tell if it was a man or a woman.

"See," the fairy said. "I told you."

"I'm beginning to think fairies are paranoid." Or at least this one was. "I don't think it was him." But when Mike buzzed her in again, a nagging doubt took seed, an ugly weed nourished by Felicity's inflexible claim that yesterday Jeff had peeked into her window.

Chapter 9

Life or death, riches or ruin, lay in the hands of ten inhabitants of Peace & Prosperity. In each of their palms rested a single white rose petal. A wizard's petal.

From the top step of the Mayor's Hall and Residence, Mayors Harradorn and Rick gazed down upon the ten grouped together at the bottom of the stairs. Midway between stood an iron brazier, its flames waiting to be fed. Attending off to the side, Peace's town council watched, Lance in the forefront.

Though most dwarfs and all of the trolls lived in Prosperity, the restless crowd filling Peace's park contained an unusually strong mix of humans, dwarfs, and trolls, with a lone elf on the outskirts, waiting to report the proceedings to the reticent elves keeping to their homes. The trees buzzed with the flittering wings of fairies and sprites, while in the shadows on the far side of the park, a handful of Sasquatch clustered together. A slight movement near the side of a building to the west revealed two of the River Folk peeking around the edge.

Lightning crackled from Prosperity. Zach was charging his tower, getting ready to go after FearfulFran. There was no point in staying, nothing he could do would stop what was about to happen. But if he captured FearfulFran, no other town would suffer because of her.

Harradorn raised both hands to call the assembled to silence. "On behalf of the town, I want to thank those who have already destroyed their petals or turned them in. For some, it was a difficult choice to make and I commend your integrity and selflessness."

Harradorn clapped in gratitude. So did Rick and the council. Applause swelled from the spectators. The ten kept quiet.

Rick spoke next. "Sheriff Caine and his deputies are scouring the town for more petals. The sprites and fairies have been checking rooftops and crannies to insure none are left to float down later. As far as we know, these ten," he inclined his head to the small group at the bottom of the stairs, "have the only ones left."

"Burn them!" someone yelled from the crowd.

"Burn them! Burn them! Burn them!" the crowd chanted. The volume grew. The ten huddled together and cast furtive glances about.

Harradorn raised his hands and called anew for silence. "This is a time for caution and circumspection. I applaud the courage it took for these ten to come forward and admit to having a petal." Actually, well-meaning and worried family members, friends, and jealous whistleblowers had reported them. "Let's welcome their brave honesty."

He clapped again to show his appreciation. Rick clapped but only half-heartedly. So did most of the crowd. Everyone knew that once someone had a wizard's petal, no one could take it away. It was part of the magic, the protective part of the gift.

Harradorn would give anything to be able to steal them all, but he might as well be asking for the moon.

But then if he had a wizard's petal, he could do just that.

He addressed the ten. "I ask you to place your petals into the fire to insure our town remains dedicated to peace and prosperity. Will you do so?"

The ten glanced at each other. No one came forward. No one said a word.

Tipsy O'Neill's husband approached the ten and pleaded with his wife. "Please, do as Mayor Harradorn asks. I love you. I really do. That's why I told the mayor you had one. Please, sweetie cakes, get rid of it. Do it for me."

Tipsy waddled forward, her tent of a dress sashaying side to side. "Oh, Pete. It's because I love you so much that I want to use it. Don't you understand, I'm doing this for us." Before anyone could stop her, she held up her petal and said in a heartfelt voice, "Just for you, Pete, I wish to be thin, young, and beautiful."

It took only a fraction of a second. The petal dried to dust and Tipsy O'Neill went from being a generously ample woman to being a large gray lump with pudgy arms and legs. It seemed the gossips were correct. She did have troll blood in her.

The crowd gasped in dismay. Her husband fainted. Rick said under his breath, "You have to admit, for a troll she is thin and fairly good looking."

With tears babbling down her face, Tipsy lumbered over to her husband and squatted down beside him. She patted his cheek, trying to wake him, but with her new larger mass and strength, she knocked him out again. "Oh, Pete. I'm so sorry."

Harradorn instructed Agamemnon to take them home. "Better carry Pete. I don't think he'll make it without fainting again."

Gently, the Cyclops lifted the limp husband in his arms and left the gathering, trailed by a blubbering Tipsy.

Harradorn turned to the nine. He hoped what they had witnessed would spur them into surrendering their petals. To his surprise, the town's aged doctor shuffled forward—not to the cauldron to burn his petal—but to mount the stairs and stand beside the mayors.

"Don't do this, Doc," Harradorn said.

"I have to. I've witnessed so much suffering both here and in the outside world. I would be remiss if I didn't take advantage of this opportunity."

"Nothing good ever came from using a wizard's petal," Harradorn reminded him. "Look at Tipsy."

The doctor shook his head. "I've thought this through. I've worded it carefully, simply. Nothing will go wrong." He faced the crowd and held out the petal.

"Don't do it, Doc," Rick said.

The doctor ignored him. With a confident smile, he said, "I wish to find a universal cure for cancer."

Like with Tipsy, once the wish was spoken, it took only a fraction of a second for it to be granted. The petal disintegrated. The doctor disappeared.

The silence was palpable. Everyone held their breath and waited for their beloved doctor to reappear. He didn't. Murmurs of "Where did he go?" and "What happened to him?" filled the air. Puzzlement turned to anger when the spot next to Harradorn remained glaringly empty. Councilmembers talked among themselves. Prodded by Lance, they turned to Harradorn for an explanation. Even Rick looked to him.

In a somber voice, Harradorn said, "From the thickest jungles to far underground to the deepest parts of the ocean, humanity has searched for cures. There's no telling where the one our doctor wished for could be found. Here," he swallowed hard, "or on another planet. Perhaps one devoid of a breathable atmosphere."

Immediately, six of the remaining eight moved to the brazier and dropped their petals into the fire. But it still left two unwilling to give up their petals: a fairy named Gloris and eight-year-old Aesa Bauer.

Like a fox slinking from the shadows, Lance approached the two mayors. He whispered, "Offer them anything: money, jewels, gold, property. Lie if you have to, whatever it takes, but get them to hand over the petals." He fixed his gaze on Harradorn and added, "It might be expeditious to use one of the petals and wish Felicity and Joy Flint back to Peace."

"Are you crazy?" Rick said. "Wizard's petal are like riptides." He repeatedly thumped Lance hard on the chest with his middle finger. "I'm certainly not going to let my brother use one." With one last thump, he glared at Lance until he backed off and rejoined the council.

Harradorn eyed Lance, wondering what the man was really after. He'd hate to think what Lance would do with a petal. But first things first. He called to Gloris. With the petal secured in her belt, the red fairy flew to him and landed in his palm.

"Gloris, you're pretty and you're smart." The fairy twittered her wings at the compliments. "The wizard's petal can grant you one wish. But I can grant you two."

Her jaw dropped. "You can?"

He nodded. "What are two things you've always wanted?"

"Well, I've always wanted to be brown, like Sheriff Caine. He's so dreamy, and red is so ordinary."

"I suppose it is." He tried to appear sympathetic while his mind raced to figure out whether it was possible to alter the fairy's color without harming her.

Maybe magic. Maybe Zach could do it.

Lightning flashed from the Prosperity side of town. Dark clouds formed. From over the tops of the buildings, he saw the black tower disappear. Rain began to fall in Prosperity. Soon the breeze would carry the rain across the river to encompass Peace. There'd be no help from Zach until he found FearfulFran.

Harradorn looked to Rick, but his brother only shook his head, plainly clueless about what to do. Seeking inspiration, he surveyed the crowd and spotted Sirena. Maybe for once she could manage to do a spell and not screw it up.

"All right, you'll be brown," he told the fairy, and hoped to Odin it wasn't a lie. With the entire town a witness, Lance would have little trouble getting enough signatures on his next petition if he failed to keep his promise. So be it. Right now he had to keep the town safe, and that meant destroying the last two wizard's petals. "What's the second thing you've always wanted?"

"A pet silkworm so I can have lots and lots of different out-fits—and not all the same color." Gloris fingered her short red dress. "If I'm going to be brown, I want a brown dress. And black. And orange. And—"

"I get the idea." *Of all things, a pet silkworm.* "Our climate is not conducive to silkworms."

"But you said you would grant my wish. If you can't, maybe I should use this." The fairy fingered the white petal in her belt.

"Oh, he can do it," Rick interjected. "He was just thinking of you and all the work you'll have to do."

"Work?"

"Lots of work. A silkworm has to be fed twice a day, and only mulberry leaves. And since birds love worms, you'll have to stand guard twenty-four hours a day to make sure your pet isn't eaten."

"I can do that," the fairy insisted, though the sharp furrow between her brow indicated she wasn't looking forward to it.

"I'm sure you can, luv," Rick said. "But to harvest its silk for all your new dresses, you'll have to kill your pet."

"Kill my pet?"

"The silk is their cocoon. When the worm becomes a moth, it uses acid on the cocoon to set itself free. To save the silk, you'll have to boil the worm alive before it transforms."

Gloris gulped. Fairies rarely killed anything.

Rick continued. "You'll have to decide what you want: the silk or the pet. Not to mention the loom you'll need to weave the dyed silk into cloth. You do know how to use a loom, don't you?"

"Well, I, uh…" Gloris looked thoroughly confused.

Rick winked at Harradorn. Harradorn smiled his thanks and said to Gloris, "Instead of going to all that work, how about a gift certificate for ten new outfits from Lucia's Fairy Faire?"

Gloris's face brightened. She smiled gleefully and clapped her hands. "For my second wish I want fifty outfits!"

"Twenty."

Rick whispered in his ear. "Are you daft? She has a wizard's petal. Give her what she wants."

"Fifty," the fairy said.

"Fifteen," Harradorn countered.

The fairy shrieked. "You wouldn't?"

"Fourteen," Harradorn said, and hoped the fairy didn't see the beads of sweat breaking out on his forehead.

"Thirty," the fairy said weakly, wringing her hands.

"Thirty it is," he said in relief. "We have a deal."

Fairy in hand, he approached the brazier. Lance lifted a hand to get his attention, probably to talk him into using the petal to retrieve Felicity and Joy. But he knew a fool's plan when he heard it and ignored the councilman. Instead, he thought of Doc and cursed the fact one petal couldn't be used to undo the wish of another.

The fairy tossed her petal into the fire and the crowd cheered in relief. Gloris fluttered her wings, basking in all the attention. "When do I become brown?" she asked.

Good question. He needed to stall for time. "When Felicity returns, you'll be brown."

Gloris twirled in the air. "Woo hoo! Wait until she sees me!" The fairy flew off to a bevy of fairies sitting in a nearby tree and bragged about the wishes the mayor had granted her.

Rick took Harradorn aside. "What were you thinking, bargaining with her like that? She might have gotten angry and used the petal."

"I couldn't appear to give in too easily, not with Aesa Bauer watching."

They glanced at the last person holding a wizard's petal: a precocious girl of eight whose parents were notorious for buying their daughter anything she wanted. Though it made Aesa the favorite customer of all the merchants, she'd bankrupt the town if offered two bottomless wishes.

"This way she knows I have limits," he told Rick.

He called the little girl up the stairs. Her parents accompanied her, their faces pale with worry. Little Aesa waved her petal back and forth for all to see. Harradorn crouched to her level and offered the same deal he had given the fairy: two wishes in exchange for the one-wish wizard's petal.

Aesa shook her head repeatedly. "I don't want to. It's mine. All mine. I'm not giving it up. You can't make me."

"Honey. Dear," her father pleaded. "Mayor Harradorn is being very generous. Two wishes instead of one. Just imagine what you can get."

The little girl stilled, thinking. A hush fell over the crowd. Behind him, Harradorn heard murmurs among the council. Long seconds dragged into nerve-wracking minutes. Aesa twisted from side to side thinking about what she wanted.

Lance stepped forward. With a flash of his white hair and red runic beads, he looked down his nose at the fidgeting little girl. "The council has just authorized the mayor to offer you three, yes, three wishes instead of two. So be a good girl and give the mayor your petal and we'll all be happy."

Rick grumbled in disgust. Harradorn silently moaned. The desperation in Lance's voice coupled with the anxious look on his face told the spoiled little girl exactly what Harradorn had been trying to hide: Aesa Bauer had everyone under her thumb.

She held up the petal and shouted, "I have something no one has! A wizard's petal! It's mine, all mine, and you can't have it!"

Lance's unpigmented skin flushed red in humiliation. He was a man used to getting his way. Before anyone could stop him, he snatched the petal away.

Aesa cried out; the crowd gasped. Lance's triumphant smirk crumbled to a grimace. He collapsed to his knees and convulsed in excruciating pain as the protective magic of the petal punished him for his transgression. All wizard's petals were to be freely given. No exceptions.

Within seconds, the petal disappeared from his hand and re-appeared in Aesa's.

"Serves him right," Rick said to Harradorn while the council-man continued to writhe.

By now the rain spawned by the departure of Zach's tower had arrived in Peace. Large drops quickly turned into a downpour and effectively put an end to the proceedings. The crowd scattered, seeking shelter. Harradorn watched in dismay as Aesa bounded down the stairs, her parents trailing behind.

Rick said, "Let's hope Aesa's petal is the only one left." With a final scowl at Lance, huddled in pain on the steps, Rick took off for Prosperity.

Harradorn stared down at the councilman. Lance had ruined any chance of getting the petal from Aesa. He could only hope her wish, when she made it, would be fairly benign and not cause anyone's disappearance or death.

Agamemnon appeared with an umbrella for the councilman. Harradorn waved him off. Turning his back on Lance, he entered the Hall, leaving the idiot to suffer alone in the rain.

* * *

At last Lance Warbird's pain eased, his mind cleared. Finally conscious of his surroundings, he squinted through the veil of rain and found a maroon-cloaked figure watching him from the doorway of a store. Sheltered from the storm, she drew back her hood and smiled.

FearfulFran.

Despite nerves on fire and muscles cramping, Lance smiled back.

* * *

Night saw the end to Zach's rain. Harradorn made three calls with the satellite phone, then grabbed Joy's plunger and left his office. He strode through the vast entryway. He usually paused, no matter how briefly, to admire the priceless works of art in the front entrance. But not now. Instead he glanced at the bare spot on the floor where Joy had wakened him with a kiss. Heat flared with the memory and he stopped. His gaze shifted to where he had taken her in his arms and felt her passion ignite. He stirred, wanting her. Wanting more.

But then Sirena's annoying chanting intruded, and the tantalizing emotions vanished. He looked up toward the fourth floor. He'd like to get rid of her before Joy returned. Rather than a mistress of quiet contentment, which her shop proclaimed, Sirena was the queen of interference. His gut told him she would ruin his plans.

And to think she wanted to be a councilmember. Not till Hel froze over.

Yet, with Aesa's wizard's petal, even that might happen.

Grumbling, he exited the building. Plunger in hand, he headed for Prosperity.

The elven subdivision on the western edge of Prosperity was still awake. In the air, glowing sprites crisscrossed amidst the beams of moonlight filtering through the humongous trees in which the elves made their homes.

Elves believed most plants sleep at night, so they gardened and harvested during the twilight hours to minimize shock to the plants. With the ground softened by the recent rain, a party of gardeners was quietly singing lullabies while planting spring flowers around the base of a tree.

Likewise, so as not to waken the spirit of the Valkyrie Oak, which might still linger within its remnants, the woodworkers had shifted to a nighttime schedule to cut and carve pieces from the enormous stack of wood. Harradorn inhaled deeply while he passed. There was something about the smell of freshly cut wood—primal, invigorating, solid—that imparted the feeling all was right in the world. He could actually smell the circle of life.

In the distance, the soft *fft* of arrows being released in the direction of the archery range indicated he wasn't the only one made restless by the torrential downpour.

With little effort, he climbed the stairs that spiraled one of the giant trees, passing a multitude of doors and curtained windows. The sound of elven children talking and giggling drifted outside, and he smiled, remembering his own childhood and all the nights he and Rick had talked for hours before surrendering to sleep.

Continuing up, he heard other sounds: the murmur of lovers,

the passionate cries of pleasure and delight, and more laughter—the endearing, intimate kind couples share. He listened, envious, his troubled mind thick with thoughts of Joy. The kisses they had shared had touched something in his heart, an empty place he never knew existed. It was the damndest thing. Since those kisses, he'd felt lonely, constantly.

In the moonlight on the topmost tier of the tree, he found Ted'ora singing while swaying back and forth in a hammock stretched between the branches. The lean, golden-haired elf was a childhood friend of his and Rick, their bonds cemented by time and the adventures only children can share.

"'Tis a perfect night for sleeping outdoors, Harradorn," Ted'ora said in greeting. Always, he left off the honorific of mayor, not out of disrespect or because of their long friendship, but because elves have no regard for titles that promote inequality of any kind.

"Care to join me?" Ted'ora added. He gestured to several empty hammocks nearby. "'Tis a long while since you and I have rocked with the sky. By the burden masking your face, my friend, you would do well to accept the offer."

Gingerly, Harradorn climbed into one of the hammocks, assailed like always with the awareness of the yawning distance to the ground. Once settled in, whatever fear the towering height engendered quickly evaporated. In the warm spring breeze, he relaxed and became one with the gentling sway of the branches.

Ted'ora eyed the plunger in his hand. "Do we have a plumbing problem I'm not aware of?"

He shook his head. "I need a favor. A quiet favor."

"A secret between friends, eh?" Ted'ora smiled with interest. "'Tis granted. By all means, proceed with your request."

"When we go camping, you often tell tales of elves being able to make the trees talk, to use words."

Ted'ora laughed. "Mumbling Maple comes to mind. In this one, a traveling band of elves granted the gift of speech to a maple so it would watch over them while they slept. During the darkest hours of the night, Mumbling Maple warned the elves that stinky gremlins were skulking nearby. Unfortunately, maples aren't the brightest trees in the woods, and the elves didn't realize she actually meant grumbling skunks were stinking nearby. When the elves snuck up on their stalkers, they were sprayed without mercy." He laughed heartily. "Mumbling Maple was lucky she wasn't used for kindling. To this day, any child suspected of exaggerating or getting a message wrong is called a Mumbling Maple."

Harradorn laughed aloud with him though he had heard the story many times before. Their merriment subsided, and he said, "I was wondering if it would be possible to make this handle talk." He tossed the plunger to Ted'ora, who easily caught it. "I only need it to say one word. And only once."

With a practiced eye, Ted'ora looked over the wooden handle of the plunger. His fingers rubbed the grain, then tapped it. "It appears to be kiln dried and several years dead. Not even a wizard could bring this back to life, let alone make it speak. Why do you wish such an impossible task?"

While the stars and the moon kept watch above, he told about his problems with the skelter mirror, Felicity, Joy, the pressure he was under from the town council, and the ridiculous payment Sirena wanted for sending him to New Jersey for the fairy and the woman.

The elf raised a golden brow in amusement. "The fog clears. Now, I understand. In case your backup plan fails, you want the other item that traveled with you, this plunger, to speak *purple*, so when it returns to Joy's home, you can tag along with it. In this way, you avoid paying Sirena for direct access to her mirror." Ted'ora shook his head in disapproval.

"What? It's a valid plan. The mirror remains activated until tomorrow night and I already paid to go to Joy's. I'm just using up my travel time, that's all."

"If I enter The Cream & Fizz and order an ice cream cone, does it give me permission to take more out of the container as long as I still have a cone?"

He frowned. "That's not the same."

"Isn't it?"

"No. Besides, I would never ask someone to appoint me to a high position for the mere price of an ice cream cone."

"If you were starving to death, the price would be more than reasonable. The question is, what do you value more: the council's order, your pride, or seeing Joy again?"

"I'm more worried about the trouble Sirena will cause being on the council."

"Even weeds produce flowers, my friend. Some quite beautiful, and many with healing properties. Never underestimate a weed. But enough on these matters. Tomorrow waits for the sun, and the sun will guide you to do what is best. For now the stars call us to sleep. Dream well, my friend. Sleep deep."

Harradorn wished he could be metaphysically balanced and unconcerned like his elven friend. But he couldn't. Instead, he stared up at the glittering stars and watched their silent trek across the sky. Eventually he closed his eyes and slept, but not before one last thought snuck into his mind, a wish that Joy was lying next to him in the hammock.

* * *

From an upstairs window in the Hall, Sirena had watched her brother head to the west side of town. His stride had been forceful, yet the droop of his shoulders had hinted of fatigue, for he carried a heavy weight in the aftermath of the wizard duel. Sheriff Caine had reported several people and a dwarf had gone missing, probably petal wishers. Undoubtedly, more would be discovered. And still there was Aesa's petal to contend with.

Sirena suspected the sag of Harradorn's shoulders also had to do with the object in his hand. Joy Flint's plunger. Obviously, he was worried about what would happen when he abducted Joy. She'd overheard him talking to Agamemnon about her brother Mike. Obeying the council's directive didn't bode well for their town.

Then there was that interesting spark in her brother's eye whose appearance coincided with Joy's visit to Peace and her wakening him with a kiss.

Must have been some kiss.

Yet it didn't solve her brother's problem. So she had chanted for inspiration, for a way to ease Harry's burden and calm his worries. And the one thing that kept coming to mind, the one intuitive solution, was the crystal ball.

She hadn't yet bonded with it for a full week, which Cynthia had dictated, and she didn't have Harry's permission to see into his future, but in her way of thinking, it would be perfectly acceptable to see into the town's future. After all, she was a citizen of Peace & Prosperity, and in that respect she'd be seeing into her own future. If Harry's actions were part of her future and the town's, well then that would be a fortunate coincidence. No one could accuse her of breaking the seer's code.

So to help her brother, she had looked into the ball.

Now she stood before the skelter mirror, nervously clicking her long nails together, afraid to get involved. Afraid not to. Her eyes were still filled with tears, her mind tormented by what she had seen.

She had done some stupid things in her life, and this might be the worst. Yet she couldn't live with herself if any harm came to Harry, knowing she hadn't tried to prevent it. Determined, she wiped the tears from her eyes and drew the hood of her purple robe over her head. Uttering Loki's prayer for fools, she stepped into the mirror.

Chapter 10

In the middle of the night, Joy's nose twitched. Frankincense and myrrh.

Harradorn! Here to take Felicity back to Peace!

With a swiftness that surprised even herself, Joy grabbed the baseball bat now kept by her bed and sat up, ready to defend the fairy's right to self-determination. But instead of Harradorn, a cloaked figure, too slender to be the wizard Zach, sat at the end of her bed.

She raised the bat. "Don't move."

"If you insist."

The woman sounded far too serene, considering Joy was about to brain her if she even twitched the wrong way. Joy reached over to the nightstand and turned on the light. She blinked in surprise. Her visitor was cloaked in a gorgeous velvet hooded robe whose purple nap rippled like water with the slightest shift in movement. The embroidery on Zach's robe had also seemed to move. Could this be another wizard? Magic would explain why Shredder lay calmly in the stranger's lap, allowing himself to be petted without clawing her hands to shreds.

Hmm. Magic versus a bat. The odds weren't good. But this was her home and she was tired of people popping in without warning. She kept the bat raised.

"Forgive the intrusion, Joy Flint. The hour is late, even more so than in Peace. Be assured, my purpose is innocent. I wish you no harm."

"Are you a wizard?"

The woman laughed easily. "A strange question. What made you ask?

"The hooded robe. Zach wears a black one."

The woman laughed again, but this time Joy detected a sadness in her voice. "Zach's robe is enchanted. This is merely a fashion statement." She scratched Shredder behind one ear and his eyes closed in blissful surrender.

"I am an alchemist," the woman added with a hint of pride.

"What's the difference?"

"One uses magic. The other elements of air, earth, fire, and water." She reached up and drew back the hood, revealing an extremely beautiful face with lush lips, exotic amethyst eyes, and classic cheekbones, all heavy on the purple and gold makeup that seemed to mar rather than enhance her features. "I'm Sirena Lawson. Harry and Rick's sister."

Sister? "Owner of Mistress Sirena's Shop of Quiet Contentment?" Joy asked.

"The same."

She kept the bat raised. The woman was a Lawson. And Lawsons ran the town. "You've come for Felicity. I don't care what Harradorn says. You can't have her."

"I am neither in law enforcement nor under anyone's dictates. Harry doesn't know I'm here."

Joy lowered the bat. "So why—" Then she remembered, and her voice hitched higher. "The wizard duel! Something's happened. Another spell. Is Harradorn all right?"

"The duel is over. Wizard Zach prevailed, though there was collateral damage of a sorts." A bitter smile crossed Sirena's face and her eyes glazed over briefly before returning to Joy. With infinite tenderness, she lifted the cat and laid him on the bed where he curled up and continued to sleep. "That's not why I'm here. I, that is, I want to… you see, I…" Her multi-ringed fingers fluttered in the air, searching for words that kept escaping. Then she sudenly smiled. "Let's go for walk."

"Now?"

"Moonlight is forgiving. It doesn't judge, nor does it take offense. It softens. Never threatens. A walk in the moonlight would be perfect."

"Do you know how dangerous it is to walk around New Jersey after midnight?"

Sirena noted her solid grip on the bat. "Fortunately, no. However, it is quite safe in Peace."

"You want me to go to Peace?" This was all very weird. "Maybe I should get Felicity."

"Please, don't. This is between you and me, and Felicity is such a busybody. Be assured, at any time you can return home as you did before by saying a certain color."

The woman sounded sincere, yet Joy continued to hesitate.

"I wouldn't have come if it wasn't important. Please. Only a few minutes."

"And if I refuse?"

"Then I'll return without you."

She was about to tell her to do just that when Sirena sighed— her entire body sighed, folding in on itself within the robe, shrinking. Giving up. Over the years, Joy had seen too many students exhibit the same body language not to recognize defeat when she saw it. Which meant only one surprising thing. "You don't have permission to be here."

"Nor do I have permission to bring you to Peace, though I'm sure the council would forgive the transgression if I claim I forced you."

Joy sized up the woman. Physically, she could take her if she had to.

"This isn't a trap," Sirena said. "I give you my word as a Lawson."

She chuckled wryly. "Rick dresses like a pirate, Harradorn tried to force me to stay, and you have a shop that's a mixture of porn and New Age gimmicks, and I'm supposed to believe a Lawson's word is trustworthy?" She leaned the bat against the night table. "I'll go but not because you're a Lawson."

"Then why?"

"Because Shredder likes you. Cats are a good judge of character." She scooted out of bed. "I'll get changed."

Sirena grinned happily. "No need." She grabbed Joy's hand and said, "Purple."

* * *

Joy exited Sirena's shop, her pajama-clad body enveloped in one of the gorgeous velvet robes Sirena sold, this one a sapphire blue, including matching slippers.

Sirena insisted she keep the hood up. "I love your purple hair, but no human in town is currently bold enough to wear the color. Someone may take notice, the fairies for sure. They'd leak word to Harry and others that you're here and get him in all sorts of trouble."

With her many rings sparkling in the moonlight, Sirena drew Joy's hood forward to hide all but her face. "I have gold ribbons in my shop that would look stunning in your hair. We'll fetch some later if we have time."

Much like old friends getting reacquainted, Sirena took Joy's arm in hers and they strolled through the streets of Peace. The quaint pole lights of the town were of a lower wattage than those in the outside world, gentler and nicely romantic, enough to see where one was going, but kind enough not to hide the stars twinkling merrily above even with the full moon.

In New Jersey, bright lights were used to scare criminals into the more murky parts of the cities. Here, the darkness felt safe. Except for one thing. "Won't we look suspicious? Two people in hooded robes roaming the streets in the middle of the night."

Sirena laughed gaily. "If this was last year, yes. But as I said, these are currently in fashion for eveningwear. We'll blend in if anyone in Peace is still up and about. Most are safely home with their families, anticipating the final results from the wizard duel."

"Sounds ominous. Is that why I'm here?"

Sirena's brow furrowed, and her ringed fingers caressed a round object in a satin purse attached to her belt. "From what I've seen in my crystal ball, my brother has a difficult choice to make, which seems to go beyond the remnants of the wizard duel. A choice that I suspect includes you. And me. I— Quick, in here."

Swiftly, Sirena pulled her into the concealing shadows of an arbor blooming with moonflowers, and motioned to remain quiet. Together they watched two figures, also wearing hooded robes, glide by on the far side of the street, talking in hushed tones. One was a shapely small, thin woman in tattered maroon robes, her hood extended so that even when she passed below a streetlight, her face remained concealed.

Her companion was much taller and larger, with a man's gait. His silken robes glossed white in the moonlight, interwoven with gleaming gold threads. A glimpse of his face in the streetlight revealed skin preternaturally white.

Human? Or one of the other fascinating creatures who lived in this equally fascinating town.

The couple disappeared from view and Sirena ventured out onto the sidewalk first. For a long time, she stared at where the two had vanished into the night. Her fingers drummed the air, the rings clicking nervously against each other, mimicking the many thoughts crossing her face.

"Do you believe the end justifies the means?" she asked Joy.

"Certainly not."

She fingered the spherical pouch. "Neither did I until recently."

Without a word, they continued their walk. Occasionally, they saw others. Many wore hooded robes, confirming what Sirena had said about them being in vogue, the rest wore contemporary garb. All nodded cordially to them yet for the most part kept to themselves. Joy couldn't help but notice how some of the men gave Sirena long assessing looks. Obviously, they recognized her, for she didn't try to hide her face, and she was a beautiful woman. But she ignored everyone and no one intruded on their privacy.

"You were saying something about your crystal ball," Joy said when they were alone. "Something about being afraid of a decision Harradorn will make."

"Aye. Fate is a terrible fabric to alter, its threads woven with such complexity only those experienced in reweaving the cause and effects of choices should tamper with. I'm too new at using a crystal ball to make major alterations with what is revealed, but I'd feel guilty if I didn't do something. The most I'll dare is show you three things. I can only hope the added threads of knowledge will give you wisdom when the time comes to make your own choice."

Sirena led her to a great silvery river. Its strong ripples produced a sound both confident and comforting. No doubt a lot of tourists came here solely for the soothing effect of the river's passage, for the river was lined with hotels, more so on Peace's side than Prosperity's.

A broad white marble bridge connected the two communities, glistening in the moonlight. Now and then someone crossed over. A gentle scattering of couples strolled along both sides of the river, intimate with their closeness, eyes only for each other. They reminded her of Harradorn's steamy kiss. Fussing with her hood, she glanced around, wondering if they would run into him, or at least see him. She hoped they would, and her heart quickened in anticipation.

Sirena must have noticed for she said, "Harry isn't here. I made sure of it." She softly laughed. "I can be very annoying when I chant. And unbearable if I chant loud enough. My brother has gone to Prosperity for the night, probably at Rick's place or up in the trees with the elves."

Joy halted. "There are elves here?"

"Of course."

Of course, Joy mentally echoed. She shouldn't have been surprised since they also had wizards and fairies.

They passed the bridge; Joy looked across to the other side. Prosperity was still awake. Sharp laughter and angry shouts hurtled across the river, along with a clash of metal, glass breaking, and bawdy strains of music. Unlike the steady constancy of the soft glow that caressed all of Peace, the lighting system in Prosperity was bright in some places and nonexistent in others. She was glad they were staying in Peace.

And yet the elves had their homes in Prosperity.

She glanced back at the bridge. "What do elves look like? Are they people-size or smaller? Do they really have pointy ears? Could I see one? Just a peek?"

Sirena shook her head. "That's best left for another time. Come. You've already noted the first of the three things I wanted to show you."

She had? Joy looked around. "The river? The bridge?"

"The difference between the community Harry is mayor of and the one Rick rules."

Joy smiled knowingly. "Rick *rules*?"

"Exactly." Sirena chuckled. "The other two things you should see are close together but on the far side of Peace."

They turned onto Easy Street, of all things, and traveled east, far past the Mayor's Hall and Residence to a residential area devoid of tourist shops and hotels. A group of teenagers crossed paths with them, talking and laughing among themselves while they kicked a soccer ball to and fro. From one of the residences, someone strummed a guitar and a woman sang an alluring ballad about life and death and young love.

The buildings here had ornate carvings and cornices that spoke of old wealth and even older ancestry. Some had stone walls carved to resemble logs. The one they stopped in front of looked like a modernized version of a Viking longhouse. Two stories tall, like most of the buildings in Peace, its white stone walls were meticulously carved and etched to resemble wood. The stone gabled roof had the appearance of white marble thatch in the moonlight, with cross pieces at the front and the back stretching up to form the top part of an X.

"This is the Lawson Longhouse, though to fit modern times for the last two centuries it's been called Lawson Manor."

Not quite a mansion but definitely larger than the average house. "You and Harradorn and Rick grew up here?"

"For the most part. Along with our younger sister Nara Erline."

Sirena crossed the lawn to the rear of the building. In the backyard, spring flowerbeds and vegetable gardens were well tended, interspersed with various water fountains, none of which were turned on. Looking up at the darkened windows, Joy got the impression no one lived here.

She followed Sirena to a small cairn of rocks under a spruce tree.

"Rick had a pet dog—Loki, he called him because he always got into trouble."

"Sounds like my cat, Shredder."

Sirena knelt on one knee by the cairn and the mysterious fluidity of her robe pooled around her feet like water. With a wistful expression, she reached out and gently laid a hand on one of the rocks. "Loki started getting into a lot of trouble. In some ways, he mimicked Rick, who was growing into a wild, fun-loving teen. Mother and Dad were having enough trouble between themselves... over an ongoing family matter."

Sirena had muttered the last part, and Joy got the impression the parents' marriage had become as rocky as the cairn Sirena was paying homage to.

"I tried to help," Sirena said. "I always wanted to help. So I made a concoction to calm Loki down—just a bit."

A lump formed in Joy's throat. Her gaze fell on the cairn. Sirena's fingers were lovingly stroking the rocks much like she had stroked Shredder a short while ago. Joy closed her eyes. This story wasn't going to end well. "You made a tranquilizer."

Sirena choked back a sob. "I wish I had." She stood and looked up at the stars as if seeking solace. "I found a spell that when used with the right minerals and herbs would make Loki controllable. Obedient. Mellow. Everything was fine. Would have been fine. I was in the midst of sprinkling the mixture on Loki and setting the spell when Rick stumbled upon us and saw what I was doing. He started yelling at me to stop messing with his dog. But I was right in the middle of the incantation, I couldn't stop, I had to finish. Rick kept yelling, wrenching Loki away, calling me all sorts of names, and I made a mistake. I couldn't help it. Instead of mellow, I said jell-O." She lowered her head. "And that's what Loki became."

Joy gasped and covered her mouth.

Sirena looked back at the cairn, her lips trembling. "A few more seconds alone and everything would have been fine. But not even a wizard can take back time. It was the last transgression of a long line of mistakes." She sighed heavily. "I was kicked out of the house. But the elves took me in." She sighed again. "Rick still hasn't forgiven me. I don't think he ever will."

Joy's heart went out to her still suffering over a tragic, senseless mistake from her youth. "And Harradorn?"

"That's the third thing for you to see."

Joy followed her to the front of the house.

"I'm still not allowed in the manor. But it's all right. I have my own place now above my shop. And for as long as Harry is mayor, I can live with him in the Residence."

She pointed up. Across the front of the house, between the first and second floors, two long rows of carvings had been cut into the stone. Each row was divided into ten-inch rectangles. A different shape filled each block. One row was full. The second had two spaces still empty.

"Every member of the Lawson family is given a bracket in which to carve their own unique image. See, the second band is almost filled in. Within another generation, we'll have to start a third band of brackets going across." She turned to Joy. "Can you pick out the symbol that represents Rick?"

Joy peered at the many images. The oldest ones on top were not easily seen in the moonlight, their carvings smoothed by the years. She'd love to get a good look at them in the sun. Toward the end of the second row, the carvings were sharper. Newer. She half-expected to see a skull and crossbones for the pirate-dressed brother but found something equally appropriate. A three-masted ship under full sail.

Chuckling, she pointed. "The ship."

"Aye, you got that right. Now, Harry, being oldest, is to the left of his."

Eagerly, Joy looked at the previous bracket, curious to what Harry would pick to represent himself on the ancestral manor for all his descendants to see. Unlike Rick's, his was less intricate. Simple. Two hands clasped.

Sirena said, "When I joined the Lawson family at the age of seven, trouble ensued. As usually happens during turmoil, someone stepped forward to take on the role of peacemaker—Harry. He's always looked out for me. When I was kicked out, Harry left in protest. Oh, he's no saint. He suffered along with Rick, grieving over Loki, angry at me like everyone else. But he refused to return until I was let back in. To this day, he hasn't set foot inside." Her gaze rose to the bracket showing the two hands joined, and she smiled. "Harry is a good man. A forgiving man when others would hold a grudge. No matter what may happen, Joy Flint, remember this: he's a man first, then a mayor."

"I don't understand," Joy said. For the life of her, she couldn't figure out the meaning behind everything Sirena had shown her. "Why are you telling me this?"

"So the choice will be easier to make. When the time comes, you must be sure to tell Harry—" Sirena stopped. Quarrelsome murmurs were heard coming up the street. The couple they'd hidden from earlier was headed their way.

Sirena whispered, "Quickly, say 'purple' or all will be lost."

Joy didn't want to. She had so many questions to ask. But Sirena looked frantic and there was no place to hide.

From near a streetlight, the man called out in greeting. Joy noticed the woman with him was gone.

While Sirena stepped in front of her, blocking the man's view and returning his greeting. Joy whispered, "Purple." Black sparkles formed around her, but not fast enough, for she saw the man crane his head to the side, perhaps aware Sirena was trying to hide someone. He drew his white hood back to get a better view. In the split second before she disappeared, their eyes met.

Her mouth opened, stunned. The man had red eyes!

Chapter 11

Late the following morning, Harradorn and the council returned from two memorial services: the previously scheduled opening of the Bjork Memorial Park, and the service-at-large for Doc Rawlins and eight others who had disappeared after FearfulFran's attack on Zach's greenhouse.

The missing were assumed to have used wizard's petals. No one expected to see them again—with the exception of the sudden appearance of a solid gold statue of a local dwarf named Nardi. Near it were found gold facsimiles of everyday objects, indicating Nardi had wished for the Midas Touch, and forgot the implications. The statue portrayed the dwarf picking his nose. His kin were in a major quandary over whether to melt him down and be rich for the rest of their lives or, out of respect, bury the golden body then guard against grave robbers for the rest of their lives. Either way, it gave a whole new meaning to gold digger.

Harradorn solemnly raised his glass of apple whiskey to lead a final toast to all the victims. He glanced at the empty chair across from him. No one had seen Lance since his humiliation on the steps yesterday.

Probably shacked up with one of his mistresses soothing his bruised ego. Asshole.

Harradorn drained his glass in unison with the council, then sat down to business.

"What are your plans for retrieving Felicity Morningstar and the outsider Joy Flint?" a councilman asked. The original mandate was to bring them back yesterday.

Another said, "We heard Sirena has requested a seat on the council as payment for sending you through the mirror."

"She has," Harradorn said. Surprisingly, she hadn't been at the memorial service. Sleeping in? Or at her shop, anticipating her transition from shop owner to councilwoman. "This morning I received a note from Councilman Warbird stating he'd agree in lieu of the restitution he owes her."

"Hmph," a councilwoman said. "Sounds like we're all being asked to pay the restitution for him." Most nodded in agreement.

"Maybe not. I have a plan already in motion which bypasses use of the skelter mirror and Sirena's payment. By evening, both Felicity and Joy should be here."

"And if they aren't?" someone asked.

"Then I guess we'll add another chair to the table." Everyone frowned. "Don't worry," Harradorn added. "It's practically foolproof." And devious, underhanded. More of Rick's way of doing things. But with Sirena butting into his life, and now threatening to invade his work, desperate times called for desperate measures.

"Now, the first item on our agenda, an advertising campaign to bring back the tourists. I've allocated twenty percent from the emergency reserves. Any suggestions?"

Immediately, the mood in the room shifted. The prospect of bringing their town's faltering economy back to life redirected everyone's thoughts and filled the room with creative energy. Harradorn took advantage of the distraction and allowed his mind to wander ahead to the coming evening. For the first time in his life, he thought about the outside world. Really thought about it. No magic. No wizard duels. No wizards, for that matter.

He envied Joy's common problems and common solutions. No wonder she seemed so balanced. So full of life. And passion. Curves and passion, an excellent combination. The tantalizing image of holding her in his arms one more time raised thoughts of how she would feel beneath him, on top of him, and all around.

I wonder if she screams during sex.

But a glance at Lance's empty seat killed the fantasy. Joy would never kiss him again, let alone have sex with him. Not after tonight. He let out a long, wretched breath. The town would never know how much he was about to sacrifice on their behalf.

Agamemnon came in and handed him a note. "We have a new problem," Harradorn told the council. "Sheriff Caine reports con artists have bought up all the white roses from our florists. They're selling individual petals as wizard's petals. We have buyers calling, asking how many wishes we'll offer in exchange, and threatening to use them if we don't."

Cries of outrage erupted on all sides.

"There could be hundreds of petals!" someone said. "We can't pay for them all. It'll bankrupt the town!"

"It's blackmail!"

"How do we know which are fake and which are real?"

"There's only one way," Councilwoman Freya said. "Someone will have to test them."

They all turned to Harradorn. He closed his eyes. It was going to be a long, painful day.

* * *

After school, Joy's classroom buzzed with teachers. The women gathered around her desk, admiring two enormous bouquets from Harradorn, while Jeff and the other men skirted the edges and joked about how the enormous amount of flowers might attract killer bees. Joy was still amazed that Harradorn had somehow managed to send her flowers. It made her eager to get Felicity alone and finagle her into revealing just how much contact occurs between his magical town and the outside world.

Dozens of purple irises and pink tulips overflowed a vase that one teacher claimed was a genuine Waterford. The second bouquet was even more exquisite, a Swarovski vase containing at least six dozen Purple Moon Carnations in several amazing shades of amethyst. Two white orchids had been inserted among the flowers. To mark their two kisses, the accompanying card seemed to insinuate. "Thank you for awakening me. For awakening us."

"You have a very romantic boyfriend," one teacher said with a wistful sigh.

Boyfriend?

Joy looked from one bouquet to the other. What was Harradorn up to? Trying to trick her into returning to Peace?

Not likely. Her visit with Sirena proved all she had to do was say purple and she'd zip home. Maybe she was being too suspicious and should just enjoy his flowers. Even old Mrs. Daugherty, the cranky, no-nonsense kindergarten teacher who'd been around since the school was built, giggled over the card that said, "Come share a moonlit walk with me."

"Looks like someone loves your purple hair," another teacher remarked, referring to all the purple flowers.

"I love pink roses," a teaching assistant said. "Maybe if I color my hair pink, my sweetie will give me some." The possibility touched off a round of laughter. Yet Jeff's frown indicated he didn't think it was funny, and his attitude didn't change when he helped carry the bouquets outside to her car.

"I'm worried about you and this Harradorn," Jeff said while they crossed the parking lot. "He barges into your home, then sends you these. It's creepy."

She laughed. Harradorn was anything but creepy. "Actually, I've seen him since then."

"You never told me." Jeff's accusing tone reminded her she'd been keeping to herself lately, a strategy she hoped would limit anyone from finding out that the *robotic* fairy was actually a living, breathing, mythological being.

"I thought we were friends," he added. They stopped at her car.

"We are." She sighed in frustration. It'd be so much easier to tell Jeff what was going on. Being vague, not sharing, wasn't her style. But her promise to Harradorn and her concern for Felicity's safety kept her quiet. Besides, not in a millions years would someone like Jeff believe in wizard duels or a curse called Blithe Mist.

He asked, "When did you have time to see this guy? You went to Mike's last night."

She jerked her head in his direction. "So, you did follow me yesterday. Have you been spying on me?"

Jeff averted his gaze. "Course not. Just had to get some medicine at the store for the kids. It's been a rough week, staying up with them all night. Once in a while I look out the window, no big deal." He blinked his puppy dog eyes, disarming her as he always did, and she felt bad for being distrustful.

"So, he came over again for a date?"

"I went to visit him." *Using voice-activated magic. Talk about high-tech wizardry.* "I did him a big favor," she added, and placed a bouquet in the back of her car. "I think the flowers are his way of saying thanks."

Immediately, there was a shattering crash. She turned and found purple carnations scattered among shards of the Swarovski vase.

"I'm sorry," Jeff said. "It was heavy and slipped out of my hands. I couldn't help it." He bent down and began gathering up the flowers. "I really am sorry."

She bit her lip. 'Sorry' wasn't much of an apology. She wanted to stomp her feet and howl at him for being so careless. But she was an adult, and accidents happen. But she wished this one hadn't. It had been so beautiful.

"I'll throw these away for you."

"Don't you dare!" She took the flowers he was crushing in his arms and placed them on the floor of the back seat.

She turned around to help Jeff pick up more and saw him step on the orchids. "Look out!"

He stepped aside. "I seem to be making a mess of things. I swear, I'll make it up to you."

"It's all right. Really." She picked up the crumpled orchids. Her first orchids. And from a daring, sexy man who made her heart soar whenever she thought about him, dreamed about him. It wasn't possible to fall in love with someone you hardly knew, and yet here she was, devastated because the flowers Harradorn had sent were ruined.

Jeff put a hand on her shoulder. "Go on home. I'll clean up the glass. It's the least I can do."

Joy got in her car. She'd barely left the parking lot when Felicity popped out of the purse. The fairy prowled back and forth on the dashboard, her wings quivering with anger, orange face dark. "He broke it on purpose."

Joy didn't want to believe it. "Accidents happen."

"You didn't see his face. He looked just like Lance Warbird when he's being mean."

"Who's Lance Warbird?" Joy asked, not really interested yet anxious to steer the conversation away from Jeff and the broken vase. Joy listened politely while Felicity prattled on about the councilman and Peace's politics, vaguely hearing something about Lance's extramarital escapades. She decided fairies told some tall tales. *Shape-shifting female dragons. Yeah, right.* But then Felicity mentioned Lance's red eyes.

Was that who saw me in Peace last night?

Felicity mentioned Lance was an albino. That would explain his white skin. If he was as much of a bastard as Felicity claimed, Sirena might be in big trouble for letting her in and out of Peace without permission. Or did people disappear into thin air all the time in Peace?

Thankfully, her head had been covered by a hood, so he hadn't seen her purple hair, which meant he probably didn't realize she was an outsider. Sirena should be okay.

She turned into her driveway and noticed the local PSE&G man on the side of her garage. "Quick, get in the purse," she told Felicity. She pulled into the garage and put the fairy in the house, telling her to go upstairs until the utility guy was gone, then went out to see what he was doing.

"One of your neighbors reported smelling gas." He swept a device along the ground. "I'm trying to find the source."

She sniffed the air. "I don't smell anything."

He checked the display on the detector. "Neither does this. I'll check the connection on the back of your house. Can't be too careful."

"Thanks." She put the intact bouquet inside, then went back for the carnations. Slivers of crystal glistened on the petals. Grabbing a trash bag, she sat on her front porch and proceeded to clean each stem. She'd gotten through the first dozen when she noticed her five-foot, ninety-year-old neighbor Gracie O'Keefe across the street, waiting for the PSE&G truck, a police car, and a small moving van to pass before scurrying across, a small padded envelope in hand.

"Oh, what lovely flowers," Gracie said.

"They're from a new friend. I think he wants me to visit him again."

"A bribe." Gracie shot her a knowing wink. "A little sugar to sweeten the pot. How nice. Too bad our neighbor isn't as thoughtful. Maybe then his wife wouldn't have left him."

"Who are you talking about?"

Gracie angled her head to the house next door. "Why Jeff, of course."

"Jeff's wife left him! Are you sure?"

With joints creaking and popping, Gracie eased herself down next to Joy. "These old bones have a habit of waking me up at all hours. Late Sunday night while I was warming them up, walking off the pain so they'd let me go back to sleep, I saw Patsy and the children leave the house, carrying backpacks and luggage. Jeff was there, shaking his finger at her, his mouth going a mile a minute. I couldn't hear a word of what was being said. It was a cold night and I had my windows closed."

Gracie shook her head sadly. "That Jeff, he was scary. Thought he was going to hit her. But he didn't. He let her go. She loaded the kids into her car and took off. Probably to her mother's. She lives in Pennsylvania, you know."

"Yes, I did."

"Poor Jeff. Nothing sorrier than seeing a man's shoulders droop to his knees. Maybe if he'd treated her to some flowers now and then, their marriage would be better. One thing's for sure, you can never tell what goes on behind closed doors."

"Isn't that the truth." Like the fact she had a fairy living in her house.

She wondered if Jeff lied about his kids being sick to cover up why they weren't in school, a way to hide his shame or protect his pride, or both. Ironic. Here she was, trying to keep secrets from Jeff when he was doing the same with her.

Gracie touched her arm. "I think you should know I saw some guy sneaking around your house last night."

The fingers picking glass from the blooms stilled. For the second time this week, Joy felt watched. "Who was it? Did you recognize him?"

"No. He kept to the shadows. The trees in your yard block most of the light from the streetlights. You should think about having them cut down. It's a shame your brother moved out. Women aren't safe living alone these days."

She looked at the petite woman sitting next to her, maybe all of eighty pounds. "You live alone."

"Bah. Who would want to mess with a cantankerous old woman like me?"

Good point. Certainly not the PSE&G utility guy Gracie had whacked with a shovel last month. He'd gotten five stitches, a result of his unannounced visit, and from the looks of his forehead a few minutes ago, still had the scar to prove it.

"Do you think it's that predator who moved into the neighborhood, the one everyone got notices about?"

"Nah." Gracie waved her hand dismissively. "You don't have to worry about him. When Tony Giuliani's wife showed him the flyer, he and his family paid the pervert a visit. Told him to move out right then and there—or else. Tony and his boys can be pretty convincing, if you know what I mean. Believe me, that raping lowlife is gone for good."

Joy hid a smile. Tony and his boys gave a whole new meaning to 'neighborhood watch.' But then she sobered. If it wasn't this known predator who had been sneaking around her place, then who?

Her neighbor handed over the padded envelope. "This was delivered a short while ago. I signed for it so you wouldn't have to go all the way downtown to pick it up."

"Why thank you. That was so thoughtful of you." She looked at the return address. L&L Specialty Stores, NY, NY. "You're such a good neighbor."

Gracie waved away the compliment, but she smiled broadly, obviously glad to be of help. And her smile grew into a happy grin when Joy gave her a dozen carnations in thanks for signing for the package. After a few more minutes of neighborly chitchat, she creaked her way home and Joy went inside. Felicity was flying through the house, releasing pent-up energy from sitting most of the day. She zoomed around the kitchen while Joy arranged the purple carnations in a vase. Since the fairy insisted the two smashed orchids were salvageable enough to eat, Joy rinsed and put them in a salad bowl, then put them in the fridge until dinner.

"What's this?" Felicity landed by the envelope. "Oooh, it's from L&L!"

Joy stared at her in surprise. How would a fairy from Peace know about a Manhattan store? "What's L&L?"

"Well, since we both swore to keep all of this a secret, I guess it's okay to tell you. L&L is Lawson and Lawson. The mayors' youngest sister runs a store here in the outside world. It sells products made in Peace & Prosperity. Tourism isn't our only business, you know."

"No, I didn't." Joy picked up the padded envelope, amazed it contained something from Peace & Prosperity—and sold only a few miles away.

"Don't just stare at it. Open it. Betcha there's something valuable inside. Something that costs a lot more than all those flowers."

"I don't know. Those bouquets are pretty expensive." Tucked inside the padded envelope was a parchment envelope and a small gold box. The box, tied with gold ribbon, had L&L imprinted in silver on it. The envelope was addressed to Joy, with the message to open it first. Her heart beat excitedly, a thousand happy bubbles brimming inside her. First the gorgeous flowers, now this.

She wasn't naive. Even Gracie had realized the flowers were a bribe of sorts. Yet Joy couldn't help but feel special. Granted, she and Felicity had helped save an entire town, but all these gifts seemed to have Harradorn's personal touch to them and so far she liked his style.

Perhaps this is what Sirena meant about Harradorn being a man first, then a mayor.

She opened the envelope and read the slip of parchment inside.

> *Dear Joy,*
> *I was wrong for ordering you to stay. I apologize.*
> *Seems like whenever we see each other, something*
> *extraordinary is going on and we're not at our best.*
> *Let's start over.*
> *The duel has ended, yet circumstances prevent*
> *my return.*
> *The mirror will still work for you and Felicity,*
> *but this will be the last night you can use it.*
> *The magic is fading.*
> *Please visit. If you're willing, I've made dinner*
> *reservations at the Red Satin Salon for*
> *eight o'clock your time tonight.*

Joy glanced at her watch. It was close to six. "Felicity, have you ever heard of the Red Satin Salon?"

The fairy flittered around the unopened box, her larcenous fingers brushing the gold ribbon. "Sure. A really weird place. You wouldn't like it."

"Why not?"

"Well, for one thing, it's too dark. The entire place is lit by candles. They're everywhere. You can't see what you're eating and you can't see who else is there. Where's the fun in that?"

Hmm. Sounds very romantic.

"All the tables are set in stupid alcoves. If you're hidden away, you can't talk to other people, find out what's going on, gossip, share meals. The whole place is very rude. I don't understand why humans like eating there."

Joy hid a chuckle. Sounded like a great place to be alone with Harradorn without a pesky fairy intruding.

She read the rest of the letter.

> *There's something special between us. I could feel it*
> *when we kissed. If you agree, have Felicity say purple*
> *and you'll be here.*
> *I'm waiting by the mirror. If you come now,*
> *I can show you my town before we eat.*
> *If there's a <u>small</u> problem, wait until seven,*
> *then open the box.*
>
> *Sincerely, Harry*

She reminded herself how the magic worked. Felicity saying purple would return her to Peace along with whomever the fairy was touching, whereas if she herself said purple, anything or anyone she was touching would return with her to New Jersey. Easy peasy.

Felicity landed on her shoulder and tried to read the letter. "What does it say?"

She quickly refolded the parchment. "Harry wants us to come for a visit."

"Harry?" The fairy raised a brow at Joy's use of his nickname. "What else does he say?"

"He wants to have dinner with me at the Red Satin Salon."

"That's it?"

For two people getting to know each other, it was perfect. "I suppose we're also going to take a moonlit stroll—that's what the card with the flowers suggested. If we leave now, he can show me around town before we have dinner."

"What about the box?"

"The letter says not to open it until seven."

"Forget that." The fairy flew down from Joy's shoulder and grabbed at the ribbons. "Let's open it now."

"Uh-uh." Joy seized it and slipped it into a pocket. "Not until seven."

"Oh, come on." Felicity flew from side to side. "Tell you what: let me open it, just me, and I promise not to let you know what's inside till seven."

"I'll tell *you* what: let me go change into something nice, then we'll go see Harry and, maybe as a reward for showing up early, he'll let you open it before seven."

Felicity stared at her as if she was some brainless nitwit. "Are you crazy? The only reward we'll receive is forty days because when we show up, Mayor Harradorn will throw us both into Dulgrun Prison. I'm not going to Peace and neither are you."

With that, she flew away.

Chapter 12

Stupid, stubborn fairy!

Hands on hips, Joy stood in the doorway of the bathroom, fuming when she should have been wondering if Harry would find her freshly painted purple toenails exotic like her purple hair—all because a certain pigheaded fairy wouldn't speak one simple word… purple.

Felicity flew above the sink, weaving back and forth in midair while she plaited the strands of hair she'd harvested from Joy's brush. She'd been making them into belts, ropes, and whatever else fairies found woven hair useful for, including what Felicity called a flying harness for mating season. The ends of her latest creation were attached to the teeth of a comb wedged behind the faucet and knobs. Water was gently running in the sink while she worked. Come to think of it, water had been running in the kitchen sink the first day she met the fairy.

Determined to show her who was in charge, Joy shut it off. "Felicity, I'm not taking *no* for an answer. We're going to Peace. Now."

The fairy ignored her.

Joy waved the note. "We're not going to prison. Harry specifically said this was a visit."

"My mother's sister's daughter came to visit me once. That was five years ago and she's still visiting. Sneaks into my stash every chance she gets. We're going to prison, no doubt about it. I'm not ready for that. I like being here. Lots of things to see." She held up the belt. "And make."

Joy crossed her arms. "And steal."

"And find," Felicity corrected her without hesitation. With a flutter of wings, she calmly tied off the ends of the belt. "Besides, Mayor Harradorn will stick you in Dulgrun Prison, too, if you leave before he says you can."

"If we're going to prison, why did he make reservations at the Red Satin Salon?"

Felicity snorted. "Why allow us to visit and then leave when no one is allowed to go to the outside world without permission?"

"He probably realizes we can be trusted. Come on. We'll spend a few hours, and when you're ready to leave I'll say purple and we'll zip back here like last time. It's a great opportunity to show off the belts and ropes you've been making."

"You mean sell them." The fairy began lining up new strands of hair for her next project.

"Look, if you think something isn't right, we'll pop right back. What do you say?"

"I say I've seen fairies during mating season less excited than you." Felicity glanced at the note in Joy's hand. With a shrewd grin, she asked, "Has Mayor Harradorn asked you to stop by and polish his rod?"

Polish his rod?

As the lewd implication sank in, Joy took a step back, shocked by the fairy's remark. She glanced at her own reflection in the mirror. Her eyes were wide, her face a bright scarlet that clashed horribly with her purple hair. She looked away. "I... that is, we... we just planned on taking a walk and having dinner." Even to herself, the explanation sounded weak.

Darn. The fairy has more smarts about men than I do. And yet she still wanted to take that moonlit walk with Harry. "Please, Felicity?"

"You've got it bad, girlfriend. Best cool off and think about what you're doing. Ask me again in the morning."

"But he's waiting for me—for us—at the mirror right now. And the note says the magic won't last much longer. Tonight may be our final chance to visit Peace."

"I guess that means I'll be here a long time." Felicity returned to her aerial weaving.

Joy pleaded, cajoled, begged, lied, made promises she couldn't keep, anything to get Felicity to comply. But the fairy ignored her and hummed merrily while she worked.

How can she be so happy when I feel so miserable?!

Joy stormed out of the bathroom to her bedroom where she perched on the edge of the bed. She scratched Shredder behind one ear. Since Sirena's visit, her cat was out and about. Sort of. He was lying on top of the covers, keeping a wary eye on the doorway, ears twitching now and then, listening to the fairy sing while she worked.

True to her word, Felicity stayed out of the bedroom. Occasionally she'd fly to the doorway to show off her latest creation and ask if it was time to open the box. Whenever she appeared, Shredder raised his hackles, yet with every instance a little less. Soon he wouldn't mind sharing his home with the small winged woman.

Unless she strangled the little obstinate fairy first.

Fudge! The best looking guy she ever kissed, the only man in the world who could face down her brother without flinching, the sexy mayor of a secret, magical, amazing town, was waiting for her—FOR HER!—and there was no way to tell him she wasn't coming.

Joy checked her watch. Almost seven. She sprang into the hall. Passing the bathroom, she said in a taunting, singsong voice, "Oh, Felicity. I'm going downstairs to open the box."

Felicity shot down the stairs ahead of her. Joy hid a smile. Curiosity was the fairy's biggest weakness.

At the kitchen table, she retrieved the box from where she had hidden it. She untied the gold ribbon and removed the lid. On top of cotton padding was a small note.

Just have Felicity say purple and you'll be here. ~Harry

Felicity danced impatiently from one tiny orange foot to the other. "What is it?"

Nestled among the padding was a small pink vial. Joy unscrewed the cap and sniffed. It smelled like roses.

Felicity flew up and inhaled noisily. "Oh! I've died and gone to Valhalla!" The fairy twirled in midair.

"Is it perfume?" Joy asked.

"That's what they want you outsiders to believe." Felicity snatched the tiny vial out of her fingers. "It's wonderful, marvelous, scrumptiously delicious, one hundred proof rose nectar! At least one full ounce of it. Wee hee! I love you, Mayor Harradorn!"

The fairy flew to the African violets in the living room and sat on one of the soft, fuzzy leaves. She tipped back the vial and drank two swallows. Smiling, she closed her eyes and wiped her mouth with the back of her hand. "Oh, they don't make it any better than this."

A scant half hour later, Joy had a very tipsy fairy on her hands. Now she understood Harry's reference to "a small problem." He undoubtedly knew it would be Felicity who'd prevent her from joining him in Peace. Forcing the fairy to wait to open the box had created a mounting curiosity, effectively destroying her suspicious nature.

Joy inhaled a nervous breath. With the magic fading, it was now or never.

"Felicity, do you believe the end justifies the means?"

"Of course." The fairy hiccupped and regarded Joy with a slurred smile. "Why? Don't you?"

"I've been taught to do unto others as I would want them to do unto me. I just wanted to make sure you got what was coming to you."

Felicity grinned and held up the vial. "I sure did." She took another swig.

Her conscience appeased, Joy hurried upstairs and changed outfits, again, opting for a dress that showed a little more skin. Remembering Harry was going to take her for a moonlit stroll around Peace, she traded open-toed heels for fancy sandals. It was tough feeling sexy and romantic when your feet hurt.

She affectionately kissed Shredder on the top of his head, grabbed a small shoulder purse, then hurried downstairs. She went around, making sure all the doors and windows were locked, then went into the living room where Felicity was lying on her back on the violets, singing a bawdy fairy drinking song.

> "She flew too high, he flew too low,
> She tried to find him, he had to sow,
> He found a flower for him to seed,
> While she and a finch clinched in a tree."

Felicity laughed and spotted Joy. "Wow, girlfriend, you look pretty. Whassup?"

"We're going to the kitchen."

"We are?"

Not sure the inebriated fairy could fly, Joy extended her palm. Felicity crawled into her hand. "Do I have to get dressed up, too, to go to the kitchen?"

"You look beautiful just as you are."

"Damn right I am." Felicity smiled and preened and let loose a huge belch. She giggled and covered her mouth with a hand while trying not to spill the rose nectar.

"Here, let me take that for a minute. I want to show you something." She put the vial on the table next to the bouquet of purple carnations, then placed the fairy on her shoulder. Felicity teetered precariously on her legs. "Grab on tight to my hair so you don't fall," Joy told her.

Felicity seized several strands. "Whoa, little dizzy here." She grabbed more hair to help steady herself. "Okay, girlfriend. What did you want me to see?"

Joy hid a smile. If she could trick Felicity into saying purple, they would be transported to Peace. Then she'd see Harry, have dinner, go for a moonlit walk, and maybe discover if kissing wasn't the only thing Harry did fantastically well.

Hot with anticipation, she said, "These flowers. I've been thinking about coloring my hair red to match them. What do you think?"

Felicity snapped her head back to look at her. Then she stared at the purple carnations. With one hand, she pointed. "Are you crazy? Those flowers aren't red."

"They're not?" Joy said, feigning ignorance.

Felicity shook her head back and forth and back and forth and back and forth. "Whoa! Stop moving, Joy. I'm getting seasick."

"Felicity, look at me."

The fairy obeyed, though it took a while for her eyes to focus.

"If they aren't red, what color are they?"

Felicity surveyed the flowers. Then she smiled, flung out her arms, and shouted, "They're purple!" Instantly, black sparkles enveloped the fairy.

"No!" Joy cried out in dismay. Felicity wasn't holding any of her hair! A second later the fairy was gone.

* * *

Elves move silently like a cat stalking across grass. On the bridge separating Peace & Prosperity, Harradorn could only guess how long Ted'ora had been at his side. Harradorn was leaning across the broad stone railing, watching the river flow past. In the water's reflection, the bright orange-pink clouds of a western sunset slowly darkened to plum, marking the passage of time. Lights were coming on in the buildings on either side of the river. The aroma of dinner drifted through the air.

Harradorn waited for the sprites lighting the lanterns on the bridge to leave before speaking. "Do you remember the day we skipped school with Rick, Leif, and Daniel to go fishing? We thought we were so clever, so smart, thinking what's one day compared to a whole year of dreary lessons."

The elf leaned on the stone railing next to him and kept quiet. The moist smell of the river rushing below filled the silence, and together they watched the water flow.

Harradorn continued. "That was the day Zach's dad took all the top students on a surprise visit to Macklin's Mark." Home of the wizards' Council of Elders. Only wizards were allowed or those accompanied by a wizard in high standing. "Our once-in-a-lifetime chance to see the Mark and we blew it."

Ted'ora studied him for a long moment, then inclined his head to the water below. "The drops flowing in the river will never be in the same configuration as they are at this moment And the next moment. And the moment after that. And yet we go about our days ignoring one unique moment after another. Because we don't know better? Or because we value other moments more?"

"I'm in no mood for philosophy."

"If not philosophy, then how about psychology? For when a friend compares a childhood mistake to an adult moment, something is wrong."

"Wrong?" Harradorn raised his voice. "How about spending the afternoon testing fake wizard's petals. Only one *wasn't* fake." He shuddered, remembering the excruciating pain for the first five minutes when he kept seizing and flinching, wishing to die. Since then, the pain returned off and on, throbbing like a toothache somewhere in his body. A little less pain each time, but annoying as Hel.

"I sympathize for the sacrifice you made so no one else would suffer," Ted'ora said. "But that's not why you're watching the sunset reflect in the river. Most nights you lift your eyes to the sky to see the real thing."

He glanced sideways at the elf. His friend knew him too well. "Once again I've missed an opportunity."

"How so? Word is Felicity returned a short while ago—intoxicated—and is safely sleeping it off in Dulgrun Prison. You accomplished what Peace's town council ordered you to do and did it well. So what troubles you?"

"The magic of the skelter mirror will soon be depleted."

"Ah. You're upset because your last chance to kidnap Joy and force her here will soon be lost."

"My last chance to *see* her one more time, to say good-bye, will be gone. I wasn't going to force her, not if I didn't have to. I invited her to dinner, hoping that if she stayed long enough to meet some of the councilmembers in an informal setting, they'd overcome their misgivings and realize what I already believe to be true—that she has the integrity to keep our town a secret."

Ted'ora arched a golden brow. "After two brief meetings with her, you already know this?"

He smiled self-consciously, realizing what he had implied. "With some people, you know things right away."

"As when I first met you and Rick. The bond was strong between us even while we climbed our first tree together though we were all of five and seven."

Harradorn grinned, recalling the first time he'd met the golden-haired elf. He and Rick had been in the forest, making believe they were fighting off a rabid werewolf. Seeking higher ground, he and Rick had struggled with their young limbs to climb a low tree when the young elf appeared. He proceeded to leap easily from branch to branch, brandishing a wooden knife, defending them from the imaginary beast. Even when Ted'ora slipped and fell to a branch below, he always landed on his feet. But then Rick fell off a high branch. Harradorn tried to catch him, only to lose his balance and fall as well. Ted'ora caught both, or tried to, which resulted in all three tumbling to the ground with bruises and laughter, their friendship cemented for life.

"Missed opportunities are like this hair." Ted'ora plucked a golden strand and dropped it into the rushing water. "Within a blink of the eye it's gone, never to be seen again."

"You know you're terrible at cheering up people. Hey!" he yelped. Ted'ora had plucked a hair from his head.

"And yet opportunities may happen again," the elf tossed the strand into the water, "as long as one remembers opportunities come in all shapes. And from different directions." He laughed when Harradorn scrunched his brow in confusion. "Perhaps this will help."

The elf drew out an object he'd kept hidden. The breath caught in Harradorn's throat. Joy's toilet plunger!

Ted'ora handed it to him. "I hollowed out the handle and inserted a dowel made from the Valkyrie Oak. It took many hours of coaxing and singing, but I believe what is left of the Oak's life force is able to read the echo of the trigger imprinted in the handle's wood."

"Will it work?" he asked, afraid to hope, yet hoping all the same.

"Everything in nature—be it rock, plant, animal, or air—reacts to movement. The passage of time, words spoken, songs sung, someone walking by, all make an impression on everything no matter how subtle."

"Like ripples in a pond," he said in understanding. "But will it work?"

"Only one way to find out."

Ted'ora grinned. Harradorn matched it. He held up the plunger, and the elf put a stern hand on his arm. "If you had said you were going to kidnap Joy, force her here, I would have thrown this in the river along with our hair. But my trust that you would see the error of your intentions has been proven correct." A smile tipped a corner of Ted'ora's mouth. "Sleeping among the stars never fails to bring out the best in us."

Harradorn tried to hide a guilty smirk. "I'm surprised you haven't figured out what was really going to happen to Joy if she came here with Felicity."

Ted'ora tilted his head. His golden eyes darkened and a rare frown sullied his elven features. "A trap. If Joy had shared a meal with you, by the time it was finished, the magic of the mirror would have been depleted. She could not have left of her own accord."

Angry, the elf moved to snatch the plunger away. Harradorn jerked it out of his reach and shook a finger at him. "Not so fast. It's already gifted. You can't take it back."

"This is not becoming of you, my friend."

"True. But circumstances allow for trickery. The town comes first."

"Do you really believe that?"

The question startled him. Of course the town came first. Why would Ted'ora ask such a thing? Yet it stayed with him like a splinter under the skin. He gripped the plunger and ordered the handle to say purple.

He had never heard a tree talk before. He expected a wooden voice or a creaking sound similar to when one sits in a dried-out chair, so he was astonished when the portion of the Valkyrie Oak implanted in the dead wood uttered "purple" with a sharp crack, the same sound the Oak had made when lightning struck and killed it. The imprint of the Oak's cry of pain was still embedded in its remaining life force. Ripples on a pond, Harradorn thought, and he deeply thanked the tree for its final gift. With the Oak's help, he was going to see Joy.

*　*　*

Hours later, Harradorn arrived in New Jersey battered and bruised. The magic powering the skelter mirror had dwindled faster than Sirena predicted. His passage had been sluggish, making him vulnerable to those who inhabit the Stygian Gap, resulting in several hit-and-runs and a few glancing blows. By morning he'd be black and blue all over. He worked his jaw until he heard the joint pop back into place. A check of his watch revealed over three hours had passed since he left the bridge. The dangerously slow journey meant he had even less time to spend with Joy. A few minutes were all he dare risk.

He was in a darkened bedroom, the air lightly scented with carnations. Moonlight peeked through a gap in the curtains, dusting the room in shades of gray and snuggling a figure beneath the covers. A cat jumped off the bed, startling him. It scrambled under the bed to hide, and Joy shifted, then settled back to sleep with a fretful sigh.

On the nightstand, he spotted one of the orchids he'd sent. The flower was wilted, its petals crushed and torn, and yet she hadn't thrown it away. A tiny fairy belt lay next to it. He pocketed the belt, then grabbed Joy's phone and took it into the hall. Lance had been right; he deleted all the photos of Felicity.

Using the phone for light, he hurried downstairs and found Joy's computer. He deleted all the files named Felicity, fairy, and Peace & Prosperity, then emptied them from the recycle bin. A quick search uncovered an assortment of tiny ropes, belts, and holsters stashed behind an African violet. He pocketed them all.

Returning upstairs, he crept toward the bed. This wasn't how he'd envisioned their last moment together. Yet waking her seemed a bad idea. By the time she got over being scared to death by his sudden presence or raging mad at him for popping into her room in the middle of the night, it'd be past due for him to leave.

But he couldn't go without satisfying his curiosity.

He bypassed a low bookshelf with a babbling water fountain and approached the dresser, eager to explore its surface, a treasure chest of what Joy valued most. Strewn amidst a thin layer of dust were garnet earrings, a plastic dragon, a castle made out of seashells, Avon perfume, a fishing lure—a Grizzly King Streamer!—and a postcard from the sister in Italy; Felicity had mentioned Merry during her interrogation. There were also five crayons, a glass-sided container filled with an assortment of beads, buttons, paperclips, and a book on mythological creatures with a fairy on the cover.

He wrote his name in the dust—he couldn't resist—then turned to Joy.

A baseball bat lay on the bed next to her.

A strange woman, this Joy Flint, going to bed with a bat. But then Rick always kept a dagger under his pillow. Everyone had something that made them feel safer: a bat, a knife, a prayer, another person in the house... or in one's bed.

What was she afraid of?

He looked out her window. The neighborhood seemed peaceful. Well lit. No sign of urban decay. A nice quiet suburban community of older houses, all in good repair. Yet the bat by her side bothered him. Maybe it was nothing. An old habit no longer needed.

He crouched down and watched her sleep. Her face possessed an innocence that belied all the feminine curves hidden under the blanket, enticing curves he had been thinking about since he first saw her. Her eyelids fluttered while she dreamed, and her breasts gently rose and fell. Her fingers twitched and she whispered his name. "Harry."

She was dreaming about him!

Amazed, he leaned closer and reached for her. But a trickle of moonlight caught his medallion, and the shine of gold reminded him of his priorities. Logic ruled over need. If he didn't return to Peace, and quickly, his absence would be noticed. More importantly, Aesa had yet to make her wish. As mayor of the town he loved, it was imperative he be there when the wizard's petal was used.

And yet he couldn't go without leaving a token remembrance of what might have been between him and this woman. Mission accomplished, his breath caressed her lips. "Good-bye, Joy Flint."

Her eyes fluttered open.

With regret, he whispered, "Purple."

* * *

Joy slowly woke from a wonderful dream about Harry. He'd been here, in her bed, breezing kisses on her lips, and then, like magic, he was gone. It had seemed so real, she swore she could smell a trace of his woodland cologne.

After Felicity returned to Peace, she had wallowed in self-pity and thoughts of Harry and what-might-have-been. Fortunately, chocolate chip cookie dough was her steadfast comfort food. Changing into ratty old sweats, she gathered all the ingredients, ready to drown her misery in sugar and chocolate, when she happened to glance at the African violet where Felicity would curl up and sleep. And it hit her. Her fairy roommate was gone.

The vivacious, mischievous little orange woman was gone forever. There'd be no fairy zooming around the place singing "good morning sunshine" tunes or "life is great" ditties and insisting they do something fun.

Her life, her home, suddenly seemed ordinary. Predictable.

Boring.

She'd torn open the bag of semi-sweet chocolate chips and munched them one at a time, wishing Felicity hadn't left without her. Or that there was some way to get over being down in the dumps without adding so many calories.

She'd asked herself: What would Felicity do?

Yet she couldn't be the fairy. It wasn't in her to be wild and capricious, flying hither and thither whenever she wanted to.

The real question was: What would Joy with a *dash* of Felicity do?

She'd gone shopping.

Now the sound of the babbling water fountain she'd bought to remind her of the absent fairy lulled her to sleep. With thoughts of Harry, she turned over and sighed wistfully, "Just a dream." Automatically, her hand reached for Shredder, but he wasn't there, only the bat. Her fingers touched the handle; it felt different. Holding it up to the shaft of moonlight stealing into her room, she sucked in her breath.

Her toilet plunger!

* * *

With the magic of the skelter mirror almost depleted, Harradorn spent the last few minutes fighting to make it through to the other side of the mirror, for he was not the only thing traversing the Stygian Gap. At the last second, he escaped and fell to his knees, exhausted. A cut burned on his forearm, the blood hot on his skin, a souvenir of his asinine jaunt to the outside world. But he was alive and he had seen Joy one last time. That's all that mattered.

To his chagrin, lights were on in Sirena's workshop. At a worktable, his sister was cutting open a long stick with an X-Acto knife. Lance Warbird stood next to her, a lustful look on his face while he raised a handful of her curls to his nose for a long, possessive sniff. At Harradorn's appearance, he let go. Sirena's look of surprise melted into a discerning smile. Without a doubt, she'd make him pay for using the mirror again. Then she noticed the blood on his sleeve. She dropped the knife and rushed to him. After a quick examination of his wound, she hurried to her medicine cabinet.

Lance's reaction was anything but concern. "You went to see that woman, didn't you! And you didn't bring her back! I'm calling a council meeting! You won't get away with this! Not by a long shot! I expect to see you in the council room within the hour!"

Lance stormed out, slamming the front door when he left.

Sirena joined Harradorn on the floor with jars of antiseptic and healing ointments and a roll of bandages. She handed him a vial. In seconds, the drink revitalized him enough to sit up straight.

"Now you've done it," she said. She deftly cleaned the wound, then applied a thin layer of ointment that tingled to the point of making him chuckle. "I don't need my crystal ball to predict the trouble you're in. I've never seen Lance so angry."

"It almost seemed faked." Exaggerated when compared to other displays of Lance's anger, but for the life of him, he couldn't figure out why. He glanced at the mirror. "The magic ran out a lot sooner than you predicted," he told her. "As if something had drained it. I almost didn't make it back."

"Oh?" She looked away and concentrated on wrapping his arm in bandages.

He checked his watch. "No wonder I'm so tired. It's been five hours since I left Joy. Hel, even if I'd wanted to bring her back, it wouldn't have been possible."

"You hadn't planned on forcing her here?"

"As you said, kidnapping is not my style."

"You're a good man, Harry." She uttered a blessing of healing, then kissed the injury, leaving the imprint of purple lips on the white bandage. After cleaning up, she tossed him a banana from a bowl of fruit and returned her attention to the worktable.

While he ate the banana, he made his way over, curious why Lance had been in the store in the middle of the night. It looked like she was splitting the bottom half of a two-foot long stick laden with thorns.

"Shouldn't you be rushing off to the Hall and planning your defense?" Sirena asked.

"When you're guilty, there's not much you can do." He tossed the peel into the trash. "What was Lance doing?"

"He's concerned one or two wizard's petals might still be around. To help find them, I've been commissioned to make a dowsing rod from a rose stem."

"Clever, but not what I asked. He was fondling your hair when I arrived." He saw her cringe. The implication turned his heart cold. "Did you and Lance—"

"That's none of your business." She refused to look at him and instead kept slicing into the stem.

He spat in disgust. "Of all the men in town, why him?"

"I needed to distract him so he'd forget someone he shouldn't have seen."

His gut twisted. Had Lance seen him take the plunger to the elves? He grabbed her shoulders and forced her to look at him. "You slept with him for me?"

"Not you." Her eyes shone with moisture. "Someone else. But it would have come back to you." She shook free of his hold and returned to her work. "Don't ask. Leave it be. Please."

After what he had just done, he had no right to quarrel over secrets, though the cost seemed high. He struggled to gentle his voice. "Wonder where Lance came up with the idea of a petal dowsing rod."

"He never said."

"Will it work?"

"If one's intent is pure, anything is possible." She cocked a brow at him. "Like finding a way to use my mirror without permission. I expected Rick to be devious, not you."

"We rub off on each other," he said, then steered the conversation back to her task. "Could it work if one's intent isn't pure?"

"Not likely. I'll soak the split handles with rose nectar to shape them into curves and enhance what is being sought—and make Lance believe he's getting his money's worth—then wrap rose vines around the junction of the split to keep the wood from cracking. The tough part is hollowing out the straight part of the rod. I'm not sure why he wants it done, but it's his money and his instructions."

"Almost as if he wants to insert something." Ted'ora had done the same with Joy's plunger to make it work magic.

"Perhaps stuff it with rose petals," Sirena said. "Like attracts like."

"Maybe." But something in his gut said it wasn't that simple. He glanced at his watch and frowned. "Time to put my head on the block."

Chapter 13

That evening, Harradorn was still mayor. Barely. The council, under Lance's manipulation, had issued a decree: Harradorn would be removed him from office if he didn't retrieve Joy by the end of the day.

Grumbling, he stomped down the central staircase of the Mayor's Hall and Residence. Agamemnon waited at the bottom with his leather jacket. "The Weather Channel indicates a chilly night in New Jersey."

"Thanks. I shouldn't be long. I'm just going to grab her and come back." Agamemnon looked doubtful, and he opened his mouth to say something, but Harradorn said it for him. "I know, I know, 'the best laid plans,' which is why I'm taking my cell."

"I'll keep the satellite phone with me." Agamemnon patted a small lump in his huge shirt pocket. "Your number is set for speed dial two."

"Who's speed dial one?"

"Joy. I figured wherever she is, you'll be there, too."

"Always the romantic, Agamemnon. But I'm afraid after what I'm about to do, she'll hate me for the rest of her life." He grimaced. "If I don't bring her back, Lance will be interim mayor until elections are held to replace me. I can't let that happen."

Agamemnon followed him outside. He handed Harradorn a sealed envelope and a folded sheet of paper. "As you requested."

"Thanks."

They stood on the steps, watching a large crowd form near the bandshell at the far end of the park. Agamemnon said, "Oprah

Winfrey says every choice in life either moves you forward or keeps you stuck."

He looked up at the wise, one-eyed giant. "I think some choices move you backwards, but only hindsight distinguishes which is which." He started down the steps.

"Watch out for Gloris," Agamemnon said. "Since Felicity's return, she's been asking to see you. She wants to know when you're going to turn her brown."

"Like I don't have enough problems." He had hoped Zach would have returned by now and could do something about the red fairy. But the wizard must still be hunting FearfulFran.

Just once he wished something would go right.

He cut through the park. The smell of popcorn filled the air as the audience took their seats. He spotted his brother leaning against a tree, eating a bag of it. The town's sheriff, Lucius Caine, stood next to him, Tonight the swarthy sheriff's black hair was tied behind his head in a multitude of thin braids, the hair style he wore when expecting trouble.

The Peace high school orchestra warmed up in preparation for their annual spring play. Rick yawned. This year it was *The Sound Of Music*. His brother hated musicals.

"Gloris has been looking for you," Rick told him.

"So I've heard. Where's Aesa?"

"Front row with her parents."

"She has the wizard's petal prominently displayed in a newly purchased crystal locket," Sheriff Caine snarled. He hated musicals, too. The next three hours would be torturous for both men.

Caine and his deputies had been keeping Aesa under surveillance, waiting for the haughty little girl to make her wish. "This afternoon," Caine said, "she was heard asking the director if she could take the part of Liesl if she had the best singing voice in the world."

"That doesn't sound so bad," Rick said. "Granted, an eight-year-old diva would be a pain in the ass, but at least the petal would be used."

"Unfortunately, the director pointed out the best singing voice in the world belongs to a male tenor in Italy. When asked if she wanted to have this man's voice coming out of her for the rest of her life, she changed her mind."

"I'm tempted to have Sirena mix up a potion that'll give Aesa permanent laryngitis," Harradorn said. "That way she'll never be able to make a wish. But with Sirena's prices continuing to escalate, I'd hate to think how much she'd charge."

"I can't believe Warbird voted to give her a council seat in exchange for sending you after Joy Flint," Rick said. "It's practically mutinous."

"Lance claimed it's the restitution he owed Sirena."

Rick sneered. "I told you to dissolve the town council soon as you became mayor." He rolled his eyes dramatically. "But no, the great peacemaker has to teach everyone how to get along and work together." Rick pointed a ringed finger at Harradorn. "Mark my words, Sirena's going to be wanting your job next."

"If I don't bring Joy back, it just might happen." He handed the folded paper to Sheriff Caine. "I'd like you to have someone keep an eye on Lance's place. The latest report from the gardeners indicate they can't get the trees in front of his house to grow at a normal rate."

Caine scanned the report. "Huh. Fertilizer had no effect. But what's this about the trees in front of Sirena's shop growing faster?"

"Probably because the skelter mirror is being used so much. Lance's trees have me more concerned."

"I agree. I'll have someone watch his place."

"Better have them keep their distance," Rick said. "Lance has a tendency to suck the life out of everyone around him."

Isn't that the truth.

"Here." He handed Rick a sealed envelope. "If anything happens to me, open it."

"Happens to you?" Rick tensed, the boredom in his eyes suddenly replaced with concern. He held up the envelope to the waning sunlight and tried to see inside. "What is it?"

"The town's insurance policy. I'm taking a page out of your book and hedging my bets." Harradorn placed a calming hand on his brother's arm and nodded toward Aesa. "Sorry to leave you with this problem, but orders are orders."

He began to leave when Rick called after him. "If you really mean that, bro, I volunteer to go in your stead. Joy Flint has a fine pair of sails, if you know what I mean."

The ribald comment stopped him. He turned and looked sharply at Rick.

Joy and his brother. The possibility taunted him, even more when he recalled Rick was the first one Joy had wakened with a kiss. There was no way he was letting his brother get near her again. "Thanks, but I don't think Cynthia would approve of you jumping ship for another woman."

Rick grumbled. "She's already mad at me. Sirena's been giving out free readings and stealing all her customers away. For some reason, Cynthia's crystal ball blames me. Crazy seer."

* * *

At Sirena's Shop of Quiet Contentment, Harradorn was anything but content, and his mood only worsened when he saw a long line of people waiting at the door. He read the large handwritten sign proudly displayed in the front window.

Newest Councilmember Sale!!!
Saturday, Dawn to Dusk
10% off all merchandise, except jade and statuary
♥ Free drinks and sweets ♥
Tell me your problems. Tell me your hopes, your dreams.
Let's get acquainted!
Free readings all weekend!

Knowing bleeding-heart Sirena, she'd show up at the next council meeting with a list of demands from everyone she'd talked to. He covered his eyes and shook his head. *Kill me now.*

It took several minutes for him to herd all the customers already inside out the door. In the backroom, he found Sirena smiling and humming a tune. By the familiar pungent odor, she was making the potion that would send him through the mirror.

Upon seeing him, she squealed in delight and rushed to give him a hug. "Harry! Mayor Harry! Brother! I'm so excited! I don't know what to call you!"

"You can call me Harry in private. Mayor Harradorn at meetings."

"You can call me Councilmember Sirena. Or Councilwoman. Either one."

He tried not to grimace. Already she was changing. "You almost done?"

"All I need is the trigger." She picked up a jar of amethyst powder. "Purple like before?"

He shook his head. "It has to be different. I can't risk Joy knowing the trigger and escaping like last time." He scanned the jars of colors on her shelves. "These are all too common. I need something obscure, a color she won't be able to guess in a million years."

Sirena looked around, then entered the front of the store. She returned with a small decanter glazed in a vibrant shade of deep blue. In a large mortar, she crushed it with a pestle, then ground it into powder. "This pigment is called smalt. I bet she never heard of that."

"I haven't even heard of it."

"Good. Because I hate to think I just destroyed a top-of-the-line aromatherapy decanter for nothing." She looked up at him and smiled. "I'd do anything for you, Harry."

He secretly winced. Here he'd been thinking what a disaster his life was going to be with her on the council, and then she goes and performs a selfless act on his behalf.

He leaned over and gave her a peck on the cheek. "Thanks." He scanned the jars and asked, "You wouldn't know anything about how to change the color of a fairy, would you?"

"Already taken care of." She held up a beaker of green liquid. "I heard about your promise to Gloris."

"But it's green," he pointed out. "She wants to be brown."

"Silly. Everyone knows red and green make brown. Trust me, it'll work. And my price is very reasonable."

He stifled a groan. "What do you want this time?"

"Well, I was thinking about asking to be seated at your right hand at the council meetings. But I'm also in need of some new outfits to wear during my official duties when councilwoman. Two thousand euros should do it."

Outrageous yet manageable. Because he'd granted Gloris her two wishes on behalf of the town, he'd pay Sirena from the public safety budget. "Agreed."

She added a large pinch of the vibrant blue powder to the potion. "Want me to check where Joy is before you go through the mirror? I've been practicing with my crystal ball, letting customers get a free reading with each purchase. I'm up to thirty percent accuracy."

Thirty percent? "That's all right. I didn't have any trouble last time."

Sirena tsked. "It's Friday night. Where do you think she is? Home? Crying her eyes out because your plan to seduce her into returning here with a drunken fairy didn't work?"

"Sure." Though when she put it that way, he really wasn't. Near the top of the mirror she wrote Joy's phone number, then dabbed some of the mixture on the back of his hand, keying the trigger to him. Like before, it burned for a second, then disappeared.

"Men can be so stupid," Sirena muttered under her breath. She sprinkled the mirror with the potion. With her other hand, she held up the crystal ball and peered into it. Her eyes glazed over. The mirror shimmered. As Harradorn stepped through, she said, "Better duck."

Chapter 14

Duck?

The instant Harradorn exited the Stygian Gap, a pie smashed into his face.

He licked his lips. Real artificial whipped cream. Laughter surrounded him. He wiped the cream from his eyes and discovered he was in a gymnasium in the middle of a school carnival. A sign indicated he'd had the dumb luck of appearing in the 5th Grade Pie Throw.

A woman in a pink and yellow clown outfit hurried over. "Are you all right, sir?"

"Did you see that?" asked the young boy at the throwing line. "He popped out of thin air. Like magic."

The clown laughed. "Children. They have such an imagination." She handed him a towel. "Sorry about your jacket."

"That's all right." Harradorn cleaned his face and hair, and wiped off his jacket. "I should be more careful where I'm going." Or listen to Sirena more.

He saw Joy a few feet away staring at him, dressed like a clown in a poufy orange wig with purple carnations stuck in it. Her hand was clapped over her heart, literally over a large red heart sewn onto her clown outfit. She smiled in amusement, her eyes sparkling in delight. She struggled not to laugh.

"Not one of my best entrances," he said with a lopsided smile. His eyes drank her in as she approached. Even in her goofy clown outfit, he wanted to wrap her in his arms and kiss her, kiss her for a long time as he had in Peace.

"I can't believe you're here." She reached up and brushed pie crumbs from his hair. A simple gesture, yet when their eyes met, it took on an air of intimacy. Her fingers stilled. "I thought I'd never see you again."

He took her hand and kissed it slowly. He didn't care how corny or outdated it might seem, only knowing how right it felt. "We still have that moonlit walk to take."

The clown holding pies to be thrown said, "Is this the guy who sent you the flowers? Ohmigod, he's gorgeous."

"You sent my sister flowers?" Mike came up from behind, holding more pies.

"Two bouquets," the clown said.

"Two?" Mike growled. "Listen here, buddy, you and I need to have a talk."

"Uh, oh. Protective brother on overdrive."

Joy frowned. "Mike, this isn't the time or the place."

"She's right," Harradorn said. There was no way he could make Joy disappear unnoticed with all these people around, especially with Mike breathing down his neck. "Why don't you and I go outside for a little talk."

"No problem." Mike handed the pies to Joy.

She whispered to her brother, "If you scare him off, I'll never speak to you again."

He whispered back, "If I can scare him off, he doesn't deserve you."

* * *

Outside, the air was crisp, scented with the sweet smell of vegetation and yet ruined by the acrid exhaust and steady rumble of vehicles from a nearby highway. Harradorn leaned against the wall of the building and calmly asked, "Now, what did you want to talk about?"

Mike faced him, stance wide, arms crossed. "I did some checking on you, Harradorn Lawson, and found out something very interesting. You don't exist. You're not in any government data base. You don't even have a social security number."

"Did you try googling me?"

"Yeah, I did. You don't even exist on the Internet."

Mike stepped closer. Harradorn fought to stay relaxed, nonthreatening. Joy's brother was a lot like Lance, always needing to be in control. But unlike Lance, Mike didn't do it to gain power but to protect others. A hardened military man.

"Only one kind of person doesn't have an identity," Mike said. "A dangerous one."

"I assure you, I'm not a criminal."

"I only have your word on that. I've known government types like you: anonymous, invisible, no background, no history, no home. Always on the move. Disappearing at a moment's notice, and sometimes never coming back. Joy doesn't need someone like that in her life. If you really like her, you should do the right thing and let her go—now—before it gets serious."

"And if I don't?"

"I'll hunt you down, no matter how long it takes, no matter what hole you're hiding in, and make you sorry you ever met my sister."

He wondered what quote Agamemnon would use to describe the situation, probably something about being caught between a rock and a hard place. Then he heard a whimper from the parking lot, followed by, "Ow!"

Mike heard it, too. "Left, twenty meters."

In unison, they headed into the parking lot. Though well-lit, SUVs and pickup trucks easily created shadows that could conceal someone who didn't want to be seen.

"Ow!" a young voice yelped again. "That hurts!"

"Don't be such a wuss," another youthful voice said.

Mike motioned he'd circle behind to the right. Seconds later, between two vehicles, Harradorn came upon five boys hunkered down. One held another's arm and jabbed it with something.

"What are you boys doing?" Harradorn asked.

Like a school of fish fleeing a predator, the boys turned as one and ran in the opposite direction, only to freeze again when Mike shone a flashlight in their face and blocked their retreat.

"We're not doing nothing," the biggest kid whined.

Harradorn raised a brow. "A double negative, which means you were doing something. Let's see your arms."

Mike trained the flashlight on their forearms. All had pinpricks forming bloody X's. Mike lowered the light to their feet. Straight pins glittered on the ground. "Okay, who has the marker?"

"Marker?" Harradorn asked.

One boy withdrew a black felt-tip pen from a pocket and handed it over. Mike explained. "Break the skin in a design, then trace over the dots with a permanent marker—instant tattoo for gang wannabes." He fixed each boy with a piercing stare. "Who started this?"

They meekly exchanged glances but no one talked.

"Fine," Mike said. "We'll go see the principal. She'll straighten this out." One boy started to speak, but Mike snapped, "Too late. Shut your mouth and go to the gym."

They herded the group back to the carnival. Harradorn asked Mike, "Why didn't you let the kid talk?"

"I don't have a degree in child psychology, but I know when someone's about to rat to save his own ass." They stopped inside the doorway. "I'll keep them here. You go hunt down the principal."

* * *

At the pie throw, Joy lifted on tiptoe, trying to see over the crowd.

"Lose a student?" Jeff asked.

"Just looking for someone." She glanced at him and tried not to grimace. His vampire-clown costume was more garish than funny. "How's it going?" She glanced at his booth. He'd done a terrible job of planning an age-appropriate game. A bean bag throw was perfect for the primary students to run, but his fifth graders were clearly bored with its simplicity. The small prizes, lollipops, weren't attracting many customers, whereas her booth had a long line for all the gift cards from local businesses she'd worked tirelessly to get.

Jeff shrugged. "It's a school carnival. What do you expect?"

"I expect to win a gift card for the local bookstore," Harry said.

At the tantalizing sound of his voice, she spun around. The undeniable pull of his gaze was like a New Jersey fog, shadowy and gray, easy to get lost in, and for a while she couldn't speak. "That will be, uh, five tickets, sir."

Harry held up a fistful. "I don't give up easily."

"Neither do I," Mike said from behind him. He held up tickets, too.

"Jeff Demarco," Joy said, "this is Harry Lawson. The one who sent me the beautiful flowers."

"Nice to meet you," Jeff said to Harry. "Sorry about the vase." To her surprise, she detected a subtle sneer of contempt under all the vampire-clown makeup. Mike's protective instincts toward her was based on brotherly concern, but Jeff's reaction to Harry was completely uncalled for. Flicking a cool glance at Joy, he muttered, "I better get back to my booth," and left.

"Weasel," Mike said under his breath.

"What's this about a vase?" Harry asked.

"Jeff helped me carry the flowers to my car and dropped one." But not accidentally, she now realized. She owed the fairy an apology.

Harry stared around her at Jeff's retreating figure, and his frown matched her brother's.

During the next hour, Harry helped with the booth, cheering and clapping for the winners, filling more pie shells to be tossed. He seemed to enjoy talking with the children and other adults.

Mike, on the other hand, quickly lost interest and left to play something else. When the carnival wound down, he returned. He and Harry folded up the tables and chairs while she and the students assigned to clean-up removed the rest of the booth. They were almost finished when the principal, in an Emmett Kelly clown costume, asked to speak privately with Joy.

"We'll meet you outside," Mike said. While they walked away, she heard her brother ask Harry, "What kind of car do you drive?"

Joy and the principal were joined by Jeff and the assistant principal. The principal said, "I assume your brother told you about the incident in the parking lot."

"The boys with the pins and marker, yes."

"Two are from your class, the same ones I suspended earlier this week. The others are from Jeff's. For the last half hour their parents have been on my back, claiming the ones from your class talked their children into getting the marks."

"There's a local gang that streaks their hair purple," the assistant principal said. "A parent says her son decided to form a gang the same day you started wearing purple hair."

"A parent is blaming my hair color for her son's actions?" Joy gawked at the principals in disbelief, then turned to Jeff and silently pleaded with him to say something about his students using pins before she colored her hair.

Jeff said. "I did warn you your hair might be considered a disruptive influence. Now you have a robotic fairy flying around your classroom, bolstering a belief in magic. I've heard parents are upset. They feel it undermines their religious beliefs."

"What?" She couldn't believe what she was hearing. To have Jeff broadside her like this in front of the principals was unconscionable. "I assure you," she told both principals, "if any parent had an objection to my fairy robot, I would have cleared up the misunderstanding immediately. As far as I know, no one has objected."

She glared at Jeff. The bastard. He was the one who had suggested using magical symbols to ensure her purple hair appeared sexless, and had inspired the idea to take Felicity to school.

"We'll look into both matters," the principal said. "In the meantime, Joy, I suggest you make some changes in your classroom. You're one of our brightest, most innovative teachers, but for the next few days you should consider using more traditional teaching techniques *and appearance* until we get to the bottom of what's causing the students' misbehavior. Now, it's been a long night. I suggest we go home and take this up again on Monday."

Joy and Jeff left the gym. Outside, the parking lot was nearly empty. Mike and Harry were at the far end next to her brother's pickup.

She glanced sideways at Jeff, her mind still reeling from the dressing down by the principals. "Why didn't you tell them your students were using pins the week before I colored my hair?"

"I don't know what you're talking about."

"Yes, you do. And what's this about complaints concerning Felicity?"

"Who?" he asked. He looked genuinely puzzled but he didn't break his stride.

"The, uh, flying robotic fairy; I call her Felicity." *Whew. That was close.* "I haven't had any objections from parents. You said yourself you were thinking about getting one for your classroom."

"I did?" He nonchalantly unlocked his car.

Anger boiled up inside; she couldn't believe what she was hearing. Then it occurred to her. "You're afraid of getting in trouble for not reporting the students in your class. Those so-called complaints about my fairy was just a diversion, a way to make me look bad while saving your own reputation."

Jeff turned to her. "The principal is right; you are very bright. So if you know what's good for you, you'll take your lumps and keep your mouth shut. With two strikes against you," he looked at her poufy clown-orange hair with the purple carnations in it, "maybe three, I have a feeling you're not the one they're going to believe."

"I thought you were my friend." She felt like screaming. "Why are you doing this?"

"Because the last thing I need in my life right now is more trouble."

"You're talking about Patsy and the kids leaving."

The areas of his face not covered with clown make-up paled. "How did you know? No, don't tell me," he sneered, his face now darkening in anger. "Patsy told you. Probably had this planned long before she left—the bitch. Can't trust any woman. Not even you."

"That's not fair. I didn't hear about Patsy until after she left."

Jeff huffed in disbelief and got into his car.

"That's no excuse for making me the scapegoat for what you didn't do," Joy said. "I'm not going to take this lying down. I'm up for tenure. If you don't tell the principal the truth, I will."

"Go ahead and try. I already have tenure. You don't." And with that, he drove off.

Joy's eyes burned with unshed tears. Up until this night, she had considered Jeff a good friend, but all the barbecues and dinners she'd shared with Jeff and his family had turned to dust. Losing his family had turned Jeff mean. Selfish. Angry.

Seething in frustration, she stared in the direction of Jeff's car and howled, "Creep!"

"Who's a creep?" Harradorn asked, coming up behind her. Joy's hands were balled into fists, her breathing hot and heavy. He noticed Mike keeping his distance and decided to do the same. Both men gave her a few moments to calm down. Then he asked, "What happened?"

In a voice a lot calmer than the emotions raging across her face, she told them what the principals had said, then what Jeff had done. When Mike offered to go inside and talk to the principals on her behalf, Joy shook her head.

"Thanks, but this is my problem. I can handle my own battles." By the fire smoldering in her eyes, Harradorn believed her.

"You sure?" Mike said. "'Cause I wouldn't mind hauling Jeff's ass back here and setting things straight." Mike's face revealed a brotherly love that was protective and endless. Growing up, Harradorn had seen the same expression on members of his own family when trouble threatened one of them. And for that he respected Mike.

Joy gazed up at her brother with an obvious smile of gratitude. "I can take care of myself."

"Yeah, but who's going to take care of him." Mike pointed a thumb at Harradorn. "The guy's got no car. Says his sister brought him here."

"Actually, I can vouch for that," Joy said, to her brother's surprise. "Look, Mike, I appreciate all your help tonight, but I'm tired and I'm going home." She started for her car.

"I'll go with you," Harradorn said. He grinned. This was perfect. Alone with Joy, he could talk her into going to Peace for the night. After what Jeff had just done, she'd be eager to get away. Two days should be plenty of time to convince the council Joy wasn't a security risk. He'd get her back to work by Monday, long before Mike got suspicious.

Pleased with himself, he started to follow her when Joy abruptly stopped and held up a hand. "You're not going with me."

He frowned. "I'm not?"

"He's not?" Mike said at the same time, only Mike said it with a big-brother grin.

"No," Joy said. "I have a terrible headache coming on. I'm tired. I've just been beaten up by someone I thought was a friend." She fixed her gaze on Harradorn. "I'm certainly not about to trust someone I hardly know. I'm going home—alone."

He opened his mouth to convince her otherwise, hating to see his perfect plan fall apart, but then she added, "Don't even try to talk me out of it, especially after what you did last night. Go back to where you came from. Next time call before you show up, like normal people."

Rebuffed, he shoved his hands in his pockets, annoyed nothing was turning out the way he thought it would. He bit out every word. "Fine. Anything you say. Except I can't go back." Not without her or he'd lose his mayorship and Lance would take over Peace.

"You can't?" Joy said. She sounded skeptical.

"Wait a minute. What's she talking about?" Mike faced him. "What did you do to her last night?"

"Nothing." The last thing he needed was for Mike to find out he'd snuck into his sister's bedroom.

Joy tiredly rubbed her forehead. "He brought back my plunger without permission."

"He needs your permission to return your toilet plunger?" Mike asked.

"Forget it. I'm not in the mood for this. Harry, you can stay at Mike's tonight." Joy stared at her brother. "Right?" It really wasn't a question, and surprisingly Mike didn't object. He figured the brother probably relished the opportunity of keeping him away from his sister for at least one more night.

"Good," Joy said. "Now that everything's settled, I'm going home."

"No, you're not," Mike said.

"I'm not?"

"She's not?" Harradorn said. Talking to these two was worse than talking with a fairy.

Mike shook his head. "It's not safe. Jeff has a key to your house. After what he just did, you can't trust him to respect your privacy."

"Then I'll go ask him for my key," Joy said.

"Uh-uh. He might have made a copy you don't know about. The guy's a weasel. You're spending the night with me. In the morning I'm going to rekey all your locks and reset the code for the garage."

"But Harry—"

"He can spend the night at a motel."

"No, I can't," Harradorn said. He had cash on him, but no *outside* ID.

"That's right, he can't," Joy said, obviously aware of his dilemma. "Look, if you insist I don't go home, I'll go to a friend's. Gina can put me up, and Harry can use your spare room. End of discussion."

Mike grumbled. He clearly didn't want him for a roommate, but he also didn't want to antagonize his sister any further. With his mouth twisted in irritation, he told Harradorn, "You better not snore." Then he looked at Joy and his demeanor softened. "We'll follow you to Gina's."

Harradorn trudged back to Mike's pickup and wondered what else could go wrong. Mike glanced at him and smirked. "Ego hurting because she'd rather spend the night with Gina than you?"

"Among other things."

"Don't take it personally. Even before what Jeff did tonight, Joy wasn't ready for any nighttime activities. And I can prove it. But first I want your promise that if I do, you'll go slow with my sister."

"Only if *you* promise not to play chaperone all weekend." That should keep Mike from getting suspicious when he and Joy disappeared to Peace for a couple of days. Delaying their departure until tomorrow was unfortunate but easily explainable to the council.

"Fair enough. Here's the thing. Whenever something's got Joy sucking wind, she colors her hair. This school year's been bad, so she's been changing the color every month. But this last dye job was only days apart. I don't know how much more her hair can take before it starts falling out, but I do know my sister's running thin. I don't want you taking advantage of her. Not after what Jeff did and the pressure she's under from the principals."

"I agree she's had a rotten night, but you still haven't proven a thing."

"Oh, yeah? What color is her hair?"

He looked over at Joy. She was at her car a few lanes away, still in her clown getup, including the poufy bright orange wig, which had some of the purple carnations he'd sent playfully inserted in it. Underneath was the erotic purple hair he'd been dreaming about. The longing to furrow his fingers through it while they made love was not going to be denied because of her brother's two-bit psychological analysis about whether his sister could handle a relationship.

With a confident smile, he said, "Her hair's purple."

Mike coolly nodded. He yelled over to Joy, "Hey, sis, take off your wig!"

Joy tilted her head in confusion and fingered her hair, but she didn't pull it off.

Harradorn stared, mouth ajar. Joy wasn't wearing a wig. The orange hair was hers!

By Thor's hammer, she was turning into a fairy!

Mike grunted. "Slow and easy."

"Whatever you say."

Chapter 15

With a six pack of beer to keep them company, Joy and Gina stayed up past midnight talking and drowning Joy's hair in conditioner to release the teased knots of her clown hairdo.

After mutually agreeing the eighth circle of hell was too pleasant a place for a dirt bag like Jeff, Gina insisted on hearing everything Joy knew about Harry. It was pure torture to keep Peace & Prosperity a secret, which meant there was little Joy could say. Harry was mayor of a small town out west somewhere; a great kisser who looked heroic even when holding a toilet plunger; he wasn't afraid of Mike, which definitely was in his favor, to which Gina agreed; and his large dove-gray eyes melted her heart every time he looked at her.

What she couldn't tell Gina was Harry was also a thief in the night, using the skelter mirror to steal into her bedroom. An event that continued to bother her hours later while she tossed and turned on Gina's couch. Her mind wouldn't stop, for she couldn't decide whether his actions were romantically clandestine or disturbingly voyeuristic.

When she'd discovered he'd erased all trace of Felicity in her home, she'd been furious until she realized what he had done might be comparable to her brother's black ops missions. She couldn't fault him for taking extraordinary measures to keep his town safe and secure. Mike did the same for their country.

She definitely should cut him some slack for agreeing to spend the night at her brother's.

Her phone played "Raindrops Keep Fallin' On My Head."

Bleary-eyed, she tried to make out the caller. Blank. "Hello?" she said.

A male voice sang a weird version of the opening song from *The Sound of Music*. Grumbling, she ended the call. It seemed like she had just fallen asleep, when her phone played "Raindrops…" again.

Another blank caller ID. This time when she answered, she said, "Hello. Who is this?"

A male sang the same song from the same musical.

"I'm on the do-not-call list. You call me again and I'll report you." She ended the call. It took a long time to fall back to sleep. She was dreaming of dancing on a mountaintop when her phone woke her.

"Not again." She glanced at the clock. It was almost four. A blank ID. And, like the last three times, the same male voice sang the same distorted version of the opening song from *The Sound of Music:*

> "Our town is alive with the sound of music,
> With songs we have sung for too many hours,
> The town cannot stop all the sounds of music,
> My heart wants to stop every song it hears."

"You realize that doesn't rhyme," she told the annoying caller.

Her thumb moved to end the call but paused when the melody changed, and the singer. Another male, but this one had a cocksure tone to his voice.

> "I'm happy to call you, I'm happy you're there,
> I wish you were here and I wish I was there,
> If you could come help us, I'm sure you'd agree
> That life would be sweeter if you were with me.

Dance with me,
Come on sweet lady and dance with me,
We'll to and fro all night/Until the morning light
If you'll just dance with me."

"In your dreams, pervert." She turned off the phone and finally managed to sleep.

Rising early, she left a note of thanks for Gina, who wasn't a morning person, and rushed home minutes before the prearranged time Mike and Harry would be there, feeling perfectly safe in the bright morning light. After taking care of Shredder, she changed into a colorful halter sundress with matching jacket and sandals.

She stood in front of a mirror and grimaced at her outrageous orange hair. "Look on the bright side," she told her reflection, "at least it matches the flowers on your dress." Her reflection didn't look convinced.

She glanced at Harry's name written in the dust on the dresser. Leaving his signature seemed endearing, and she'd traced over it numerous times, hoping to elicit insight about him. Returning her plunger was also romantic, if in a quirky way. Even though she had taken the bat downstairs to kill another spider, the plunger was still in her room next to Harry's name—a fitting symbol of their weird yet scintillating relationship. She blinked in surprise. A tiny green bud was growing on top of the plunger's handle.

The doorbell rang and she hurried downstairs to find Mrs. O'Keefe on her doorstep.

"Don't you look nice," her neighbor said with a shrewd wink. "Have a hot date?"

Joy laughed softly. "As a matter of fact, I do."

"Well, then, it's a good thing I came over before you left. My aching bones got me up again last night. Saw someone prowling around your windows. Almost caught a glimpse of his face when your motion-sensing porch light came on, but he was too quick for these old eyes to get a good look at."

Joy glanced over at Jeff's house. Felicity had accused him of peeping in the window, and he'd followed her to Mike's. Perhaps Jeff had developed some unsavory habits since his wife and kids left. Or maybe they were the reason Patsy decided to leave. The thought made her shudder. She was about to ask if the prowler had Jeff's height and build when Mike pulled up with Harry. Joy introduced him to her neighbor.

"Having a man around should scare away that prowler," Gracie said with a nod of approval. "You two kids have fun. And watch out for the police." She squinted up the street to where a patrol car had pulled over a speeder. "Must be behind on their quota of tickets. I've never seen so many around."

"Good to know," Joy said, and made a note to be extra careful driving. Having the police run a background check on Harry would be disastrous.

With a parting wave, Gracie scurried across the street to her home.

"What's this about a prowler?" Mike asked.

"Nothing rekeying the locks and setting a new garage code can't take care of," Joy replied. "You know Mrs. O'Keefe. Even a strange bird in the neighborhood gets her attention."

Harry shifted around Mike to her side, "But just in case, I'll keep a close eye on Joy."

He did just that, slowly looking her over, his smile twitching a bit when his eyes took in her orange hair. His gaze was hooded and sensuously inviting, yet held a question he seemed hesitant to ask. What was it about this man that made her excited to be with him, not knowing where he might lead yet willing to follow?

"Joy,—" Mike began to say.

"Mike." Joy wrenched her gaze away from Harry and focused it on her brother. "When you pick up the rekey kit, why don't you get that indoor motion alarm you've always wanted us to have. And use the year you were born for the garage code. Harry and I are going out for coffee. Maybe do some sightseeing."

She waited for Mike to object. Normally, he would. So she was surprised when he shot Harry a look. A silent message passed between the two.

"One more thing," Harry said. "My phone."

With a grunt, Mike removed the item from his pocket and tossed it to him.

"What's going on?" Joy asked.

"Damn phone was going off all night," Mike said, "so I took it away."

"After he broke it," Harry added. "Caught your brother trying to bug my phone. Whatever he did made it keep ringing."

"Just practicing with a few toys from work."

Joy scowled in disapproval, and he sheepishly looked down at his feet. "His damn phone plays opera," he said. "What kind of guy has an opera ringtone?"

"'The Ride of the Valkyries' is more than opera." Harry checked for messages.

Joy laughed. Anything that irked her overprotective brother was fine by her.

She and Harry stopped at the new Coffee & Buns and got coffee and cinnamon scones, then drove up to Garret Mountain. While she parked the car, Harry took in the four-story round tower on the crest of a cliff.

"Are we visiting Rapunzel?" he asked.

"The Observation Tower is one of my favorite places," she said. They headed for it. "I love the turrets and crenellations. Wait until you see the view. Lambert Castle is below, built by a silk tycoon at the end of the 1800's."

Harry chuckled and they climbed the stone stairwell. "There's a fairy in Peace who wanted a pet silkworm so she could have lots of silk dresses."

"Oh, no. She didn't know the worm's killed?"

"Nobody ever said fairies were smart."

"Felicity seems extremely clever."

"Sneaky, devious, and shrewd, but not smart."

"How much schooling do the fairies get?" she asked, remembering Felicity had little knowledge of biology.

"The drop-out rate is high. After all, they're fairies. Always on the move."

"Maybe I can help. I took two years off from college to be a VISTA volunteer and teach the disadvantaged."

"That's a very selfless thing to do."

She loved the admiration so clear in his voice. It was nice to be appreciated. "I learned a lot of teaching strategies that incorporate movement with learning. If you like, I can copy the info for your teachers to try."

Harry shrugged indifferently and took a sip of coffee. "Thanks, but I don't think Peace & Prosperity could handle having smart fairies. They cause enough problems the way they are."

"Or maybe they're the way they are to compensate for a poor education."

He raised his brow. "I hadn't thought of that."

They had reached the top of the tower. The windows on the east side looked out over northeastern New Jersey, taking in the expansive skyline of New York City in the distance.

"Beautiful," Harry said. "You can even see the George Washington Bridge."

"You know about the GW?"

"Just because I live in a secret town, doesn't mean I don't get out."

"Of course. Your sister lives in New York City." His mouth fell open in surprise, and she chuckled. "Felicity told me about her when your package arrived. Originally, I was planning on checking out the store this weekend. We still could. Would you like to see her?"

He turned his back on the spectacular view and said, "I'd rather look at you."

There it goes again—the rest of the world. He looked at her as if she was the only person who mattered. That and he'd come all this way to see her, even put up with her brother last night to be with her. She'd be a fool not to take advantage of the situation.

"Do you mind?" Grabbing his jacket, she pulled his mouth down to her level. "I've been wanting to do this ever since I left Peace." Then, she kissed him, really kissed him: lips parted, tongue inserted, emotions exploring at will. It was brazen and unexpected, but she didn't care. She had orange hair like Felicity, and the fairy had three husbands. It was time to be wild and crazy, at least for the moment.

The taste of his mouth, the sumptuous touch of his lips, was everything she remembered about their last kiss. And more.

Harradorn wrapped his arms around her and drew her close. A laugh rumbled deep in her throat. So this is what it was like to be a fairy, adventurous, sensual, more alive than she'd been in a long time. The fire from his lips poured into her, melting her from the inside out. Her heart spiraled out of control. She was his, and by the longing in his kiss, Harry was hers.

Harradorn couldn't believe what the woman in his arms was doing to him. He wanted to stay in control. Needed to stay in control. After Mike's warning about Joy being in an emotionally fragile state, he'd spent the night convincing himself to do the right thing, keep his promise, and take things slow.

Plainly slow was the last thing on Joy's mind.

But it was wrong. He shouldn't be doing this until he confessed why he had come to see her. She had a right to the truth before they went any further.

With a restraint he wished he didn't have, when all he wanted to do was press her against the wall and make her moan with pleasure, he placed his hands on Joy's shoulders and gently eased her mouth away. She looked at him, her brown eyes dark and smoldering. Bedroom eyes. Let's-have-sex-all-day eyes.

He took a determined breath. "You're an extraordinary woman who I would love to get to know better. And I don't just mean physically."

Instantly, her demeanor changed. Her hands ceased their erotic pulsations on his back. Her face turned cool and guarded. "Why do I have the feeling there's a huge 'but' about to come between us?"

"You're also very perceptive."

She stepped back, wrapping her arms around herself. She looked down at the stone floor. "I'm sorry. I'm being too bold."

"No." His heart fell. The vibrant, sexy woman before him was withdrawing, turning shy and insecure. "For the love of Freya, don't do that." Angry at himself, he lifted her chin to look at him. Mike was right. With everything going on in her life, she didn't need him mucking up her emotions. "Don't you dare be ashamed about what just happened. I'm not. I'm glad you made the first move. I barely slept a wink last night; all I could think about was you. Ever since you woke me in Peace, I haven't been able to get you out of my mind."

His fingers slowly traced the outline of her lips, and he was glad to see her gaze spark with heat. "Any man would be a fool to say no to a woman who wants him. But this is different. You're not any woman. You're Joy Flint, a beautiful passionate woman who's also smart, brave, changeable, cheeky, and..." he fingered a curl of orange hair, "quirky."

"Not erotic like purple, huh?"

He grinned. "No, but it is enticingly playful. I can't lie to you, not when you've been so honest with me. *But* before this goes any further, I want to show you my town, take that walk I promised you and get to know each other better. And what knowing each other involves."

"The trials and tribulations of a long-distance relationship?"

"It's more than that. You live in a place where you keep adding locks to your doors. In Peace, nobody locks their doors. In fact, we don't have any locks."

"Really? Not any?"

"Bathrooms and bedroom doors. More for privacy."

It sounded safe and wonderful, like a fantasy.

But that's not where she lived. "Mike wants to put a deadbolt on my bathroom door, and not for privacy." She looked out at the view. Millions of people and all of them needing to feel safe in their own homes, using bars, locks, security systems, even guns, whatever it took to make their personal castles secure.

"I remember my great grandmother saying nobody locked their doors when she grew up. They even left the keys in their cars." She glanced at Harry. "But that was then. I don't know if I could live in a house where I couldn't lock the doors. I wouldn't feel safe."

"For me, having to live in a place where people imprison themselves in their own homes would be stifling."

The stirring melody of "The Ride of the Valkyries" played on his phone. "Sorry. Let me check this and then I'll turn it off." From her angle, the screen looked blank. He held it to his ear. "I swear, your brother owes me a new phone. I can't hear a thing."

"If I were you, I'd pick the most expensive one on the market and send him the bill."

He chuckled and pocketed the phone. "Now, where were we?"

"You were being honest. Hold that thought while I make sure mine is off, too." She dug her phone out of her shoulder bag. "I don't want any more interruptions. Not like last night."

"You got a lot of calls last night?"

"Tons of them. All the callers sang, and not very well, either. Worse than a karaoke bar. Hmm. Twelve messages. Strange, there's no return number on any of them, exactly like on my caller ID last night."

Harry became suddenly still. "May I hear one of them?"

"Sure." She played the first message. It contained one of the songs from last night. She noticed his eyes widen in recognition. "You know who that is?"

He nodded grimly. "Play them all, please."

The songs were all the same, except for the last one, which was a duet. The two male voices weren't perky, playful, or cocky like the other times. They were mournful.

"We've called and we've called for Harry
But he never answers his phone
Where, oh where has our mayor gone?
Oh where, oh where can he be?
If he'll just come home/So we're not all alone
Oh where, oh where can he be?"

"By Thor's hammer, it's Rick and Agamemnon!" He clenched his fists. "There's trouble in Peace. We have to go."

"We? Go where?"

"Peace. I just hope it's not too late." He took her hands in his. "Ready?"

"I'm going with you?"

A shadow crossed his face, and his gray eyes hardened to steel. "If there's one thing I know, Joy, it's that I want you with me when I return to Peace."

Her heart warmed, glad he wanted her help. *How can I refuse him at a time like this?*

She nodded. Harry's smile tightened, whether in relief or in apprehension of what they would find, she couldn't say.

With her hands firmly in his, he said, "On a count of three, say purple. One. Two. Three."

"Purple," she said, though her mind questioned why she was saying the color. The other times, the person who had traveled from Peace had said the trigger to initiate the return.

Black sparkles surrounded them and her anxiety grew, for she had noticed when she uttered the trigger, Harry had murmured something under his breath. And it wasn't purple. The movement of his lips hadn't matched hers, which meant he had spoken a different word. A word he didn't want her to hear. Why?

He must have sensed her unease, for he squeezed her hand and said, "You all right?"

"It's so dark." *And I can't see your eyes to figure out what you're not telling me.*

"Hold on. We're almost there."

His voice sounded concerned, and she truly believed he cared about her. And yet a traitorous thought slipped into her mind: too bad Mike failed to plant a bug in his phone.

Similar thoughts continued to plague her, and her misgivings grew. As soon as they exited the mirror, Joy pulled free of his grip and said, "Purple!"

Nothing happened.

Fuming, she backed away from Harry. "I was right. You lied to me, just like you lied in your note. You said you couldn't visit me because the magic was fading, but then later that night you returned my plunger and took all of Felicity's stuff. Then last night you show up at the carnival with no problem at all."

She examined the mirror and noticed her phone number was written in blue this time. "Blue," she said.

Nothing happened.

"Sapphire. Navy. Indigo. Dresden. Cyan. Cerulean."

Nothing happened.

She tried every color of blue that she knew. Still nothing. "What's the trigger? Tell me! I have a right to know!"

Harry raised his hands in an appeasing gesture. "Calm down and I'll explain what's going on."

She'd dealt with enough misbehaving students to recognize the guilt stealing across his face. She planted her feet and crossed her arms. "Explain."

"Look, it's not what you think. The thing is…" He paused and tilted his head. "Do you hear that?" He walked to the lace-curtained doorway leading to the front of the shop. "It's singing. We should find out what's going on."

"Go ahead. I'm going home." Furious at herself for being such a romantic fool, she spun toward the skelter mirror and decided she would find her own way back. The surface shimmered like the last time she had used it. Her hand reached out.

Harry yelled, "No! Don't touch it!"

Like I'm going to listen to you.

Fingers tingling, her hand passed through the surface as if it wasn't there. Harry rushed to stop her, but it was too late. With a yank on her hand, the mirror sucked her in.

Chapter 16

Black. Everything was black.

She couldn't even see her own hand in front of her face.

Fudge! She could be right next to the mirror and wouldn't even know it.

Her hands flailed in all directions, trying to find the mirror, and found nothing. Nothing. Nothing except the overpowering black closing in. Filling her lungs. Suffocating her.

She panted, scared. Tried to catch her breath. And couldn't.

Miracle of miracles, her training kicked in, and the mantra both her self-defense instructor and her teaching mentor believed was essential for survival popped into her head.

Don't panic. Stay in control. Don't panic. Stay in control.

She took a short steadying breath, then a longer steadying breath, and forced herself to calm when what she really wanted to do was scream hysterically.

Concentrate. Evaluate your surroundings.

Think through it.

"All right," she whimpered. "Where am I?"

The sensation of movement she'd experienced during her previous passages was missing, which meant she must be standing still. Or floating. Maybe if she tried making a short circuit, she'd be able to blunder back through the mirror. She pointed herself in what she hoped was the right direction and began walking in a tight spiral. Or was she? In absolute darkness, there was no frame of reference. She couldn't tell whether she was even moving.

Something brushed her bare leg. Something hairy. She jerked back. "Ohmigod! What was that?" She wrung her hands together. "Please, please don't let this place have spiders."

Something scaly grabbed her arm.

She shrieked, shook it off, and ran, believing nothing could grab her if she wasn't standing still.

Something clawed the bottom of her shoe, and she stumbled and fell. Only she didn't hit ground. Her hands reached out. To her horror, there wasn't any ground. No surface at all. She was suspended in midair. Or freefalling. "Aaaah!" she screamed.

Someone poked her in the back, hard. And then something cold slithered across her leg. From all sides, fingers—large, small, rough, smooth, scaly—touched her face and hair and legs and arms, groping and grabbing. Scratching.

In a panic, she resorted to flight *and* fight. She whacked, slapped, punched, and elbowed her way through the flurry of grasping hands until she broke free and ran. Ran with all her might.

From far away, someone called her name.

She stopped. "Harry?"

"Joy! Follow the sound of my voice! Hurry before it's too late!"

Too late?

"I'm coming!" she answered. Immediately, something latched onto her jacket. What felt like claws combed through her hair. Harry called her name, his voice a beacon of hope. In a flurry of movement, she disentangled herself from whatever was rummaging in her hair, then ripped her jacket free from whoever was holding it. She raced in the direction of Harry's voice.

"Joy! Don't say a word! Sound attracts them like moths to a flame! Keep quiet and move toward my voice! Whatever you do, don't stop!"

But that's exactly what she did do, stop, for she could swear his last sentence had come from below. Harry kept talking, and it confirmed her worst fears. His voice was coming from underneath her! How was that possible?

He called her name again. He sounded further away than before!

How could that be? She wasn't moving.

Unless… There must be eddies to the blackness. She must be caught in a riptide like the treacherous currents along the Jersey shore. If the darkness was akin to water, maybe she could use that to her advantage.

"Joy!" His voice barely reached her.

She dove in his direction, kicking her feet, swimming toward him.

"Joy! Hurry!"

His voice was closer and straight ahead. Something brushed her leg, but she didn't dare shrink back. In the blackness, any jerk, a slight turn, might cause her to veer away.

But then she bumped into something soft and squishy, slimy, and reeking of vomited butterscotch. Yuk! Her stomach threatened to heave. There was no helping it; she had to back away. With her hands, she wiped the gunk off her face and flung it into the darkness.

Uncertain which direction to go, she waited for Harry's voice to show her the way. A tentacle wrapped around her ankle. At the same time, she heard Harry's voice from straight above. Her heart leapt. He sounded so close!

No slimy octopus is going to stop me! She dug her nails into the tentacle and squeezed. It squealed and released her. She thrust herself overhead in the direction of Harry's voice and swam madly, reaching out with her hands until she barreled into a warm, firm body.

"Joy?"

"Harry!" Burying her face in his chest, she wrapped her arms around him and held on tight.

"Hold on. I've got to pull us back through."

She felt his muscles strain, his arms climb. A cloth brushed her face, the rope Harry was using to draw them out of the blackness.

Something grabbed her foot. She tried to shake it off, but it held on tight. With her other foot, she kicked it. It yelped and let go, but then something snagged the hem of her dress.

In a flash of light, they were back through the mirror. Joy tumbled to the floor on top of Harry, and they smiled at each other in relief. But then his gaze shifted to her legs. His eyes widened. She looked. Hanging onto her skirt was the ugliest, foulest smelling creature she'd ever seen. Eight inches of moldy green, with needlelike teeth jutting out of its mouth.

She squealed. "Eww!"

The creature's beady yellow eyes leered at her. It peeked under her skirt and grinned. Shocked, repulsed, she yanked her skirt away and tucked it around her legs.

The lecherous creature puckered its drooling mouth and blew her a kiss.

"Catch it!" Harry yelled.

"Not on your life."

"Don't let it get away!" He grabbed for it but missed. The noxious beast popped onto its three-toed feet and dashed to the front of the store. The door chimes signaled its escape.

"What was that?" she asked.

"A skratta. A goblin." He reached down and helped her up. "Probably stuck in the Stygian Gap for ages, driven insane by the constant darkness. Now it's loose in my town. Thanks to you." From a nearby table leg, he untied what looked like the lace curtain from the doorway. It was knotted to scarves, skirts and whatever else he had found to create a lifeline. He pulled the rest of the makeshift rope out of the mirror and piled it on a table.

He sounded angry. Looked angry, too. She gasped. And torn. His jacket was in shreds, his shirt slashed. One pants leg was ripped, his leg bloody. There were red scratches on his arms and hands and a bleeding gash on his cheek.

"You're hurt!"

"Me? Look at you!" Ignoring his own wounds, he inspected a

cut on her hand. The sleeves of her jacket were ripped in two places, and there was a long tear in her skirt, but it was minor compared with how bad Harry looked.

"It's nothing," she told him. But he was past listening. Grabbing her by the waist, he sat her on a table and ordered her to stay, then hurried to a cabinet loaded with medical supplies. Sirena must have a lot of accidents.

With tender care, he used a cleansing wipe on her hand, then opened a small porcelain jar and dabbed the cut with a shiny ointment smelling of cinnamon and lemon, a curious substance that made her skin tickle for a few seconds. She laughed. She couldn't help it.

"They say laughter is the best medicine," he said with a knowing smile. "It'll speed the healing."

"Someone figured out how to bottle laughter?"

Harry nodded. He saw a scratch on her calf and moved to take care of it, but she brushed his hand away. "It's fine." She scooted off the table. "Now sit so I can tend to you." With a nudge that became a push when he balked, she shoved him into a nearby chair. She started taking off his jacket when her fingers stilled. "Harry! What happened? You're scratched all over."

He shrugged dismissively, acting macho cool, the same false bravado Mike used when he came home injured. But the way he flinched when she carefully removed his torn shirt and cleaned his wounds indicated the magnitude of the pain he hid.

"In the Stygian Gap," he said, laughing when she applied the tingling ointment, then wincing when she applied two butterfly bandages to the cut on his cheek, "the only signposts are sounds. Those stuck in the Gap wait for any noise made by passing travelers, then zero in and latch on to get out, much like the skratta did."

"That's why you told me to be quiet. So I wouldn't attract them." She covered her mouth with a hand, aghast at what he had done to save her. "You were holding our only lifeline with no way to defend yourself, yet you kept saying my name over and over. Oh, Harry, I should have listened to you. I'm so sorry." Careful not to touch his injuries, she hugged him, her heart aching in misery. He'd gotten hurt for her. Tears of guilt filled her eyes.

"It's all right," Harry said.

"Is that why you told me to follow your voice before it was too late?"

"Not exactly. If they realize you're stuck like they are, you're no longer a ticket out. You're prey. Even those in the Gap get hungry."

She shuddered at the thought. "I'm sorry. I didn't mean for any of this to happen. I had no idea the mirror would suck me in. I was just so angry with you." She pulled back and wiped her eyes. "This is all your fault, you know."

"Mine? You're the one who entered the mirror when I told you not to."

"Yeah, well, how could I believe you? You lied to me. First your note about the magic running out, and now the trigger."

His jaw firmed, and the gray in his eyes took on the hardness of flint. "Let's get something straight. What I said in the note was correct: the magic *was* fading. When I returned your plunger, I barely made it back. Yesterday the council allowed me to use a new spell—fresh magic—to visit you."

"All right, I'll give you that. But you did lie about the trigger."

"I've never lied to you."

"Purple is not the trigger."

"I never said it was."

She groaned and fisted her hands. "But you led me to believe it was. You had me say purple while you whispered the real trigger. You're a real bastard, Harradorn Lawson."

"But a lovable bastard." He wiggled his eyebrows.

He was also half-naked, lean, and sexy, but that didn't let him off the hook. "A lie of omission is still a lie."

"Huh. You should talk. Every time you get mad at me, you

leave. If I had told you the trigger, you'd be back home."

"If you had told me the trigger, I wouldn't have gotten angry at you and wanted to leave."

"The point is, this is the second time you've used the mirror to avoid a confrontation. It's cowardly."

"Yeah, well, maybe you're right about that. Maybe," she repeated, countering the smug look on his face. "But that doesn't make you any less guilty for deceiving me. Admit it: the real reason you didn't tell me the trigger is because you didn't want me to leave without your permission."

He raised a finger for emphasis. "Without the *council's* permission. Being mayor, I was ordered to bring you back to Peace to provide assurances you'd keep our town a secret. But even if they hadn't, I would have done it anyway. Because I like you. And I really do want to show you my town." His gaze softened; his voice gentled. "As mayor, I'm always asked out. But you… you've never treated me anything more than as a man, and I like that." He leaned close. "What do I have to do to convince you how special you are?"

His gaze was a caress, seductive and irresistible. Don't give in, she ordered herself. Don't think about the musky scent of his warmth or the muscled bare skin waiting to be touched. For heaven's sake, don't start imagining what he would feel like lying next to you, completely naked.

Her heart pounded in breathless expectation. "Tell me the trigger."

"Tell me the code to your garage door. You only alluded to it in my presence: your brother's year of birth. If you don't trust me, why should I trust you?"

And here she had accused him of keeping secrets. Ashamed, her cheeks burned.

"Trust is a two-way street," he added.

"Then it seems we're at an impasse."

"For now. But I have high hopes."

A truce of silence descended on them and Joy finished treating his wounds. While she applied a final, thin layer of salve to a scratch on his neck, she asked, "If going to the outside is such a security risk, why did you answer my call for help?"

At first, he looked like he wasn't going to answer. But then he said, "Since honesty is the only way to restore your trust…, I'm cursed. I have to help all damsels in distress."

"Cursed?"

"The last mayor of Peace was a major sore loser. He blamed the women in town for losing the election, claiming they chose me for my good looks. To get even, he secretly had a spell put on the medallion of office." He fingered the large gold pendant hanging from his neck. "As soon as I put it on, a curse took hold. A Damsel In Distress curse. Whenever a female asks for help, I have to answer the call."

"So the first time we met, your heroic rescue was nothing more than being forced to answer my call for help?"

He nodded.

"What if you had refused?"

"Once activated, the curse pumps adrenaline into my system. The level stays manageable if I try to help. If I refuse or drag my feet, I start burning up with unused energy—the curse's way of forcing me to take action. According to Sirena's books, if I fail to respond in a timely manner, my body could literary burn itself up and I die."

"How horrible. Isn't there some way to remove the curse?"

He glanced down at the medallion. "Zach tried, but only the spellcaster knows how, and the ex-mayor disappeared before I could force him to reveal who that is. There's an arrest warrant out for both, but that doesn't do me any good unless they're found."

"Wow. Politics here can be dangerous." Then something occurred to her, and she smiled slyly. "So, if I ask you to help me get home, you have to do it?"

He playfully tapped her nose. "Only if you're in distress.

Wanting to get home doesn't qualify. Caught in the Gap, yelling for help, does."

She stared at him in sudden realization. "The curse forced you to stay and be injured until you rescued me. Ohmigod! Suppose I had never found my way to you?"

"I would have died trying, unless you died first, which would release me."

"So the curse forces you to be a hero."

"In your case, no." He took her hand in his. "From outside the mirror, I couldn't hear your cry for help. It was my decision to go in after you, not the curse. If anything, the curse helped me hold on to the lifeline and ignore the attacks while waiting for you to reach me."

He lifted her hand and kissed it. His mouth lingered, heating her skin. He looked at her, asking for something she wasn't sure she should give. It'd be so easy to give in and lose herself to the growing hunger so plain on his face.

But he didn't trust her, not enough to tell her the trigger. She pulled her hand out of his. "Now what?"

"Now we find out why people are singing outside." He tossed his shredded jacket and shirt in the trash, then rummaged through a supply closet and pulled out a blowsy white shirt, much like the one she had seen his brother wearing. Loose and soft, it wouldn't irritate his wounds. He slipped it on. The V-neck opening plunged just shy of his waist. The gold medallion rested appealingly on his chest.

They sure don't have mayors like this in my world, she thought, her admiration based not only on how he looked but his determination to help his people. Commitment to a cause, to a people, his town, was sexy. So was the pair of black silk pants he quickly exchanged for the torn pair he had on.

He proceeded to enter the shop but stopped in the doorway. "Are you coming?"

"In a minute. I want to freshen up a bit."

He glanced at the shimmering skelter mirror. A wave of apprehension crossed his face.

"Don't worry. I won't go anywhere near it. I promise."

"You're one in a million, Joy. Don't let what Jeff did ruin what we might have. You may not trust me, but from this moment on I'm going to trust you to keep your word." With that, he left. She heard the chime on the front door of the shop when it opened and closed.

He was putting it all on her. Whatever might happen to their relationship, it was in her hands now. Her stomach was in knots, her mind confused. Liking a guy shouldn't be this hard. It should be slow and easy, a long get-to-know-each-other period of weeks or months. With Harry, she had the feeling they were dating in overdrive, condensing everything into bursts of intense moments.

A laugh stuck in her throat. Considering how they first met, how could their relationship be anything else?

On a worktable sat several jars labeled with colors, some in hues of blue. The urge to discover if one was the trigger was huge. Yet if one worked, it'd prove Harry right: she was a coward. More than that, the trust he'd professed for her would be shattered by her own doing.

Fudge!

Leaving temptation behind, she entered the shop. Through the windows, she saw Harry on the street, surrounded by at least forty people singing and dancing. By the frustration building on everyone's face, no one was communicating well. Harry grabbed one man and tried to make him stand still and talk, but the man kept singing and dancing with the others.

She exited the shop and made her way through the dancers. She had to hop, skip, sashay, and slide through various dance routines until she made it to his side. "What's going on?" she asked.

"From what I can gather, Aesa used the wizard's petal." He gave Joy a brief summary of what had happened after the wizard duel and what a wizard's petal can do.

"She used it while you were gone to see me?"

Harry nodded, so did all the people dancing in unison around them. "I'm not sure how to fix this. It might help if we knew exactly what she wished for."

They heard a shout. Harry's pirate brother, Rick, came leaping and spinning down the street, accompanied by a troupe of pirate dancers who appeared to be reenacting a scene from *The Pirates of Penzance*. Rick tried talking to Harry by singing, but the bothersome rhymes made him difficult to understand.

It also didn't help that Rick's feet seemed cursed to keep dancing. Harry tried to match his steps so they could converse, but the whole situation was too awkward to be helpful. It seemed hopeless.

Joy had an idea. She began a waltz. "Rick!"

The pirate's blue eyes sparked in recognition. He smiled and slowed his steps. By the time he reached her, he was doing the same waltz. He took her in his arms.

"I'll be back," she told Harry, and was surprised to see him frown when Rick waltzed her away.

Chapter 17

In the spotlight of a bright morning sun, Joy waltzed down the street with a pirate in her arms. They were soon followed by other waltzing couples. Everyone looked tired yet all had forced smiles.

"How long has everyone been dancing and singing?" she asked Rick.

He sang:

> "I must have danced all night
> And I've danced all day
> But with you I could dance some more."

"All night and morning." She shook her head, astonished.

They passed others doing everything from a two-step to a polka. Even the fairies flying in the air danced: looping and twirling, changing partners and singing, performing their own version of *Peter Pan*.

If the circumstances weren't so dire, she might have been enjoying herself. She loved musicals. To actually be part of one in real life with a handsome pirate as a dance partner was like a dream come true, fun because she could stop whenever she wanted. For Rick, it must be a neverending nightmare.

Rounding a corner, they came upon a dancing elderly couple who stumbled and fell. Other dancers helped them to their feet. The woman's knees were bleeding, the man's trousers torn, and yet with smiles on their faces they returned to dancing.

The gravity of the situation chilled her to the bone. A Danse Macabre had taken hold of the town. If they didn't find a way to stop it, people might die from exhaustion.

"Harry thinks it might help if we knew the wish Aesa made," she said.

Rick shrugged, plainly dubious it would remedy the problem.

"Okay. Maybe *where* Aesa made her wish will help us figure out *what* she wished."

Rick grinned. He twirled her around a corner to dance up another street. They passed a group of teenagers doing a hip-hop dance version of *Grease* and waltzed to the park. In the bandshell, people were performing *La La Land.* Joy noticed all the chairs had been pushed aside or overturned. Whatever had happened last night, happened suddenly.

"Aesa was here? On stage?" Rick shook his head; they continued to dance. "All right then. She was in the audience, watching something on stage?" He nodded.

By now, Harry had caught up to them, along with the prancing troupe of pirates and anyone else who had noticed their mayor along the way. Clearly, everyone hoped he would save them. The entire park became filled with dancers singing for help, each group doing a different play. *Hello Dolly* was converted to Hello Harry. *Jesus Christ Superstar* became Harry Lawson Supermayor. *Cats'* "Memory" was turned into a haunting rendition called Harry. The discordant singing frayed her nerves.

She noticed Harry flinch repeatedly. His hands fisted, muscles tightened, lips thinned as if in pain. The curse! All the singing women were asking him for help. If he didn't find a way, the curse would kill him.

She quickly asked Rick, "What was Aesa watching on stage?"

Rick grimaced and rolled his eyes. Then he smiled, flung out his arms, slowly twirled, and began singing the opening song of *The Sound of Music.* So did everyone else, young and old. The entire park.

She and Harry stared in amazement at all the Julie Andrews copycats.

"How old is Aesa?" she asked Harry.

"Eight. "Why?"

"Most girls love musicals. I wouldn't be surprised if she got caught up in *The Sound of Music* and accidentally wished life was like a musical."

"It certainly would explain what's going on."

"Harry!"

In tandem, Joy and Harry turned to the woman who had yelled his name—and without a song in her voice. Walking, not dancing, a stunning woman with perfectly coiffed red hair entered the park from the east, outfitted in a gray designer silk suit and platinum and gold jewelry. Even in stilettos, she strutted easily across the grass.

"Kathy!" Harry said in surprise. "When did you get to town?"

"About two hours ago. It's like this all over. Even Prosperity. Best stay away from the elven subdivision. Half are doing *Flower Drum Song*, the other half *Spamalot*. I barely avoided a band of dwarfs doing a dreadful version of *The Wizard of Oz*. They wanted to make me Dorothy. What the Hel's going on?"

Harry quickly explained about Aesa and the wizard's petal. "Have you seen Lance?"

"He's home performing *West Side Story* with our servants. Doing all the major roles, I might add. The bit with Maria in front of the mirror, saying how great he looked, was too much, so I came searching for you."

Kathy edged toward Harry. The unmistakable gleam of interest in her smoky green eyes seemed lost on him, and yet his smile indicated he enjoyed her presence. Old girlfriend or the town's femme fatale? When the woman placed a proprietary hand on his arm, Joy instantly disliked her.

"Dressing more like Rick, I see." Kathy surveyed his tight silk pants and low-cut shirt. "Always knew you had a pirate in you. But what happened?" Her fingers stroked the cut on his cheek. With a foxy smile, she arched one brow. "After all these years, you finally like it rough. Told you you would."

Harry's face darkened. Embarrassed, annoyed, or both, he glanced sideways at Joy and said, "A little accident with the skelter mirror. I just returned from visiting Joy." He reached for Joy's hand and entwined his fingers with hers. At his touch, a frisson of heat sped through her.

The gesture wasn't lost on Kathy. Her teasing smile drooped for a split second before returning to its dazzling breadth with a mouth full of too-white teeth. Had to be veneers, Joy thought, then scolded herself for being so catty. It wasn't like her.

Harry made the introductions. "Joy, this is Kathy Warbird, a childhood friend of mine. Kathy, Joy Flint. My, uh,—"

"Prisoner," Joy cut in, hoping to startle the woman, and wasn't disappointed when Kathy shot Harry a questioning look.

"A prisoner of love," he promptly added. He subtly tugged Joy's hand, indicating she was to behave herself. "Joy is my fiancée." He turned to Joy, a glint of warning in his smile.

Joy almost choked. *Fiancée?* She tried to untangle her fingers from his, but he refused to let go. If anything, his grip tightened. He glanced at Kathy. Joy followed his lead and saw Kathy's aristocratic facade crack.

With frost in her voice, Kathy said, "Since when did your tastes run to *outsiders?*"

Kathy didn't wait for an answer. Instead, she assessed Joy with a cool once-over, and snickered at her orange hair. "Very gauche, my dear. And I see five-dollar sandals are still available in the outside world. By the way, you have slime on your dress."

Joy's face burned with indignation. She was about to tell Kathy that being a value shopper had its rewards when Kathy dismissed her with a snobbish turn of her shoulders and faced only Harry. With one hand on a hip, she gestured at all the singers and dancers. "So, mayor, what are you going to do about our town becoming Bollywood?"

"I've never heard of anyone being able to undo a petal's wish."

"Any chance of recalling Zach?"

"Already tried. He's traveling by magic, and since magic blocks manmade signals I can't get through."

"What about contacting a wizard in another town, have him get in touch with Zach?"

"Too risky. Zach's tower is damaged. If a rogue wizard finds out what FearfulFran did, Zach might be considered weak, vulnerable, and our town ripe for another wizard to move in and take over."

Kathy rested a hand on Harry's shoulder. Joy stiffened, remembering all the times Jeff had done the same. Not out of friendship, she now realized, but a patronizing gesture of being superior.

"Don't get me wrong," Kathy said. "Zach's a luv. But maybe he *has* grown weak. Wizards are supposed to protect their towns. From the look of things, Zach's been slacking off."

"He was in the midst of a wizard duel," Harry countered. His grip on Joy's hand loosened and she slipped away, giving the two some space. "No one could have foreseen FearfulFran's treachery. I was there. I saw it. There wasn't any warning."

"Of course not. What I'm saying is: if Zach had a better reputation, say for being a mean fighter or a sore loser, no one would dare duel him. None of this would be happening."

Harry fiercely shook his head. "Zach's always done his best. No defense is foolproof. If it was, our ancestors would never have been forced to cross the seas and establish this town."

"Still, if he doesn't find FearfulFran soon and repair his tower, the point will be moot." Kathy patted his shoulder and removed her hand. "By then another wizard, maybe a lot of wizards, may lay claim to us. We are a prosperous town."

"And peaceful."

"That too might change."

The quarrel continued. It was like watching two old lovers fight, and it solidified Joy's suspicion that they were more than childhood friends.

Oh, great. Ex-lover. New lover—prisoner—fiancée. The town a menagerie of neverending musicals. What else could go wrong?

The ground shook. Leaves on the trees jiggled. Dancers and singers gaped at something behind Joy—at something really tall behind her. She froze in fear. From the terrified looks on their faces, she expected the worst. Everyone sang "Help" from the Beatles' movie. Harry repeatedly flinched while the curse responded to their pleas. The townspeople scattered. Joy wanted to run, too, but she remembered Harry's criticism and stayed put.

I am not a coward. I will not run away.

The tremors grew closer.

She gulped. *I am not a coward. I will not run away.*

Harry looked up. His mouth opened. His eyes went wide. Kathy, on the other hand, backed up in fear.

Joy held her breath. *Oh god, I am a coward. But I will not run away.*

From behind her, a man bellowed a horrible rendition of "Just In Time" from *The Bells Are Ringing*. The guy must be using a bullhorn, Joy thought. It drowned out all the other singers. Cringing, she covered her ears and turned to see who was singing.

Stomping toward them in a shuffling hop step was a twelve-foot tall giant with one huge hazel eye in the middle of his forehead. She gasped and backed into Harry, who grabbed her and held on tight.

Ohmigosh! An honest to goodness Cyclops is dancing right in front of me. In a great looking suit no less! And he's singing, badly.

> "Just in time/ The mayor came just in time
> Before you came my time/ And hopes were low.
> The town was lost/ The losing dice were tossed
> The council all were crossed/ I had to go.
> Now you're here/ And now I know we'll all be fine
> No more doubt and fear/ You'll find a way.
> 'Cause you came just in time

The Mayor came just in time
To save our town/ This lovely day."

In disbelief, Harradorn stared at Agamemnon while he danced around them. His huge feet flattened the grass; after three circuits, a rut was already forming. One false move and the towering Cyclops would crush anyone nearby. The possibility increased as many joined the singing giant and sang the lyrics over and over again.

It was maddening.

With his arms wrapped protectively around Joy, Harradorn called over to Rick, who was singing along with everyone else. "Rick, clear the area! Keep to the song but do a different dance!"

"A line dance," Joy suggested while keeping a nervous eye on Agamemnon.

"Great idea. A line dance, Rick! Go out on the street and circle the park!"

Rick pleated his brow in concentration. Sweat broke out on his forehead, but eventually he forced his feet to change rhythm. Within minutes, he had everyone including Agamemnon doing a line dance around the park. The place emptied. Harradorn righted three chairs near the bandshell and motioned for Joy and Kathy to join him.

They sat, and Joy kept track of the Cyclops. "Who is that?" she asked. "I think I recognize his voice. He kept calling and singing all night."

"That's Agamemnon, my assistant. He's usually a lot more graceful with his words, and his feet."

"Poor guy. Everyone must be exhausted by now. Aren't there any musicals where people sleep?"

"*Mary Poppins* has a song," Kathy said. "Ironically, it's called 'Stay Awake.'"

"Good. Let's try an experiment." He pointed to several children line dancing between their parents. "There's the Anderssons. Get them to follow you onto a grassy area of the park, maybe with a 'Ring Around the Rosie' hand-hold. When they *all fall down*, switch to 'Stay Awake' and see what happens."

Kathy rose to her feet with sinuous grace and smoothed imaginary wrinkles from her clothes. "It's worth a try," she said, though she sounded skeptical.

They watched her approach the line-dancing family. "I hope it works," Joy said.

"I fear it's only a stopgap measure. After they wake up, they'll start singing and dancing again." Out the corner of his eye, he saw Joy surreptitiously pick slime from her skirt. He frowned in sympathy. She wasn't the first woman to feel the sting of Kathy's hauteur, nor would she be the last. *Welcome to the Warbirds of Peace.* "I have to find a way to break the wish."

"What if you can't? The curse will kill you, too."

He shook his head. "I'm all right for now. When everyone asked for help to save them from Agamemnon, it cancelled the initial calls for help from Aesa's wish. When Agamemnon started line-dancing around the park, the curse deactivated. I'm fine until the next call for help."

He dreaded when that might take effect, but it didn't lessen his need to rescue his town. "We have to undo Aesa's wish."

"Is that possible?"

"I don't know. But she might." He inclined his head to Sirena. Always one to march to the beat of her own drum, she ignored the line dancers and entered the park, clad in an array of scarves. With hair loose and wild, she performed a seductive dance from *The Bolero*. Many of the male line dancers broke off to follow her.

"Sirena," Joy said.

He noticed her smile of recognition. "How do you know who she is?"

Joy gulped. "She was in the Mayor's Hall, asleep on the floor during my first visit. Remember?"

"Yes, but I never told you her name. Exactly how many times

have you been to Peace?" It would explain the unaccountable drain of magic from the skelter mirror when he visited Joy's bedroom, and the continued rapid growth of trees in front of Sirena's store.

Joy dragged a hand through her bright orange hair, clearly nervous. But when she raised her gaze to him, her eyes flashed. "You said trust was a two-way street. Since when did we become engaged? I didn't even know we were dating."

"I needed to keep Kathy off balance and her hands off me."

"Why?"

"Because she lied. She didn't get here two hours ago. She's been here all night."

"How do you know?"

"She's wearing silk. She only wears linen when she travels."

"Maybe she changed clothes."

"In two hours without servants." He shook his head. "Not likely. Besides, the sheriff has standing orders to shut down all the portals if the town becomes defenseless. Even dancing, he'd have them closed by midnight. He knows if word got out about what's going on here, thieves would strip the place clean while everyone's off dancing and singing."

"Huh. So, that's how the tourists get here, portals. From other towns like this?"

He nodded. "The skelter mirror is currently assigned to me. The only other way in is by car, and Kathy never drives. Too slow. Too boring."

"Sounds like you know her very well."

"As well as you know my brother by kissing him."

She slanted him a look. "Is that a hint of jealousy from my fiancé?"

"No more than the scowl on your face when Kathy touched me."

"Oh."

Their eyes met, and held. There was something in Joy's gaze that hadn't been there before. It sucked him in much like the skelter mirror, and wouldn't let go. To be honest, he could have picked a dozen scenarios to throw Kathy off, none having to do with marriage. And he realized that when he thought of having children with Kathy, he'd always pictured whiney little Kathy's running amok. But when he thought of children with Joy, he pictured little Joys, all of them smiling and laughing, with different colored hair: purple, yellow, orange, blue.

He couldn't have picked a worst time to get interested in a woman. "I don't even know the true color of your hair."

Her laugh was almost fairy-like in its carefree tone. It matched her hair perfectly. With a mischievous smile on her face, she leaned close and whispered, "There's one way to find out."

The ground trembled. Agamemnon danced by on the street, shaking them apart. "Always bad timing with us," Harradorn said.

"Look!" Joy pointed to where the Anderssons slept on the grass. "It worked." Already Kathy was getting another group to "Ring Around the Rosie" with her.

"That's one problem solved. I'll go talk with Sirena." His scantily-clad sister now had several partners, not all of them men.

"I bet Sirena has never worn linen."

He chuckled. "Sometimes I wish she would."

He cut in and danced Sirena away from her current partner and asked if anyone had ever reversed a wizard's petal wish. She shrugged and shook her head, not knowing or not caring. Behind all the makeup, she was practically asleep on her feet.

"I'll figure it out," he told her. Somehow, he would. He lifted one of her hands. "Do you mind if I borrow a ring?" Puzzlement creased her brow and he added, "It's a long story. I'll explain later." He removed one of her many rings and was about to rejoin Joy when Sirena came to an abrupt stop. Her entire demeanor changed. She was now tall and primly. With hands folded demurely at her waist, she sang in a falsetto voice.

Joy came up beside Harry. "What's she singing? It sounds familiar."

"It's 'Marian The Librarian' from *The Music Man*." He turned to Joy. "Books. She's telling us there may be something about reversing the spell in the library. Or not," Harry added when Sirena suddenly sang one verse louder than the others, something about whispering the news to Sirena—Mistress Librarian.

He grinned in understanding. "Not the town's library. Hers. Over the years, she's accumulated a lot of books about magic, potions, and alchemy. I bet she's trying to say the answer may be in her collection."

With a nod of approval, Sirena continued singing, adding a simple dance. Many of the men lost interest and rejoined the line dancers circling the park. Most of the women stayed and imitated Sirena.

A green fairy suddenly flew in front of Harry and sang "It's Not Easy Being Green."

"Gloris!" Harry stared at the pitiful fairy whose tears were also green. "Don't cry. I'll fix the color, I promise, soon as I figure out how to stop Aesa's wish."

The fairy didn't look convinced. Still singing her sad song, she disappeared among the trees.

Joy asked, "What was that all about?"

"Gloris used to be red. Sirena was supposed to make her brown in exchange for surrendering a wizard's petal. Obviously, it didn't work."

"I'm guessing Sirena used a green liquid to attempt the color change?"

"How did you know?"

"I'm a teacher. Even my students know the difference between mixing colors and dyeing." She fingered her orange hair for emphasis. "I assume your sister never took basic chemistry in high school."

"Towns like ours have a high drop-out rate. Homemade crafts and magic take precedence."

"Then I suggest you get a new superintendent of public

instruction."

"Would you like the job?"

The offer took her by surprise. Just then, Kathy yelled from the other side of the park. With both hands, she gestured at the people lying on the grass. The Anderssons were awake and rising to their feet. Harry motioned Kathy to join them and told her about the books.

"I'll help," Kathy said, "though I'm not sure I'll understand half of what we'll be reading. I've never been much into magic." She glanced at Joy, clearly questioning whether an outsider could comprehend any of it.

So this is how it feels to be a special ed student.

To prove herself to Harry, she smiled confidently and said, "Don't worry about me. I've read all the Harry Potter books. Even *The Tales of Beedle the Bard.*"

Kathy and Harry exchanged amused looks.

Great. When it comes to magic, they probably consider Harry Potter a preschooler.

"You two go on ahead," Joy said. "I have something to ask Sirena."

Harry glanced from her to his sister. Suspicion clouded his face, like when he had asked how many times she had visited Peace. Very little got by the mayor.

They were still keeping secrets from each other, and this would be one more.

Harry moved close. Breathless anticipation raced through her. He took her left hand and snugged it between their chests. Hidden from Kathy, he slipped a ring onto her finger. Joy looked down at it. Two silver dragons encircled a blue sapphire, the gem a tiny version of the larger one in Harry's medallion. Already she loved it. He raised her hand and kissed the ring, then kissed her, sending a delicious tremor through her as if he really had proposed.

Kathy coughed, loudly.

Harry ignored her and kissed Joy once more. He whispered, "I still want to know what my kisses tell you about me." Then he winked and added, "I hope you're taking notes."

He and Kathy left in the direction of Sirena's shop, pausing to talk to Rick while he line-danced by them, probably telling him not to follow, since Rick kept the dancers circling the park.

By now Sirena was back to dancing the bolero, not the easiest dance for extracting information. In memory of their last meeting, Joy sang the song from *Sleeping Beauty* about walking with someone in a dream.

Sirena noted the silver ring on Joy's finger and grinned. Instantly she slowed her steps and hummed the song while Joy talked.

"I understand my phone number on the skelter mirror sends Harry to me, to my phone. But how does it work if I have the phone with me? Where will it take me? Or won't it take me anywhere because my phone is already here?"

Sirena scrunched her beautiful brow in thought. She hummed, her hands fluttering, mimicking her mind at work. Then she sang:

> "When you wish upon black glass,
> Makes no difference where you're last,
> When *you* wish upon black glass,
> Your dreams come true."

"Really?" Joy said. "Are you sure?"

Sirena shrugged and returned to singing, "I know you, I walked with you once upon a dream."

Joy watched her dance away, uncertain whether Sirena's info was based on fact or wishful thinking. After all, Sirena had thoroughly goofed up her attempt to change the red fairy brown.

Full of misgivings, Joy headed to the store. She contemplated the ring on her finger. Engaged—but not really—to a fascinating, exasperating man whom she didn't trust but who claimed to trust her. Yet not enough to tell her the trigger.

She had the sudden urge to dye her hair green.

Joy stopped in her tracks. *Where did that come from? And why now?*

Had Harry been right about her running away? It definitely was a bitter pill to swallow, and it didn't go down easily. Changing hair color was a form of running away from herself. A clever distraction, especially the latest wild colors, which kept her so busy looking in the mirror at her hair that she failed to take a good, long look into her own eyes and see the truth. The truth even Mike had tried to make her see.

The challenges of being in charge of a classroom had its ups and downs, sort of a microcosm of what Harry had to deal with as mayor of Peace. Of course, in her case she didn't have to contend with errant magic. And yet what she was going through with Jeff and the principals, having to drastically alter her teaching style and put up with students who didn't want to learn and parents who never bothered to attend parent-teacher conferences, all created a form of errant magic in her psyche.

It was a wonder she hadn't shaved off all her hair and gotten a tattoo.

Near Sirena's shop she heard a painful cry. Remembering the elderly couple who'd fallen, she traced the sound down an arched alleyway to an outdoor café. Sweetheart Café, a sign said. Beyond the umbrella-topped tables, she discovered a middle-aged woman swaying back and forth, her gaze fixed on one of several hanging pots overflowing with pink flowers. Her black hair was long and ragged, and her thin maroon robes hung on her gaunt frame like clothes on a hanger. Amidst sobs, she sang a perverted variation of a song from *Wicked*:

> "No good deed goes unpunished
> That's my lot in life
> The road of good intentions
> Always leads to strife."

Joy said, "Excuse me, do you need help? Are you hurt"

Startled, the woman spun toward her. Joy stepped back in shock. The woman's nails were broken and bleeding. Behind her, bloody fingerprints streaked the white wall of the café and marked where the woman had tried to jump or scratch her way up to the planter. Chairs were overturned. Like the rest of the town, dancing made even the simple task of standing on a chair difficult to accomplish.

"I'll get some bandages for your fingers," Joy told her. Sirena's workshop had plenty.

The woman moved fast. She twirled around Joy, blocking her exit.

Joy's skin prickled in warning, exactly like when she spots a spider. It didn't help that the woman had an ivy tattoo at her throat with tendrils climbing up her neck, along with a macabre harlequin mask on her left cheek. She gulped. Was that a tattoo of a scorpion circling her left eye?

Joy backed away, putting space between her and the creepy woman, who sang:

"Please help me, you pretty little thing
A favor, please, such a very small thing
From up above, if you will bring
From the pinks, a little white thing."

The bloody fingers pointed to the pink blossoms.

The woman must be crazed with exhaustion, Joy thought, yet she decided to play along if only to calm her. She scanned the flowers. To her surprise, she spied a thin white object among the blossoms. "There's something there."

The woman shrieked with laughter and rushed forward.

Joy raised a hand and stared her down. "Stay back or I won't get it."

The pathetic woman grimaced and grumbled, but she moved away swaying and singing her somber song, "No good deed goes unpunished…"

Directly under the hanging plant, Joy placed a chair, then looked for something to extend her reach. A long forked stick on the ground seemed perfect. She picked it up and got jabbed by thorns. "Ow!" She threw the stick away. Licking blood off her finger, she searched for an alternative. One of the umbrellas seemed the best bet.

She yanked one from a table and stood on the chair. Several jabs and a few nudges later, a single white petal fell, slowly drifting toward the crazy woman's out-stretched hands.

Chapter 18

No good deed goes unpunished, Joy thought while the flower petal floated toward the woman's bleeding fingers. She noticed yet another tattoo, a blue-white flame on the back of her right hand.

The hag reached for the petal and cackled with glee.

> "Sentimental I am, I am a fool
> As everyone knows, life can be cruel
> A token of love, the wind took on high
> A token of love among pinks on high."

The woman did a jig, bobbing happily while the petal got closer. Like everyone else in town, she couldn't help but keep dancing, which provided the split-second Joy needed to snatch the petal away.

Joy held it to her nose. The scent was unmistakable. A rose petal.

"You may be a fool," she said, "but I'm not. You're the only one in town who's not on the street singing and dancing with a group. Instead, you're hiding and obsessed with finding a petal. I may be the new kid on the block, but I'm laying odds you're FearfulFran. The one who attacked Zach."

The woman shrieked and performed a frenzied pirouette of rage. When she came out of the turn, she leapt at Joy. Bleeding fingers lashed. Joy jumped back but not fast enough. Broken fingernails raked her hand. They seized her thumb and wrenched it back. The sudden, excruciating pain automatically opened Joy's hand. FearfulFran stole the petal.

"No!" Joy shouted.

The woman gripped the petal in her blood-stained hand, a maniacal grin of triumph on her face. Then her mouth opened wide in an icy scream. Her body convulsed, her limbs twisted. With what looked like a break-dance drop, she fell on her back and did a spin. Her hands splayed open. The petal was gone.

Joy's palm tingled like a Fourth of July sparkler and the petal appeared in it, white and clean, not a trace of the woman's blood on it. How about that. Not only did the wizard's petal have its own anti-theft magic, it also had a cleaning spell.

FearfulFran breakdanced in agony on the ground. The woman had to have known what would happen if she tried to steal the petal. After all, she'd attacked Zach's tower to get one. What on earth could have motivated her to take such a painful risk?

Must be one hell of a wish.

Then it hit her: she was dealing with someone who could use magic. A wizard!

Joy shrank back in fear. Any second she expected to be turned into a frog or hairball. And yet, like a teacher with a C student who suddenly starts to get all A's, she knew something wasn't right. Why hadn't FearfulFran used magic to dislodge the petal from the flower pot? Creating a strong breeze, a gust of wind, should have been easy for her. At the very least, the wizard should have been able to magically blast the petal from her hand.

Unless…

Unless Aesa's spell—the way it forced people to think in tuneful rhymes—prevented her from formulating the right sequence of thoughts, the mental concentration required to cast a spell—if that's how wizard magic worked. She had to remember to ask Harry. Maybe the local chamber of commerce had a newcomer's manual.

FearfulFran continued to writhe in agony. She glared at Joy and tried to sing:

> "Mine, mine, mine
> I've waited all this time
> Though Fate decrees it's thine
> It's mine, mine, mine."

Gradually, her spinning contortions slowed. Her limbs stopped twitching. Grunts of pain eased into whimpering moans and she got to her knees.

Someone else might have felt sorry for her. But not Joy. "Harry told me about you. The whole town was put to sleep just so you could get a wizard's petal."

By now FearfulFran was on her feet, wincing in discomfort as she shuffled back and forth in a mournful one-step.

> "Sentimental I am, I am a fool
> As everyone knows, life can be cruel
> A token of love, the wind took on high
> A token of love among pinks on high."

"Yeah, I heard that before, but I'm not buying it anymore."

Fudge! Her words had rhymed. She tried again. "You're responsible for Aesa finding a wizard's petal, for trapping the entire town into doing musicals for the rest of their lives. I'm getting Harry. He'll know what to do with you."

She started to leave.

FearfulFran wailed and sang a woeful tune:

> "My flesh is torn, my hands leave stains,
> To save this town, heed my refrain,
> To stop the spell, to break the chains,
> I know how to stop their pain."

Joy halted.

Don't listen to her. You can't trust her.

All true. And normally she'd listen to the voice of reason. But curiosity got the best of her—along with the sound of several people passing by on the street singing a sad tune from *Hamilton*—and she had to ask, "You know how to undo a wizard's petal?"

FearfulFran sang:

> "To free the town, to break the spell
> Two ways only, so heed me well
> A secret we keep, free of blame
> In exchange, the petal I claim."

It had to be a trick. But if it wasn't, if she could get FearfulFran to tell her how to break the spell, she could save the town. Harry would be pleased with her. Very pleased. Already she could think of several interesting ways he would show his thanks.

The only problem was, FearfulFran wasn't stupid. The sly hag wanted the wizard's petal as payment. There was no telling what she might wish for and what harm it would do. "Forget it. I don't need you. With this petal, I'll make a wish to reverse the one Aesa made."

FearfulFran cackled so hard, Joy was surprised a troop of flying monkeys didn't show up to join in.

> "Petal, petal, toil and trouble
> One to one creates a bubble
> Solar flare, crater deep
> All is lost, none to weep."

Joy's eyes widened in alarm. "Using one petal to negate another would destroy the town?"

FearfulFran did a little jig, and the foul smirk on her face indicated she wouldn't mind seeing it happen.

"I can't take a chance you're lying, and I can't take a chance you're not. This is Harry's town. He knows about magic. I'll let him decide."

FearfulFran snickered.

"Save the town, that's a fact
If you agree, a secret pact,
If Harry, the curse will act."

Someone must have told her about Harry's Damsel In Distress curse, which meant FearfulFran knew he would have to help her or die. If so, why wasn't she dancing to Harry and asking for help in order to activate the curse?

The answer was obvious. Harry would rather die than help the wizard who'd endangered his town. For all intent and purposes, FearfulFran held a gun to Harry's head, threatening to kill him if Joy didn't concede.

Crazed eyes studied her face.

"Save the town, that's a fact
If you agree, a secret pact
Tell no one, that's the tact
Reveal me, I won't be back."

A deal with the devil. The only way to save Harry.

"There you are." Kathy entered the garden courtyard. FearfulFran twirled and hid the side of her face covered with tattoos.

"Harry's been worried sick about you," Kathy said. "He's been looking all over for you. We have work to do and you're wandering around like a tourist."

"Sorry." Joy hid the petal in a pocket. She expected to feel a tingling in her palm like before, but it seemed the petal didn't need to stay in direct contact. So long as no one else had it in their possession, it was content. "I thought I heard someone in trouble."

She glanced at FearfulFran. "I was wrong."

Kathy regarded the haggard woman with obvious disdain. "Prosperity riffraff. Never know when to keep to their side of the river." With an insolent snort, she turned away. But then she wheeled around and peered at the woman. "Do I know you?"

Joy held her breath. She couldn't let Kathy find out she'd been talking with FearfulFran, the one person everyone in town must hate, and ironically the one person who might hold the solution to saving them. She had to keep her presence a secret or FearfulFran might go after Harry.

She brushed her thorn-pricked hand against Kathy's designer outfit. "Oh, sorry."

Kathy grimaced at the blood smudged on her silk jacket. "That was clumsy."

"I hear spit is good at cleaning blood. Here, let me try." She worked up a mouthful of saliva, exaggerating the effort. Kathy recoiled in disgust.

"You sure you don't want me to try?" Joy asked, while doing her best not to roar in laughter at Kathy's horror-stricken face.

"We have more civilized ways of cleaning stains."

She'll probably throw the entire outfit away, Joy thought. A shame, really. It's such a great looking suit. But at least she was no longer interested in FearfulFran.

With a manicured hand, Kathy gestured toward the street. "We should go. Harry's looking for you."

* * *

Harradorn hurried into Sirena's store and found Kathy calmly descending the stairs from his sister's apartment, carrying two tote bags full of books. "Did you find her?"

"She's in the workroom." Kathy handed him the totes, then dusted off her hands on a Pashmina shawl on display. "Like I said, nothing to worry about. Just doing some sightseeing." She started for the front door.

"Where are you going?"

"The Sweetheart Café. From the size of Sirena's library, we'll need all the caffeine we can get. And a bit of chocolate." With a wave good-bye, she left.

Harry scratched his head, perplexed by her offer to play waitress. The Kathy he knew in high school might have volunteered, but not Kathy Warbird. She hated getting her hands dirty. That's what servants were for. Then again, never the studious type, fixing coffee probably seemed less like work than reading.

He entered the workroom and noticed a coffee machine. Obviously Kathy preferred gourmet take-out to Sirena's home brew.

Joy looked up from the book she was reading. Her welcoming smile and the mango-coconut scent of her hair reminded him of secluded tropical beaches, tiny bikinis, and making love in the moonlight. Easy to imagine Joy in all three settings.

"Where were you?" He set down the bags of books.

"Helping a woman at an outdoor café."

"Is that where Kathy found you?"

Joy nodded. He glanced at the coffeemaker again.

She slid a hand into a pocket. "Harry, do you think it's possible to use one wizard's petal to undo another?"

"I've been told it can't. But when it comes to magic, nothing is certain. It might make everyone stop singing and dancing, or it might create a black hole." He noticed her yank the hand out of the pocket, plainly troubled by the possibility. He tried to reassure her. "I doubt any petals are left, which is why we need Sirena's books."

With a gentle touch, she fingered the cut on his cheek. "This looks a lot smaller."

"Sirena's healing potions work fast. Yours are probably already gone." He raised her bandaged hand to show her and noticed several fresh scratches. "What happened?"

"I, uh, accidentally scraped it on something while helping that woman. Don't worry. I already put some of the laughter potion on it." She eased her hand out of his. "Do you think Zach would know whether it's safe to undo one petal with another? Or another wizard? Someone like, uh, FearfulFran would know the answer, wouldn't she?"

"I can't get in touch with Zach. And being a wizard doesn't make one all-knowing or wise. As for FearfulFran..." He fought to control his temper, thinking of all the harm she had done and was still doing. "I wouldn't trust anything she said."

"But if we found a petal..."

He emphatically shook his head. "Too risky. Plus we don't have a petal. What we do have are a lot of books to read."

"Felicity and her team could find another petal. She's tenacious when she wants to be. I bet if we have her sing a search song, she'd find one. If you want, I'll go look for her."

"That won't be necessary." He handed her a book to read. "I know exactly where she is."

"You do?" Joy's eyes brightened. "Where is she?"

"Dulgrun Prison, probably singing 'Jail House Blues,' so you can forget about using a petal. It's the books or nothing."

"Prison?" Joy stared at him in shock. "What's Felicity doing in prison?"

"Serving her punishment for leaving town without authorization."

"Ohmigod! That's exactly what she told me would happen." She backed away from him. "I didn't believe her, but she was right. Your invitation for dinner *was* a trick. How could you?"

By the look on her face, he was in for it now. Only moments before he'd been fantasizing about making love to a bikini-clad Joy. If only he could turn back time.

With a firm resolve, he said, "Like it or not, as mayor I'm supposed to uphold the laws. And the laws here are strict when it comes to the safety and concealment of the town."

"What about leniency? Felicity's responsible for bringing me here and waking the town."

"I assure you, we're all very grateful for that."

She planted her hands on her hips. "But not enough to pardon her."

"The law is the law."

She stomped to the other side of the table. "If Felicity hadn't let go of my hair, what were you planning on doing with me? Throw me in prison, too?"

"Actually, after dinner, I was going to put you under house arrest until I convinced the council to forgive your transgression. By the way, you're also charged with harboring a fugitive."

Her jaw dropped. "You mean Felicity?" She slammed the book he'd given her down on the table. "Here I am, trying to rescue a town that's going to have me arrested as soon as I save them— again—and you're going to let them."

It had always been tough for outsiders to acclimatize to towns like his, especially to the rules which must seem archaic and restrictive. Yet a town with such diversified inhabitants— creatures some might call them, freaks of nature others might say—would sink into anarchy without strict rules to offset everyone trying to do what they thought best for their own kind. Compromise created tolerance. To keep the town harmonious and secure, rules had to be followed. "I assure you the council will learn of your efforts. I'm sure it will garner a commuted sentence."

"Commuted? That means I've already been found guilty. Haven't you people ever heard of the Bill of Rights? Innocent until proven guilty?"

"Doesn't work that way here."

"Fine!" She shoved the book across to him. "Save your own damn town! I'm out of here!" Bristling with anger, she glanced at the mirror, then headed for the doorway.

"Running away again?"

With a groan, she spun around, hands raised as if she wanted to strangle him.

"Wouldn't you rather face your accusers?"

"Yes! But the council is out there singing and dancing!" She clenched her fists. "I have half a mind to get them all together and initiate a few songs from *Sweeney Todd*."

"You wouldn't!"

"No." She uncurled her fists and lowered her hands. "But it sure felt good to see your reaction." She grabbed a book and opened it. "I'll help your town. But then I never want to see this place again."

"And me?" The seconds passed unbearably slow while he waited for her answer.

"The law is the law," she threw in his face.

When Kathy returned with a tray laden with food and coffee, he was on one side of the workroom, Joy on the other, both looking through their own stack of books, the silence between them frosty. He glanced at Kathy. Her discerning gaze shifted from him to Joy. She winked.

He scowled. *Women.*

*   *   *

An hour later, the three of them were still perusing the books. Joy had barely touched the turkey club croissants, too upset with Harry to be hungry, and too nervous when she noticed the coffee containers had the Sweetheart Café logo on them. Harry's remarks about how dangerous it might be to use one petal to undo another seemed to corroborate FearfulFran's song. Still, she'd like to find another petal to practice with, a small experiment to determine whether she could use a petal to save the town while keeping the one in her pocket in reserve. But with Felicity in prison, there wasn't much chance of finding another petal.

Joy sighed. If they couldn't find a solution in all these books, she might have to make that horrendous deal with the wizard—and without Harry's knowledge. Even if Harry was a stubborn, law-abiding bastard, she couldn't let him die from his curse. She had to find some way to keep FearfulFran away from him.

First, she needed to see if FearfulFran was still at the outdoor café or if Kathy hadn't scared her off. And without drawing suspicion. So she waited an hour. Just when she was about to say she wanted to go for more coffee, Harry declared he'd found something.

He read, "As everyone knows, the two standard cures for reversing the effects of Cupid's arrow are far more viable than the one for reversing a wizard's petal."

Joy blinked in surprise. *Cupid's arrow?*

Harry smiled. "Now we know for sure we can reverse Aesa's wish."

"But not how." Kathy walked over to the skelter mirror and checked her hair.

Huh, Joy thought. To Kathy, it was just a mirror, whereas for someone like herself who had traveled through it, its surface shimmered like glowing water, not reflecting anything. She rubbed her eyes. The strain of reading handwritten books in various fonts and sizes was taking its toll.

Her eyes were dry and itchy, and she rose to her feet. "Let's take a break." This was her chance to check on FearfulFran. "I'll go to the café for coffee. Maybe find some scones"

Kathy waved her off and headed for the doorway. "I'll go. I'm in need of something cold and without caffeine."

"That'll be nice for change." Harry stood and stretched. "Sounds quiet out there."

Every few minutes they had heard people singing when they passed the shop, a constant reminder that the tedium of skimming through the books for a solution was easy compared to what the town's inhabitants were going through.

"Want some help?" he asked Kathy.

"Thanks, but I can manage. Besides, you have some make-up sex to attend to." She lifted a hand and admired the huge blue diamond on her finger. "Not as good as diamonds and gold, but almost. See you two lovebirds later." With a naughty chuckle, Kathy left the store.

Joy stared after the insensitive woman, shocked by her brazen remarks. Harry shifted and cleared his throat. She looked at him, and he at her.

They returned to their own stack of books, and the next hour dragged on. Once in a while she caught Harry glancing at her. She ignored him and read the instructions for making a sow's ear into a silk purse. *Purate maggots. Marinate the mash in fresh sulfur dioxide from an active volcano. Coat the sow's ear with the paste and set it in the moonlight for seven nights and the ear will transform into silk.*

This is really outdated, she thought. Nowadays you can just buy a silk purse on the Internet.

Out the corner of her eye, she saw Harry get up and grab something from a shelf. He stood there, looking at it. Then he started towards her. She gulped, not sure whether to expect make-up sex, any sex, or another argument.

He stopped beside her. This close, his heat, his scent—a mixture of earthy male and mountain forest—radiated across the space between them. She heard his long, torturous sigh. Look at me, he seemed to be saying.

She pretended not to see him and kept reading.

Another long breath. He placed a small jar on the page she was reading. It was filled with a bright deep-blue powder.

"Smalt," he said.

Puzzled, she raised her eyes to his.

"The color, the trigger, is smalt."

Tears came to her eyes. The most precious gift in the world was the color in this jar. "I can use this to avoid the council's punishment."

"I realize that."

"And it would be all right with you?"

"If that's what you want—yes."

"What if they send you or someone else after me, force me to return here?"

"I'd break the mirror first so they couldn't."

Stunned by his ferocity, she searched his face. His lips were firm, his jaw set, not a hint of hesitation in his stone-gray eyes. This wasn't a romantic gesture or a spur-of-the-moment means to gain her favor. "You would do that for me?"

He nodded.

"Why?"

"Because of what happened to you in the Gap. Because you're trying to help my town even though you may be punished afterwards. Because you have orange hair and still look sexy. Because you can't keep your eyes off my chest—No, don't look away."

He drew her chin back around, forcing her to meet his gaze. "Because my brother and sister are out there in a never-ending musical, my town stuck in a nightmare I may never be able to end and I don't want you to be stuck in it, too. I want you to have what they don't have, a way out.

"But mostly because someone's jewelry reminded me no one should have a hold over someone else, no matter what each gets out of it. Despite the advantages, manipulating others invariably leads to heartache and ruin, even if it starts out with good intentions. With what we have, we don't need it."

"What do we have?" Joy whispered, overwhelmed by the depth of his honesty.

The hand under her chin slid up to caress her cheek. "Let's find out."

Maybe it was all the caffeine. Or the argument they'd had. Or his gift of truth. Or the terrible secret she had hidden in her pocket. But when Harry claimed her mouth, she willingly surrendered all thought, all feelings, to the desire boiling up inside to take and be taken.

"What about Kathy?" she murmured, loving how his mouth traveled down her neck, licking and nipping.

"The door chime will warn us."

She arched her head back, overwhelmed by the sensuous pleasure his fiery lips bestowed, but when he moved to savor her mouth again, she placed her finger on his lips The next level in their relationship was not going to be built on lies and mistrust. Or omissions.

"Wait," she said. "There's something I have to tell you first." She slipped a hand into the pocket holding the wizard's petal. Harry had trusted her with the trigger word. Now she would trust him with her secret.

From outside the store, they heard Kathy yell, "No, I don't want to climb every mountain!" followed by the chimes and the door slamming shut. Joy quickly straightened her clothes.

"I look forward to finishing this later," Harry murmured, and returned to the book he'd been reading.

Kathy entered the workroom, grumbling. "It's getting worse out there."

Joy kept her head down, knowing from her students how to look lost in a book. If this town wasn't in the middle of a crisis, she'd grab Harry's hand, say the trigger, zip him back home to her bed, and make love to him for the rest of the weekend.

Kathy put a large frosty glass of what looked like cherry Italian ice on the table by her.

"Thanks," Joy said, relieved to see Angie's Trattoria emblazoned on the glass and not Sweetheart Café. Kathy's arm knocked over the drink. Icy red fluid spilled onto Joy's lap. She shot to her feet.

"How clumsy of me," Kathy said. "Looks like I've ruined your outfit."

She glared at Kathy, certain it was payback for smearing blood on her suit. This was a dangerous woman. A woman who always got even. Even if it wasn't right away.

With her fingertips, she peeled away the wet material sticking to her skin. Cherry Italian ice pooled around her sandals.

"What a shame," Kathy said. "Ruined your shoes, too. I'll find something for you to change into."

"I'll get a mop," Harry said and left to find one.

Kathy returned from the front of the store with an armload of clothing. "Sirena doesn't carry many of the larger sizes but some of these should fit."

Joy wrung out the lower half of her skirt, imagining it was the woman's neck, then followed as Kathy led the way to the restroom. Thanks to Kathy, she'd gone from feeling sexy and desirable to looking like a melting cherry popsicle.

Kathy set down the clothes. "I'll wait outside. Give me your clothes and I'll rinse them before the stain sets."

Alone, Joy peeled off her jacket and added her sticky dress to the pile. Suddenly, her palm itched like crazy.

What the... ? Oh, the petal.

She dug it out of the pocket. The itching stopped. "I'm putting you on the shelf while I get dressed," she said, feeling silly talking to it yet hoping that somehow the magic understood. "I promise to pick you up when I'm done." She put it on the shelf. At once, her palm itched, bordering on pain the longer the petal stayed separated from her. "All right already." She grabbed it and the itching ceased.

"Who were you talking to?" Kathy asked when Joy opened the door to hand over her clothes. Kathy shifted to see inside.

"Just myself."

The woman raised a brow.

Great, now she thinks I'm a loony outsider who talks to herself. But if it keeps the petal a secret, I can live with that.

Joy closed the door and started toward the sink when her foot stepped on something wet. Her panties. She must have dropped them. Hoping to catch Kathy before she left, she reopened the door. Kathy was already on the other side of the room at a sink, prying into all the pockets. Cleaning the pockets before rinsing the clothes? Or looking for something.

Paranoid. You're becoming paranoid like your brother. Even if Kathy had seen her slip something into her pocket at the café, there was no way for her to know it was a wizard's petal.

Joy washed the sticky residue from her skin, then sorted through Kathy's selection of clothes. All were too large or too small. They'd either make her look fat or in need of losing weight. Fortunately, having a sister whose clothes were a different size, Joy knew how to make do. She used safety pins on the broomstick skirt. The yellow tube top was tight, making her breasts bulge—Harry should like that. She layered it with a large green silk shirt, the ends tied at the waist. While dressing, she noticed Sirena's healing cream had worked miracles. All her cuts and scrapes were gone, the fresh scratches from FearfulFran already fading.

When she rejoined the others, Harry was putting the mop away. His gaze fell to her breasts straining against the tube top and he grinned.

Oh yeah. Back to feeling sexy and desirable.

They returned to reading. Sometime later, Harry said, "Listen to this: 'As referenced in *Butcher's Compendium of Clinical Trials of Common Antidotes For Magical Mayhem,* the Great Redux is the only foolproof solution to vampirism, rabid werewolves, gremlin gum, orc-blood poison, and wizard's petals.'"

"What's the Great Redux?" Kathy asked.

Harry knows what it is. The haunted look in his eyes, the droop of his shoulders, were clear indications. Yet all he said was, "We should ask Sirena to be sure."

"Lots of luck," Kathy whined. "She could be anywhere."

Joy said. "Then we better get started. I'll grab a pair of shoes."

The store's only footwear were slippers. While Joy put on a pair, a group danced by singing "Colors of the Wind" and tossing flowers in the air. Birds flew above, chirping in harmony. Even the animals were affected by Aesa's wish.

Harry and Kathy were discussing a search grid to find Sirena when two soft tones filled the air. "What was that?" Kathy asked.

Joy raced outside.

"There it is again," Harry said. He and Kathy joined her on the street. "It's coming from all directions, indoors and out. Maybe some sort of magic."

"I could swear I've heard it before," Kathy said. "I just can't place it."

Heart pounding, Joy looked up and down the street. Except for the tones, the street was quiet and empty. Chills ran through her. She turned to Harry. "They're gone. The people singing on the street, they were right here. I saw them. They vanished. Even the birds." She wrapped her arms around herself. "What's going on?"

Chapter 19

The streets were deserted, not a soul in sight while Harradorn and Joy circled the block and returned to the store after searching the surrounding area. Kathy soon joined them. Her puzzled shrug plus shake of her head indicated she hadn't found anyone either.

Shadows lengthened. Soon the sun would flee behind the mountains to the west and darkness would envelop Peace & Prosperity like a shroud. This was his beloved town, but without people, without the sights and sounds of the living, the buildings seemed more like mausoleums.

Joy leaned into him, holding his hand, providing comfort. Hard to believe they'd met only a few days ago, and yet their two forceful personalities had forged an enchanting intimacy, a passionate friendship—fragile because of its newness but full of lifelong potential.

"It's so quiet," Joy said. "Spooky. Like when Felicity and I found everyone asleep."

Kathy looked at her in surprise. "You know Felicity?"

"Strange as it seems, Joy and Felicity are best buds." Their friendship still amazed him. Perhaps once in a generation a human could claim a fairy as a friend. And he wondered what other interesting traits she would surprise him with while they got to know each other better.

"Best buds? That explains the orange hair."

From Kathy's tone, she didn't mean it as a compliment, but Harradorn let it slide. "I wouldn't have her any other way. Except purple." He shared a smile with Joy, her erotically-colored hair and their fairy-tale kiss foremost in his mind. Town historians would soon write a modern-day version of *Sleeping Beauty* starring him and Joy.

If they could *find* the historians.

Kathy sniffed the air. "I smell food."

"She's right." Joy raised her nose. "Hot dogs. Cinnamon rolls. Fried chicken. Tacos."

"I'm detecting lobster, apple bourbon pie, and paella." Kathy licked her lips. "Hmm. Coq au Vin and rakfisk. What an impudent variety. I wonder where's it coming from?"

"The Sweetheart Café is the closest restaurant," Harry said. "We should check it out."

They entered the arched alleyway. When they neared the patio, he noticed Joy slow and hang back. "What's wrong?" he asked.

"Nothing." Yet her timbre was nervous, her tone high-pitched, and she hesitated before anxiously peeking around the corner. The place was empty. With a long sigh, she visibly relaxed.

"Looking for someone?"

She laughed uneasily. "In this town, I never know what to expect, including a dancing Cyclops. It pays to be cautious, that's all."

Kathy came out of the café munching a carrot. "No one's in there, but the smell of food is all around."

"Like the strange tone we heard." It hadn't sounded for a while, yet the silence was equally disturbing. Even the air seemed becalmed. Something under a table caught his eye and he bent to pick it up. A forked rose stem with the end hollowed out. The dowsing rod Sirena had made for Lance so the councilman could find wizard's petals. What was it doing here?

Both women eyed the object in his hand, Kathy with simple curiosity. But Joy was surprisingly pale. "Do you know what this is?" he asked Joy.

She shook her head.

He believed her, and yet he had a feeling she'd seen it before.

Kathy glanced at her platinum watch and said, "I wonder when Aesa made her wish."

"I might be able to help with that," Joy said. "When I asked Rick what she was watching onstage, everyone in the park began singing the opening song to *The Sound of Music*."

"Gawd, what an annoyingly sweet musical," Kathy said. "Thank Odin for intermissions." A shrewd smile crossed her face. "Now I know where I heard that sound before. The chime to signal intermissions. No wonder I couldn't place it. It belongs in theaters and concert halls, not out on a street."

Harry nodded. "Intermission. That makes sense. It's almost twenty-four hours since the play began. Maybe the wish gives everyone a break once a day."

"So where is everyone?"

"Perhaps where they were when the wish was made."

Joy looked about. "If that's true, shouldn't this place be filled with diners?"

He chuckled. He'd forgotten she was an outsider. "In Peace, everyone attends a school play—even if it's a musical. Nothing is more important than supporting the children of the community."

Joy appeared stunned. "Everyone?"

"Unfortunately," Kathy muttered.

"If my theory is correct," he said, "all of Peace is in the park. Let's have a look." He put the dowsing rod on a table, then thought better of it and picked it up again.

The park was deserted. His stomach clenched. He was so sure everyone would be here. The town was his responsibility and he'd lost them all. Some mayor he was.

Kathy put her hands on her hips. "Where could they be?"

"There!" Joy pointed at a nearby tree.

"Everyone's up a tree?" Kathy said.

"Of course not. But a bird is." Joy craned her neck to get a better view. "I know this bird, or rather Felicity does. It's Richurp.

He's up there eating a worm. From what I can see, every time he gulps one down, another worm appears in his beak."

Harradorn watched in amazement. "The magic is replenishing his need for food, making it appear out of thin air." He started for the nearest building. "Let's see if people are in their homes eating."

Joy and Kathy hurried after him. "Won't the door be locked?" Joy asked.

"Remember, no one in Peace locks their doors."

"What about Prosperity?"

Kathy produced a very unladylike snort. "You'd be a fool not to. I should know, I grew up there."

The building belonged to the Anderssons, the ground floor a fabric store where they sold the best velvets, lace, and silks in town. If you got on Lana Andersson's good side, she'd make a designer outfit that rivaled any in the outside world.

Upstairs in the residence, they found the entire Andersson family at the kitchen table, eating and drinking—eating their favorite food, he surmised. Lana was finishing up a Caesar salad, Lars a steak with all the trimmings. Young Lynda had half a pizza left on her plate and was digging into a dish of chocolate ice cream while Lars Jr. was eating a cheeseburger, fries, and apple slices. Everyone looked reassured by their mayor's presence, and yet no one stopped eating. Perhaps the magic wouldn't let them.

"Mayor Harradorn," Lars said between bites. "Good to see you." Munch. Munch. "Can you help us?" Munch. "Please, help us."

The man gazed around at his family. The desperation haunting his eyes tore at Harradorn's heart. "We may be close to a solution," he told them, giving them hope while hoping it wasn't a lie.

Another two-note chime sounded. The food vanished. As one, the Anderssons stood Zombie-like and walked to their bedrooms. Within seconds of lying down, all were asleep.

"Hmph," Kathy said with a disapproving frown. "This magic is crude. Everyone is sleeping in their clothes."

Harradorn tried to wake Lars, but couldn't.

"I'm worried about the children," Joy said. "I can't see them surviving if this happens only once a day."

"I agree," he said. These were his people, but he could do nothing more for them here. Back outside, he looked to where the Valkyrie Oak once stood, tall and stately. Solid. And he remembered Kathy saying all this was Zach's fault.

"I wonder how long they stay asleep," he said. "If the children aren't getting enough rest, we may need to restrain them, strap them to their beds."

"That would keep them from dancing but not singing," Kathy pointed out.

"Every little bit helps."

"You know how many brats there are in this town? And not just humans. Dwarfs, elves, fairies, sprites, trolls, not to mention Sasquatch. It'd take days to find them all. How do we keep releasing them so they can eat or go to the bathroom?" Kathy shook her head at the impossible task. "It's a waste of time. But if you insist, let's go to my house. I need to change my outfit. Then we can tie up Lance."

"You go on without us. Joy and I have to locate Sirena."

Kathy asked Joy to go with her, whining that she wanted some company, but Harradorn insisted Joy stay with him. Kathy nagged twice more before she left with a disappointed sniff. He gestured for Joy not to talk until Kathy was out of earshot.

After Kathy exited the far side of the park, Joy asked, "What was that all about?"

"Did you notice, she didn't seem worried about the intermission tones or the people disappearing. It confirms my suspicion she arrived last night." He'd never equated danger with his former lover, but the chill of foreboding creeping up his spine said Kathy couldn't be trusted. He certainly wasn't going to let Joy be alone with her.

"When we heard the tones," he said, "I think she knew exactly what was going on and didn't tell us until she got bored. I'll lay odds Sirena reveals the intermission happens more than once a day, but first we have to find her." They cut across the park to the Hall

"Sirena lives with you?" Joy asked.

"In payment for my coming to your *rescue*, I allowed her to move into the Mayor's Residence."

Joy stifled a laugh. "How much is saving me worth in free rent?"

He thought about the pungent incense his sister used, the gongs, chants, and sitar music she played endlessly, and he muttered, "As long as I live there, she lives there."

Joy put a hand on his arm, and he stopped. "You really are a boy scout."

"So I've been told. But you're the first one who's meant it as a compliment."

"I don't have any badges to give you," she said in a teasing voice, "but maybe this will do." She leaned toward him, lips parted, a promise of sex, lots of sex, in her bewitching smile, but stopped when a pink rose petal floated down between them. He snatched it out of the air.

Joy gasped. "A wizard's petal! You have a wizard's petal!" The guilt gnawing at her for keeping her petal a secret was gone. At last, she could ignore FearfulFran's horrible blackmail and let Harry use his own petal to find a way to save the town.

She felt like dancing even without being under Aesa's wish. But then she noticed the ugly black veins streaking the pink petal. "What's wrong with it?"

"Diseased," Harry said. "Sick. Only pure white ones can be wizard's petals." He tossed it away. "It would seem only those cured of their illness can be entrusted to help others." The faraway look in his eyes matched his odd explanation. Then his gaze settled on her and he returned from wherever his mind had taken him. The worry on his forehead eased, and he put his arm around her. "At least I can trust you."

She wanted to curl up and die.

If she told Harry about FearfulFran now, not only would he never trust her again, but the hag might force the curse on him. But if she didn't tell Harry and he found out she'd been keeping the woman's presence a secret, he would still never trust her again. And if he couldn't trust her, they could never be friends. And if they couldn't be friends, then they certainly couldn't be anything more.

Life was so unfair.

They climbed the steps of the Hall, and Joy wondered if she could slip away and meet with the wizard. Problem was FearfulFran was no longer at the café.

Joy asked, "If there was a visitor in town, where would the magic send her during intermission?"

"Maybe a hotel or the home of the people she's visiting."

They passed the door carved with people being guillotined. Would he allow the town to do that to FearfulFran? She didn't think Harry had it in him. But the council might, especially Kathy's husband, Lance. Despite all the heartache FearfulFran had caused, Joy couldn't condone such a punishment. One thing was certain, there was no way she was going to let FearfulFran get her hands on a petal.

"Harry, how do you destroy a wizard's petal so it can't be used?"

"Tear it up, smash it, burn it. Why do you ask?"

"In case the next petal that floats down is white."

"The fairies and Sheriff Caine did a good job of scouring the town. If one does show up, don't touch it. They get very attached to their owners. Best let me take care of it."

Great. Now he tells me.

Frankincense and jasmine scented the air of a large fourth floor suite colorfully arrayed with floor pillows and metaphysical wall hangings. Scarves lounged over tables and chairs while suncatchers cast the last rainbows from the sun disappearing behind the mountains. They found Sirena asleep on a purple bedspread. They tried everything to wake her, including water sprinkled on her face, aerosol spray on the bottom of her feet, and vinegar and ammonia by her nose. Other than a twitch in annoyance, all failed.

Harry sat on the edge of the bed. "We're going to have to wait until the magic wakes her. With any luck, she'll be able to talk before she resumes singing."

Joy's stomach rumbled. She glanced at Harry. With an easy smile, he said, "I'm hungry, too. If you don't mind, I'll stay and keep an eye on her."

She followed his directions to the kitchen. The facility was vast. In one of three refrigerators, she found several prepared meals ready to be heated. All the lights came on. Out a window, she saw all the street lights on, too. With night approaching, the magic insured no one would sing and dance in the dark.

Soon she headed upstairs with a tray of food. Magic tones filled the building, signaling the next stage of the intermission. Or the end to it. When Joy entered the suite, Sirena was doing an operatic promenade around the bed and singing in German. She stopped before Harry, flung out her arms, and bellowed words in German.

Harry sprang to his feet. "No! There has to be another way!"

Joy set the tray down. "What's she singing?"

"It's from *Götterdämmerung*—the 'Twilight of the Gods.'" He grabbed his sister and shook her, and for a moment she stopped singing. "Are you saying the wishcaster has to die to reverse the wish?"

Tears poured down her face and Sirena nodded. She resumed singing in German.

Harry wrenched himself away. He dropped to his knees, his face twisted in agony. "But Aesa's only eight years old."

Sirena switched to English and sang a sorrowful version of "Somewhere" from *West Side Story:*

"There's no place for us,

237

This dooms all of us.
Tears and sadness and mournful air
Wait for us
Everywhere."

With one long last look at her brother, Sirena left. Her singing faded as she descended the stairs. Through the open window, Joy heard people singing happy show tunes in the park. She shut all the windows. In the silence that followed, she hugged herself, hating magic, hating the town, hating wizards and wizard's petals, hating the fact that at one time she thought this place was wondrous and exciting.

Harry knelt bent over, heavy with the burden he carried. In an eerily calm voice bordering on madness, he said, "I think you should go home—now—before things get worse."

Before I do something you'll never forgive me for, is what he meant. Horrified, she rushed to his side and knelt beside him. "You can't possibly consider killing a child. There has to be another way."

"Only one solution, the book said."

"But, Harry, you can't."

"No, I can't. Not now. But in the weeks and months ahead, when other little girls start dying from exhaustion, along with the old and sick and infirmed, will it seem as monstrous as it does now?"

"What about Zach?" she suggested. "When he comes back, he could help. Surely, he can help."

"And do what? Hold Aesa down while I strangle her, smother her, inject her with a fast-acting poison? Make him an accomplice? It's bad enough having one person do it. He's my friend. I won't share the guilt."

She moved to touch him, hold him, share his grief, but he jerked away and stood.

"Maybe Zach knows of another solution," she said. "Let's wait and see what he says."

"He won't be back until he's found FearfulFran and punished her. What if children start dying while we wait?"

Blood hammered in her ears. All this misery might have been avoided if she had told him right away that FearfulFran was in town.

She had to make amends, set things right. "Is there some way to contact Zach?"

"Magic interferes with electronics, communications—and his tower uses a lot of magic."

"What about using the skelter mirror to go to him?" If Sirena was correct, having the phone with her would allow them to travel anywhere in the mirror.

"It's never been done before." For a second, his troubled face calmed, and she saw a spark of hope in his eyes. But then his lips firmed and he closed in on himself. "His tower defenses would have to be down. And he won't lower them while FearfulFran is on the loose. No, the die is cast. Go home, Joy. This is my problem, not yours. Leave me be."

She stood up and went to him. "I won't abandon you. This isn't your fault. It's Zach's petal, his responsibility. Don't take it on as your own."

"It's not his fault!" His hand sliced emphatically through the air. "FearfulFran is to blame. I swear by Thor's hammer, if I ever lay eyes on her, I'll strangle her to death with my own bare hands." He clenched his fists. "I will. Odin help me, I will."

She drew back. "You don't mean that."

Chest heaving, he stared at her. Hate raged in his eyes. "Yes, I do."

Plainly, he felt backed into a corner. But still…

Her fingers reached into her pocket and touched the wizard's petal. FearfulFran said there were two ways to undo the wish, not just the one mentioned in the books. It might be a lie, a trick. Harry said she couldn't be trusted. But in her lust to have the petal, what if she had told the truth? Maybe the magic kept people from lying while they sang? If so, it meant there was an alternative to the Great Redux, perhaps one that wasn't fatal.

Harry crossed to a window and looked out on his town, his people. If she revealed FearfulFran's presence, the wizard had promised never to disclose the other solution to Aesa's wish.

There was only one thing left to do.

While Harry stared out at his town slowly disappearing into twilight, she quietly slipped from the room.

Chapter 20

As soon as Joy left the Mayor's Hall and Residence, she heard Kathy's voice yell from a distance. Joy ran to the large trees in the park. Concealed behind one, she observed Kathy in the evening light. The woman strolled into view from the west, sipping a drink and occasionally yelling at bespelled singers to back off. Given the dire circumstances, Kathy sure didn't seem in a hurry. From the look of her container illuminated in a nearby streetlight, the drink was from the same trattoria she had gone to before.

Interesting.

Kathy climbed the stairs of the Hall. In the waning light, Joy squinted at the map she'd taken from the visitors table. It showed all the businesses and residences on Harry's side of town. According to the listings, there was only one Italian tavern in Peace. Angie's Trattoria was a good eight blocks from Sirena's store, a long trek in Kathy's four-inch heels, and suspiciously in the opposite direction from where the map showed she and her husband lived.

Kathy entered the Hall, and Joy took off for the trattoria. Perhaps she was on a fool's quest, but she suspected the woman's preference for Italian ice had nothing to do with her love of the beverage.

Joy had gone two blocks when the ground suddenly shook. Not an earthquake, but a rumbling two-step. The dancing Cyclops!

She thought of hiding, but the streetlights were magically bright and she'd already been spotted. Agamemnon danced toward her. A flock of fairies circled his head. All sang a ditty from *Enchanted*.

> "How do we know Harry loves her?
> How do we know he cares?
> Love is all around, love is in the air,
> That's how we know he cares."

With the song bellowing from his mouth, the giant pranced right up to her. The fairies landed on his lofty shoulders and danced merrily.

Joy tilted her head back and yelled up to him. "Agamemnon, I need a favor from you! Two favors!"

The Cyclops switched to humming. He swayed from side to side and waited to hear her request. The fairies, on the other hand, looked like they were going to be seasick from the rocking and took off singing. They disappeared high up into the night.

Joy said, "I need you to tell me my hair is green."

His one eye stared. He frowned.

"Yes, I know it's *not* green, but I need you to say it is. Please."

He filled his massive chest with air. She covered her ears just in time while he sang in a soft roar:

> "It's not easy being green
> But orange is how you are seen
> You'd think it'd be prettier being the color of grass
> Or leaves or mold,
> But being like fruit is just as keen."

Joy laughed at the words and also with relief. Her theory was correct. The magic did force people to tell the truth while they sang, which meant FearfulFran hadn't lied when she said there were two ways to undo a wizard's petal. With any luck, the other solution would be less horrific than turning Harry into a murderer.

"Thank you, Agamemnon. You did great."

The Cyclops smiled broadly, displaying huge, perfect white teeth that would make any dentist in the outside world swoon.

"Now for my second favor. If Harry asks about me, tell him I went to Dulgrun Prison to visit Felicity. Okay?"

The gentle giant blinked his huge hazel eye and nodded. Huh. She expected him to object, but apparently the prison here must not be dangerous or difficult to get into like those in the outside world.

To insure Agamemnon wouldn't follow her, she waved goodbye and sang a variation of the children's song from *The Sound of Music*:

> "So long, big guy, *auf Wiedersehen*, goodbye,
> To prison I go, to visit my good friend
> While you will dance
> And sing to your heart's content."

The Cyclops joined in, repeating the verse and waving goodbye to her. She sang and waved and danced away, and hoped he'd do the same. He did. She glanced back and saw him dance out of sight around a corner.

She promptly dashed up Happy Street for the trattoria. Yeah, she'd lied, a habit she'd picked up since Harry and Felicity entered her life, but this was no time for regrets. If Agamemnon ran into Harry, the magic would force him to tell Harry she was going to prison to visit Felicity. Since Agamemnon didn't know she'd lied to him, he could only relate what he thought to be true.

Unless the magic was more astute than she gave it credit for. In that case, the wild goose chase she was about to send Harry on would never happen. He'd track her down and stop her. And she couldn't let him do that. No matter how many lives it might save, she wasn't going to let him become a killer.

She ran the rest of the way to Angie's Trattoria.

Upon opening the stained-glass entry door, she heard a familiar song.

> "Sentimental I am, I am a fool
> As everyone knows, life can be cruel
> A token of love, the wind took on high
> A token of love among pinks on high."

She followed the voice through the ragu and wine-scented interior, past etched-glass dividers to an indoor garden situated in the back of the restaurant. Underneath an arbor of red roses, FearfulFran swayed, a wand in one hand conducting music only she could hear. Yet by the frenzied look on her face, Joy decided the woman was actually trying to cast a spell, for every time she flicked the wand and nothing happened, she grimaced and repeated the verse.

FearfulFran was unpredictable. Violent. Once released from Aesa's wish, she'd be a dangerous force. Giving her a wizard's petal might increase the threat a thousandfold. Who could say what wish she would make, how many lives it might affect. Maybe even those in the outside world. Her world.

She wished Zach was here. She even wished Mike was here. But they weren't. It was all up to her.

She took out the petal and regarded it with loathing and awe. All her life, wishes had had a hopeful quality. Wish upon a star. Wish before blowing out birthday candles. Wishing wells and wishing stones. There was even a Make-A-Wish charity for children battling life-threatening illnesses.

Wishing should be a good thing. A miracle on earth. An answer to one's prayers. It should bring happiness, laughter, smiles, and joy.

If she gave the petal to FearfulFran, her wish might bring sadness and pain, maybe even death. But if she didn't, it would bring sadness and pain to Harry and death to Aesa.

She stared at FearfulFran and recognized her for what she was.

A bully. Capable of great magic and great harm, but underneath it all someone who needed to be put in her place. To be confronted without fear, yet with respect.

Tough assignment, considering this bully could probably turn her into a toad.

No matter. Life was a school, she was a teacher, and Fearful-Fran a student in need of a few lessons on how to get along with others.

She put the petal away and stepped forward. "I'm here."

FearfulFran spun around with a smile... until she recognized her visitor. Her lips twisted into a distasteful frown.

"Expecting Kathy?"

The wizard's frown deepened.

Joy moved closer and was glad to see FearfulFran shift back. Bullies hated being on the receiving end of confrontation. "You've been talking to her, haven't you? At the Sweetheart Café when she made sandwiches, and then here for drinks." It was the only way Kathy would have known to look through her pockets for the petal.

FearfulFran cackled and sang:

> "No good deed goes unpunished
> That's my lot in life
> My road of good intentions
> Always leads to strife."

"Yeah, well, you get what you give," Joy said. "Somehow you convinced Kathy to steal the petal from me. What I don't understand is why you thought she'd succeed. I saw what happened when *you* tried."

The wizard tightened her lips, struggling not to answer, not to sing, clearly knowing only the truth would come out. Her lips twisted and stretched, and she clamped her hands over her mouth, fighting to keep it shut. But the magic was too powerful to resist.

Her hands left her mouth, her arms opened wide, and with a snarl she sang:

> "A petal wants to be found
> A petal wants to be needed
> Send it away, the thread frays
> Keep it away, it's free."

Joy nodded in understanding. "Kathy dumped the drink on me, hoping I'd forget about the petal and leave it in my clothes. It's why she offered to rinse them out while I changed. She wanted to get the petal far enough away from me that the petal would break its connection. Then she'd be free to take it without being attacked by pain." It also meant FearfulFran didn't know everything about wizard's petals, particularly that they used itching and pain to warn their owners about being separated.

"You said there were two ways to undo a wizard's petal wish," Joy said. "Is one of them killing the wishcaster?"

FearfulFran smiled and danced a jig.

> "No good deed goes unpunished
> That's my lot in life
> My road of good intentions
> Always leads to strife."

"I gather that's your standard song for yes." Joy sighed. She was about to make the worst compromise of her life. "I need the other solution that will cancel Aesa's wish."

The wizard's lips curled with malevolent delight. She switched from the jig to an expectant sway.

> "To free the town, to break the spell
> Two ways only, so heed me well
> A secret we keep, free of blame

In exchange, the petal I claim."

Joy held up the wizard's petal. FearfulFran cackled with glee and danced another jig, her gloating a sharp contrast to the war being fought in Joy's conscience.

A wrong to prevent a wrong didn't necessarily make it right. Yet she would do this for Harry and for a little girl named Aesa, and let the chips fall where they may. Hopefully in the end something good would come from all of this.

Voice trembling, every nerve on edge, she told the wizard, "I'll give you your wish if you tell me the second way to undo Aesa's wish."

Laughing, FearfulFran twirled. She leapt into the air, and twirled again.

"But only after we have everything we need to nullify Aesa's wish," Joy added. She remembered all the weird ingredients some spells utilized. It might take days, weeks to find them all. She didn't want FearfulFran to have the petal before the town was freed.

The wizard snarled. With a menacing glint in her bloodshot eyes, she shook her wand at Joy and sang:

"Mine, mine, mine
I've waited all this time
Though Fate decrees it's thine
It's mine, mine, mine."

Joy heard a commotion from outside. People wandering the streets must have heard FearfulFran's singing and were coming to join her.

Quickly, she lowered her voice and said, "Look here, wizard. I know you don't like it. Neither do I, but it's the best we can do given the circumstances. Is it a deal?"

The wizard sang:

"Blood is strong while words are weak
Heart's are bound by oaths we keep
Blood is spilled, and I'll spill mine
You'll be mine and I'll be thine
Lick your promise, I'll lick mine
No way out for all time."

Joy widened her eyes. "You want us to swear on our own blood that we'll keep our word?"

FearfulFran nodded.

"No good deed goes unpunished
That's my lot in life
My road of good intentions
Always leads to strife."

Joy shivered in revulsion. A blood oath. Yuk. Could this get any worse? "What happens if one of us breaks their promise?"

The wizard swayed in rhythm with the song:

"Petal, petal, toil and trouble
One to one creates a bubble
Solar flare, crater deep
All is lost, none to weep."

"I get it. Mutual destruction. Crap! We really are in this to-gether, aren't we?"

FearfulFran nodded grimly while swaying side to side.

The deal hadn't been sealed and already she had a bitter taste in her mouth. "All right. Let's do it before I lose my nerve."

She grabbed two knives off a nearby table and was about to hand one to the wizard when the woman bit down on her own hand and drew blood. *Wow. She really wants this.*

Instead of doing the wild thing, Joy elected to be a total wimp and delicately nicked the pad of one finger. FearfulFran grunted and raised a brow in suspicion. Joy showed her the bright red bead of blood on her finger.

"Who goes first?" Joy asked.

The wizard held up her hand.

> "A way to break the petal's spell
> I give to you, I will tell.
> When the spell is near its end,
> Your vow to me you will tend."

FearfulFran licked the blood dripping from her hand. Instantly, she was jolted by a bright white light, her part of the bargain sealed with magic.

Joy gulped. The entire situation was surreal, something that might happen in a dream, a nightmare. Her job, her home, her mundane life in New Jersey, all seemed light-years away. Her insides knotted in dread, every breath faster than the last. She could feel the panic building, threatening to undermine her resolve. The longer she hesitated the worse it became.

Just do it.

In a tremulous voice, she said, "If FearfulFran reveals the second way to undo a wizard's petal and we have everything needed to nullify Aesa's wish, I promise to give her her wish."

She raised her bleeding finger to her mouth.

"NO!" Harry rushed forward, Kathy behind him. "Don't do it!"

"I'm doing this for you," she told him. "This way you won't have to kill Aesa."

"I promise I won't kill her," Harry said. Yet the desperation in his voice made her realize he'd say or do anything to stop her.

He inched toward her. She shifted toward FearfulFran. He stopped. "I promise, I won't do anything to Aesa," he said. "I'll find another way. Please, in Odin's name, don't."

Harry had his hands raised toward her, his stormy gray eyes

silently pleading with her. Joy's heart went out to him. She wanted to walk into his welcoming arms, have him hold her and make her feel safe and warm and loved. He was right. Making a deal with this wicked wizard was crazy. What had she been thinking? How could anyone possibly control FearfulFran once she had the petal?

Stupid. Stupid. Stupid.

She lowered the bleeding finger from her mouth. They'd find another way.

Kathy smirked. "All this over a snot-nosed brat when an entire town is at stake. I've always said kids are a dime a dozen, easily replaced. You're actually smarter than I thought—for an outsider."

"Kathy!" Harradorn said in shock.

"That's not why I changed my mind," Joy said. "Every child is precious."

"So, you're just a second-class wimp. A child dies because you're a coward?"

"That's not—"

"I guess it's true: Stupid is as stupid does. Run on home to your spineless, ordinary life and let the true heroes like Harry and me take care of this."

Joy stared at Kathy. Her gaze hardened. She licked her finger.

Like being punched in the gut, she was jolted by a bright white light. In seconds it eased. She'd just caught her breath when a sizzling yellow aura enveloped both her and FearfulFran, smelling of sulfur. She could swear a thousand fire ants were crawling all over her skin, biting, burning, eating her alive. FearfulFran twitched and moaned. It didn't take a wizard to understand what it meant. If either one reneged on their promise, they'd both go to Hell.

The yellow light vanished; the pain subsided.

Kathy snickered. "I guess she's not as smart as I thought."

Harradorn turned to Kathy. Every muscle in his body vibrated in fury, every condemnation he'd learned over the years ready to fly off his tongue. But he didn't get to be mayor of Peace and stay mayor by letting emotions control him.

His words came out cold and smooth like ice. "Shut up, Kathy."

Kathy took a step away, either stunned by his abrupt command or disarmed by his lack of anger. Lance was a raging tyrant when angry. After years of marriage to him, she probably wasn't used to someone who didn't resort to fire and brimstone.

Satisfied he'd silenced her—for now—he glanced at Joy. She looked scared.

She should be.

"The oath is deathly bound," he told the wizard, steel in his voice. "Now abide by your half of the bargain and reveal the second way to undo a wizard's petal wish."

The woman shrank back, her bravado when dealing solely with Joy gone.

> "Secrets and lambskins covered with hide
> Hide from us all except Silver's tide
> Under the peaks, out on the plains
> Into the Mark is where your search ends
> Pamela's Choices and Pamela's Chances
> No one to blame if you wish the same
> No one to blame if you wish the same."

"I've heard drunks make more sense," Kathy said. Harradorn motioned for her to keep quiet, but she continued anyway. "Well, I have. Someone should force her to be more specific."

"I agree, but this is not the time or place." He shot FearfulFran a stern look that warned her to stay put, and another that warned Joy to do the same. Then he told Kathy, "Come with me," and started for the front door.

"Harry, you can't believe anything she says," Kathy whined. They stepped outside. He wasn't sure if "she" meant FearfulFran or Joy. At this point, he didn't care.

The street was filled with groups whispering songs under their breath. Most were from *Les Miserables, Miss Saigon, Sweeney Todd,* and *Phantom of the Opera.* Their mood, like his, was sullen and angry. Rick and his troop of pirates looked particularly murderous.

"I'm confining FearfulFran and Joy to Dulgrun Prison for the night," he told the crowd. "Agamemnon!" he called out. The crowd parted and his faithful assistant danced sadly to the front. "Take Kathy home. I want all of you to go with them and make sure she gets there safely."

Kathy protested. "I want to stay with you."

He shook his head. "You need rest, and I need time alone to think. I'll meet you at the Hall during the morning's intermission." He gestured for Kathy to go with his assistant while at the same time he set the tone for the crowd by singing the opening line, "You're off to see the wizard!"

Everyone cheered and sang the lyrics from the *Wizard of Oz.* With Rick and Agamemnon leading the way, the happy crowd followed. Kathy went with them accompanied by everyone in sight, all of whom took turns linking their arms with hers to dance her away. Harradorn grinned. It was going to be a long dance home, especially in high heels.

The street soon cleared. From a distance, he could hear Kathy yelling at everyone to leave her alone. But he had given orders and everyone obeyed. Sometimes it was good to be mayor. He turned to the trattoria.

And sometimes not.

Inside, two women waited for him. One he hated. The other... he no longer knew what he felt.

Chapter 21

In the trattoria, Harradorn found Joy sitting hunched over at a table in a corner, hands clasped in her lap, looking for all the world like a little kid waiting to be yelled at for doing something bad. As for the wizard, the troublesome hag rocked somberly under an arbor of red roses, mumbling a song to herself while eyeing him with contempt.

Joy glanced his way and explained. "We overheard about us going to Dulgrun Prison."

No hope of reprieve brightened her eyes. She'd already accepted the punishment. But for what? He was almost afraid to ask. "What did you promise FearfulFran?"

Her voice trembled in misery. "What do you think?"

He remembered what she had been holding when he first entered the restaurant. "Not the wizard's petal?!"

She nodded and turned away.

She might as well have promised a nuclear bomb to a terrorist. "What the Hel were you thinking?"

Joy flinched. "I wasn't thinking. I was feeling—your anger, your pain, your terrible choice, the Great Redux. I couldn't let you do it. There wasn't any other way."

The brittle silence that followed condemned them both. The magic of the blood oath would kill Joy if she didn't fulfill her side of the bargain. And FearfulFran might kill them all if the wizard got her hands on the petal.

Blood pounded in his head. He turned to FearfulFran. All of

this was her doing: the wizard duel, the blast that had unleashed the wizard's petals, the disappearance of those who had found and used them—their names were burned into his memory, never to be forgotten. And now the blood oath with Joy.

Furious, he stormed toward the wizard, hands clenched, voice ringing with murderous intent while he fought the urge to strangle her. "The streets are clear for the moment. I want you gone before the crowd returns." He paused, trying to think of a good place for FearfulFran to hide. That's when he noticed she was standing among flowers.

He asked Joy, "Where did you first encounter FearfulFran?"

"The patio of the Sweetheart Café," she murmured with regret.

Where he had found the dowsing rod. In an area full of hanging flowers.

Flowers.

When it came to wizards, there was no such thing as a coincidence. Flowers. What it meant, he couldn't say, but his intuition told him to stick to the pattern.

"Heather's Secret Garden has a greenhouse on the far side of Peace," he told FearfulFran. "Take Good Times Avenue all the way east to avoid those dancing Kathy home. Wait there until I get back, no matter how long it takes.

"And wizard," he added, pointing an uncompromising finger at her, "if you talk with Kathy or Lance before then, if you're not there when I return, you'll never see Joy again."

FearfulFran reared back, her fingers curled into claws, ready to strike.

> "Die, die, die
> Miss America dies—"

"No. She won't." Harradorn stood his ground despite her threatening nails. "Joy may have made a pact with you, but I didn't. I'll find a way to keep her alive and away from you if you don't do as you're told. Understood?"

Without her magical powers, the wizard didn't dare refuse. With her standard singing refrain for *yes*, she performed a death march out of the restaurant.

"She's not going to prison?" Joy said in surprise. "Am I?"

"I haven't decided." He plowed fingers through his hair, trying to control his temper. "I should. By Thor's hammer, if I had thrown you in Dulgrun Prison as soon as we arrived, none of this would be happening."

"But then I wouldn't have found FearfulFran and learned there was a second way to undo a wizard's petal. You'd still be thinking of killing a little girl."

"Maybe," he said, in no mood to argue.

"Maybe? I just bargained my life for a maybe?"

Joy was on her feet, hands fisted, spoiling for a fight, her stance reminiscent of her brother, Mike. By the fire in her eyes, the guilt over her secret meet-and-greet with FearfulFran had morphed into righteous martyrdom. By Odin, she was beautiful when she was angry. But that didn't let her off the hook.

"That's the difference between us, teacher. If something doesn't work in the classroom, you can always try something else. Being mayor, I don't have that luxury. I need to anticipate what stands the best chance for success with the least amount of harm. If I screw up, they can throw me out of office. Lance has tried three times and already has a fourth petition going. This time he might succeed."

"Sounds like he's after your job." Joy's hands remained fisted, but some of the fire left her eyes.

"That's what I thought. But he says he doesn't want to be mayor, and I believe him."

She loosened her fists. "Then why try to get rid of you?"

He shrugged. "I assumed it was Lance being Lance—a pretentious bastard who enjoys making my life difficult. But now…" He shook his head, trying to make sense of it all. "Then there's Kathy. Just today she suggested the town needed a new wizard."

"I remember." Joy lowered her hands, her brow furrowed in thought. "What would happen to the town if you were gone?"

"Rick would still be mayor of Prosperity—that wouldn't change. He'd fight and draw blood if he had to."

"I gather they don't believe in petitions on his side of town."

"Why use paper when you can use a cutlass."

Joy grimaced. Clearly, she didn't approve of how things were done in Prosperity. Neither had Doc, who'd spent most of his days suturing cuts and setting bones.

"Lance owns several restaurants in Peace. With me out of office, he might persuade the council to allow casinos in his eateries. He's tried before."

"So, Peace would no longer be so peaceful. And what would happen to the town if both you *and* Zach were gone?"

He stared at her, unsettled by the question. He couldn't imagine Peace & Prosperity without his childhood friend watching over them. "I don't know," he told her. And yet a chill coursed through his veins. Why, he couldn't say. He'd love to talk with Rick. His brother had a special insight when it came to guile and intrigue. But talking was impossible while singing and dancing under Aesa's wish.

"Come with me." Harradorn took Joy by the hand and they exited the trattoria. Usually at night the lights were soft and muted, but nothing was as it used to be. Lights shone full force in all the windows and lanes. Not even a mouse could move about undetected. He had to get Joy under wraps before anyone saw her. And he knew the perfect place.

But then they passed the Bjork Memorial Park and he had to stop. Their deaths were too fresh, this token of affection too new to ignore. There should never come a day when he could pass this spot without pausing to pay his respects.

"How lovely," Joy said, taking in all the red flowers of the small park situated on what used to be Bjorks Beautiful Blooms. She walked over to the plaque and read the inscription. "Oh. This is so sad. Did you know them?"

He swallowed past the lump in his throat. "I was their son's godfather."

"I'm sorry." She backed away, giving him some space, and wandered over to the circular marble labyrinth in the center of the park. She took several steps along the convoluted path. "I've never seen a labyrinth laid out in the shape of a blossom."

"The Bjorks were florists. It's only fitting." Other than the walkway and labyrinth, the entire park was covered with red blooms. Appropriate, but it would have been nice to have some green grass and a bench or two. "Everything was arranged by an anonymous donor. I would have preferred more calming hues, but condolences in whatever form should never be rejected. I was thinking of adding several white flowering bushes to break it up."

"That would be a nice touch. All this red reminds me of the red lightning zipping through my house when I tried to call my brother and got you instead."

"You saw red lightning in your home?" Yet another chill shot through his veins.

"Made my phone go bonkers. Thought it was going to taser me, but it just drained the battery."

He considered the implications. Every one of them filled him with dread. "FearfulFran was attacking Zach with red lightning when I got your call. He deflected the strikes. Several must have bounced off the atmosphere and reached where you live. Must be why I was able to get your call."

"Well, I guess that explains that."

"Not at all. The red lightning and what Zach used to deflect it were created by magic. I only have a rudimentary understanding of magic, but from the little Zach has told me, it's a living energy, somewhat sentient."

"And that's upsetting you because…"

"Because I don't think it's an accident we met. Of all the people in your area, why did I get a call for help from a female who would activate the curse and force me to go rescue her? The one person able to befriend a fairy, and an irascible fairy at that. Someone who'd figure out how to free my town from a sleeping spell and then return again to help save my town from Aesa's wish."

Joy's face paled. "And offer to give FearfulFran the one thing she wants, a wizard's petal. Omigosh! All of this was set up by FearfulFran to get her a petal! She's been manipulating me all along!" She lowered her head. "I feel so stupid."

"You shouldn't." Gently, he lifted her chin to look at him. "Remember, Zach's lightning deflected her magic and sent it to you. I don't think that was an accident either. I believe you were meant to be here from the start. Zach's magic and FearfulFran's magic battled each other. The question is: which won? Which magic actually wanted to bring you here, Zach's or FearfulFran's?"

"What do you think?"

"I think the oddsmakers in Prosperity would get stinking rich trying to figure it out." He stroked her cheek. "Knowing the answer might help us decide what to do next, but I don't think that's going to happen." They heard singing coming their way. "We have to get indoors."

Within less than a minute they were inside a shop and he was closing all the blinds and curtains. He kept the lights on. With the magic ensuring all the buildings and streets were well lit, a darkened store would draw attention.

"We're hiding out in the Cream & Fizz Soda Shoppe?" Joy asked. She took in the chrome stools lining a long white counter, and the shiny red booths. On the walls, memorabilia spanning hundreds of years caught her interest. She seemed particularly fascinated by the mother-of-pearl battle-ax.

"Not as fancy as the Ice Cream Emporium," he said, "but the malts are the best in town." He went behind the counter. "Would you like one?"

"I haven't had a good strawberry malt in a long time."

"One strawberry malt coming up."

She was about to sit at the counter when she nervously glanced at the closed doors. "You said there aren't any locks here. What's to keep someone from barging in and finding us? I'm supposed to be in prison, remember?"

"This is Peace. No one enters without permission during off hours. It's ingrained into our social fabric. Unless we start singing or play the jukebox, no one will bother us."

"And the owners? Won't they get mad?"

He chuckled. "You promised to give FearfulFran a wizard's petal, and yet you're worried about helping yourself to a strawberry malt? Joy Flint, you're priceless." He slid a menu with the name of the owner across the counter to her. He watched her out the corner of his eye while he worked on the malt.

Her eyes went wide. "This is yours?"

He wiggled his brows. "I wasn't always mayor."

Joy angled her head and studied him as if seeing him for the first time. She must have liked what she saw because a smile finally broke through the frown that had been haunting her since the trattoria. "What made you decide to become mayor?"

"It's in our blood, an obligation to our ancestors who established the town to keep it safe and well for future generations. Since the beginning, every Lawson has taken a turn being mayor."

"That explains why your brother is also mayor. What about Sirena?"

"She has aspirations to office, but with her the tradition would best be left to others."

"No administrative skills?"

"She'd either bankrupt the town with frivolity or alienate everyone with her promiscuous demands."

Joy chuckled and for a while a comfortable silence settled over them. "That thing you told FearfulFran—can you really find a way to keep the petal from her without it killing me?"

"I already have."

She blinked and sat up straighter. "What is it?"

Something that would doom their relationship. But she'd be safe. That's all that mattered. He forced a smile. "We'll discuss it later. After you've had your malt." With a flourish, he added a strawberry garnish, inserted a straw, and placed it in front of her. "You're going to love this."

"Why are you being so nice to me?" she asked.

"Consider it my way of apologizing. Hel, my idiotic rambling after finding out what the Great Redux was would have had anyone believing I could kill a little girl. But I'm an old fan of Star Trek and I believe its adage that the need of the many never outweighs the need of the one." But it didn't absolve Joy of her foolish deal with FearfulFran, and he turned away to clean up so she wouldn't see his frown. A moment later, he heard her suck the malt through the straw, followed by a long, happy "Ahhh."

He glanced over his shoulder. Her eyes were closed, face beaming in delight at the taste. She lowered her lips to the straw to draw up more into her mouth, and he felt himself stir. He'd give anything to have her suck on him—just once. Make love to her. Just once. While there was still time.

Instead, he donned a Cream & Fizz apron and stood in the open door of the refrigerator, cooling off, trying not to think about Joy going down on him while she continued to suck and *ahh* over the malt. "What's your favorite dessert?" he asked, and hoped he sounded calm and in control when all he kept thinking about was laying her on the counter, naked and aroused, coating her with whipped cream, then taking his time licking it off.

He shook his head. Thoughts of having sex in his shoppe had never happened before, and it caught him by surprise. Must be her orange hair. The fae-like color had him associating her with the breezy anything-goes sex life of fairies. While she continued to suck her drink, the thought came to mind that his tongue would really make her moan.

"Is that all you serve here?" she asked. "Dessert?"

"I make a mean carrot and wheat-grass shake, but generally I don't compete with Joanne's Juice-It Joint." He leaned across the counter. "I consider this my own pleasure palace."

She stopped sucking and raised a brow.

"I can transform even the stodgiest sourpuss into a fun-loving kid with one of my confections. It never fails."

Her brow arched higher. "Never?"

"Of course, Lance has never been in here."

She laughed, then returned to sucking, which only made him ache in longing. In dire need of a distraction, he said, "So, what can I tempt you with?"

"Anything with chocolate chips," she replied. "And cookie dough."

"Gotcha."

He gathered all the ingredients, but paused when they heard singing from outside. His gaze met hers. Their eyes stayed locked until the singing faded. He returned to creating his masterpiece, and Joy brought up the subject they both had been avoiding.

"I should have told you about finding the wizard's petal," she said.

"Yes, you should have." That came out a lot harsher than he meant. Joy was back to frowning. He swallowed his anger and tried again in a more neutral tone. "Sorry. This hasn't been one of my better days."

"I don't think you've had a good one since we met."

"That's for sure, and it's about to get a whole lot worse."

"You figured it out," she said in sudden realization. "You understood what FearfulFran said. So why don't you look pleased?" She covered her mouth with a hand. "We don't have to kill someone else, do we?"

"We won't know for sure until we find *secrets and lambskins covered with hide*, FearfulFran's reference to a book that has the answer to our problem. Which is a problem in itself."

"Finding the book?"

"Oh, I know where the book is, though not the title. She was quite specific: *under the peaks, out on the plains, into the Mark is where your search ends.* The big problem is gaining access to it. We're going to the one place we're not allowed to go—Macklin's Mark. City of wizards."

Joy almost choked. "Really? A whole city of wizards?! Really?!"

Omigosh! She was living in a Harry Potter world—with enough wizards to make an entire city. It was so fantastic, so amazing. She looked across the counter to the mirrored back wall and saw her own silly smile. And it became even sillier when she thought about the city of wizards all over again. Omigosh! A city of wizards!

"How do we get there?"

"We'll take my car." He poured glossy chocolate syrup on something behind the counter.

"You have a car?" Joy studied him among their surroundings. She'd always considered Harry a sexy, astute, influential head of state—Mayor of Peace. Now she was trying to picture him an ordinary yet sexy fun-loving dispenser of sodas and sundaes. Harradorn Lawson had more layers than a Dobosh torte. And she loved Dobosh tortes. This layer added an intimacy that had nothing to do with sex yet made him even more attractive. And she wondered if this playful, sweet side of him carried over into bed.

He added, "How else did you expect to get there?"

"Oh, I don't know. Maybe a flying carpet or a winged horse. Or the skelter mirror. I mean, who'd expect there would be a paved road leading to a secret city of wizards?"

"Actually several interstate highways. We're going to Denver."

"Denver, Colorado?"

He nodded.

"A city of wizards is in Denver?" Her eyes narrowed in disbelief. "Don't you think somebody would have noticed wizards all over the place by now?"

"As Zach explained it, the Mark occupies a slight temporal

distortion amidst the city of Denver. It can be seen if you're not looking straight at it. Like when you catch something out the corner of your eye, but when you look directly at it, it's gone."

"My brother said he once saw purple lightning near Denver."

"Probably from the Mark."

She shook her head in wonder. A city full of magic and wizards! Would they be nice like Zach or nasty and unpredictable like FearfulFran? Considering what magic had done to Peace & Prosperity, the last place on earth they should be going to is a place full of magic users.

"When Sirena first woke," Harry said, "she told me there's a morning intermission. We'll sneak out of town while everyone's asleep. My car's not far."

He lifted a shiny, flat silver bowl and set it before her.

Her mouth opened in astonishment. In the bowl was a vanilla ice cream castle surrounded by a moat of chocolate fudge syrup. Pellets of chocolate chip cookie dough formed the crenellation on the parapets. Each tower was topped by a bright red cherry. Above the gatehouse, a tiny plastic princess waved to the knight below on the graham cracker drawbridge while a red licorice dragon stalked from the side of the castle.

He sprinkled the structure with fine sugar, making everything sparkle like diamond dust, then retrieved a small piece of dry ice from the freezer and set it inside the castle grounds. Soon a soft, dreamy mist enchanted the scene.

"It's beautiful," she gushed. "I've never seen anything like it."

"A Harry Lawson original. Made with homemade ice cream from Crago's Creamery." With a grin, he handed her a long silver spoon. "Enjoy."

"Oh, I couldn't. It's a work of art." She looked up at him. "It's too wonderful to eat."

"Women," he muttered. He grabbed another spoon and dipped it into the chocolate moat. Ignoring her protests, he scooped a section of parapet, and held it to her mouth. "Open."

"Well, since you've already ruined it." She accepted the spoonful, and was immediately overwhelmed by the most incredible taste of chocolate, vanilla, and creamy, gooey goodness she had ever experienced. Eyes closed, lips parted, she breathed, enraptured by the tastes seducing her senses. If food could produce an orgasm, this was it.

"That good, huh?"

She heard the amusement in his voice. Reopening her eyes, she found him on her side of the counter, inches away, apron gone, his mouth descending to hers. He rotated her stool toward him. He kissed her, lifted her, sat her on the counter, and kissed her some more. She dropped the spoon, overcome by a whole different form of seduction.

He shouldn't be doing this. They didn't have time for it. But this was his one chance, maybe his only chance to be with the woman he had fallen head over heels with the first time he saw her. The possibility of living happily ever after had been taken off the table the moment Joy made the blood oath. For both of them, it was now or never.

Her milky brown eyes had changed to dark chocolate, and her sultry gaze asked for more. "I bet you know how to do a lot of interesting things with whipped cream," she purred.

He flashed a knowing smile. "You're about to find out."

His touch was rough and passionate, acting more like the dragon than the knight in the sundae, which was fine by her. But then from outside she heard singing.

"This won't do." Harry swept her up into his arms and carried her to a side door with stairs leading up to the next floor. They entered a large apartment. Without stopping, they moved to a bedroom. He kicked the door shut with a foot, locked it, and carried her to the bed.

He lowered her to her feet, his gaze hungry. "You smell good," he whispered, nibbling her neck while his fingers teased her blouse apart. Quivers of excitement raced through her while he slipped the blouse off her shoulders and let it drop to the floor. He reached for her tube top. Her palm itched, turning into pain that made her shriek. "Ow!"

"What's wrong? Is it my medallion?" He readily placed it on the night table. "I'm sorry."

"It wasn't you. The petal inflicts pain when it's too far away." She retrieved her blouse and dug it out. The pain ceased. "Such a simple little thing."

"Yet potentially the most dangerous thing in the world."

He lightly stroked the petal and she noticed what looked like a scar on his palm. A lot of scars. She took his hand in hers. Not random cuts. More like an intricate pattern.

"What's this?" she asked.

He looked down at his palm. "A reminder that doing the right thing sometimes hurts. Hurts a lot." He sighed deeply and glanced at the petal in her hand.

"You're expecting me to die." Incensed, she backed away from him. "That's why this was so great, why you were so great. This was to be my last hurrah. My going-away gift. One last night of glorious sex in case I die of the blood oath."

He winced, and she knew she'd hit upon the truth.

"You're right," he said. "A going-away gift. But not the way you think." He picked up the medallion and put it back around his neck.

"You still haven't forgiven me for making the deal with Fearful-Fran," she said.

"It's never far from my mind, but forgiveness is not what this is about."

"Then what?" she demanded. Tears filled her eyes. Something beautiful was dying and she didn't know how to stop it.

He lowered his head and refused to reply. And still he wouldn't look at her.

Her heart hurt; her insides were tied up in knots. Maybe she had been wrong about him.

She tried to sound mature, sophisticated, unemotional, as if being rejected by a lover happened all the time. But the words kept catching in her throat and her misery came through. "For the love of… Peace, Harry, tell me what's going on."

He stared at her, at the tears falling from her eyes, and for a second his stance softened. His hand reached out to her. But then his face hardened and he curled the scarred palm into a fist. "You bargained your life to save me and my town. A noble act. Except when you promised to give FearfulFran the petal, you did just the opposite. You doomed my town. Her wish might be a hundred times worse than what's going on. "

He took off the silk clothes he'd gotten from Sirena's and threw them in the trash, then changed into canvas pants and a cotton shirt, his mayor clothes. "What's done cannot be undone, not by you or you'll die for sure." He glanced her way, and his gaze pierced her soul. "I won't let that happen. I refuse to let that happen. It's up to me to make sure you never get the chance to live up to your promise, which is why I wanted to give us one beautiful memory of what might have been. Odin knows, we deserve it."

"I don't understand."

"After we find a way to nullify Aesa's wish, you're going into hiding. It'll have to be by force—you can't have a say in the matter—that should keep the blood oath from taking effect and killing you. Once Aesa's wish is over, FearfulFran will have her powers back. I can't protect you from a full-fledged wizard. You'll have to return to the outside world. Wizards can't use their powers there. I'm not sure why. Maybe because it truly is *outside*. You'll be safe in your world, and the petal with you."

While she had been reacting to everything, feeling sorry for herself, feeling guilty, Harry had thought it all out and found a solution. And yet he looked as miserable as she felt. "Why do I have the impression you're pronouncing my death sentence?"

"Because this is it for us, Joy. Once the town has returned to normal, you can never come here again." His voice broke, his hands shook, and he shoved them in his pockets. "If you did, the petal would activate and start killing you for not giving it to FearfulFran."

"But you can still come visit me, can't you?"

He shook his head. "She'll have spies follow me whenever I leave town. Like hounds on the scent, they'd follow me to you and bring you back to Peace or some other town like this and force the blood oath to take effect."

"There has to be another way." She couldn't imagine not seeing Harry again. "Don't wizards have prisons? After what FearfulFran did to Zach and your town, I'd think someone in that city of wizards would lock her up."

"Sure, if they can find her. But nothing short of death will dissolve the blood oath. Maybe not even then." His voice turned cold. "I've heard if someone kills a person under a blood oath, the oath is transferred to the killer."

"Is that possible?"

"I don't know. But I won't take that risk with you." He looked at her, and his face reflected the agony boiling inside.

She wiped tears away, but more just took their place. "I think I love you."

He swallowed hard and looked down at his feet. "I know. It's the only explanation for why you made the blood oath."

"And why you told Kathy we're engaged."

His mouth twitched, remembering. "That was merely a ruse. But it stuck in your head, didn't it?"

"At the time, the thought was appealing."

"And now?"

"Now I would risk death to see you again."

"That's not going to happen, teacher." He unlocked the bedroom door. "This is it for us."

She rushed to him and grabbed him by the arm. "Please, Harry, don't let it end like this."

The mere touch of her hand did him in. He grabbed her, held

her, never wanting to let go. She trembled in his arms, crying. He wanted to kiss away her tears, carry her back to the bed, and make love to her all night, every night, for the rest of their lives. But he couldn't. And he wouldn't. Her life meant more than a thousand nights of passion. He had to find the strength to let her go.

She drew her head back to look at him. The fierce determination in her tear-filled eyes made him love her even more. "I refuse to believe this is it," she said. "I'm not going to run away. I'm going to face this and do it my way."

He gaped. "Did you just rhyme?"

"Don't change the subject."

"All right then. Let's face facts. I love you. I think I'll always love you. But too many people's lives are at stake for you to be selfish."

She stiffened. "Selfish?"

"We're not going to think of ourselves. This is still my town and I'm still the mayor. And as my guest—"

"You mean prisoner," she angrily cut in.

"You're going to do as you're told and stop being so bold."

Her mouth dropped open. Surprise supplanted anger. "You rhymed."

"Dammit, I did. I was afraid this might happen. The magic from Aesa's wish must be seeping into us, like an infection."

She caught the edge of fear in his voice. "How long before we start singing and dancing like everyone else?"

"Hard to say. We should be fine if we leave by morning." He caressed her cheek. "This will be dangerous. From the tales I've heard, Macklin's Mark isn't easy to traverse even for a wizard. If you hadn't made a blood oath with FearfulFran, I'd do it alone and send you home."

"We're in this together," she said, and hoped she sounded brave.

"Which is why I have to leave and find everything I can to insure our safe passage."

Harry pulled her close. He slowly rubbed his hands up and down her back, and she closed her eyes. The heat of his touch, the tender strokes, made the world recede, and the night returned to just the two of them. She sighed in longing. Much like Felicity weaving her belts, a strong thread of love wrapped around them, tying them together.

"Get some rest. The drive is long, at least a full day." His gaze shifted to the bed. "No other woman has been in this bed." With one long, last, torturous kiss, he released her. "Keep the lights on and lock the bedroom door. No matter what you hear, what anyone might say, don't open it except for me."

Then he was gone.

From below, she heard the door to the soda shoppe open and close. Miserable, she looked down at the spot of dried blood on her finger. A tear splashed on it. If only crying could wash her foolish oath away.

Chapter 22

Men are idiots.

If Harry thought to alleviate any misgivings she might have about using his bed by revealing he hadn't made love to anyone in it, he was wrong. Sure, it was comforting to know she was the first woman in his bed, but all she could think about, toss-and-turn and grow hot and feverish about, was the miserable certainty they would never make love here or anywhere else. How did he expect her to get any sleep knowing that?

With longing, she admired the fake engagement ring on her finger and wished it were real. But she might as well believe in fairy tales for all the good it did.

Dawn grayed the sky. On the street below, she heard Rick and his troupe of pirates sing "Oh, What a Beautiful Mornin'" from *Oklahoma* while they passed by. Harry had been gone all night. Where could he be?

Obeying Harry's admonition to stay put, boredom set in. While the sky brightened to baby blue, she rearranged forty-two fishing lures in a rack on the wall—twice—once according to size and then in a flower pattern based on their colors. Harry would have gotten along great with her dad. George Flint was an avid fly fisherman. She could easily see the two admiring each other's lures and trading fish stories for hours.

She'd just decided to build a house out of a stack of *Magic: The Gathering* cards when she heard a familiar voice at the bedroom door singing "I Won't Grow Up" from *Peter Pan*.

"Felicity!"

Joy unlocked the door and flung it open. Harry stood before her, a stuffed gym bag in one hand and another shouldered on his back. His other hand held a large gilded bird cage. Inside danced her small orange friend. The fairy wore a copper diadem. She pointed at Joy's orange hair and then her own hair and laughed.

Harry frowned. "I thought I told you not to open the door."

"I missed you, too," Joy replied, and gave him a long, sweet, sympathetic kiss on the lips, which told him she understood why he was so grouchy. The fairy could easily get on anyone's nerves. That and he'd been up at least twenty-four hours, longer if she considered his rough night with her meddling brother. "Who else would think to use Felicity as bait to unlock the door?"

His eyes turned to stone. "Kathy. I told her you two were best buds, remember?"

Inside the cage, Felicity cartwheeled and sang "Sisters" from *White Christmas*.

Harry set down the cage. Joy moved to open it, but he put a hand on her arm. "She's still serving her sentence. Because of her size, this is her cell in Dulgrun Prison. I moved locations, that's all."

"Oh, come on, Harry. Let her out."

He stubbornly shook his head.

"Your town is cursed doing nonstop musicals, I'm under a blood oath, we're going to sneak into a city of wizards, and you're concerned about bending the rules for Felicity?"

"The law is the law."

She was about to tell him where he could stick his law when she noticed the dark circles under his eyes and his day-old whiskers. She held his face in her hands, wishing she could ease his worries. In a tender voice, she said, "If the law is the law, why did you bring her?"

"We're going to need a lie detector in Macklin's Mark. Since the magic won't let Felicity lie, she'll be perfect."

"Wizards do a lot of lying?"

"You've talked with Zach. Did he ever say anything straight out?"

"Most of the time he spoke in half-truths and innuendoes."

"Now imagine an entire city full of wizards talking the same. Not only will Felicity be our lie detector, she'll be able to cut through the crap and let us know what everyone's really saying." He glanced at his watch. "According to Sirena, the morning intermission starts in fifteen minutes. Once everyone's asleep, we'll slip out to my car." He hefted the gym bags and handed her the lighter of the two.

"Why do we have to sneak out if everyone's asleep?"

"Kathy." He grabbed the cage and they went downstairs. He placed the cage and his bag on the counter, then crossed to one of the shaded windows and peeked out. "I'm almost certain Kathy and Lance are working against us. If they are, I don't want to take a chance of her seeing us leave."

He set out fruit and yogurt and together they sat down for a quick breakfast. "Not much fun eating on the run," he said. "I'll be glad when this is done."

Joy stopped eating and stared at him.

"I rhymed, didn't I?"

She nodded.

"It's getting worse. During the night I caught myself singing 'Without You' from *Rent*."

Easy to guess why he'd been singing that particular song. Her finger wiped some yogurt from a corner of his mouth and she slowly licked it clean. "Harry,—"

"Wait. I have something for you." From a pocket he took out a small box. "I planned on giving you this later, it's part of our cover story for getting into the Mark, but I want you to have it now." He slipped a ring on her finger next to the engagement ring.

"It's beautiful." Platinum with tiny gold oak leaves and acorns. "This is a wedding ring."

"The best way to avert suspicion when we try to bring Felicity into the Mark is to pose as a married couple." He held up a matching ring. "The Valkyrie Oak symbolizes longevity and strength. It decorates many of our products. On wedding rings, it symbolizes the enduring strength of love."

"Enduring love," she whispered. She took the ring and placed it on his finger. The moment felt sacred, as if they had just taken marriage vows. Thoughts of wedding gowns, bridal showers, a colorful outdoor wedding, and a joyous reception danced through her mind with happy possibilities.

She looked at him and he at her, and the warmth filling her turned to ice. There'd be no fairy tale wedding. It was all make-believe. A sham. The blood oath insured there would never be anything more than this shadow of what could have been. She wanted to cry. Instead, she tried to make light of her feelings. "Fastest betrothal in my family."

He stroked the ring on his finger. "Given the circumstances, this is all the time we have."

She choked. "Or will ever have."

"Don't cry." He put his arms around her and held her close. "Hel, I didn't mean to upset you. I should have waited until we entered the Mark."

"I'm glad you gave it to me now. A good memory to cherish in the days ahead." *When I'll be comparing every guy I meet to you.*

He kissed the rings on her finger, sealing a promise they would never be able to honor except for this moment.

"Oh, Harry. What are we to do?"

"Save the town. Save you. Go on living as if we had never met."

They sat holding each other, their heartbeats marking the passage of time.

She sniffled and wiped her nose and tried to think of something else. "What makes you suspect Kathy's husband might be involved with FearfulFran, too?"

"The trees in front of his house haven't been growing as fast as the other trees in town."

"You keep track of tree heights?"

"With the exception of the Hall and Center Park, all the buildings and trees in Peace are of uniform height, the buildings all the same color."

"Definitely a planned community."

"Peace's tourists come here specifically to vacation away from magic and its inherent problems. Centuries ago, the Council figured correctly that mandating consistency in style and substance would drive any reckless magic users out of Peace and across the river to Prosperity. Somehow my brother's side of town thrives on irresponsibility, though they do have a large number of accidents."

"Accidents?"

"Mood rings that change the mood of the wearer. Good luck charms, bad luck charms. Then there was the love potion. Nine months later Prosperity had a population explosion. The trolls doubled within six months. As for the dwarfs, well, rumor has it all of them are now related—to each other."

Harry wagged his brow and Joy laughed. Felicity began singing about babies. Harry hushed her and told her to hum. She obeyed but couldn't stop dancing.

Joy asked, "How does having buildings and trees all the same size prevent what happens in Prosperity?"

"Similar to electricity emitting EMF fields, magic tends to ooze and subtly alter the color, shape, and size of things in the immediate surroundings."

"Like Aesa's wish infecting us."

"It's why Zach lives in a tower. The thick stone walls insulate the town from the magic he uses, keeping us somewhat safe."

"Somewhat?"

Harry shrugged. Clearly, magic wasn't an exact science.

"What about Zach?" she asked. "Doesn't the magic affect him?"

"No one knows. It could be why he talks the way he does. He

certainly didn't talk like that before he inherited his father's position." Harry glanced at his watch. "Almost time."

He went to peek out the window. "A few years ago, a mattress maker in Peace was secretly commissioned by several unhappy spouses to insert a magical aphrodisiac into the padding to spice up their marriage beds. Fortunately, we knew something was up when The Sleep & Slumber Shoppe began turning a light shade of red."

"What about trees?"

"Trees are more quickly affected than stone. Depending upon the magic, they might grow faster, slower, gnarled, or sickly. I've been receiving reports the trees in front of Sirena's store were taller than they should be, probably because of the skelter mirror being used so much. Lance's trees are hardly growing. I suspect FearfulFran visited him long enough or repeatedly enough to affect his trees. Maybe if I hadn't been so distracted by the wizard duel and a certain feisty teacher," he winked at her, "I would have realized sooner what was going on."

"Hindsight is always 20/20."

"Now you sound like Agamemnon." He shouldered his pack and grabbed Felicity's cage. "When I found the divining rod at the café, I knew Lance was involved. He'd commissioned Sirena to make it so he could find a wizard's petal."

She raised her brow. "So that's what that was."

"Obviously he gave it to FearfulFran. She probably inserted her wand into the hole in the base to augment its range of detection. Once I realized that, I wasn't going to let Kathy take you home to meet Lance. I hate to think how they planned to get the petal away from you."

He checked the street in both directions, and swore. "Kathy's headed this way. Hurry. Out the back door."

Behind his shoppe, they sped down a flower-lined alley to Happy Street. Harry checked around. "A group of singers are dancing away from us. If we're quick, they won't see us."

They zipped across the street, and were about to enter the next alley when from the other end they heard male voices singing the belligerent "Jet Song" from *West Side Story*.

"Lack of sleep must be putting some in a fighting mood," Harry whispered. "We better keep to the streets." They raced around the next corner and took shelter in a doorway. "I don't think they saw us."

"How much time?" she asked.

He checked his watch. "Two minutes. After that, we just have to avoid Kathy."

Crouching behind flower boxes, they scooted past a fabric store with people inside singing "Buttons and Bows," then ran to the next corner. Harry peeked around the building. He turned back and nodded the way was clear when he suddenly grabbed her arm and yanked her around the corner with him.

"What?" she whispered.

"Kathy. And she's not alone." He stole a glance. "The skratta's with her, sniffing the air, trying to catch our scent." Quickly, he surveyed the surrounding stores and hotels. "We've got to hide, but nothing can hide our scent."

"I thought you said the skratta was crazed. Wild. How could it be working for Kathy?"

"She probably offered it what you refused." Joy looked at him, not quite sure what he meant until he added, "Sex."

"Oh, yuk! She wouldn't!"

"No, but she made the skratta believe she would. Sometimes that's all it takes—a promise. Kathy's very good at it. Comes with being a consummate liar."

They heard a screech.

"It's picked up our scent!" He hurried her to the nearest door. "If Kathy sees our bags, she'll know I figured out FearfulFran's song. She'll have the town stop us from leaving, or follow us herself." They entered a candle store. "We'll stash everything here and come back for it later."

They hid their bags behind a counter.

"What about Felicity? Won't the skratta pick up her scent?"

"I'm going to release her for now." He fiddled with the cage's lock. "By Loki's luck, it's jammed. I can't get it open." He tried again. "It's no good. We'll have to leave her."

"We can't."

"If Kathy finds us together and asks what we're up to, Felicity will reveal everything. She can't lie." He hid the cage behind a display of votive candles.

"We can't leave her!" Joy said. "The skratta's hands are small and sharp. It can reach through the bars and harm her. I won't let that happen." She grabbed the cage. Harry did, too.

From outside, they heard the skratta's nasty laugh and the click-click of Kathy's heels.

"Leave it," Harry said.

"Never." With a firm hold on the cage, she grabbed his arm and said, "Smalt."

* * *

Kathy entered the candle shop with the skratta, expecting to see Harry. The place was empty. The skratta snuffled and snorted, knocking over candles and glassware while it searched for its prey. It sniffed two black bags, then went outside and sniffed some more. It had lost their scent. But how?

The skratta must be crazier than she realized. She'd been idiotic to think it could help her find Harry and that dim-witted outsider.

She fumed and followed it outside. All her plans were falling apart.

Harry had lied about meeting her at the Hall. He was probably in one of the hotels, screwing his brains out with that worthless bitch. Damn her! Who would have thought Joy would be stupid enough to make a blood oath with FearfulFran.

The skratta turned to her. It licked its thin lips and leered at her, its claws flexing, itching to tear off her clothes.

"Our deal was for you to find them," Kathy said firmly. "You haven't."

The skratta shrugged, not caring, and started for her, wanting to be paid anyway.

With the long, pointy tip of her shoe, she kicked it against the side of the building. It fell, stunned. She walked over and stepped on it, piercing it with a stiletto heel until it stopped squirming and was dead.

Unfortunately, its pungent dark blood had stained her heel. "What a waste of a good pair of shoes." Heel To Toe Cobbler was up the street, respectable shoes but off the rack. They'd have to do until she got a decent pair from home.

She yanked the shoe out of the skratta, her mind already devising a search grid. She'd find FearfulFran and make a new deal with her.

Or kill her.

Her back-up plan. Kill the hag, Joy dies from not fulfilling the blood oath, and the wizard's petal becomes free for the taking. She laughed out loud, thoroughly pleased with herself, glad she had goaded Joy into taking the blood oath.

Chapter 23

"Our bags are back in the candle shop," Harradorn said when they exited the Stygian Gap. "Everything we needed to get into Macklin's Mark." Annoyed, he glanced around. They were in Joy's living room. "We shouldn't be here. The mirror should have returned us to the location of our original departure."

"True," Joy said. "But the mirror is keyed to my phone. Sirena said it'll take me anywhere I want as long as I have the phone with me."

"If I'd known that, I certainly wouldn't—" he stopped. He'd just heard someone chamber a bullet. He looked over his shoulder. "Hello, Mike. Bit of an overreaction, don't you think?"

With a steady aim at Harradorn's heart, Mike grabbed his sister and pulled her away. He scanned her from head to toe. "Are you all right? Are you hurt? What did he do to you?"

"Nothing," Joy said. "I'm fine. For heaven's sake, put the gun away and let me explain."

Mike wasn't listening. Harradorn recognized the look on her brother's face. The soldier was a predator fixated on what he could see, not on what anyone would say. Mike glanced at the orange fairy flitting in the gilded cage, singing the "Gun Song" from *Assassins*, but his gun stayed trained on Harradorn.

"This isn't about us showing up out of the blue, is it?" Harradorn said. So as not to appear threatening, he eased himself down on the couch, hands raised to show they were empty, all submissive movements that established himself a willing prisoner. "What's happened here?"

Suddenly, Felicity stopped singing. Everyone looked at the cage. The fairy sat cross-legged, eating fruit and sipping from a tiny flask. She smacked her lips. "This rose nectar tastes better than what you sent, Mayor Harradorn."

"Mayor?" Mike lowered the gun. He let go of Joy and waved at the cage. "What the hell is that?"

"A toy. A robot." Joy set down the cage and began to tell him a crazy story about educational gadgets. Mike seemed to be buying it. But then he snatched her hand and held it up.

"Is that a wedding ring? You're married?" He scowled at Harradorn and the matching ring on his finger. "Sonofabitch! To him?! Jeez Louise, you just met the guy!"

Harradorn raised his eyes to Valhalla. *What else could go wrong?*

Someone opened the front door. "That's it, Mike," a male voice said. "Can't do anymore here."

Mike's gun disappeared into his jacket and Harradorn hid the cage behind the couch. Bad enough Mike had seen Felicity. Anyone else and they'd end up selling the story to Disney.

A man in a police uniform entered the house.

"Kasey?" Joy said. He was Mike's ex-army buddy. A year ago, he'd joined the local police force after opting out of re-enlistment so he could spend more time with his family. But his military haircut and trim physique indicated his heart still remained with Mike and their team.

Kasey stared in surprise. "Joy? Holy shit! Am I glad to see you. Mike's been going nuts ever since he found blood on— Say, how did you get in? I was right outside." He noticed Harry, and his voice turned flat, professional. His hand reached for his gun. "Isn't this—"

"Yeah," Mike grumbled. "The last one seen with my sister."

"Thought so. Matches the description you gave the sketch artist perfectly. Is he—"

"Not a threat," Mike said. "For now."

Kasey lowered his hand from the gun, but he kept his body angled toward Harry. "All right then, let's take this one step at a time. Joy, I'll start with you. Where have you been for the last twenty-four hours?"

"We were just getting to that," Mike said.

"Kasey, what are you doing here?" Alarmed, Joy glanced at her brother. "What blood?"

Kasey looked her over just like Mike had done. "Not yours, obviously. Excuse me while I cancel the BOLO on you. And him," Kasey added, looking at Harry. He reached for his shoulder mic and went into the kitchen where they could hear him report Joy Flint had been found alive and well.

"BOLO?"

"Be On the Look Out for," Mike said. He clenched and unclenched his hands. "We assumed you were abducted. Or worse. We found your car abandoned on Garrett Mountain."

Crap. In their haste to get to Peace, she'd forgotten all about it. Worse, the torment lingering in her brother eyes, the tired lines etched around his mouth indicated she'd put him through hell. She felt awful. "I'm sorry. We used Harry's, uh, transportation. A spur of the moment thing. What blood?" Then it occurred to her, and she quickly glanced around. "Where's Shredder?"

"At the vet." She covered her mouth with her hands and Mike quickly added, "He's okay. The vet gave him something to calm him down. She's keeping him overnight, just to be sure." Mike wrapped her in a bear hug. She could feel his muscles trembling as he held her tight. "Oh, God, I was so worried. You sure you're all right?"

"I'm fine. Fine." She tenderly patted his back, trying her best to soothe him. Kasey reentered the room. Mike gave her one last squeeze, then let her go.

"That's one mean cat you have," Kasey said. "Guess the blood belongs to the burglar, now that we know it's not yours."

"Someone broke into my home?" Her mind reeled. While she'd

been dealing with one disaster after another in Peace, her own world had been rocked.

"Slit the screen and entered through the kitchen window," Kasey said. "Found a few fibers where he squeezed through. Dusted, but most of the prints are small, likely yours and Merry's, the larger ones Mike's, but we're running them all to be sure. Intruder probably wore gloves. Cat must have nicked him on the wrist. Most of the blood is upstairs in your room."

Joy gasped. "Why my room?"

"Well, uh." Kasey's mouth twitched. His feet shifted uncomfortably, and he looked away.

"What he's not saying," Mike growled, "is that the break-in three weeks ago in the house behind you wasn't just a burglary. The woman was assaulted. The police kept it secret. And two others in the area."

"We have a serial rapist in the neighborhood?" she said, stunned. Then she got angry. "You should have told us." She shook a finger at Kasey. "Everyone in the neighborhood has a right to know."

He held up his hands. "Hey, not my doing. The detectives in charge didn't want to scare the guy off, afraid he'd move to another town and start up again before they could catch him. We were ordered to keep quiet. You might've noticed we've been patrolling the neighborhood more."

Now that he mentioned it, she had. Yet it hadn't kept her home from being broken into. Her temper flared, furious at being kept in the dark. Then she remembered a night not too long ago when it was dark and stormy. She looked at Mike. "The screen in the garage!"

"Already told Kasey about it. Good thing I came by that night and scared him off. If I hadn't..." He fixed his gaze on Kasey, looking as if he wanted to throttle him for putting his sister in danger.

"If you hadn't," Joy said, "someone else was already on his way to rescue me." Harry came up from behind and slipped his arms around her, his hold steady and secure. *My hero.* Right from the start, her heart if not her mind had realized Harry was one in a million, and not because he came from a magical place. She angled her head back to look at him. "Looks like I really was a damsel in distress."

The turmoil in Harry's eyes indicated he was all too aware of how badly that night might have ended. He kissed her temple, his lips lingering, assuring her, and maybe himself, that she was safe. But not for long. The blood oath was as real and menacing as the man who had broken into her house.

"May we see her room?" Harry asked.

Kasey held up a hand. "First things first. Mind telling me where you and Ms. Flint have been for the last twenty-four hours?"

"We've been together," Joy answered. "That's all you need to know."

Mike glanced at her wedding ring, looking hurt that she'd excluded him from one of the most important events in her life. If only she could tell him where she had been and why they wore matching rings. But she had given her word no matter how hard it was to keep.

Mike started for the stairs.

Harry stayed behind. "I need to make a call," he said. Kasey eyed him with suspicion equal to that of Mike's. Harry pulled out a phone for all to see. "I'll catch up."

Joy caught his eye. He probably wanted to hide Felicity better so Kasey wouldn't catch sight of her. Or hear her. If the soft snoring from behind the couch got any louder, he'd find her for sure.

Upstairs, Joy did a quick survey of her room. Not bad. No gallons of blood, just bright red splotches on the floor by the bed. Most items had been knocked over or swept onto the floor, including the white orchid Harry had sent. She shivered and hugged herself. It could have been so much worse. At least

Shredder was all right.

"Thank God, Merry's in Italy."

Mike nodded bleakly in agreement.

"How's her room?"

"Untouched," Kasey said. "Which suggests he was specifically targeting you."

"Why me?"

Kasey shook his head "So far none of the victims fit a pattern. How about looking around, see if anything is missing."

"Sure." Anything to catch the bastard.

She skirted the areas spattered with blood—Shredder deserved an extra treat for being so ornery—and inspected her closet and drawers. The room felt different. All the vibes that made her bedroom feel cherished and cozy had been taken away by the intruder. The good memories of her late night laugh sessions with Merry while sharing a bowl of chocolate chip cookie dough, including their silly debates over whether college or elementary students made the best excuses for not doing their homework, had now been replaced with violation and blood. Though full of furniture, the place seemed empty.

She didn't think she'd every feel safe here again.

"Strange thing to keep in your bedroom." Kasey held up the toilet plunger. He glanced at her clown orange hair and she could see it in his eyes: his pal's sister is a nut.

For Mike's benefit, she dredged up a smile and said, "It's a traveling joke between Harry and me." She took the plunger and held on tight. It was the only thing in her room that didn't feel tainted.

"What's it made of?" Mike asked. "Bamboo?"

She followed his gaze, amazed to see the green nub she'd noticed the other morning had become a two-inch shoot. The rest of the surface of the wood was lightly splattered with green buds.

"Is everything here?" Kasey asked. "Sometimes rapists take trophies from their victims."

"The Grizzly King Streamer is gone." Harry stood in the doorway and nodded toward the dresser.

"A what?" Kasey asked.

"A fishing lure." Mike crossed his brawny arms. With a scowl that would have lesser men shaking, he asked Harry. "How would you know what was in her room?"

Joy gave Mike a look that said "not now" and told Kasey, "Harry's right. It's gone. And my blanket."

"Forensics has it," Kasey said. "It was slashed. Probably out of frustration that you weren't here."

"He also took your bedspread," Mike said.

She shook her head. "I threw it away a few days ago when I returned from—" The breath caught in her throat. She looked at Harry and felt the blood drain from her face. Her limbs turned ice cold. "The bedspread was shredded when I came home. I thought Shredder had done it. He's been upset lately. But now…"

Her legs gave way. Harry's strong arms swooped her up. Her teeth were chattering, her limbs trembling. She looked up into his worried eyes. Above the mad thumping of her heart, she vaguely heard him say, "She's going into shock."

In a flurry of movement, Mike covered her with a thick bathrobe from the closet. Under her brother's direction, Harry carried her next door to Merry's room where he sat on the bed and gently rocked her back and forth. With her eyes closed, she breathed in deeply of his scent, and for a few moments forgot about everything but being held in his arms.

"I'll be right back," Mike said. He headed for Joy's room where they could hear him talking with Kasey.

"It's all right," Harry said softly. "I swear to Odin, I'm not going to let this guy get anywhere near you." He lowered his face to hers. "You mean everything to me."

He kissed her, claiming his right to protect her above all others. The kiss lengthened, deepened, and her trembling eased, her body warmed. The distant conversation between her brother and Kasey drifted away and she only heard the steady beat of Harry's heart and the soft sound of his breath.

He held her closer, about to kiss her again, when he suddenly flinched and said, "Either you're into kinky sex or that's a toilet plunger in your hands."

Joy gave him the plunger. His lips parted in surprise. "It's alive!"

Mike and Kasey entered the room. "Tell him no," Mike ordered Joy.

"Come on, Mike," Kasey said. "It's a good plan."

"You're not using my sister as bait."

"Look, we could use a policewoman as a decoy, but I don't think it'll work. My gut says he knows Joy personally, so he's not going to be fooled by a look-alike. We'll keep Joy safe, use plenty of undercover. She'll never be alone."

"You got that right because she's coming home with me. And she's going to stay there until you catch this sicko."

"Mike's correct," Harry said. "It's too dangerous for Joy to stay here."

"See. I'm not the only one who thinks so." Mike nodded his thanks to Harry.

"It's also too dangerous for her at your place," Harry added. "He's been here three times, which means he wants her bad. A small change of location isn't going to stop him. No, the best thing for Joy is to leave the area completely and go out west with me where he can't find her."

The doorbell rang.

Mike pointed a finger at Harry and said, "We're not done with this," then went to answer the door.

Kasey stayed and tried to convince Joy to agree to his plan. She refused. "Believe it or not, I have a bigger problem to deal with."

Kasey left. Joy watched from a window while he walked to his police car. Across the street, Mrs. O'Keefe stood on her porch, waiting for her chance to scurry over and find out what all the commotion was about. Her neighbor turned to stare at something.

So did Joy. Her jaw dropped. Pulling up behind the police car was a gorgeous gold stretch limo with New York plates.

Harry joined her at the window and smiled. "You can always count on family to answer a call for help."

* * *

An hour later, Joy sat at the kitchen table and slapped a spider on the back of her hand.

Crap!

"I hate this tattoo," she said. "I keep thinking it's real."

"Be glad it's only temporary," Harry said.

She blew on the fresh coat of black nail polish and watched Harry's sister who ran the L&L store in Manhattan, draw a coiled snake on the back of his right hand with a permanent pen. Having met Sirena, this sister was definitely not what she expected.

Nara Erline Lawson was fashionably dressed in a modest turquoise cashmere sweater, white pearls, and white wool slacks. Her long fingers were perfectly manicured in the demure French style. Though she might pass for an upscale New Yorker, her flat shoes and flowing curls in shades of gold, amber, and hearty ale were casual and country. The easy smile she always shared when Harry looked her way revealed a loving bond with her brother. Certainly not the begrudging tolerance Harry showed toward Sirena.

Upon her arrival, Nara's driver had filled the downstairs with an assortment of bags, boxes, and cosmetic cases, "to replace what had been left behind in Peace," Harry had told Joy.

To forestall questions, Mike had been commandeered to get everyone food from the deli. While he was gone, Harry had explained that the fashion mavens of Macklin's Mark changed styles every 10 years, something about security and mystical currents. Joy guessed it was related to how magic changed the color and shape of buildings and trees in Peace.

Macklin's Mark was in the final year of a modified Goth look. It's why she was in an outrageous costume composed of black boots, black embroidered satin skirt, and a black leather bustier that made her breasts bulge in a way that screamed porn or dominatrix rather than a statement of feminine empowerment. Shiny silver chains accented her breasts and crisscrossed her back, and matched the silver skull-and-crossbones necklace and earrings.

Nara had wanted to dye Joy's hair black, but Harry insisted on only a few black streaks, claiming Joy needed to keep the orange color. Likewise, he had his sister add a few black streaks to his own hair.

While Nara finished the fake tattoo, Joy studied his appearance. Obviously, male wizards didn't show as much skin in the Mark as women. The silver-studded black jeans with chains, the opened black silk shirt, silver-embroidered black vest, and black duster created a whole new look for him. Dangerous and bad. Sexy.

You'd never guess he moonlighted as a straight-laced mayor or a soda jerk.

She tugged at the top of her bustier. Harry looked a lot more comfortable than she, except for the pierced earrings his sister had just installed. The bleeding in his freshly-pierced ears had stopped but Joy could tell by the way Harry kept fidgeting with the diamond studs curving up the helix of one ear that he was in pain.

From what Harry was telling her, tattoos among wizards were status symbols and identification marks. Anyone entering the Mark without them would be suspect. The tattoo on the front base of the neck proudly proclaimed one's family connections. Harry was going to pass himself off as a distant cousin of Zach's, so his sister had drawn a stylish black hawk below his neck.

A wizard's strongest magic was displayed on the left cheek. With what little he knew, Harry had decided to depict his major magic the same as Zach's—a white masculine-looking rose. To signify his secondary magic, an orange sunburst circled his left eye, different than Zach's so as not to arouse suspicion.

To get the fairy into the Mark, Joy and Felicity Morningstar would be related, so Nara had drawn stars and suns below Joy's neck, readily seen above her bustier, plus small colorful flowers on her cheek. Nothing around her eyes except a heavy dose of black liner.

Tattoos on the right hand denoted one's enemy, a constant reminder to never let one's guard down. Spiders and their webs were bane for free-flying fairies, which was why Joy had one on her hand.

While Nara finished the tattoos, Mike entered the kitchen with the deli sandwiches. He walked around the room, his gaze scornful of all the ear piercings and body art. His steely-eyed disapproval of the outfit Joy wore was offset by his repeated glances at Nara. For her part, Nara's glimpses at Mike indicated something was going on between the two. Curiosity? Or mutual attraction? Poor guy. Knowing where Nara came from, he didn't stand a chance. Joy swallowed hard and looked at Harry. Neither did they.

"I wish you would tell me where you're going," Mike said.

Joy sighed. "I told you, a rock concert in Denver. A once in a lifetime chance to see the wizards of the Mark."

"Never heard of them."

"I have," Nara said. "Many times." She touched her brother's arm. "It's a once in a lifetime event. But I don't envy you, Harry. I wish there was another way."

"You mean streaming live feed?" Mike asked.

"I mean an undiscovered passage," Nara replied. She pulled out something from the back of her brother's vest and tossed it to Mike. "One without bugs."

Joy recognized the tiny object. "You didn't."

Mike crossed his arms. "What did you expect? Ever since you met this guy you've been acting like a starry-eyed, love-struck nincompoop."

"Have not."

"Really? Then I guess you didn't forget about work tomorrow. Or that your principal wanted to see you first thing in the morning—without orange hair. What's going to happen when she sees your tatts?"

Joy cringed. She'd completely forgotten what day it was.

"You haven't missed a day of work in three years. Now you're flying off with a man you only meant a week ago, dressed like a witchy Goth—"

"Wizard Goth," Nara cut in with an amused smile.

"Whatever," Mike tossed back. "There's something wrong going on here. You sure as hell aren't telling me everything. Like, if you're going to a concert, why are you taking that singing robot in the cage?"

"You want the truth?" Joy said.

"Please."

Harry stood up in alarm. "Joy, don't."

"I have to. He's my brother." Harry gave her a long searching look, then threw his hands up in the air. She turned to Mike. "While we're in Denver, we're taking her to a place where we can get her fixed so she's not singing and dancing all the time."

"Why don't you just turn it off?" Mike asked.

"I wish," Harry muttered.

"It'll, uh, damage her circuitry," Joy said, "if she's not powered down first."

"Are you going with them?" Mike asked Nara.

Nara shook her head. "I'm afraid to fly, which is why I had to attire them before they left. But you're not afraid." Her long finger stroked her own cheek, mirroring the fresh scar on Mike.

Mike looked startled. "How did you know—" he began to ask when the doorbell rang. He left to answer it.

While he was gone, Harry helped Joy into the black hooded cloak she'd wear into the Mark, then got Felicity. She sang "We're Off to See the Wizards." He covered the cage with a black cloth, and the singing faded into silence.

"I wish I could tell Mike what this is all about."

"I know." He hugged her close. "But you can't. His loyalty rests with your government. He would be obligated to report all of this. And then Peace & Prosperity would be invaded by your country's darkest version of national security. The nonhumans would be caged and interrogated, perhaps even tortured into revealing secrets of magic that are best left unknown. I cannot allow Mike to be aware of even a hint of my town's existence."

She nodded silently in agreement.

"You have your phone?" he asked. She checked her pocket and nodded.

Nara summoned her driver to pack her things and take everything out to the limo. She hugged her brother. "You really think this is going to work?"

"We don't have any other choice."

"But you left all your magic tokens back in Peace. How will the two of you ever pass for wizards if the gatekeepers can't detect any magic?"

Joy turned to Harry in dismay. "That's why you were gone all night?" The bags they'd left in the candle shop were far more valuable than she'd ever imagined. Since Peace restricted magic, he must have spent hours scavenging Prosperity. "I'm so sorry."

"It's all right," he said. "We'll manage."

"But how?" Nara asked, her smooth brow wrinkling with concern.

"Joy has a wizard's petal." Nara caught her breath; she looked at Joy in surprise. Harry continued. "If I stand close, the magic should bleed over and make it seem like we both have magic." He kissed Nara on the cheek. "If you don't hear from me within three days, contact Mom and Dad. Tell them what's happened. Whatever you do, don't go home."

Mike returned. "That was Kasey. They're going ahead and using a policewoman to catch that creep. While you're gone, she'll use the house, wear your clothes, work at your school. The police will contact your principal and arrange things. She'll even have orange hair like yours so as not arouse suspicion."

"My principal will love that," Joy said sarcastically.

"Yeah, well, we don't have a choice. Merry will be home in a week. If he's not caught, there'll be two Flints he can target."

Joy shuddered. Horrible enough thinking he was after her. The thought of him going after their sister was far worse.

"We'll ride with my sister to the airport." Harry grabbed the cage. They headed into the living room where he opened the front door.

"I'm going, too," Mike said. "To see you off," he added, sporting a far too innocent smile.

Harry and Nara exchanged glances. With a coy smile, Nara batted her long lashes and asked Mike for help with something she'd left in the kitchen. The transformation of her brother was almost magical. Completely disarmed by Nara's delicate charm and gentle hand on his arm, he smiled, really smiled, and accompanied her to the kitchen.

As soon as they were out of sight, Harry waved at the limo to leave. "Mike will think we left for the airport without him." He took her hand and said, "Smalt."

Chapter 24

Within seconds, they appeared in Sirena's workshop. "Why are we here?" Joy asked.

"The magical trigger with your phone will only work in Peace. From here you can transport us to Denver and the secret entrance to Macklin's Mark."

"Very clever."

Harry drew her close. "I thought once you were home, you'd be safe—no blood oath, no wizard's petal wish. Now I'm going crazy thinking about this guy stalking you. He's been so close. A shift in timing and he could've had you—twice that we know of."

"I can't stay here," she told him.

He leaned his forehead against hers, the gesture intimate as a kiss. "I know."

"Peace is your home. You belong here."

"Not while you're in danger."

"I can fight my own battles. And I have Mike and a good chunk of the Clifton police force watching out for me. Besides, you said it yourself, I shouldn't run away."

He groaned, hating having his own words thrown in his face. "This is different. You—"

She silenced him with a kiss, gentle yet sad, and felt the fight go out of him.

She tugged his hand and tried to smile. "The sooner we do this, the sooner we save your town." *The sooner we say good-bye.* She saw the same thought reflected in his eyes.

She sighed in misery and asked for the address.

"1313 North Macklin Avenue, Denver, Colorado."

She raised a brow.

"Nothing like hiding in plain sight," he added.

She concentrated on the address and said, "Smalt."

When they exited the Gap, the lights were bright, the air filled with playful music and children's laughter, plus the scent of peppermint. "We're in a toy store."

"Toy Paradise & Magic Emporium," Harry said. "Quick, outside for a sec." Upon exiting the store, he asked for her phone. She complied—and wailed when he smashed it with his foot. "Wizards never use anything electronic," he explained. "Having any would be a dead giveaway, and I doubt we'll be coming back this way." He smashed his own phone and tossed the parts in a nearby trash bin. He left his watch on a bench for someone to find. She did the same.

"The first of three gatekeepers is in here. Remember we're people of magic, so nothing we're about to see or experience should surprise us. Follow my lead."

They reentered the store. It was merry and colorful, while they were dark and clothed in black. *Talk about standing out like sore thumbs.* In her cloth-covered cage, Felicity began singing "Toyland" until Harry insisted she hum. With the numerous distractions of a toy store, no one paid them much attention. They skirted the more cheerful areas and entered the magic section where the subdued colors helped them blend in.

The young woman behind the counter smiled at Harry. "Cool tatts. Where'd you get them?"

"My sister." He smiled. "Anyone here fix robot fairies?"

"You must want Nick. I'll get him."

A few seconds later, a tall, lean, middle-aged man with long curly white hair and a trim white beard approached wearing jeans and a t-shirt with the logo of the store. If ever there was a modern embodiment of a virile, health-conscious Santa Claus hiding out in a toy store, Nick was him. The top edge of a dagger tattoo was visible on his left cheek above the beard, but there was no hiding the Christmas wreath encircling his left eye. Her friend Gina would love to find this guy under her Christmas tree.

He scrutinized their face and hand tattoos, then gestured to their throats, a silent request to be shown their family symbols. Joy opened her cloak and Harry his duster. Nick moved closer to inspect her stars and suns, and she held her breath.

"What can I do for you?" the man asked in a smoker's rough voice.

Harry put an arm around Joy and snuggled her close. "We were late getting back from our honeymoon and missed our ride. Not a big deal, but then my wife's relation became ill. We need to get in to see a healer." He put the cage on the counter and lifted the cover enough so Nick could see the fairy. Felicity must have noticed the man's eye tattoo because she started singing Christmas carols and prancing around the cage.

"She won't stop singing and dancing," Harry said. "Some kind of spell. It's driving everyone nuts. Can you let us in?"

The man stroked his beard. From a mirrored cabinet, he took out a top hat that magicians wear and rabbits are known to frequent, and motioned Joy to put it on her head. Remembering not to question anything, she readily complied. In the mirror behind Nick, she noticed the black silk band on the hat was now glowing white, its edges a bright blood red.

"Passable," the man said. He gave the hat to Harry.

Joy stood by his side and crossed her fingers, and hoped the magic from the petal in her pocket would extend to Harry and make it seem he had magic.

On Harry, the hatband barely glowed, not white or red like with her, but a green that flickered like a flashlight whose battery is going dead.

The man frowned. "Never known a Blackhawk to be so weak. Who's your sponsor?"

"Zacharias," Harry said with a broad smile. "He'll vouch for me."

The man continued to hesitate

"Zach is such a sweetheart," Joy said, forcing a smile. "Best man at our wedding. When he kissed me to welcome me into the family, I thought, 'Wow!' For a second, I wasn't sure I'd married the right Blackhawk."

Harry laughed and pinched her butt. She jerked up in response, heaving her breasts forward, straining the bustier and attracting Nick's attention. For the first time, the man actually showed signs of life. He licked his lips.

"All right. You can pass, but I don't think Ssiv Sssi will be so lenient. Chances are she'll send you back—without the fairy. She loves fairies. Considers them a delicacy." His rakish smile led her to believe he'd tasted fairies too, and liked them.

He invited them to try the disappearing booth—one at a time. Harry went first with Felicity, who was singing, "We're off to see the wizards…" When the door reopened, they were gone.

Joy stepped in. A crystal amethyst hexagon covered the floor. She turned and waited for Nick to close the door. A glint appeared in his snowy blue gaze. "I bet you're naughty *and* nice. If you ever get tired of loverboy, I've got some presents you'll like, toys I've never shown anyone else."

She tried to appear shocked by his audacity—she being a newlywed and all. But it's tough looking insulted when wearing a skimpy Goth outfit with chains and skulls all over. And Nick knew it. He winked and shut the door.

* * *

A cloud of lavender sparkles deposited Joy in the middle of a columned rotunda. From all sides, a cloying grey mist spilled into the circular room. Vomit green light pervaded the area while a thick, musky odor made her want to gag. She drew the cloak over her nose.

"Lovely scent, don't you agree?"

Harry stood several yards away, straight and stiff, cage held high. His eyes glanced down. In the shifting mist, snakes slithered around his feet. Several of the serpents leapt up trying to snag the cage. With Joy's arrival, half the nest broke off and slithered to her, tongues out, sensing her presence.

"Stay still," Harry warned.

She rolled her eyes and proceeded toward him. The serpents scattered. Their roiling thick mass cleared a path through the mist. "Snakes are inherently shy," she explained. "Growing up with a brother like Mike, we had a lot of unusual pets in the house. Worst were spiders. I never got used to them." She got to Harry's side and saw beads of perspiration on his forehead. "Really? Snakes?"

"We all have our demons."

"But not much magic," a sleek voice said.

A wisp of a woman glided toward them. In spite of the tight black dress covering her from shoulders to feet, her curves shifted effortlessly like the snakes. Her tongue flicked—split, with two silver piercings. A coiled snake tattoo adorned the base of her neck, more stylized than the one on Harry's right hand, the symbol of Zach's enemy. Since Harry was posing as Zach's relative, she was his enemy, too.

This couldn't be good.

Ssiv Sssi slid up to Harry. Her scaly green fingernails plucked the cloth covering the cage and tossed it away. "Ooh! A fairy!" Her tongue flicked excitedly. Felicity flew to the opposite end of the cage, singing a frantic version of "Will You Miss Me When I'm Gone."

The woman gazed happily at Harry. One hand slithered around his neck up into his hair. "A gifffft? For me?"

"Not on your life," Joy answered when Harry kept quiet. Seemed he really was afraid of snakes, even in human form.

"You may procceeed," she told Joy. She flicked her hand in the direction of the hexagon which the mist and the snakes avoided. "But thisss one doesss not have enough magic. He will have to go back. Or ssstay and feed my love." Her head flexed sideways and Joy saw a giant python slowly curl around one of the columns. "Long sssince a Blackhawk dare visssit me. With ssso little magic, thisss one won't be misssed."

The woman's fingers slithered through his hair. Harry shuddered.

"But he does have magic," Joy said.

"Not enough to passs," Ssiv Sssi hissed. She glanced down at the snakes.

Joy noticed they stayed a respectful distance from herself, yet got up close and personal with Harry. Magic detectors.

"Then we'll both go back," Joy said.

Ssiv Sssi's eyes slanted her way. Her tongue flicked. "You have already been given passsage. Or do you wisssh to duel? Ifff you lossse, my love will have two sssnacks. Isss thisss Blackhawk worth it?"

There was no way she could duel a wizard. If she tried, Ssiv Sssi would discover she was a fraud, and then both she and Harry would be swallowed whole by the python eyeing them with ravenous interest.

Kathy would know how to handle someone like Ssiv Sssi.

Desperate, Joy did her best to impersonate the confident snob. With bored disinterest, she studied her nails. "Perhaps I drained my husband too much of his magic on our honeymoon. You know Blackhawks, always wanting more. We haven't slept in days."

Ssiv Sssi regarded her, then flicked a glance at the python. Her mouth twitched in understanding. Yet her fingers still snaked around Harry. She wasn't going to give him up.

"Perhaps you're right," Joy said. "If he doesn't have enough magic to keep me satisfied, maybe I should find me a new husband." She drew Harry's face into her hands and kissed him. She caught Ssiv Sssi slinking excitedly from side to side while she felt him up one last time—and secretly slipped the wizard's petal into his pocket.

Instantly, her palm itched. "I'll always love you," she told Harry. She took Felicity's cage and hurried for the hexagon, wincing in pain as the distance between her and the possessive petal increased.

Like before, the snakes avoided her, but their distance was no longer respectful. Her magical connection to the petal kept them at bay, but they were definitely slithering closer. And though they were partially hid by the mist-covered floor, it was only a matter of time before Ssiv Sssi noticed she had less magic—and a lot of excruciating pain.

An invisible knife stabbed her palm. She flinched, almost cried out. The pain unbearable, she raised the hood of her cloak to hide the tears streaming down her face. Her mouth twisted in agony, the petal punishing her for leaving it behind. Pain sliced up her arm into her chest and she almost doubled over. Nerves on fire, muscles flinching, she glanced over her shoulder and saw Ssiv Sssi looking at the snakes slithering at Harry's feet. They were all retreating.

Ssiv Sssi hissed. "It ssseems your lusssst for her hasss recharged your magic. You may go with her—thisss time. But come thisss way again, Blackhawk, and you'll not be ssso lucky."

It seemed to take forever for Harry to join her on the platform. His smile of relief swiftly turned to shock when he looked at her face inside the hood. "Joy!" he whispered.

"The petal!" She gasped. "Pain… killing me." Blackness fogged the edges of her vision. She barely saw his eyes widen, his brow shoot up when he finally realized what she had done to save him. He frantically searched his pockets. Ssiv Sssi hissed esoteric words and lavender sparkles swallowed them. Harry caught Joy as she collapsed in his arms.

* * *

Having a sister who's a professional caver, Joy had gone on a few trips underground to see what Merry found so fascinating. Truthfully, she still didn't know, but if her sister loved it, that's what counted. So when Joy regained consciousness, she immediately knew she was in a cave. The scent of moist earth and rock was infinitely more pleasing than the repulsive musk of snakes.

Harry moaned. In the dim light, she found him in a fetal position by her side, twitching in agony, whereas her own pain was gone. "What happened?" she asked.

"No one can touch a wizard's petal without paying the price. You were unconscious, couldn't take it out of my pocket, so I did it for you."

"Oh, Harry." She gathered him up in her arms and held him close until the pain subsided.

"Where are we?" he asked, wincing now and then but every time a little less.

"In an underground tunnel. There's light around the bend."

Several growls and barks erupted from the same direction.

"How are you with dogs?" he asked.

"I'm a cat person. You?"

"Our sheriff is a werewolf." They got to their feet. He picked up Felicity's cage and checked the fairy. She was singing "Batman" and fluttering her wings nervously. He looked at Joy. "Ready?"

Hands grasped together, they headed for the last gatekeeper.

* * *

Under strict orders, Joy stood apart from Harry while a crusty old man with mushrooms growing in his filthy hair, wanded him with a clear crystal rod. The rod barely glowed. The man circled him. "Not much magic."

Harry nodded sadly in agreement. "As I said, I'm a distant cousin of Zach Blackhawk. Always thought in another generation my descendants wouldn't be allowed in, but then I found Joy Morningstar." He reached for her hand and kissed it. "The love of my life. My wife."

The gatekeeper eyeballed Joy, particularly her breasts threatening to pop out of the bustier. Like the first guard, he was plainly mistaking her tight clothes and breathlessness for the energetic sauciness of young love when actually she was scared stiff that after getting this far, something would go horribly wrong and they'd be denied entry.

Or worse.

Nearby, a two-headed dog the size of grizzly bear kept licking both his chops. He—they—appeared hungry, and the two leg bones they gnawed on looked awfully human.

The man wanded Joy a second time. The crystal glowed brighter than for Harry. The gatekeeper scrutinized her orange hair and the matching color on the woman in the cage. "And you claim this fairy is your sister?" the man asked Joy. She could see his mind trying to figure out the logistics of whether sex between a fairy and a human was possible.

Fortunately, Felicity decided to sing "Sisters" with a joyous, energetic dance. Acting as if happiness might be contagious, the grumpy guard retreated. "Destination?" he asked.

Harry said, "We're researching the magical properties of white tomatoes that have been crossbred with wolfbane for use as an ingestible pesticide against werewolves." The guard's eyes glazed over. Harry glanced at Joy. With a furtive wink, he continued. "We hope anyone who regularly uses the potion will no longer need fear an attack."

"Could have used some of that myself forty years ago," the gatekeeper said. He scratched cruel scars on one side of his neck, then scratched his crotch. "I'll shoot you to the Archives."

"Actually, I think we'll find what we need at Pamela's."

The gatekeeper eyed him suspiciously. "Don't think you're going to find what you're looking for there. Just full of New Age gobbledygook. Not a lick of magic."

Harry frowned, echoing her own doubt they'd find what they needed in the one place without magic. But FearfulFran had been specific—Pamela's Choices and Pamela's Chances. The magic infecting Peace wouldn't let her lie. It had to be there.

"Worthless junk, I tell ya." The scarred gatekeeper spat a mass of green phlegm out the side of his mouth. "Place run by a bunch of no-good liberals. Surprised the Council of Elders let them set up shop."

Harry shook his head. "Disgraceful. But my sources tell me what I'm looking for is there." He shrugged. "If not, we can always check the Archives."

The gatekeeper grunted. "Let me know when that potion comes on the market."

"You'll be the first," Harry said. With Felicity's cage in hand, he and Joy stood on the amethyst hexagon like those at the last two guard posts.

"You sure now?" the gatekeeper asked Joy. He scowled at the enemy tattoo on her right hand. "Pamela's is the last place you oughta be going to."

She looked down at the spider tattoo and shuddered. Harry reached over and took her hand, covering the spider. With a gentle reassuring squeeze, he told the gatekeeper, "I'll keep an eye on her."

"So be it." The gatekeeper stretched out his hand toward them and burped from the gut, assaulting them with the stench of partially digested sausage and eggs. Instantly they were covered in lavender sparkles, headed to Macklin's Mark, city of wizards.

Chapter 25

Within seconds, Joy and Harry appeared in a large circular store full of feel-good banners, kites, aromatherapy, and floor water fountains babbling merrily.

Crystals of every shape, size, and color dripped from an array of clear strings from the ceiling, giving the impression they were surrounded by motionless raindrops. Enya music breezed through the place. Not surprisingly, Felicity danced and sang along.

"Not what I expected," Joy said.

"The gatekeeper must get his jollies frightening visitors," Harry replied.

"I still can't figure out how you got past him and Nick. They both detected magic on you."

"Elven magic." He opened his black duster and pulled out the handle of the plunger. The green buds had grown twice their size. "Part of the Valkyrie Oak was inserted into the center so I could visit you that one night. Most likely the magic of nature spirits was invoked to make it work. Not powerful like wizard magic, but enough to fool two of the guards."

"What if it hadn't?" She shuddered. Ssiv Sssi had almost killed him. She reached up and tenderly touched his cheek. "You took a big chance, *husband*."

"No worse than a blood oath."

She looked away. Just her luck to fall in love right before she died. "Now what?"

"Beats me. But the answer is here. Somewhere."

Their task seemed hopeless. The large store was packed with so much merchandise, it would take days to look through it all.

She pivoted to survey the store— and flinched, startled to see a beautiful woman standing behind them, head tilting from side to side, studying them. Her long black hair was interspersed with tiny braids that joined and split apart to rejoin others, creating a natural net over the rest of her hair. Likewise the soft fabric of her black velvet dress was richly embroidered with silver threads in a floral fishnet pattern that accented her voluptuous figure.

Her face eased into a serene smile. Her arms opened to greet them, and the flowing sleeves of her dress rippled like the water fountains around them. With a tranquil voice, she said, "Welcome to Pamela's Choices And Pamela's Chances."

"You must be Pamela," Harry said.

She lowered her arms and graciously shook her head. "Pamela made her choice and took her chance. I'm the new owner—Wyrna Ashdapa. How may I help you?"

Felicity suddenly began singing at the top of her little voice, "Food, Glorious Food."

Wyrna frowned. "A fairy? Ordinarily, they're not permitted in the Mark. I'm surprised they let her in."

"The guard said it would be all right as long as we kept her in the cage," Joy said. "She's my, uh, sister."

"And you have three eyes."

Joy sucked in her breath. Somehow Wyrna knew she was lying, which meant they'd be thrown out of the Mark. Or worse.

But then the shopkeeper added, "And yet your third eye is barely open. It would explain why you look so lost. Is there something I can help you find?"

"My wife and I are looking for anything on wizard's petals," Harry said.

Wyrna drew herself up and peered at him. "How odd. I wasn't talking to you, yet you answered. But what is even more interesting is that what *you* are searching for is not the same as what *she* is searching for."

She spoke to Joy. "What is it you want? Or should I attend to his needs first?"

"I want what he wants," Joy said.

"Do you really?" Wyrna glanced at the wedding ring she wore, and smirked. "Lying doesn't suit you, but I will concede until you're ready." She turned to Harry. "Info on wizard's petals? How strange. This is not a magic shop."

"So I've been told."

"And yet you believe everything you hear." She tsked. "It would seem you are as lost as she. But you are my first customers of the day. Of the week, actually." She laughed dryly and her smile broadened. "This honors me and honors you. Come. Let us see what we may find."

They followed her, not in a straight line, but in an ever widening spiral that had them circling the store several times before they came to a stop at a kite-making station.

"What you seek is here," the woman told Harry. "The fairy may stay with you. As for your *wife*, what she seeks is not far."

Wizards, Harradorn thought while the woman led Joy away through the forest of colorful banners, water sounds, and prism rainbows. Why can't any of them talk like normal people? But that was the problem, wasn't it. With all their magic, wizards were inherently freaks everywhere except in Macklin's Mark.

He looked about uneasily. The place was too happy. Too cheerful. And his mood only worsened when Felicity began singing a strange version of "Candy Man."

> "Who can take tomorrow, dip it in a kiss,
> Separate the sorrow and collect up all the bliss?
> The Candymaid can 'cause she mixes it with love
> So we all taste good…"

Harradorn grumbled. "Go back to humming."

Felicity complied, but she didn't seem happy about it. He scanned all the worthless kite-making material in front of him. How the Hel was he going to find the solution to a wizard's petal among kites? He set the cage on the counter. Inspired by her surroundings, Felicity pranced and sang "Let's Go Fly a Kite."

It was too much. Tired, his patience at an end, he was about to tell her to shut up when a young woman, barely out of her teens, came out of a back room carrying a bolt of brilliant red fabric.

"Sorry to keep you waiting," she said. "I'm LucklessLu. How may I help you?" She took one look at Felicity and gushed. "Oh! A fairy! And she's singing my favorite song." She smiled shyly at Harradorn. "You're so lucky. I'd give anything to have such happiness as my companion."

Any other time he might have taken the woman up on her offer. But her appearance struck him speechless and for a moment he could only stare.

An albino wizard!

Her waist-long white hair was pulled back into a single braid interwoven with red ribbons that reminded him of Lance Warbird. So did the slant of her dark pink eyes. The crystal above the young woman rocked back and forth. The one above him did, too. Must be a breeze up by the ceiling.

He shifted to get a better look at the family tattoos below LucklessLu's neck. But her fluttering gothic robes blocked his view while she swayed in time with the song.

"Any kites in the shape of a fairy?" he asked.

Still smiling, she stopped and looked at him.

There. He peered closer. Was that—?

She laughed and clasped her hands in front of the tattoos. "What a wonderful idea! I can make one for you if you like."

He had to get her to move her hands. "Sounds great. Perhaps orange to match my friend here."

"Super!" LucklessLu grinned and clapped her hands several more times in delight, still blocking her tattoos. But then she leaned down to get a better look at the fairy. For an instant, her robes shifted. Two symbols were below her neck: a sprig of English Ivy and a red triangle.

Frowning, he watched her select a bolt of bright orange fabric. FearfulFran had an English ivy tattoo twining its way up her neck, which meant this woman was a blood relation. Yet his suspicion that she might also be related to Lance Warbird didn't match the triangle. The tattoo should be a predatory bird akin to his last name.

When she turned to grab scissors, he noticed the primary magic tattoo on her cheek—a red rune, an exact copy of the one Lance had etched on the beads in his hair! Encasing the rune was another red triangle like the one below her neck. There was no tattoo near her eye to denote secondary magic.

"I don't have much time," LucklessLu chatted amicably, oblivious to his keen interest in her markings. "I have to get back to work."

"Don't you work here?"

"I should be so lucky." Her hands moved faster than a hummingbird's wings, cutting fabric, fitting dowels, tying string, drawing something, sewing something else, and all the while her mouth moved almost equally fast. He only caught snatches of what she said. "I love making kites... work of my heart... lunch break... Wyrna's so nice... makes me happy... just a touch... the others don't understand."

He was about to ask in what way she was related to FearfulFran—and if she knew Lance—when she abruptly handed him an orange kite. It looked exactly like Felicity.

"There you go. Sorry it took so long. Got to pop. Bye."

Before he could thank her, she disappeared with the soft sound of a bubble popping.

He glanced up. The crystal that had been rocking back and forth above her slowed to a stop.

* * *

In the clothing section of the store, Joy stood within a circular dressing room composed of thick fabric. On the outside, it looked like a white cocoon hanging by a rope from the ceiling, but the interior was a mirrored fabric, giving her a perfect three-hundred-sixty-degree view of the outfit Wyrna Ashdapa had insisted she try on, declaring it crucial protection for what lay ahead.

Joy studied the silken one-piece silver bodysuit that fit her like a second skin Not tight, not confining at all compared to the bustier and tights she had been wearing. Its neckline only low enough to let her tattoos be seen. So wonderfully light she almost felt naked. Definitely sexy. It accented all her curves, even smoothed out a few to make her body seem perfect.

"Knock. Knock," Wyrna said before entering. There was just enough space for two in the wraparound dressing room. She handed Joy a pair of low-heeled slip-ons that matched the bodysuit. "You look beautiful," she said after Joy put them on. "Absolutely beautiful."

She moved around Joy. Fingers flittered close to the fabric, like a ghostly cat slinking, fingers sweeping here and there, including places she shouldn't be near. Unnerved, Joy drew away from the woman and the feather-light touch of her fingers.

"Sorry." Wyrna simpered. "I didn't meant to offend. Just making sure it fits."

The woman creeped her out. Fear tingled up her spine similar to whenever she spotted a spider. This was a mistake. She should return to Harry.

"I don't think this is me." She reached for the hidden zipper at her neck.

"Oh, please don't take it off. It suits you. Go on. See for yourself with your own hands."

Figuring it was the quickest way to appease the woman and get out of the dressing room, Joy ran a cursory hand down the silken sleeve of one arm, and found herself slowing her movements, taking her time, caressing the fabric. She slowly ran her fingers back up, loving the feel of it. It made her happy. Warmly excited. Slightly turned on.

She ran a hand down the other arm and almost purred at how good it felt. With both hands, she slid fingers over her flat stomach, then down her thighs, sighing with pleasure when she ran her hands back up the curve of her hips.

Joy noticed the woman followed her hands with more than casual interest. And why not. They were both two good-looking women. It's certainly all right to appreciate the female figure. She met the woman's smile with one of her own. "I'd love to take it, but I don't have much on me." She laughed at her own pun. "How much is it?"

Wyrna calmly folded her hands. "A touch."

Joy's eyes hardened.

"Plus the clothes you were wearing. Not what I normally sell here, but I know several who would look good in them."

A touch.

Wyrna cocked a knowing smile. "Afraid of taking a chance?

"Why no. It's just—"

"Your heart wants only one." Wyrna shook her head. "Pity. At times like this I wish I were a man, yet some things even a wizard can't change. A touch." She held up the bustier. "Or you can go back to wearing this *man*made girdle for breasts."

Joy hated the thought of squeezing back into the bustier and its painful restriction for who knows how many more hours. But still...

"I will also reveal the book your *husband* is looking for."

Her stomach clenched. Somehow the woman knew why they were here.

"And where you can find it," Wyrna added. "He already lost his chance. The choice falls to you."

Not much of a choice. The alternative was to search endlessly throughout the Mark, maybe for weeks, endangering the children of Peace & Prosperity who might not even last a few days longer.

Maybe it was worth letting the woman cop a feel. After all, who would know.

Joy swallowed uneasily. "A touch."

Wyrna's smile twisted into a smirk of assured pleasure.

"But first the book and its location."

"Of course. The Archives. And the book will come to you."

Wyrna approached. The air within the cocoon changed. It grew heavy with a sense of sultry nights and long-suffering arousal. She had never been turned on by a woman before, and she wondered if Wyrna was using magic to make her feel stimulated.

The tattoo on the woman's cheek denoted her strongest power: a symbol for female inside a white circle, whatever that meant. Wyrna raised a finger between their faces. Joy stared at it. That's when she noticed the tiny tattoo by the corner of the woman's eye and marked her secondary magic. This close, there was no mistaking the red hourglass. Like that on a black widow!

"No!" Joy never had a chance to say it. The woman's finger touched Joy between her eyes slightly above the nose, a deceptively light pressure that shot a bolt of energy through her. Every nerve tingled. Her arms spread open of their own accord, then stopped, caught against something.

Wyrna edged closer, a spider stalking its prey, her fingers undulating back and forth like feelers testing the air, close but not touching, traveling up and down Joy's torso. Joy stared at her in horror. She couldn't move. Her back, arms, legs were snared in an invisible spider's web.

The gatekeeper was wrong about there not being any magic in the store. Yet he was right about warning her not to come here. Perhaps another magic user would be able to resist, but she had no defense, like the enemy tattoo on her right hand indicated.

Wyrna lowered her hands and licked her lips. "Don't be afraid. This won't hurt a bit. In fact, you'll enjoy it immensely. No one has ever complained—until it's over—so you might as well relax and enjoy. I'll take my time. Let it last."

The woman lifted a slim hand between them. The heat was palpable. She reached for Joy's left breast.

No! Joy desperately tried to call for help. Her mouth opened but her voice remained silent. She screamed in her mind. *Harry! Help me!*

"He can't hear you, love. There's only you and me in here. Let's begin."

Her fingers moved above Joy's breast and fluttered in the air, close but not touching, near where she had hidden the wizard's petal.

"Ah." The woman closed her eyes and moaned, unequivocally being pleasured. "So pure," she murmured. "Small yet powerful." She squirmed, her lips parted, acting like she was the one being touched. "Yes! So potent."

Joy panted. The magic was taking her over. She wanted... needed... desired Wyrna's touch. Not just where her fingers teased the air, but on her everywhere. Wyrna was beautiful, and dangerous. Sensual. And hungry.

Joy panted harder, aroused—and repulsed—wanting to let go, enjoy, while also yearning to flee. The seconds passed, and she no longer wanted to resist. But she had to. There were so many lives at stake.

She thought of Harry and whimpered.

"Don't cry," Wyrna said, a rapist soothing her victim. "You know you like it. Stop fighting and we'll have a good time."

And still Wyrna hadn't touched her. Not physically. And yet her legs trembled, her body grew weak. Something was being siphoned out of her, and she couldn't stop it.

"Yes." Wyrna's eyes were half-opened, dreamy, drugged with pleasure. "I would recognize Zach's work anywhere." Keeping the finger above where the petal was hidden, she arched her back and gasped. "Oh. He must think you're very special to give you part of himself."

More like cursed. Joy wept, tormented by what the petal was costing her—her family, her home, the man she loved. She was going to die here, cocooned in Wyrna's trap until she was drained of life and love.

"And now Zach is part of me." Wyrna removed her hand. It seemed to be throbbing, glowing faintly. She swept back her hair and lustfully licked her lips. "That was good. Let's do it again."

Eyes ravenous, she raised her other hand to plunder more. But her hand stopped. Her head jerked. Had she heard something?

Please, let it be Harry.

Joy struggled to move. But she was still caught. *Hurry, Harry! I'm in here! Help me!*

The woman's hand twitched. The fingers flitted and slowly moved down Joy's arm to her hand where they rapidly tested the air.

"What's this?" The woman peered closer and spotted the small scab on Joy's finger. Her fingers fluttered madly. "Oh, I don't believe it. A blood oath." She tilted her head at Joy and grinned like a cat about to eat a helpless bird. "You're full of delicious surprises. I must have it. Let me touch."

Joy moved her mouth, but she still couldn't speak.

Wyrna paced back and forth, talking to herself. "A big risk, letting her go. She may not be willing if I set her free. Yet so much to gain. I've never had a blood oath before. A once in a lifetime treat. Dare I take the chance?" She chewed on a nail, thinking. "Who would have thought an outsider would provide such a choice." She turned to Joy. "I can't resist."

She tapped a finger between Joy's eyes. Immediately, Joy could move. She backed away from the woman, hands raised in self-defense.

"I let you go," Wyrna said. "Now let me touch."

"No." Afraid to turn her back on the woman, Joy reached behind and searched among the folds of mirrored cloth for the exit. She couldn't find it!

She circled around twice. Wyrna followed, pleading to touch her again.

"Not on your life," Joy said.

"What about your life?" Wyrna answered. "I can see the two roads before you. If you take one more chance, your choices will be easy. If not, you may die, and then the other dies in his heart."

"I don't believe you." Frantic, she tried to find a way out of the dressing room.

"I cannot lie. As part of my gift I am obligated to help all who enter my store."

"Is that what you call what you just did to me?"

The woman raised and lowered one shoulder, making the silver embroidery on her dress glimmer like fresh dew on a spider's web. "There is nothing to prevent me from helping myself. I did not force myself on you. Permission was granted."

"If I'd known what you were going to do, I never would have agreed."

"And now you do. No harm done. Please, let me touch. I've never had the magic of a blood oath before."

"Not in a million years. Now let me out of here."

The woman mewed sadly. "If you insist." She reached for the nearest side of the cocoon and drew back the cloth to reveal an opening. Joy rushed for the exit, but halted when the woman blocked her way. She extended a hand toward Joy's forehead. Joy backed away.

"Before you go," Wyrna said, "there are two things you will need that I'm obligated to give. I cannot let you leave without them or I'll be in trouble with the Council of Elders."

Wyrna slipped out the opening and straight away closed it behind her. Joy tried to follow but found the cloth had reformed, cocooning her again. She tried lifting the cloth to go under, but it was fastened to the floor and refused to give.

She screamed repeatedly for Harry, but when the cloth opened, it was Wyrna who entered. The cloth closed tightly behind her. "He didn't hear you," she said. "The dressing rooms are soundproof."

Though scared, Joy tried to sound defiant. "If they are, how did you know I tried? Magic?"

"I have no magic."

"I don't believe you."

"That's your choice. Here." She handed her a black chain-mail mini dress whose thin links gave it a gossamer appearance. "You can't go around the Mark only in the bodysuit. If you do, every wizard in the place will want to exchange magic with you, and you already belong to your *husband*. This will protect you long after you leave the Mark. Consider it my gift, a token of what might have been."

Eager to escape, Joy slipped it on. The sleeveless dress wasn't made of metal but of some strange fabric, light yet hard like armor. A modest slit between her breasts allowed her fake family tattoos to be seen.

"This is my second gift to you." Wyrna held up a small red plastic whistle on a silver necklace. She lowered it over Joy's head and positioned it around her neck.

Joy's breath hitched when the woman boldly tucked the whistle into her cleavage, hiding it from view. She thought about grabbing the woman's wrist and yanking her hand away, but stopped at the last second, keenly aware Wyrna had avoided skin contact. Perhaps initiating a touch of any kind was equivalent to granting permission. The thought of another *session* with Wyrna made her skin crawl.

The shopkeeper's beautiful catlike eyes stared into Joy's and she removed her finger. "Still afraid," she purred. "I like you. I like you a lot. Which is why I took a chance with you—and lost. But I see choices before you and I will ease your fears with this one question. When we were exchanging energies, where did you feel me inside?"

Joy searched, remembering the lust that had churned secreted and low.

The woman nodded, clearly aware of what Joy had discovered. "Notice where you feel *him* the next time you touch, and you will know whether you have made the right choice. Or want to return." With a light tap of her hand on the mirrored cloth, the dressing room walls opened. "I could just eat you up. But then what would your *husband* think. Come along before he finds out you've been cheating on him."

*   *   *

Cage in hand, kite in the other, Harradorn had been searching a long time for Joy. Strange how easily he kept getting turned around in the circular store, almost mazelike in its layout. He had just returned to the amethyst hexagon, his gaze darting here and there, about to call out and admit he was lost, when he noticed a few of the crystals hanging from the ceiling begin to rock, moving in a line toward him. For the first time he noticed all the strings were connected to what looked like a huge crystalline spider web on the ceiling.

Wyrna and Joy approached in the same direction of the rocking crystals. The shopkeeper greeted him with her usual serene smile.

Joy, on the other hand, rushed toward him. She had changed outfits. He missed the bustier and its generous view of her breasts, yet the bodysuit was equally arousing, the silvery fabric shimmering over curves asking to be stroked, whereas the gossamer, chain-mail overdress was merely a challenge to be breached. Very sexy.

"We need to go," Joy said.

His hands full, she wrapped one arm around him and hurriedly guided him onto the transport crystal. Felicity began singing the strange candymaid song. He glanced up and noticed the crystals above them moving. Then he looked at Joy, solely at her face this time, and saw terror.

"We need to go," Joy said in a tight voice. "Now."

"She's correct," Wyrna added. "The time for questions has come and gone. As we speak, the magic of the skelter mirror depletes. If you wish to have a chance, you must hurry and finish your task."

Skelter mirror? He turned to Joy. "Did you tell her—?"

315

"Enough already." Wyrna shook her head and said to Joy. "He'll be a handful if you live through the day. In case you do, take this." She pressed a small booklet into Joy's hand. "You have a friend, Gina, in need of this, though she doesn't know it yet. Made for children but it will help her with her own choices and chances."

With a final look of longing, Wyrna stretched out her hand toward them, and yawned.

Instantly he and Joy were surrounded by lavender sparkles, then quickly deposited elsewhere. The lighting was dim, the air cool and dry, scented with old leather, sweet inks, parchment, and the iron hint of blood. Aisles of books radiated from the hexagon, stretching far as the eye could see and then some. Harradorn looked up. A well of floors soared far above them. They stood in an enormous tower filled with books.

He said, "Is this the Archives?"

Joy nodded. To his surprise, she pulled him off the platform to behind one of the bookshelves where she removed the kite and cage from his hands, flung her arms around him, and said, "Kiss me."

She didn't wait for a reply but kissed him with an energetic mix of passion and desperation that made him want to stop and ask her what the Hel was going on. But the feel of her lips, the yearning stroke of her tongue, erased all questions. He wrapped his arms around her, felt the annoying ripple of the chainmail dress, and decided to ease his hands up and under the strange garment. The sleek feel of the bodysuit when his hands slid over her hips ignited a longing for her that made him wish they had been transported to a hotel.

Her tongue ravished his mouth and he groaned, and groaned again.

"I felt you," she gushed, a happy smile on her face. "I felt you everywhere. I don't think there was anywhere I didn't feel you— deep and hot, inside and out."

Harradorn was thoroughly confused. But at least she no longer looked afraid. "What happened back there?"

"Welcome to the Archives," a familiar voice whispered. To his surprise, the albino kitemaker stood meekly before them.

"Hello again," he said.

"Quiet voices," LucklessLu whispered, her cadence slow and distinct. Her eyes flicked from side to side, as if afraid of being seen, then she leaned forward and added in the lively voice she used at the store, "Hi! Nice to see you, too."

There was a faint rustling from among the books nearby. Immediately, she shifted back to her original stolid demeanor. "I am LucklessLu, fourth level curator of all the knowledge of magic. By your infraction on noise, I suspect this is your first visit here."

"Yes," he said.

"Only whispers permitted, soft footfalls, slow movements. No visiting. No talking with other researchers. And, of course, no food, drink, or magic except in the designated areas." She looked at the fairy, who was singing "Marian The Librarian," and frowned. "Absolutely no singing or I'll have her removed."

Harradorn whispered to Felicity to hum. The fairy complied but kept dancing.

"No dancing either," the woman sternly whispered.

"She's under a spell," he explained. "It's the reason we're here. We need to find out how to remove the wizard's petal wish from her so she'll stop singing and dancing. Can you help us?"

LucklessLu's face lit up, excited to assist, yet kept her voice forcibly calm. "Follow me." She disappeared with a meek pop.

Harradorn swore. If they couldn't act like wizards, they'd be thrown out of the Mark, his town damned forever.

Chapter 26

LucklessLu popped back into view. "Sorry. Keep forgetting not everyone can do that. Well, hardly anyone. Please, don't report me. One more mistake and I'll be demoted to blood inking again."

"No problem," Harradorn replied, not sure what blood inking entailed yet sympathizing with her plight. When he had cleared out most of the staff left behind by his predecessor, he'd quickly learned to assess the right job for the right personality. LucklessLu's artistic creativity and seemingly boundless vitality made her totally unsuited for working in a library. He couldn't imagine what had made her decide to work here.

LucklessLu tapped two index fingers together. A second later, all of them were on an upper floor by some windows.

"You did that so easily," Joy said, marveling they'd been transported without sparkles or a dark passage. "It was wonderful."

"No one has ever said that before. Thank you." LucklessLu blushed at the compliment, her pigment-free face turning a brilliant shade of red. "I believe what you seek is down this aisle."

She led the way, skipping every once in a while, catching herself and walking sedately, only to skip again, giggle, and return to walking. Harry followed, but Joy stayed behind. They had appeared near a curving bank of windows and she just had to take a peek. This might be her only chance to see what the wizard city of Macklin's Mark looked like.

Joy stared out in amazement. The entire city was composed of towers. All the same height, about seven stories, except for the one she was in, which was higher than all the rest, matched only in height by an outlandish crystal tower in the distance. To her surprise, all the towers were narrow, maybe fourteen feet in diameter.

Huh. Each level must have only one room.

Felicity sang, "On A Clear Day You Can See Forever." Joy reminded her to whisper.

Towers stretched to the horizon: round towers, square towers, triangular towers, plus hexagons, pentagons—each a different color—no two exactly alike. There were also skinny versions of the Transamerica Pyramid of San Francisco, the Eiffel Tower, along with the Leaning Tower of Pisa, a ziggurat, and the clock tower of Big Ben.

Her lips parted in awe when what looked like a slim version of the Burj Al Arab Hotel in Dubai—easily recognizable with its distinctive sailboat shape—suddenly appeared amidst a flash of purple lightning, popping into view much like LucklessLu had done. Seconds later off to the side there was another flash of purple lightning, only this time a yellow tepee-shaped tower disappeared. Two more lightning bolts followed and both a golden pagoda and a short, skinny version of the Freedom Tower materialized.

"What are you looking at?" Harradorn joined her by the windows.

"Everything. It seems when wizards travel, they take their homes with them."

"Cuts down on hotel fees."

"They all look so narrow."

"An illusion. A basketball court could easily fit inside Zach's greenhouse."

"If buildings in the outside world had that ability, it would definitely cut down on urban sprawl. Oh!" She looked off to the side. "I could have sworn I saw Coors Field. Just for a second. Then, like a ghost, it was gone."

"Denver and Macklin's Mark occupy the same place but a slightly different temporal shift. The other can be seen only when you're not looking directly at it. Twice I've caught sight of the Wells Fargo Center." He surveyed the city. "All my life I've wanted to visit here. But the longer we stay, the more likely we'll be found out. LucklessLu thinks she's located the book we're looking for. She's scanning it now—with her mind."

"She's so amazing. The perfect research librarian. But I get the feeling she doesn't like working here."

He held up the kite he'd been carrying around. "She loves making kites."

Joy laughed. "It looks exactly like Felicity!"

"She'd be rich if she opened a shop in Peace." His voice trailed off, his attention captured by the disappearance of a tower out the window, in particular the empty platform that marked the place where it had stood. He looked around at all the empty platforms that earmarked the home base of traveling towers.

Zach's platform in Prosperity was a plain circular stone of black granite, smooth and flat. Over the years when Harry had visited other towns like Peace & Prosperity, the local wizard's tower had always been present, so he'd assumed tower platforms were basically like the one in his town. But from here, he could easily see that wasn't the norm. Though some were plain stone disks, some had designs etched into their surfaces: an animal, a face, a geometric shape, a crown, a flower.

Every hair on the back of his neck rose in horror.

The marble donated anonymously for the Bjork Memorial Park had a flower labyrinth etched into its surface, the same diameter as Zach's tower and all the platforms he was seeing below.

He staggered back. Vomit crawled up his throat. The park in honor of his friends was actually the landing pad for a wizard's tower! A wizard who liked being among flowers, like at the Sweetheart Café and Angie's Trattoria.

"Harry, what's wrong?"

"Library voices." LucklessLu appeared in front of them, her hands empty.

"I guess you weren't able to find what we were looking for," Joy said.

LucklessLu pointed to her forehead. "It's all in here," she said.

Joy remembered what Wyrna had said: The book will come to you.

"Before we continue," Harry said, his voice suddenly sharp, "I need to know who your parents are."

LucklessLu opened her mouth, plainly eager to answer. But then she must have remembered where they were and her face grew long and solemn. "I am not allowed to answer questions of a personal nature at work."

"Of course not. My mistake," Harry whispered in a cold, thunderous rage that scared Joy. And it didn't dissipate when he added with polite ferocity, "When we're done here, we'll all go outside. Have a nice chat."

Not sure what was going on, Joy slid between the two and asked LucklessLu, "So, how do we reverse or undo a wizard's petal wish?"

The librarian's eyes shifted back and forth as if reading something only she could see. "Most gardeners report the easiest way to negate a wizard's petal is by use of the Great Redux. When this is not desired, the mirror's silver tide is the best alternative, though this is considered time-consuming and inconvenient. Still, most wishcasters prefer the latter to the former. A poll taken by the Wizard's Board of Magic Licenses reports that—"

"Stop," Harry said.

LucklessLu complied, her hands clasped serenely together, eerily mimicking Wyrna. Joy shivered and looked out the window, hoping to drown the memory of what she had suffered at the spider woman's hands by concentrating on the sea of towers.

Harry said, "Define what is meant by 'mirror's silver tide'."

The librarian's dark pink eyes repeatedly shifted back and forth.

"There are exactly 4,687,219 passages in the library that contain a reference to your request."

"Is that all," Harry whispered cynically. "How about cross-referencing that with wizard's petal?"

Her eyes shifted. "33,347 passages."

"Better. Now let's add—"

"Excuse me." Joy raised her hand. "Are there any two towers that look the same?"

LucklessLu's eyes shifted. "Wizard Emma's Guide to Modern Wizard Etiquette clearly states it would be an unforgivable faux pas for any tower to mimic another, thus no two towers have been alike for the last six hundred years."

"Uh-oh," Joy said. "Guess who just popped in?" She pointed out the window to a solid black circular tower.

Harry swore. "By Odin's eye. Zach. We have to get out of here. Now."

"Why? I'd think he'd be the perfect person to help us."

"Not if he finds us in the Mark. Friendship with a wizard only goes so far. There are some laws even he can't break without retribution." He addressed the librarian. "Please cross-reference 'mirror's silver tide,' wizard's petal, and—"

"Jersey girl!"

All three pivoted in the direction of the ominous voice. Zach walked towards them, hooded like always, white staff firmly in hand.

LucklessLu whispered, "Library voices, please." Then she answered the question. "There are zero passages that reference 'mirror's silver tide,' wizard's petal, and Jersey girl."

"Are you aware of the penalty for being here?" Zach asked, voice rising in anger. He drew steadily closer.

"It's so hard to find a good kite," Harry replied flippantly. He transferred the kite to the hand holding Felicity's cage, grabbed Joy's hand, and said, "Smalt." Instantly, black sparkles covered them. Zach's roar of frustration followed them into the Stygian

Gap.

"That was close," Harry said.

Felicity sang "Music of the Night." No one told her to be quiet. Joy suspected Harry found her singing comforting, much like she did, even though a few hands and paws—attracted to the song— brushed her arms while they soared through the dark. Their transit seemed to take twice as long as when they traveled back and forth to New Jersey, or maybe she was just tired and depressed, her heart heavy. After all they'd been through, they had failed miserably.

"Our passage is sluggish. Like swimming against the tide." Harry held her close and shielded her from those trying to latch on. "I've felt this before. The mirror's magic is almost depleted. I'd say another hour and the magic will be gone. We're lucky it's lasted this long."

She didn't feel lucky. The perilous trek to Macklin's Mark had been a tremendous waste of time.

They exited the skelter mirror. The bright lights of Sirena's workshop temporarily blinded her and she was grateful when Harry took Felicity's cage from her hand. But then she heard Harry swear, and the fairy sang, "We're Off To See The Wizards."

"Wizards?" Joy's vision began to clear.

Squinting, she saw Zach before her, Felicity's cage in one hand, white staff in the other. Next to him, LucklessLu gazed all around, clapping her hands in delight, her pink eyes admiring the various items in Sirena's workshop.

"How did you beat us here?" Harry asked Zach. "Towers are fast, but not that fast."

"LucklessLu obliged. She doesn't get to travel much, and it's been a while since she's seen her mother."

Her mother? Joy studied the librarian. The small sprig of English ivy tattooed on her chest was almost imperceptible compared with the extensive tattoo snaking around FearfulFran's neck. "You don't mean—"

Zach raised a finger for silence. The black-hooded face stared at

Harry. "She's here, isn't she?"

A muscled jerked in Harry's jaw. "How did you know?"

"Before we play twenty questions, let's clear the room." He turned to LucklessLu and handed her the cage. "Please take the fairy into the front of the store. We'll be along shortly." The young woman shifted excitedly from one foot to the other. He placed a calming hand on her shoulder. "I'm sure you'll find many things you can make into pretty kites."

Much like a child given free access to a candy store, LucklessLu grinned with unabashed glee. "Thank you, Wizard Zach." She dashed into the store where they could hear her giggling and squealing in delight.

"I can explain," Harry told Zach.

"Really?" Frost coated his voice, and Joy noticed the hand holding the staff repeatedly clench and unclench. "I suggest you be quiet for a while, unless you want me to turn you into a bush."

Harry stiffened. He shut his mouth.

"Good," Zach said. He looked from one to the other. "You two took a terrible risk. Time to come clean and undo what has been done."

Softly, he murmured the words of a spell, strange words, mystical words that gave her goose bumps. Then he raised his staff and thumped the end on the floor. White light shone from the sigils carved into its surface, hitting her and Harry like a sudden gust of wind. When it passed, the spider tattoo on her hand was gone, so was her black nail polish. She looked down at her chest, then at Harry. All their tattoos were gone, as were the black streaks in Harry's hair and the painful diamond studs in his ear.

Harry looked at her. A smile of approval settled across his face. He touched her hair. "Beautiful. Golden. Like the first rays of sunlight on a spring morn. Absolutely beautiful."

She blinked in surprise. The strands being caressed were no longer orange and black. Zach's magic had returned her hair to its normal shade of blonde. If Harry kept loving her hair as he did now, she might never color it again. Then again, she might never have the chance, for she suddenly remembered the blood oath.

Zach cleared his throat with an impatient growl; Harry let go of her hair.

"How did you know we were in Macklin's Mark?" Harry asked.

"I sensed someone tampering with one of my petals." Zach turned to Joy. "Danger can be very beautiful, isn't that true, Jersey girl?"

She swallowed hard and nodded, the terror of being cocooned with Wyrna still fresh in her mind.

"What's he talking about?" Harry asked.

Grumbling, Zach raised a finger in his direction. "Really, Harry. Silence or a shrub. It's your choice." Harry remained silent, but the concern in his eyes told Joy he'd ask her again later.

The wizard shifted closer to Joy. "Choices can be deadly. How did you escape?"

Joy shuddered, remembering. "She wanted something else."

"Did she ask to touch you again?"

Joy nodded. Harry looked alarmed. He opened his mouth but shut it again when Zach raised a finger in warning.

"What did you reply?" Zach asked.

"No," she breathed heavily. "I told her no."

"Lessons learned are better than lessons taught. Do you understand what happened to you?"

"She overpowered me with her magic."

He shook his head. "Wyrna has no magic."

"But how did she..." Joy glanced at Harry, then looked away, ashamed to admit what had happened, how she had felt. What a complete idiot she had been.

"In New Age circles, she's called an energy vampire. A reverse empath. Normally one of her kind steals energy from others without either party aware of what is happening—except for a feeling of tiredness. In Wyrna's case, she's very aware of what she does. She and her predecessor Pamela primarily consume magical energy. As such, they were permitted to set up shop in the Mark under the stricture the *donor* must be given the choice of refusal." He lifted Joy's chin to face him. "She gave you that choice, didn't she."

"Yes."

"In exchange for?"

"The name and whereabouts of the book that would set Peace & Prosperity free from Aesa's wizard's petal wish. From one of your petals, I believe." The last came out with more vehemence than she thought herself capable.

"I see." Zach released her. "You blame me for your encounter with Wyrna."

"I don't see anyone else here giving out petals." It felt good to be angry, even if she was substituting Zach for Wyrna.

"FearfulFran gave them away, not I." He passed his hand over the black obsidian ball in the crown of his staff. "But I do see." He turned to Joy. "Everything that has happened, and will happen, has you at its center. Wyrna was correct. Choices lead to chances. Be very careful with what you are about to do."

He angled his head to Harry. "And you, my friend, take care. In the end, there's really no choice at all. It will be easy."

He turned to leave.

"Wait a minute," Harry said. "I don't know what the Hel is going on, but you have to fix what's happened to my town."

Zach stopped. "*Your* town?"

The air sizzled with a buildup of static electricity. "Our town," Harry quickly amended. The air calmed. But the storm gathering in Harry's eyes said the confrontation wasn't over yet. "You have to undo the wish."

"If a wizard's wish can be taken back, then it's no longer a wish."

"Then at least tell us how to undo it."

"Again, a wish is a wish. Only the one who makes it should determine whether to end it." Zach continued toward the front of the store.

"Hold on." Joy dashed around the worktables and blocked his exit. "If Wyrna is such a threat, why do you and the other wizards allow such a gullible young woman like LucklessLu to work in her store? Don't you care?"

"Care is a four-letter word."

"So is crap, and that's what I'm getting from you."

"She didn't mean it," Harry said, coming to her side.

"Yes, I did." Seething with resentment, she decided Zach wasn't such a great person, magic or no magic, if he allowed LucklessLu to be in constant danger of abuse from Wyrna.

Even with the face hidden within the cowl, his stare intimidated. She expected flames to shoot out from the hood. Instead, he spoke calmly, gently. "Love is also a four-letter word. So is life. For all her innocence, LucklessLu is the most powerful wizard the world has ever known. Ever," he emphasized. "She has the power to pop here and there and everywhere with a mere thought of doing so.

Joy opened her mouth in amazement. "You mean quantum tunneling?"

By Zach's movements, he seemed taken aback.

"Public school teacher," Harry explained.

"Impressive." Zach squared his shoulders as if confronting an equal. "As I was saying, LucklessLu has unbelievable power. And yet she is only at half her strength."

"Half?" Joy said.

"Even with Wyrna's insatiable appetite, she cannot fully deplete LucklessLu's power. Pamela tried. Pamela died."

The immensity of the problem finally hit home. "Macklin's Mark tolerates Wyrna's presence in exchange for her keeping the young woman manageable."

"More than that. For keeping her alive." The black-robed wizard sighed deeply. "Wyrna is a necessary evil. LucklessLu's power is almost godlike in strength. If she wasn't so guileless, so unaware of what she is capable of, she would have been killed long ago to save the planet. But all she wants to do is make kites."

"And work in the Archives," Harry added.

Zach shook his head. "That's her mother's doing, in hopes she'll acquire enough knowledge to leave the Mark, acquire a town, and lead a different life—with her mother as adviser, of course. Fortunately, the young woman's Olympian magic has feebled her mind. Her goals will always be simple, for which all wizards are grateful."

"How sad for her," Joy said.

"And a blessing for us all, including those in the outside world."

"It sounds like an ideal solution, and yet..." she glanced nervously at Harry.

Zach must have noticed her distress, for he said to Harry, "I suggest you check on the other two. Fairies have a corruptive influence on the naive, even if they're only singing and dancing, and some of your sister's statuary might be too enlightening for our young librarian."

Harry's brow shot up in comprehension. He started to leave, but he held back and looked at Joy, his concern, his love for her so plain on his face that she wanted to hug him. But she didn't feel worthy of that love, not after what had happened with Wyrna, so she simply said, "Go ahead. I won't be long."

After Harry left, Zach put an arm around her, a gesture that imparted protection and personal privacy, for which she was grateful. "We are alone," he said. "You may speak freely."

"I can understand Wyrna keeping the world safe and all." She stopped, too mortified to continue.

The wizard gently drew her closer. "When Wyrna was sampling the magic of the wizard's petal, you felt aroused. You enjoyed it."

She bowed her head.

"Perhaps it would help if I explain what happens when Wyrna takes. From what I'm told, when she drains someone's magic, some of the magic bleeds out, shifts into a level that induces lust within the donors, an orgasmic enticement, a reward for giving up some of their power. There's no need to feel shame for feelings magically induced."

Alarmed, she glanced at him. "LucklessLu."

"Have no fear. Her massive power creates a buffer, preventing Wyrna from inciting arousal. It only tickles—happily. We made sure."

"I'm glad. I was afraid she was being abused." Joy raised her head and saw the caring smile in the shadow of his hood. "But why did I feel turned on before she touched me?"

His head jerked. "Are you sure?"

"I thought maybe it was the clothes she gave me, that's when it began. Kind of like the way the embroidery on your robes mesmerized me the first time we met."

He surveyed her outfit. "These clothes?"

"The bodysuit, yes. She gave me the chainmail later."

"Wyrna is obligated to provide aid to all who enter her store, a standard covenant for shopkeepers in the Mark. She must have foreseen your need for these clothes." He rubbed a finger on the sleeve of her bodysuit, sniffed it, then lifted her arm and licked the fabric. A wicked grin appeared inside the hood. Its savage cruelty made her shudder. "However, trickery is not permitted. But look." He turned her hand over. "You're bleeding."

The scab on her finger must have gotten torn off. A small drop of blood oozed, followed by another.

"A blood oath!" Zach seized her shoulders. "With whom?"

She cringed. He wasn't going to like this. "FearfulFran."

Zach released her and bellowed a slew of epithets that would have impressed her brother. Harry ran into the workroom.

"What did you promise?" Zach asked, his voice shaking with fury.

"The wizard's petal," Harry said. He stood by her side, her defender, her champion—she looked at the wedding ring on his hand—her *husband*—and her heart swelled with love.

Harry added, "The oath was the only way to discover how to undo the wish. It's how we knew to go to the Mark and meet LucklessLu. But it's okay. Joy's going to the outside world so she doesn't have to live up to her side of the bargain."

Zach pointed to the blood dripping from her finger. "She's bleeding. The oath seeks fulfillment."

"I know," Harradorn said sadly. "She has to go."

He lovingly held her face in his hands, trying to memorize her eyes, her mouth, the curve of her brow, the sunlight shade of her hair. "I thought we'd have more time. There's so much more I want to say. I love you, Joy. I'll always love you." He kissed her, committing to memory the feel of her mouth, her taste, her warmth. But it was all bittersweet. Choked with emotion, he barely got the words out. "Go, before it's too late."

"It already is," Zach said. "She's bleeding."

"It'll stop once she's in the outside world. You've told me before there's no magic there."

"I've told you wizards can't use magic there. But magic still exists. The second stage of her oath was activated when she returned from the Mark. The magic will persist no matter where she goes. Even home, she'll continue to bleed until not a drop remains."

Joy's face paled. Harradorn pressed her bleeding finger to stem the flow. Blood continued to leak out. "We can cauterize it." Frantic, he raced to Sirena's medical supplies and searched for something to use.

"No scab will form," Zach replied. "Only two solutions to a blood oath. Fulfill the oath or die. I'm sorry, but within hours she'll be dead. I'll summon my tower. There's a room there where she'll be made comfortable, free of any pain."

"I'm not going to let her bleed to death."

"And I am not going to allow her to give FearfulFran one of my petals."

Harradorn sized him up. Wizard or not, he wasn't going to

allow his friend to harm Joy. "I'll stop you."

"My friend, her fate is sealed."

"There has to be another way."

"There isn't. But the choice is no longer ours. We had our chance. And lost."

Harradorn stared at him, confused, wondering if he'd missed something.

"She's gone," Zach said.

He spun around. His heart sank. She must have whispered the trigger word while he was arguing with Zach. "She went home to die."

"That would have been the smart thing to do." Zach gestured to a trail of red drops leading to the front of the store.

The implication hit him all at once. "She wouldn't." He hurried into the store. Zach followed. They found Felicity free of her cage, flying around the store singing "Take Me Away."

"LucklessLu is gone as well," Zach said. "Perhaps to find her mother."

"I told FearfulFran to wait for us in Heather's Secret Garden greenhouse."

"Then that's where our Jersey girl has gone." Zach opened the front door. Felicity zoomed out.

Harradorn gripped the wizard's arm. "Wait. There's something I need to know."

"More questions?" Zach said impatiently. "Our fair teacher is having a bad influence on you."

"Are there wizards who feed off things like Wyrna?"

"If they did, they wouldn't be wizards."

Zach tried to shake free of his grip, but Harradorn refused to let go. "FearfulFran seems to prefer being around flowers. That's the reason I sent her to the greenhouse. It seemed the right thing to do though I don't know why."

"Harry, you have your father's practicality but your mother's intuition. FearfulFran has the wizard's form of ADHD. Those with the disorder find relief around large bodies of water. For a rare few, the energy of flowers is the best treatment. Their presence calms urges, tames wild magic—not permanently, which is why FearfulFran stays in close contact with as many blossoms as possible."

"Then we can't let Joy hand over the petal."

"I agree. Giving it to a vicious person like FearfulFran would be disastrous."

"It's not that. It's the price already paid." Harradorn released him and formed a fist. "I wasn't completely sure in the Mark, I didn't realize until I saw all the empty landing pads. It was such a monstrous thought, I didn't want to believe it." He stared at Zach. Just this once he wished he could see his face. "The Bjorks, the Memorial Park—there's a tower platform in its center with a flower etched into it."

"Are you sure?"

"The same anonymous donor also filled the park with flowers—not because Kelly and Ragnar were florists as I thought, but because someone needs to be surrounded with flowers."

"Generations of Bjorks have owned a florist shop on that location," Zach said. "The ground must be saturated with the latent energy of centuries of blooms. Exactly what someone like FearfulFran would need to stay in constant control." Zach gripped his staff, knuckles white. "FearfulFran murdered the Bjorks."

Harradorn nodded in agreement.

"But they died over a month ago," Zach said. "Weeks before the duel. It makes no sense. She had to have known she'd fail. Her magic is too wild and unpredictable to win a duel."

"Don't you get it? She never wanted to win. She only wanted to steal a petal."

Zach grabbed his staff with both hands. "A fool I am. She knew I'd lower my shields during the concession ceremony, the petals free for her to find. One wish, the right wish, and all her dreams come true."

"And Joy's going to make sure it happens unless we stop her."

"I thought you didn't want her to die."

"I don't. But I can't let the murderer of my friends go free."

"Agreed."

Harradorn shucked his Goth coat. On second thought, he removed the sprouting stick from the coat's pocket. The damn thing was becoming a good luck charm for him and Joy, and right now they could use all the luck they could get.

Zach exited the store. He hitched up his robes. "In high school, you always beat me at track. Can you still run a four-minute mile?"

"Watch me."

*　　*　　*

Heather's Secret Garden greenhouse was heady with humidity, fertilizer, and a sickening, thick abundance of floral scents. It was like standing in a perfumed sweaty armpit. Joy almost gagged. With the gardeners out singing and dancing, there was no one to regulate the fans and windows.

The vast array of flowers made LucklessLu's mouth spread open in a huge O. "So lovely," she said. Grinning in delight, she turned to Joy. A splash of red on the floor caught her eye and she cried out. "You're bleeding! Oh, how awful. I can heal it, if you like."

Joy's heart filled with hope. Zach said this was the most powerful wizard ever. If anyone could heal her of the blood oath, it was LucklessLu. She held out her hand. "That would be wonderful."

LucklessLu twirled her pinky at the wound. Smiling, she said, "All better."

Drops continued to splash on the floor. The young woman frowned. "I don't understand." She tried again, and still the finger bled. Tears welled in her eyes. "My magic has never failed." Red splotches of frustration smeared her face; tiny sizzles of energy glinted from the woman's pores. Joy stepped back in fear. Zach's description was correct. LucklessLu was a loose cannon.

"I guess some things can't be healed by magic." This was it, then. Her life near its end. No more tomorrows, her future gone. She ached to see her parents one more time, one last hug from Merry and Mike, one last stroke for Shredder, one final kiss with Harry. Hell, make that a lot of final kisses. And sex. God, they hadn't even made love. She sniffed back tears. How pitiful was that?

LucklessLu leaned toward Joy, face scrunched in worry.

"It's all the pollen," Joy said. A feeble excuse, but she didn't think LucklessLu could handle the reality of the situation. "My sinuses are swelling up fast."

She thought it would stifle the girl's apprehension. It did the opposite. LucklessLu wrung her hands together, even more distraught. "I've never known anyone with so many problems. There must be something I can do to help."

"Maybe you could conjure up some kind of force field to keep out the pollen." The young woman seemed bewildered. Obviously science fiction wasn't big in the Mark. "You know, like the covering of a snow globe."

"Oh, I love snow globes!" LucklessLu flung out her hands. Instantly she and Joy were encased in a two-person-sized clear glass dome. And, like a snow globe, it was snowing inside.

Large flakes quickly covered them both. Joy shivered. "Without the snow, please."

"Sorry." The young woman waved a finger. The snow disappeared.

"That's better." Joy let out a satisfying breath. The air was free of hothouse odors, crisp and clean like after a snowstorm.

Harry had probably already figured out where she had gone. Zach also, and equally furious. Thankfully, neither men had LucklessLu's ability to pop about. Even if they ran, she had a good five minutes to finish what she had come here to do.

Blood steadily dripped from her finger. One wrong to make a

right before any more of her life seeped away. She was going to stop FearfulFran once and for all.

First, she had to get rid of LucklessLu.

"Would you mind waiting outside for Wizard Zach and let him know I'm in here."

LucklessLu nodded happily in agreement. But then, from the far end of the long, hazy greenhouse, Joy heard the murmur of two familiar voices—FearfulFran... and Kathy!

With glee, LucklessLu shrieked, "Mommy!" and popped away. The dome vanished.

"Oh, crap!" Joy raced toward the voices.

Chapter 27

FearfulFran swayed back and forth singing a nursery rhyme while holding LucklessLu's hand. One glance at her daughter and her harsh features gentled, wrinkles melted, and her body grew soft and ageless. She actually smiled.

Kathy, on the other hand, sported a tight, brittle frown, like a dried-up bloom. Next to her, she clasped the wrist of a frightened young girl who sang "Tomorrow" from *Annie*.

"My stupid husband risked everything for you!" Kathy yelled at the wizard. "Reveal the other cure or the Great Redux is what I'll do!" She pressed a pair of trimming shears against the girl's throat.

Alarmed, Joy held her breath and cautiously approached. The girl must be Aesa; the Great Redux would only work on her.

FearfulFran pointed her wand at Kathy, a useless threat since the petal's wish still prevented her from formulating whatever mental concentration was necessary to cast a spell.

FearfulFran cackled and sang:

> "Secrets and lambskins covered with hide
> Hide from us all except Silver's tide
> Under the peaks, out on the plains
> Into the Mark is where your search ends
> Pamela's Choices and Pamela's Chances
> No one to blame if you wish the same
> No one to blame if you wish the same."

Kathy hissed in anger and aimed the shears at the wizard. "I've heard that before and you've shown me the door. But it doesn't get me closer—to Joy and what you told her."

"It's the same thing she told you," Joy said. While they were gone, the magic must have continued to infect Kathy. She wasn't singing yet, but she was rhyming.

FearfulFran chortled in welcome. She held up a hand. It was bleeding. Joy raised the finger dripping blood, acknowledging what she had come to do.

The wizard smiled and did a jig. LucklessLu blithely copied her mother.

"You can't go through with it." Kathy pointed the shears at Joy. "You don't know what she'll do with it."

"True. So let's ask her. But first let's tone down the child abuse before Harry throws you in Dulgrun Prison." She did a swift clutch release on Kathy's grip that she'd learned in self-defense class and pulled the girl away. "You okay, honey?" she asked, and kept a wary eye on Kathy and the shears still pointed in her direction.

Aesa plucked a flower and sang "Edelweiss."

Joy asked her to hum the words. The girl stubbornly refused, but at least she sang softer.

Joy turned to face the wizard, and staggered. The steady blood loss was making her feel faint. She'd give anything to lie down and take a power nap. "What wish did you plan to make with the petal?" she asked. "And don't try to lie, the magic won't let you."

FearfulFran raised her arms and sang:

> "Wizards come and wizards go,
> A town's worth is more than gold,
> One thing all good parent's know,
> For a child, they want the best,
> For a child they want respect."

"You're going to wish that LucklessL—uh, that Lu" Joy quickly amended when FearfulFran scowled at the derogatory moniker, "be given Zach's position as wizard of Peace & Prosperity."

FearfulFran twirled and sang Three Dog Night's version of "Joy To The World."

Away from Macklin's Mark and Wyrna's drain on her magic, Lu would become a lightning rod of power, unmanageable even by her mother, though FearfulFran probably believed she could control her child.

"See," Kathy told Joy. "You should be on my side. Only I can turn the tide." She pointed the shears at the wizard. "Her words are a singing muddle, what good to her to have the petal?"

"As if you could do any better," Joy said.

Just then, an orange fairy swooped in front of her. Felicity sang, "Anything You Can Do I Can Do Better." She must have escaped when Harry left the shop. Time was running out.

Joy turned to Kathy. "Your husband has been helping FearfulFran all along. Why? What does he have to gain?"

Kathy refused to say, so FearfulFran answered for her.

> "Wizards come and wizards go,
> A town is worth more than gold,
> One thing all good parent's know,
> For a child, they want the best,
> For a child they want respect."

"Lu is an albino," Joy said. "So is Lance. She's his child."

The wizard danced a jig.

Kathy whined, "God, she's all Lance talks about, the lout." She waved the shears at LucklessLu. "His dimwitted wizard lovechild. Isn't that wild?"

"But Lu's not just any wizard," Joy said.

Kathy's blank look confirmed she didn't know how powerful her stepdaughter was, or how much danger she was in if she continued to threaten the young woman or her mother.

"This is your hometown. Do you really want Lu and her mother in charge?"

Kathy shrugged. Her exquisite jewelry glittered with the slightest movement. Of course. This was about power. For FearfulFran, it was using her daughter's power to gain respect not only for her child but for herself. For Kathy, maybe even Lance, this was about the power of wealth, of control. Greed was a terrible addiction.

In the end, all of them were selfish. Not one had asked Lu what she wanted. Certainly not being responsible for an entire town.

Dizzy, her hand shaking from the steady loss of blood, Joy drew out the wizard's petal. Blood from her finger quickly coated it.

"Wait!" Harry rushed forward, gasping for breath, the plunger stick in his hand like a long relay baton.

Kathy and FearfulFran moved between him and Joy. Kathy aimed her shears at him, the wizard her wand. Joy didn't doubt he could handle them both, but he took a precautionary step back when Lu came to her mother's side.

"Joy, there's something you need to know," he said. "The memorial park I showed you. My friends, the Bjorks, my godson— FearfulFran killed them. Murdered them to establish a pad for her tower. That petal you're holding has been paid for with their blood. Don't let her win. Don't give it to her."

Joy drew back in revulsion. Wanting to help one's child was one thing. Doing it by murdering innocents was another.

FearfulFran waved her bleeding hand, a reminder to give her the petal or die. Joy swallowed a sob. Harry's desire for justice grappled with her own desire to live. A terrible choice.

Would he understand her decision? Would he ever forgive her?

"FearfulFran didn't kill them," Kathy said. "It was an accident, not a whim."

He stared at Kathy. "You knew the sewer was going to collapse?"

"More than knew." Zach strode forward. "Magic leaves traces. I would have noticed the presence of another wizard in town, so

FearfulFran used an accomplice to scout locations and carry out her plan."

"Lance," Harry snarled angrily. "The magic unleashed during the wizard duel left traces of FearfulFran all over town so you wouldn't be able to tell she'd been visiting anyone. But the trees did. It's why those outside the Warbird residence were getting sickly."

"But Kathy tried to steal the petal from me, twice," Joy said.

"FearfulFran had two accomplices," Zach said.

Harry shook with rage. He glared at Kathy. "You and Lance killed the Bjorks."

"An accident." Kathy waved the shears in a dismissive gesture. "No death was meant. To make them vacate without their consent, we blocked the sewer, let it ferment. It was Founders Day. In the park they were to play, safe from harm and not in the way."

"They *were* in the park. My godson was colicky. He wouldn't stop crying, so they decided to take him home early."

Kathy didn't even fake regret. "Their deaths we can't negate. Stop the wish and death is Joy's fate."

"She's right." Joy held up the petal, magically clean of blood, to FearfulFran.

"Joy, don't," Harry said.

She smiled tiredly, feeling her life bleeding away, wanting all of this to end. "You were right, too, Harry. Sometimes doing the right thing hurts. Fran wants her daughter to be happy." She turned to the wizard. "Don't you?"

"I forbid it." Zach raised his staff and pointed it directly at her.

"Sorry, Zach, but I can't have you zapping my *wife*." With ease, Harry imitated the move she'd used on him the first time they met. He swiftly hooked the stick behind one of Zach's knees and pulled. The wizard landed flat on his back with a pained "Oof."

Harry thrust the rod at his chest. "There has to be another way."

"There is none." Zach knocked aside the stick. Among a tangle of robes, he scrambled to his feet and raised the staff to ward off any more attacks.

Harry planted himself between Joy and Zach. With an icy smirk, he brandished the plunger stick, daring the wizard to test his resolve.

"That's what I love about you, Harry," Joy said. "Your uncompromising duty to your town, to family, to your dear friends who died."

"And to you," Harry said.

His love for her burned fiercely in his eyes, melting her resolve. "I know. Which makes this even harder. Lu, my sinuses. The covering, please."

Always happy to help, Lu complied. A clear dome encased Joy, Lu, and those closest to them: Aesa, Felicity, FearfulFran, and Kathy. A huge dome, and without snow this time. The humidity of the greenhouse soon condensed on the exterior of the glass.

Harry ran his hand over the glass, then smacked it in frustration. Zach raised his staff and fired a burst of lightning at it. The bolt bounced off and ricocheted around the room. Harry and Zach ducked until it found an open window and shot outside.

"It's all right," Joy assured them, barely able to keep her hand up. So tired. So very tired. "FearfulFran lived up to her part of the oath. She told us how to undo Aesa's wish. If she hadn't, her hand and mine wouldn't be bleeding. I should have realized it sooner. We had to go to the Mark to discover the answer was right here all along. You said it yourself when we were returning from the Archives. Traveling through the Stygian Gap felt sluggish, like we were swimming against a tide. And what's the backing on mirrors? Silver."

Harry's brow shot up in understanding. "Hide from us all except Silver's tide," he said, reciting the line from FearfulFran's song. "That's it. Having Aesa go through the skelter mirror will remove the wish."

Joy nodded. "We had to go to the Mark and use the skelter

mirror to make the connection. Even if we had figured it out sooner, I'm glad we went. It was important we meet Lu.

"No, Zach," she swiftly added. She had noticed his staff. The end glowed bluish white while he powered up his magic. "Not until I've fulfilled my part of the oath."

Kathy snagged Felicity and squeezed the squirming fairy. "You do and she's through."

"No! Don't!" Joy yelled.

Zach aimed his staff at Kathy and pressed it against the dome like a blowtorch. The end sizzled; the shield held.

Kathy noted the blood dripping from Joy's finger. "You're already dead. Give the wish to me instead." Joy shook her head in refusal. Kathy scowled. She crushed the fairy; Felicity screamed in pain.

"Stop!" Joy cried out. "You can have the petal!"

Kathy loosened her grip, but not by much.

The bitch is all heart, Joy thought, and she considered siccing Lu on her. But Lu was biting her nails, distraught over the sudden turn of events. Clearly, she had never experienced any violence in her protected life in Macklin's Mark. There was no telling what she might do, how she might overreact, or how powerful her magic might get. Best not to involve her at all.

"If I promise not to give FearfulFran the petal, will you let Felicity go?"

Kathy laughed. "Of course. With no remorse."

"Fine. I promise not to give FearfulFran the petal. Now release her."

"Give me the petal first."

Joy shook her head. "A simultaneous exchange."

"If you insist." Kathy put down the shears and held out both hands, one with the squirming fairy, the other palm up to receive the petal.

"Joy, think about this," Harry warned.

She dropped the petal smeared with blood in Kathy's hand and grabbed for Felicity. Kathy moved quicker. With a malicious laugh, she snatched up the petal while simultaneously throwing the fairy away. Felicity banged into the inside of the shield, then fell into a flat of petunias. Joy rushed to her. The crumpled fairy dragged herself out of the flowers, her copper diadem askew, one wing horribly bent in the wrong direction.

Joy reached down. "Are you all right?"

Whimpering, Felicity staggered into her palm, tears in her tiny eyes. Joy lifted her to one shoulder where she gingerly grabbed strands of hair for support. Once steady on her feet, the fairy flipped Kathy the finger.

Furious, Joy faced Kathy. "I never promised you the wizard's petal. Only *a* petal." Joy held up a clean white petal. "A lot of flowers in here. A lot of white petals."

The petal in Kathy's hand was still smeared with blood, not magically cleaning itself. Not even a rose petal. On the other side of the dome, Zach chuckled.

"I don't believe it!" Kathy shrieked. "You won't get away with it." She lunged at Joy.

FearfulFran blocked her attack, singing, "Mine, mine, mine, I've waited all this time," and jabbed the wand into one of Kathy's breasts. Kathy screamed in pain and backed off, cradling her breast in both hands.

With new respect for the wand, Joy eased away from it and told the wizard, "I also never promised you the wizard's petal." All looked surprised. "But I did promise to give you your wish and that's what I'm going to do."

FearfulFran cackled with glee.

Intent on stopping her, Zach pressed his staff harder against the shield. Already he'd made a dent.

"Joy!" Harry said in alarm.

"Trust me," Joy said. Please, she silently pleaded, knowing she was asking him to place his life and the lives of everyone in his town in her hands.

The struggle within Harry played out on his face. Surrendering control of his town was hard. She watched his eyes, those beautiful stormy gray eyes, and saw the sudden shift, the change from fear to calm certainty—and love, strong and steady, like the sacred Oak and its symbols on their wedding rings.

Harry placed a hand on Zach's arm and urged him to lower his staff. After a long moment, the wizard acquiesced.

She had never loved Harry more.

Exhausted, her hand trembling from the loss of blood, she held up the petal. "On behalf of FearfulFran, I wish her daughter the best, I wish Lu happiness."

The petal disintegrated into ash and LucklessLu disappeared. So did the dome. Joy's finger stopped bleeding along with FearfulFran's hand. But the wizard never noticed, too busy casting about for her daughter. She wailed in dismay. "Where's my Lu? What did you do?" Face twisted, ugly in rage, she pounced on Joy, nails like claws aimed at her throat.

Harry moved. Zach moved faster. He tackled FearfulFran, pocketed her wand, then seized her long hair and viciously yanked her head back. With cold fury, he said, "You and I are going to visit *my* greenhouse." He glanced at Kathy and in the same icy voice said, "Harry will see to you." He hauled FearfulFran to her feet and tapped her on the shoulder with his staff. The two vanished in a dark column of smoke, leaving behind a scent of roses, which inspired Felicity to sing, "Everything's Coming Up Roses."

"It's how he travels to his tower, a magical zip line." Harry reached for Joy. But he stopped in his tracks when Kathy grabbed Aesa around the waist and held the trimming shears to the girl's throat.

"Not so fast, Harry. I'm not going to tarry. And I'm not going to prison, so you better just listen." Kathy edged toward Joy. "The one you would marry, through the Gap she will carry: me and Aesa makes three."

"There are worse things in the world than a few years in

prison." He looked anxiously at Joy. "Besides, there's not enough magic left in the mirror for all of you."

"I'll take that chance. You can have Lance." Kathy pressed the shears into the little girl's throat. Aesa yelped and began crying.

Joy held up her hands. "Stop! I'll go!" She nodded to Harry. "I'll make sure nothing happens to Aesa."

"It's you I'm worried about. Stay."

The irony of the situation made her smile. They'd come full circle since her first visit to Peace. "Is that an order from the mayor?"

"From the one who loves you."

Dreams of a life together flooded her mind, invoking wishes that would never come true. "Whatever happens, I'll never forget you." She swallowed the misery in her throat and glanced down at her shoulder. "Felicity, you should stay and get your wing fixed."

The orange fairy shook her head and sang "Sisters."

Joy grasped Aesa's hand. Harry raced to stop her. Before he could reach them, Joy said, "Smalt." Black sparkles surrounded them.

"Here! Take this!" Harry pitched the rod to Joy.

She reached up to grab it, but it bounced off the sparkles and stayed behind while she entered the massive darkness of the Stygian Gap, headed for home. Joy held on fast to Aesa. From the other side of the girl, she heard Kathy say, "I've been rhyming for so long, let's see if the wish is gone. In the Year of Withdrawal, to avoid another brawl—Aah, I'm such a jerk! After all this, it didn't work! "

Joy thought back to what FearfulFran had sung. She and Harry had done everything in the song. Or had they? "FearfulFran said 'No one to blame if you wish the same.' She sang it twice. I thought it was because she had to rhyme it with the previous line and couldn't think of anything else to add. But maybe she meant to say it twice. Maybe it means the wishcaster has to make a second wish while traveling through the skelter mirror—a wish to take back the wish, and no one will blame her for changing her mind."

In the blackness, she patted the little girl's hand. "Aesa, sweetheart, if you want to return to home, you have to wish life was no longer like a musical. Can you do that for me, honey? Please?"

"I wish," Aesa said. "I wish… When you wish upon a star…" The girl cried, blubbering uncontrollably.

Kathy said, "It's taking too long. Now what's wrong?"

"She's a little girl. It's easier to sing a song she already knows than to make one up."

"Well, shit, I can do that. I'll figure it out in one second flat." Kathy paused. And paused.

"Not so easy, is it? The thing is not to overthink it." She patted Aesa's hand. "Sweetie, sing with me to the tune of 'Let's Go Fly a Kite:' Let's go make a wish, life's not a musical wish."

It took several tries, she had to get the girl to stop crying first, but eventually with she and Felicity singing along, Aesa sang, "Let's go make a wish, life's not a musical wish."

"Let's see if it worked," Kathy said. "In the Year of Withdrawal, the Founders of Peace & Prosperity traveled to the shores of the West…. It worked! For an outsider, you're pretty smart."

Joy sighed in relief. Peace & Prosperity was back to normal. But then Aesa cried out in pain. "Kathy, stop hurting her!" Joy pulled the little girl closer.

"It wasn't me," Kathy shot back. "There's all sorts of beasts trying to grab on. Ouch! Get away!" There was a nonhuman growl followed by a shriek of pain. Kathy snorted. "That'll teach you."

A claw raked across Joy's back, barely noticeable thanks to the chainmail Wyrna had given her. Zach was right, the woman was gifted with prescience and had foreseen her need of it. A furry hand tried to latch onto Joy's forearm but lost its purchase. The slick fabric of her bodysuit, another gift from Wyrna, repelled any creatures hoping to snatch her legs and arms.

Aesa wasn't so lucky. Joy knocked away paws, claws, and

tendrils trying to snag the girl still gripped around the waist by Kathy.

Being a larger target, Kathy was having a worse time. "We're going too slow. Harry was right, the magic can't handle all three of us. We've got to lose some weight or we'll never make it to the other side."

Without warning, Kathy's arm wrapped around Joy's waist from behind and held on fast. The tug on Aesa felt lighter. Joy gasped. Kathy had let go of her! The girl's only lifeline was now Joy's hand.

From behind her, Kathy said, "We're almost at a standstill. I can barely feel any movement. Face it, Joy, her usefulness is over. It's her or us."

Kathy tried to yank Aesa out of her grip. A deadly tug-of-war ensued. Joy held on fast, all the while Aesa sobbed and cried for her parents. Just one tiny speck of light, Joy wished. Just enough to see Kathy's nose and punch some sense into her.

"Release the brat or I'll slit her throat," Kathy said.

There was a tug on Joy's hair. In the pitch black, Kathy shrieked—twice. Her arm disappeared from around Joy's waist.

"Help!" Kathy screamed. She grappled for Joy's arm, but the slick fabric repelled the manicured nails seeking purchase. Seconds later, she heard Kathy hollering in the dark from a distance. Since Kathy was no longer holding onto Joy, the magic thrusting them to Joy's home no longer included her. The poor woman had been set adrift.

"That'll teach her," Felicity said.

"What did you do?"

"Poked her in the eyes with my crown. Twice," said the fairy proudly. "I tied your hair around my waist and let her have it. No one messes with my girlfriend."

"Thanks."

Kathy yelled from farther away. A twinge of remorse nudged Joy's conscience. But Kathy had injured both Felicity and Aesa, and Joy decided life was too short to worry about abusers.

Occasionally, creatures in the Gap brushed by or bunked into them. Joy hunched over the girl and shielded her, grateful for the chain mail. Their passage through the Gap felt a little faster, enough to keep the creatures from latching on and hitching a ride out. Or snatching a traveler for a meal. Poor Kathy. Those shears were going to come in handy.

After what seemed like hours, the Gap finally let them go. Still hunched protectively over Aesa, Joy raised her head to get her bearings. They were in her bedroom, the house dark, no lights except for a strange red glow from outside.

Thanks to the absolute darkness of the Gap, her eyes adjusted immediately.

On the bed, a woman in Joy's clothes was handcuffed to the headboard, twisting and turning, trying to fight off a man intent on assaulting her. With a gag in her mouth, she futilely yelled for help.

The wig on the floor, maybe even the handcuffs, indicated this was the policewoman assigned to pose as Joy and trap the rapist preying on the neighborhood. Something had gone horribly wrong. Where was her backup?

The scent of smoke answered the question. The red light from outside the window wasn't glowing but flickering. From the firehouse down the street, Joy heard the approaching sirens of fire engines. Strobing lights diffused the red; police sirens added to the din. Muffled shouts filtered in through the closed window. A house was on fire. Maybe Jeff's.

No one would think to check on the policewoman until the fire was under control. By then, her attacker would gone and she might be dead.

Aesa straightened from her crouched position. "Where are we?"

The man on the bed momentarily froze, listening, then resumed his attack on the woman. In spite of the uniform, Joy would recognize him anywhere. The PSE&G guy who serviced her utilities, the one Mrs. O'Keefe had whacked on the head with a shovel when he entered her home. The thought of him trying to rape her elderly neighbor twisted her stomach in disgust.

She spun Aesa around, keeping her innocent gaze away from the bed. Joy swiftly took off the chainmail and lowered it over the girl's head. The adult size made it a long armored dress. Protection for what was to come.

There was no time for explanations. Not enough magic left in the mirror for all of them to flee to Peace. Already the assault taking place on the bed was causing horrendous flashbacks about being cocooned with Wyrna. She wouldn't leave another woman to face a similar fate. Heart pounding madly, she shoved Felicity into Aesa's hair and whispered, "Get her out of here. Now!"

The fairy shook her head and fought to untangle herself from the strands.

"Who's there?" The man's voice was sharp, edged with lust.

Joy heard the bed squeak, then a heavy footfall on the hardwood floor. The gagged woman screamed a muffled warning as another footfall headed in Joy's direction.

The fairy struggled to free herself from the mass of frizzy hair. Even with a damaged wing, Felicity's face showed her fierce determination to stay and fight. But Joy couldn't take any chances with Aesa. She grabbed the girl by the shoulders and looked into her frightened eyes. "If you want to see your Mommy and Daddy, say 'smalt'—now—or you'll never see them again." She let go of the girl. In her sternest teacher's voice, she ordered, "Smalt."

"Smalt," Aesa dutifully replied.

Black sparkles formed. Felicity yelled, "Nooo!" Then they were gone.

"Who are you?" The man's thick voice made her shudder in revulsion. "Who you talking to?" he demanded to know. He grabbed Joy's arm and reeled her around. Or tried to. The slick material of the bodysuit made her slippery as an eel.

Most household items can be used as a weapon or deterrent, her self-defense instructor had said. She was about to find out if that was true.

Chapter 28

In Sirena's workroom, Harradorn tried his best to assure Aesa's parents their daughter was safe and sound. He would personally bring her home. The council had sanctioned one last journey to the outside. Already, Sirena was mixing a new potion to reactivate the skelter mirror, using the original color that had started this whole escapade. Purple.

With its magic almost gone, Harradorn could see a wisp of his reflection in the mirror, the surface nearly solid. Evening was upon them, hours since the four had gone through the mirror. Felicity and Aesa should have returned by now. Joy would have sent them back if she could. He refused to think the weakening magic had prevented them from reaching Joy's home, and they were lost in the Gap.

From across the crowded room, he caught his brother's eye. A tankard of ale in hand, Rick gave the impression he was imbibing liberally, celebrating like many of the partygoers out on the street whose cheers could be heard. But Rick's eyes were keen and alert. They swept the room, studying everyone present: the parents, councilmembers, Sirena, the sprouting rod Harradorn still clenched in his hand, but mainly the fake wedding ring on Harradorn's finger.

A commotion was heard from out on the street. Angry shouts followed Sheriff Caine inside while he hauled in the one missing councilmember—Lance Warbird.

"What's the meaning of this?" Lance asked. He shucked the

sheriff's grip. "Where's Kathy?"

"You mean where's FearfulFran?" Harradorn replied, ice in his voice. "You conspired to betray our town and Zach so she and your daughter could take over Peace & Prosperity. You can't deny it. I've seen Lu. A young albino wizard with your runic marking tattooed on her."

Lance's eyes barely widened. "Nonsense. Just try and prove it."

"FearfulFran admitted everything."

"Then bring her here and let her confess. Oh, wait. You can't." Lance glanced slyly at him. "By now Zach has meted his own punishment."

He knows about the rose bushes. FearfulFran must have told him.

Lance's smugness twisted like a knife in his gut, only to cut deeper when Lance added, "It's your word against mine."

"Joy saw you and FearfulFran walking together."

Lance addressed the council. "Would you believe an outsider over one of your own?"

"Sirena also witnessed the two of you together." He turned to her. "Tell them."

Everyone stared at Sirena. But his sister only glanced at the crystal ball in her hand and said sadly, "I can't be sure. It was dark, the night full of shadows."

Harradorn gaped at her, shocked that she would betray him.

What the Hel is going on?

"Sirena?" he pleaded, but she refused to look at him. He turned his back on her and told the assembled, "Felicity also heard FearfulFran confess to what she and Lance had planned."

"A fairy?" Lance chuckled derisively. "Who would believe the word of a fairy?"

Everyone snickered, and Harradorn's heart sank. No one trusted fairies. Except Joy. And now him.

"What about the withered condition of the trees outside of your house?" he said. "The town gardeners are certain only magic prevented your trees from growing straight and tall."

Lance lazily straightened his clothes. "You got me. I confess. Take me away." He laughed and looked around the room. "Yes, I admit using magic contraband in my home. I've been experimenting with potions to add pigment to my skin. It's not easy being the only albino in town." He shrugged dismissively. "Call it vanity, but I wanted to try looking like everyone else for a change. The potions didn't work. I threw them away before Aesa made her wish, no harm done except to the trees, and they'll soon recover. If you wish to charge me for my transgression, I accept whatever fine you may impose." He glanced at Harradorn, a sneer on his face. "Anything else, *mayor*?"

Harradorn stared at Sirena, hoping she'd confess, but with shoulders bowed and a tear sliding down her cheek, she refused to look at him. As for Rick, his clenched jaw indicated his mutual frustration, but there was nothing he could do to help.

Lance raised his head high. "Now, if you're done throwing stones, where's my Kathy?"

"She threatened to kill Aesa if Joy didn't take her through the skelter mirror." Harradorn smirked. *Got you.* If albino's could turn any whiter, Lance was doing it now. "When Aesa returns, she'll tell everyone what happened, what she heard, and so will Felicity and Joy. A citizen, a fairy, and an outsider, all with matching stories about how Kathy agreed to help you and FearfulFran take over the town. How will you counter that, *councilman*?"

"Again, we have only your word on it. For all we know, no one survived the Stygian Gap, not even my dear Kathy."

Aesa's parents wailed and crumpled into each other's arms, crushed by the callous remark concerning their daughter's fate. Several councilmembers moved to console them. Harradorn fingered the rod in his hand, itching to beat the snot out of the man, when a soft whisper from behind said, "Make me mayor and I'll tell the truth."

He turned to Sirena. Tears peppered her face. She glanced at the ball. "Resign and appoint me in your stead," she whispered.

A sucking sound came from the skelter mirror. Little Aesa reached into the room, struggling to break free of the semi-solid mirror as if it were quicksand. A slimy green tentacle shot out and wrapped around her waist. She screamed as it dragged her back into the Gap.

Harradorn rushed past stunned onlookers and grasped her arms. He held on fast while Rick pulled out his dagger and sliced through the tentacle. The appendage dropped to the floor, yellow blood spewing out. As one, Harradorn and Rick pulled Aesa into the room where her parents picked her up and smothered her with kisses.

Felicity escaped from the girl's hair. Wing damaged, she zigzagged to Harradorn. "Joy's in trouble! A villain's in her room, attacking her and someone else! You've got to save them!"

The curse took hold. Harradorn's heart pounded, readying him for action. He whirled toward Sirena. "Send me!"

She lowered her eyes and shook her head. "It's not ready."

He grabbed her by the shoulders. "Why are you doing this?"

"Because I love you." She sniffed back tears. "And this town, though it has never loved me."

"What's she talking about?" Rick asked.

"Doesn't matter. I resign as mayor and appoint Sirena in my stead."

"Are you daft?"

Harradorn ignored him and told Sirena, "Joy no longer has her phone. You'll need to use her address." While he recited it, Sirena dipped her finger in the potion and wrote on the mirror.

"You don't have the council's permission to go," Lance said. "Aesa and the fairy have returned, so the dispensation to use the mirror is negated. With your own words, you're no longer mayor. As an ordinary citizen, any rights to ignore the council are void."

"That's true," one of the councilmembers said.

Harradorn sputtered, seething in anger and dismay, anxious to get to Joy before it was too late. "But—"

Lance interrupted him. "Sheriff Caine, if he tries to go through the mirror, arrest him." He noticed Sirena dab a spot of potion on the back of Harradorn's hand in clear violation of his mandate. "Better yet, let's get rid of temptation."

While Sirena quickly sprinkled the mirror with her feather caster, Lance seized one of the decorated walking sticks in her workroom and struck the mirror, shattering it. Dozens of pieces fell to the floor.

"No!" Harradorn dropped to his knees. He grabbed the shards, desperate to put the mirror back together, heedless of the edges cutting his fingers and making them bleed.

"Now we've both lost someone we cared about." Lance tossed the walking stick away. "I'd say we're even."

"I'd say we haven't even started." Rick stepped forward. "I swear to Odin, Peace is worse than Prosperity. That's about to change." He opened his palm. Two white rose petals glistened in the light.

Stunned, Harradorn rose slowly to his feet. "Where did you get those?"

"Zach. During our visit, he offered us both two. Of course you refused. While you calmed our wizard, I claimed my booty and decided to save them for a rainy day. I'd say the swells of a tempest are about to swamp us." He raised a brow at Sirena. "*Mayor* Sirena, for making the divining rod in exchange for a seat on the council, knowing Lance would give it to FearfulFran—"

"My ball said no harm would come from her having the rod," Sirena interjected.

Rick snorted in derision and continued. "But mostly for extorting our true mayor when you know a person will give up anything for love, I sentence you to three years community service in the outside world."

Sirena paled. "Rick, don't do this. Please. I did it for you."

"You did it for yourself. Now you'll have to work only for others." He held up one of the petals.

Sirena grabbed his wrist. "Please, Rick, not the outside world. Anything but that."

He shook her off. "I wish Sirena Lawson be banished to the outside world to do community service for three years."

The petal crumbled to dust. Sirena wailed, "Remember me!" and vanished.

"A bit harsh," Harradorn said.

Rick dismissed his rebuke with a wave of his hand. "Better than the ten years I was thinking of. Now for you." He held up the other petal. "I wish the skelter mirror be restored and remain open for five minutes." The petal disintegrated. From the floor, the silvered pieces rose and reformed like a jigsaw puzzle into a mirror.

Harradorn raised one brow. "Five minutes?"

"Enough time to get there."

"But not get back." He could see the surface shimmer, indicating it was open for travel. "Thanks." Gripping the plunger stick, he started for the mirror.

Rick grabbed his arm. "Forgetting something?" He inclined his head to the medallion on Harradorn's chest.

Without a second thought, Harradorn removed it and handed it over. He flinched, and a cool wave of relief flooded his body.

"You okay?" Rick asked.

"The curse. It's gone."

"Aye. But by the look on your face, you still want to rescue your damsel."

"Easiest decision I ever made." Zach had been right.

"Wait a minute." Lance barged forward. "Who said Rick can be mayor of both towns?"

"I did." Harradorn backed toward the mirror. "Before leaving to kidnap Joy, I signed a decree, an insurance policy, that if for any reason I ceased to be mayor, Rick would take the position until elections were held. Sheriff Caine will attest I gave it to my brother in the park."

Sheriff Caine nodded in affirmation, but there was no mistaking the sardonic twitch of his lips. He detested Peace's town council almost as much as Rick. Lance in particular.

"Then that means—" Lance started to say.

"Sirena was never mayor, not officially. Agamemnon knows where a copy of the decree is filed." Harradorn clasped the plunger stick and leapt into the mirror. Or tried to. Lance grabbed his arm and wrenched him back.

"I say he stays," Lance said, and grappled with Harradorn to prevent him from leaving.

"And I say he goes." Rick shoved both men into the mirror.

* * *

"I've never had a threesome before." The rapist sniggered. He tried to latch onto Joy, but her body suit continued to deter any chance of him grabbing hold.

"I know someone scarier than you," she said in defiance. Wyrna Ashdapa. The thought emboldened her, kept fear from paralyzing her, kept her fighting for what seemed like forever. From the dresser, she snagged her jewelry box and bashed him on the head. Like everything else she had used, it barely slowed him down. The room looked like a war zone of destruction. Everything movable had been used against him. The guy must be on drugs, oblivious to pain.

He wiped the blood from the fresh cut on his forehead and chuckled. "Feisty, huh. I'll teach you to behave."

He jostled for purchase. She kicked and elbowed, punched, then slipped away, deciding her best chance to save herself and the policewoman handcuffed to the bed was to run for help. But then he found something he could grab hold of. Her hair.

Laughing, he yanked her around and slammed her face against the window. She saw stars. Then her vision cleared, and she saw Mrs. O'Keefe's home on fire across the street. Down below, Mike held a comforting arm around the woman while her house died among the rampant flames. Kasey stood nearby with several uniformed cops, watching.

"You set the house on fire as a distraction." So he could break in and rape the policewoman while everyone looked the other way.

"Payback's a bitch." He slammed her face into the window again. "No one bashes me on the head with a shovel and gets away with it."

"Help!" Joy screamed to the people below. With the window closed and more fire engines arriving, no one could hear her.

He hooked his arm around her neck and pulled her back from the window. She dropped and used his own weight to roll him over her shoulder onto the floor. She ran to the stairs and raced down. He tackled her on the bottom step, knocking the breath out of her. She squirmed out of his hold, crawling to the living room. He tried to grab her wrist, her hair, anything not covered by the bodysuit. She kept twisting and squirming, frantically avoiding his grip.

A strobing light from an emergency vehicle illuminated her spider-killing bat. She sprang for it but was pulled back when he grabbed her ankle. She turned and kicked him in the face with her other foot, but he refused to let go. Catching her other foot, he dragged her toward him.

Don't give up, she thought as his body covered hers. His weight held her in place, pinned her to the floor. She grimaced as his sour breath panted in her face. But then something between her breasts jabbed her with pain. Wyrna's little red whistle. She'd forgotten all about it.

He tried to tear off her clothes, but the body suit wasn't only slick. It was strong. He growled and cussed in frustration. She lifted her head, clamped down on his ear, and ground her teeth as hard as she could. Disgusting yet effective, he screamed and let go long enough for her to squirm away and grab the bat. She got to her feet and swung it back and forth, ready to kill him if he got close.

She grimaced and spat out his blood from her mouth. Her attacker stood between her and the front door.

He fingered his ear and his hand came away bloody. His face twisted in rage. "Bitch!"

The only thing worse than a rapist is an angry rapist.

Which is why instead of swinging the bat toward him and fighting her way to the front door with the risk of being pinned to the floor again, she swung the bat at the front window. The glass shattered. Someone would notice. Mike would notice.

Eventually.

She dug out the tiny whistle, put it in her mouth and blew as hard as she could and—*ohmigod!*—screamed in pain, overwhelmed by the fiendish noise the tiny whistle made. Such unbelievable pain.

Groaning, the rapist covered his ears and dropped to his knees. With two hands, she raised the bat to knock him out, only to see him bowled over by two men appearing out of thin air, wrestling each other while an orange fairy shot away from the two. Joy watched as Harry drew back a fist and knocked an albino to the floor. Had to be the infamous Lance, Kathy's husband.

Lance lay stunned on the floor. Harry quickly looked around and found her. "You okay?" he asked.

She smiled with relief. "Always nice to have backup. Look out behind you!" Her attacker was sneaking away.

"Trade you." Harry threw her the stick and she tossed him the bat. He wielded it almost like a sword. In a flurry of stylized moves, he struck the man repeatedly here, there, and everywhere, sending him to the floor, groaning, moaning, barely conscious.

"I knew you'd come." She threw her arms around Harry and hugged him tight, never wanting to let go. He kissed her for a long time, passionate and hard, releasing all the terror from her attack, trading them for the love of the man in her arms. "Those were some moves," she murmured. He nestled her close. "Karate?"

"Tie-dye Tai Chi. Fast-forward version. I practice every evening to relieve stress."

She laughed. That explained the tie-dye outfit he'd worn the first time they met.

"Hey!" Felicity yelled. With her crooked wing, the hitchhiker zigzagged over to Joy. "Just in the nick of time, huh?"

Joy grinned. "What are friends for?" She held out her hand. Felicity landed in her palm.

Mike's face appeared outside the broken window. "What the hell?"

Joy quickly put her hand behind her back so Mike wouldn't see the fairy.

He studied the broken pane, then peered inside. "Hey, when did you two get back?"

"Just now," Joy said.

"We need to talk about you going AWOL, but later. What happened to your window?"

"That's some of what we need to talk about. Right now there's a woman upstairs in need of paramedics."

Mike looked genuinely startled. "Officer Ranfield? What happened to her?"

Joy swallowed hard, barely able to talk, her mind replaying the horrible events. Harry put a steadying arm around her and held her close. Joy said, "She was attacked. Harry and I took care of him. Knocked him out."

Harry waved the bat.

Mike grunted in approval. "I'll get Kasey. Don't go anywhere." He pointed a stern finger at her. "Promise?"

"Promise."

"Good. Nice to see your hair's back to normal." Mike disappeared.

Harry looked down at Felicity. "You and Lance have to get out of here."

"Aw, mayor, I just got here."

"It's just Harradorn, remember?"

Just? "Oh, Harry, you didn't." Joy felt for the medal of office beneath his shirt and discovered it was missing. "For me?"

"For us. Believe me, the choice was easy."

They heard shouts from outside; people headed to the front door. At the same time, they noticed Lance start to get up. Harry leaned toward Felicity and said, "Lance wants to find Kathy. Why don't you give him a hand." He quickly whispered something to the fairy.

A mischievous smile crossed her face. Felicity waved to Joy. "See you later, girlfriend." She grabbed one of Lance's long braids and said, "Purple." Both disappeared in a cloud of black sparkles.

Mike and a throng of cops and paramedics burst through the front door. Joy and Harry backed out of the way. She asked him, "What did you tell Felicity?"

"I told her to let go of Lance as soon as they entered the Gap." Harry tossed the bat on the couch and then snugged Joy safely in his arms. "And also to have Agamemnon plan a reception for us for when we get back. Say, two weeks?" He looked at her and a devilish grin spread across his face. "Better make that two months. We'll take an extended trip back to Peace so I don't have to share you with anyone for a long time."

"Is that a proposal?" she asked.

"Is that a yes?"

She was about to agree when she remembered the bodysuit and what Wyrna had laced it with. "Ask me again after I've changed my clothes."

"Ask you what?" Mike said. He stayed close while they watched the police haul the rapist away.

Joy said, "Ask me whether I'd quit my job and move someplace where it doesn't matter what color a teacher's hair is or how many tattoos I have. Where everyone sings and dances, castles are made of ice cream, and magic is in the air."

Mike grumbled. "Sounds like a fairy tale."

"It does, doesn't it." She laughed. Harry winked, his gaze overflowing with love, and she laughed again, so happy. "I wouldn't have it any other way."

Epilogue

In the wizard's tower, Zach tended two freshly potted rose bushes, their gold nameplates shiny and recently engraved.

"There, there, ladies. Don't fret. I'll take good care of you." He fingered the blackened petals of the rose bush labeled FearfulFran and tsked at love turned selfish. "It may take years, but I won't give up on you.

"Nor will I give up on you," he told the rose bush named Wyrna Ashdapa whose red roses were thickly veined in black. "Lust is never a substitute for love. You'll learn. You may fight me all the way, but in the end you'll learn."

He whistled a tune from *Wicked* while he worked, and set about rebuilding his greenhouse.

* * *

Rick Lawson, mayor of both Peace and Prosperity, fingered the two jeweled medallions on his chest, waiting for the five minutes of his wish to be up. He emptied his tankard of ale and glanced at his watch. On cue, the mirror shattered like before, littering the floor with shards. He smiled in satisfaction. His brother had decided love was more important than being mayor. The fool. Now he had control of the entire town. Life didn't get any better.

A movement by the mirror caught his eye. To his surprise, Felicity squeezed through the largest shard still attached to the frame. He stared at her in dismay. "Harradorn?"

"Safe and sound with Joy. Can't say the same for Lance, but that's his problem. See you later, Mayor Rick." Felicity zigzagged to the front of the store and out to the street where she could be heard yelling for her team.

"Help!" An albino hand reached out of the same piece Felicity had squeezed through. Lance screamed in horror as a green tentacle wrapped around his wrist and drew him back into the Gap.

With his booted foot, Rick kicked the large shard free of the mirror's frame and smirked in satisfaction when it broke into pieces on the floor. Turning his back on the fate of the councilman and his wife, he strolled out of Sirena's store.

Daylight waned. Evening stars peeked from the sky. Those still celebrating the end of Aesa's wish greeted Rick with cheers and drinks while he sauntered through Peace, surveying his domain, confident he'd do a better job of running the town now that he controlled both sides of the river.

Three hours later, with a heady alcohol buzz and a need to get off his dance-weary feet, he started toward Prosperity. On the way, he passed a store in Peace he didn't remember seeing before. The windows displayed a colorful assortment of kites.

He looked at the shop's sign: Lucky Lu's Kite Emporium.

Appalled, he entered the shop. Harry had told him Lu was the most powerful wizard in the world. In trepidation, he cautiously approached the young albino woman at the kite-making station. With a joyful smile, she glanced up from making a rainbow kite that proclaimed Peace & Prosperity.

"Looking for a kite?" she asked.

"I have a model of a ship in my library. Could you make a kite like it?"

"I'd have to see it first, but chances are I can."

"How about popping over to take a look?"

"Popping?"

"You know, snap your fingers and be there for a look-see, then *pop* and your back."

"Oh, you mean magic." Lu laughed merrily. "Wouldn't that be nice. You're very funny. I have to finish this kite for a customer, but if you leave your address, I can probably be there in about an hour, depending on where you live and how fast I can walk."

Rick threw his head back and laughed. "Don't worry about it. I'll have my assistant bring the model here in the morning. Have a good night, Lucky Lu."

"Thank you. You, too."

Chuckling about how Joy's wish had turned out, Rick headed for Prosperity. On the bridge separating the two communities, Sheriff Caine caught up to him. He had heard the fairies gossiping about Lance and Kathy Warbird, and offered to rescue them.

"Very noble of you," Rick said, "but I don't think they're worth risking your life. Finding them in the Gap would be worse than finding a drop in the sea." He clamped a friendly hand on the sheriff's muscular shoulder. "Besides, you're needed here."

"I've traversed the Gap before, with minimal injuries." Caine tapped his nose. "Tracking their scent will be simple. There's a skelter mirror in the Seychelles I could use."

"Wait a week. No, wait two." He slapped Caine on the back and together the two friends headed into the raucous community Rick loved so well, Prosperity. "When you return, make sure they share the same cell in Dulgrun Prison."

Caine's chuckle resembled a growl. "They may find it worse than the Gap."

Rick laughed. "Nothing worse than married life." But then his thoughts turned to Harry and Joy and the love blazing for each other in their eyes. Maybe they would prove him wrong.

Author's Note

I have had many people ask me why, if I write psychological thrillers, do I also write romantic fantasy. The answer is easy. My brain needs balance. After months writing a fast-paced thriller about murder and mayhem, danger and testy relationships, it's nice to take a mental vacation and write about love and humor, magic and mayhem. Yes, mayhem is a constant because without conflict, a book would be boring. At least in my romantic fantasies, the mayhem isn't so hard-edged and desperate. Plus it's fun to visit the magical town of Peace & Prosperity and explore its wide range of eccentric and mythical citizens, its back alleys, crazy laws, and fantastic shops. One never knows who or what is waiting around the corner. With pesky, playful, fun-loving fairies around, it's never a dull moment.

About the Author

Liz Roadifer is an award-winning author, poet, and columnist whose work has been published in newspapers, magazines, and literary journals. Born in New Jersey, she now lives with her family in Wyoming.

Thank you for buying my book. If you enjoyed this story, please consider posting a favorable review on book review sites such as Amazon, Barnes & Noble, Goodreads, and Smashwords. For independent authors like myself, good reviews help us compete with the big name publishers.

You can reach me at lizroadiferbooks@gmail.com
I'd love to hear from you.

Peace & Prosperity Book 2

The Trouble With Pirates

Rick's story. Being mayor of both Peace and Prosperity is more than Rick bargained for, especially when Joy's feisty sister, Merry Flint, shows up to rescue her.

Printed in Great Britain
by Amazon